Forest of Forgotten Vows

Dreams of Faerie Book One

Grace Carlisle

Moth & Crown Press

Published by Moth & Crown Press

Cover designed by Spurwing Creative.

Paperback ISBN: 978-1-971568-00-3

eBook ISBN: 978-1-971568-01-0

Contents

Contents

Chapter One

WE DON'T DRIVE BY any monsters on the way to my grandmother's house. Brambles and other undergrowth encroach on the long dirt driveway that winds between the trees, growing thicker and wilder than they had when I'd last set foot here, seven years ago.

But there are no monsters in the woods.

"What?" my rideshare driver asks from the front seat. I didn't realize I'd spoken those words out loud.

"Nothing important, sorry," I say. The mantra is not something I'm eager to explain, or could if I wanted to. I don't remember when I started using those words to comfort myself, or why they were the ones I chose.

Eventually the woods give way just enough to form a freshly-cut yard encircling a two-story brick house, but the once-loved vegetable garden and flowerbeds that run along the side of the house now sit unweeded. The dirt drive loops around in front of the porch, where an old tan Ford truck sits. Ribbons of ivy make slow but unimpeded progress up the brick walls.

When I lived here, Grandma was industrious about keeping her property tidy. The stark change gives me an uneasy feeling in the pit of my stomach. Grandma sounded so dismissive on the phone, I wanted to believe her doctor really was overreacting by suggesting I move back here.

My last memory of this place is staring out the rear window of Grandma's truck at fourteen, watching the only home I'd ever had vanish as we round the first bend. From there it was boarding school, a few semesters in a college dorm, and then a tiny apartment I shared with three other people. Even during school holidays and between semesters, Grandma never wanted me to come back and gifted me excuses on semester breaks and holidays: the water was out, the house was being fumigated, she had the flu.

The bouncing ride down the driveway comes to an end as we pull up in front of the house. My driver helps me get my suitcase out of the trunk and swiftly drives off, probably annoyed he had to drive this far out of town. I don't have a lot of cash left, but I give him what I hope is a good enough tip for the inconvenience, waving halfheartedly as he turns and disappears back down the drive.

I don't go inside right away. The sight of Grandma's front door only amplifies the mucky feeling in my gut. Instead I stand in the drive until the sound of the engine fades and I'm left alone with the trees. A breeze gently rustles the branches overhead; the birds, bugs, and other tiny animals call out to their own in the late-May frenzy of activity.

They should be comforting—the sounds and sights of my childhood; the very woods I grew up playing in. But they're not. Something unpleasant slides around in my brain and I can't quite grasp onto it. I force myself to stare until my eyes water, studying every gap in the branches, honing in on every sound, to try and figure out what it is that's bothering me. But there's nothing strange at all.

"There are no monsters in the woods," I whisper to myself. Satisfied as if I've won a dare, I relent and drag my luggage up the porch steps. The possessions I deemed worth keeping fit into a single suitcase and backpack.

I don't have a key, so I knock on the door and wait. The porch holds a few weedy flowerpots and a porch swing. A large orange cat sits near the far edge of the porch, watching me with yellow eyes. I wonder when Grandma got a cat. We'd never had pets when I was growing up.

"Here, kitty," I say, crouching down and putting out my hand. It jumps up, twitches its tail, and darts around the side of the house and out of sight.

"Alright, then," I mutter. While I'm still crouched down on the porch, something moving beneath the warped planks catches my eye. The shape darts under me and to the stairs; I whirl as it emerges from a gap between the steps. It's a tiny man less than a foot tall, with giant, pointed furry ears and wide, round eyes. His clothes look made of patchwork animal skins.

"Young Miss, you came back!" he squeaks excitedly in a high-pitched voice. The creature smiles widely up at me, displaying a mouth full of tiny, sharp teeth.

This isn't happening. Averting my eyes and without speaking a word, I straighten up, stare at the door, and ignore the creature completely. I've barely arrived and it's already starting. I had countless imaginary friends growing up, well past the point believing in them was appropriate. I didn't realize how weird it was until I went to boarding school and none of the other kids had similar stories. But they're not real, I understand that now. Even if I see and hear them, I'm not crazy if I don't talk back. There are no monsters in the woods.

"Young Miss? Can you hear me? Can you see me? Has your Sight gone away again?" the creature says, ears drooping and eyes growing large and sad. It makes me feel terrible and I immediately want to turn around and talk to him, but I force myself not to. It will go away. It has to go away. Adults don't have imaginary friends. There are no monsters in the woods.

The doorknob turns before I can knock more insistently. Grandma opens the door and glowers at me from behind thick glasses. The last time I saw her, her hair still had streaks of brown, but now gray has taken over. She wears a handmade patchwork quilted skirt and an old denim work jacket and leans on an old-fashioned wooden cane, hands shaking slightly. She never used to shake.

"The door was unlocked," she says. Her sharp, vaguely accusatory tone sends me directly back to my childhood. We sometimes talked on the phone while I was away, but only enough for her to make sure I was still alive.

"Sorry. Not used to people leaving their doors unlocked," I say.

"Right," she says. "City life. Tamsin, if someone came all the way out here just to rob me, a deadbolt isn't going to stop them." She moves aside to let me in.

"Did you get a cat?" I ask, looking for something light to talk about. Grandma looks at me strangely.

"Did you forget? That old thing's been around at least fifteen years."

"Oh," I say. After she reminds me, I vaguely recall seeing the cat around years ago—flashes of an orange streak between the trees—or maybe that's just my brain trying to fill in blanks I'm supposed to remember. The cat looks healthy for being so old.

"It have a name?" I ask.

"I usually just call her, 'hey, you' but her official name is Tansy."

"Is that from the same hippie baby name book you got my name?" I ask. Grandma snorts.

"It's a flower. When I went to school, there was always at least one other girl in my classes with the name 'Mary.' I decided that won't happen to anything I have a hand in naming," she says. "Anyway, the cat comes and goes. I leave food out for her, but I suppose you should be doing that now. I'm not supposed to be bending over. My doctor will probably also be wanting you to chew my food and clean my behind."

"I can leave after a few weeks if you don't want me here, assuming you don't fall again," I say. I realize immediately I shouldn't have said the last part, even if it was true. Grandma harrumphs and heads back into the house, leaving me to shut the door and resist the instinct to lock it. "And I'm sorry I haven't visited. I should have." It's a meaningless statement. We both must know why I eventually stopped asking.

Grandma just shrugs, as if brushing my comments off. She hobbles determinedly back to her armchair in the living room and eases herself into it before it occurs to me to offer to help her, or if that's even what I'm supposed to do. I feel bad that the only person she can turn to for help is me.

I follow her into the living room and stand behind the tartan couch, resting my arms on the back. The thought of sitting feels like a violation of a space that isn't mine. Something about being in the house makes the back of my neck prickle. I don't feel welcome here.

"Well, how are you?" Grandma asks after an awkward silence. There are multiple levels to that question.

"Good," I say, mulling over how much I want to tell her. "I've been good. Normal. Nothing much to report. I've been off meds since I graduated high school and I've been doing well without them." Grandma nods, though seems preoccupied.

"You still tell people about your 'friends'?" she asks.

"No. I know that's all stupid," I say.

"Good to hear you've finally outgrown that phase."

"How are you?" I venture. She scowls at me.

"Fine," she says, "Dr. Gupta was being paranoid, begging me to call you."

"Well, he thinks it would be a good idea for me to help out at least until your bruise heals up. After that, he says we can talk about all our options." I try to sound light, but Grandma's scowl deepens. I think we both know this won't just be for the summer. Grandma, Dr. Gupta, and I had a brief conference call before I left Boston. He said the weakness, the risk of falling, they would only get worse. I want to ask the burning question: how long does she have? Is it measured in years, months? That was something we didn't discuss. But before I can figure out how to broach the subject, Grandma speaks.

"You didn't have to pause your life to come back here. Don't tell me you didn't have a job, friends, a boyfriend. A bunch of things you shouldn't have given up just to come babysit me," she says.

"I didn't have anything I couldn't walk away from for a while." A retail job, no close friends, no romantic attachments.

"That's why you should have stayed in school. Then you could send me to a nice old people's home to die in and you wouldn't have had to bother yourself coming back here," she says.

"College degrees are a lot of money and they don't even mean good jobs anymore," I say, waving my hand dismissively. Not that that was the reason. I had no idea what I even wanted to study and flunked most of the classes I signed up for.

"I'm sure it means better jobs than dropping out," she says pointedly. "Employers are going to see that and think you don't have drive. And how do you not have friends? With all the people at that boarding school, college, and the city? Were you even trying?" Her tone is grating.

"I didn't really meet anyone I clicked with." Because I didn't try. She's right.

"And you're a smart, pretty girl. You could have a boyfriend if you wanted one. Or do you have a girlfriend? That would also be fine."

"Grandma, please. I didn't connect with anyone. That's not a crime," I say. Her face softens, and she looks sad. "I went out," I continue, just to reassure her. "I went out and talked to people. I didn't just sit in my room. I did things. You don't have to worry about that." I did things sometimes. But most of my free time was spent alone.

"Is that what all your clothes look like now?" she asks, gesturing to what I'm wearing—a baggy T-shirt, very ripped jeans, and slip-on flats.

"I guess this is what happens when I don't have you to dress me," I say. As a child, she decked me out in dresses and floral prints. Even playing in the woods I'd be dressed like a proper little lady. But as I grew, I shied away from wearing anything that would draw attention or make a statement. The older I got, the more I wanted to disappear. I don't want to tell her another reason I dress like this is that I can't afford anything nicer. She'd bring that right back to not going to college.

"I hope you at least own a nice dress for job interviews," Grandma says. "Do you ever wear makeup?" she asks, studying my face. "That could help make you look more professional."

"It would if everything I've ever tried didn't make me break out," I say.

"Why didn't you let your hair grow out? It's so pretty." My hair is just long enough to tie back, and it now sits messily at the nape of my neck, which is as long as it's been since I graduated high school.

"Long hair is a pain in the ass."

"I know you didn't learn words like that in my house," Grandma says.

"No, just from every other kid at school. I've heard worse. Your house looks very nice." I say. It does, though the main point of bringing it up was to end the interrogation on my life choices. The living room has hand-quilted pillows and blankets piled on every soft surface, and the mantle over the fireplace has a row of framed photographs and a ceramic figurine of an elephant I bought her for Christmas years ago. She has my mother's baby photo, my mother's high school graduation photo, sepia toned photos of her parents, and a line of my own baby-to-graduation photos.

It was always shocking to see how little I looked like both my mother and grandma. Side by side on the mantle, my mother and I smile at the camera in our respective high-school graduation photos. My mother had dark hair that framed a strong face with a square jaw and dark, piercing eyes. My face is angular and my chin narrow and pointy, and my blond hair and watery gray eyes both light-colored in comparison as if the photo had been left out in the sun. Maybe I took after my father in terms of looks, but I wouldn't know because I've never met him. Questions about his identity were always met with a shrug from Grandma. Whoever he was, my mother—Skye—was the only one who had that information.

In every one of my mother's photos, she looks ready to take on the world; I look drawn and sickly. I've always wished I could command the same energy she did, even just for a day, or a photograph.

"I don't suppose you heard anything from her," I say.

"Not in twenty years, Tamsin. I suppose I'd be notified if she died, so I assume she's somewhere. But no, nothing."

"I guess that's not a surprise." My heart falls, anyway. I don't know why I expected anything different. I have no memories of my mother. Just the photographs.

"I left your room the way it was," Grandma says. "It might be a bit dusty up there, though. I haven't had time to get upstairs to clean." Grandma's retired, but I let the lie go because I don't want to think about her struggling and failing to get up the stairs.

"I've been cleaning on my own for years, now. I got it."

"And I suppose you'll need to go to town and get groceries and other things when I need them. You can use the truck. And just so you know, I won't need your help in the bathroom," she sniffs. "I'm not *that* helpless." Even if she did need help, I don't think she'd admit it to anyone. I hope she's right.

"Do you want me to go shopping today?" I ask.

"We have plenty of food right now. I'll bake some chicken breasts for dinner tonight," she says.

"I can do that if you want."

"No," she says firmly. "I've been cooking for more than fifty years. I don't need your help."

"I didn't mean to offend you," I say. She grunts in response. With that, she picks up a book from the side table next to her chair and opens it, signaling an end to the conversation. For a moment, I just watch her, looking for tremors in her hands as she turns a page. This is how it was for so much of my childhood. Grandma took care of me, fed me, clothed me, made sure I did my homework, but always at a distance, it seemed.

"What?" she asks, catching me staring and glaring at me from over the rim of her glasses.

"Nothing. Sorry," I say. "I'm going to unpack."

I lug my suitcase up the stairs and down the hall to my old room, the room I was born in. The February twenty-second of twenty-one years ago bore witness to one of the worst snowstorms in recent memory, and my mother, who was living with Grandma at the time, couldn't make it to a hospital. Grandma was a nurse, luckily for us. It wasn't an event Grandma ever went into detail about.

My old bedroom has a twin-sized bed covered in a white bedspread adorned with curling blue flowers. A burgundy blanket knitted by Grandma lays over the foot of the bed, while the head is overloaded with more pillows than anyone could ever need. Grandma often recycled her old clothes into quilted projects. The wooden bed frame was my mother's from when she was a child; the frame has a collection of gouges on the side closest to the wall that

I suspect she carved. The side of the dresser features a pen drawing of a poorly proportioned dog with immense fangs. I don't remember if it's hers or mine.

I put my suitcase on the floor and sit on the bed. There's a large window that would frame a beautiful view of the backyard if it wasn't instead dominated by a giant oak tree growing right next to the house. Grandma doesn't have a fence, and the backyard itself seems to have steadily been eroded away by nature, now down to the shed and a small patch of grass.

I lay down on the bed and look at the ceiling, where a few glow-in-the-dark star stickers remain to remind me that this used to be a child's room. Looking at them triggers a flash of memory: Grandma standing on the bed to affix stars to the ceiling while I sat exhausted in the middle of the floor, away from any shadows. Right, I used to have nightmares. My old night light is still plugged into the wall by the door. It's shaped like a whale.

My roots are here, but I don't feel at home the way I should. My grandfather bought this house and built it up from the tiny brick cottage it once was, with his own hands adding more to the first floor, an entire second floor, and and attic. Even though part of him is in every brick and board of this house, he passed before I ever got the chance to meet him. I want to feel like this place gives me a connection to my family; I want to feel comfortable here, safe. But I don't. Laying here in the bed, I start to fill with nervous energy. I take several deep, slow breaths, trying to empty my mind, to think of nothing instead of whatever it is that's nagging at the back of my mind, except I can't place the feeling of general unease being here gives me.

As I lay on the bed, I get the sudden sense I'm not alone. When I open my eyes, everything in the room looks washed out and gray. Even the stars on the ceiling, which should glow in the dark, are muted and dull.

My sense is correct. There's someone else here: a tall figure facing away from me, examining the vandalized dresser. They're dark, almost appearing as if merely a silhouette.

"Grandma?" I say, sitting up. Maybe she just looks tall because of the shadows, though I don't know what she would be doing in here. As I fumble blearily for the bedside lamp and switch it on, the figure turns around, and the sudden light—though strangely dulled—momentarily reflects off the figure's eyes and makes them shine like a cat's. In the light, this person is clearly not Grandma—the comparison is laughable. The man now looming above my bed is well over six feet tall. Black hair falls well past his shoulders, and his eyes glow a sickly shade of yellow in the gloom. He's dressed in a long fancy robe like he's on his way to a Renaissance faire, which is the final straw that launches the vision from terrifying to simply absurd. I can't help but let out a strangled laugh.

The man does not seem amused. "Who are you?" His voice is quiet and smooth, but there's an unsettling edge to it. Something about him makes the back of my brain prickle.

"Tamsin? Mary's granddaughter? I'm staying with her?" Did Grandma forget to tell me there's a guy staying with her? Where could he have come from if he wasn't already here? I'm nervous and confused, but then I wonder why. Even if he isn't trespassing in the house, he *is* trespassing in my room. "This is my room. You see a closed door and you just walk in? Get out," I demand.

"You're very mouthy for a figment," he says, almost to himself. "But I have enough of my mind at the moment to know that this is my dream, not yours. I don't know which unfortunate brain dreamed up this hovel, but I know it's not mine; I know this isn't real. It can't hold me forever." He takes a step forward, cutting the distance between us in half; the light from the lamp better catches his face, it's eerily perfect, blemish-free, and perfectly symmetrical.

I want to scream, but the only person who would hear me is Grandma, and it would accomplish nothing but putting her at risk. I came here to take care of *her*. I don't want to risk him hurting her. Though, now that I've had a moment to think, his presence makes no logical sense. He didn't come from anywhere, he just appeared, talking nonsense.

"Oh. I get it. *You're* the figment. This is one of those imaginary friend things I do," I say. "Which means I've already messed up. I told myself I would just not talk to any of you. You're going to just go away. Now." But he's still here. And I'm pretty sure telling them to go away never worked.

"You will not trick me, creature." He takes a step closer so he stands next to the bed, forcing me to crane my head up to see his face, which suddenly looks thoughtful, almost uncertain. "You look so familiar, and yet ..." he reaches out toward my face. I scream and cover my ears and eyes, falling back on the bed.

"It's not real it's not real it's not real it's not real—"

"Tamsin? What happened?" Grandma calls from downstairs. I open my eyes; the lights are back to normal and the man is gone. I'm alone in my room. There are no monsters here. It was nothing.

It was nothing.

Please be nothing.

"I'm fine!" I call back. At school and in the city, there were no people only I could see. No imaginary friends telling me stories and getting me in trouble. I'd thought that meant I'd grown out of the phase, but it appears not. Grandma would be furious if she found out I'm talking to myself. But she doesn't have to know. I'm not a kid anymore. I know what's real, and I know what I just have to ignore.

Except I thought that man was real, for long enough that I would have looked insane if anyone else was in the room. I can remember every detail of that man's face—the high cheekbones sharpened by the shadows cast by the dim light; the creepily flawless, blemish-free skin. Something about him was familiar. I remember hearing something about how faces in your dreams all come from your memories, so I wonder if I've seen him somewhere before. Maybe in a TV show. I'll have to make sure my night light is working before I go to bed tonight.

"No monsters," I whisper, taking a deep breath and bracing myself to face Grandma.

I slink back downstairs and Grandma is waiting at the foot of the stairs, leaning on her cane. She looks relieved when she sees me.

"What happened?" she asks.

"I laid down, but I had a bad dream or something," I say.

"Or something?"

"Must've been a bad dream," I correct.

"That didn't take long," she sighs. "Were they bad when you were at school, or in Boston?" She stares hard at me.

"No, I didn't really have them then. I actually forgot all about how bad I slept when I lived here until I saw my room again," I say. Grandma tried to give me all sorts of teas and natural supplements to help me sleep. None of them worked. There were many nights I didn't sleep, instead going downstairs and watching TV until the sun came up. Sometimes Grandma would still be up, and we would sit together and pass the night in silence.

"Do ... you need to talk about it?" she asks. I can tell by her apprehension she doesn't actually want to hear it.

"It was just a dream. I'll be fine," I say.

"Well, let me know if you want to talk to someone. Dr. Webster still has a practice here," she says. My therapist from the time I was about seven to when I moved.

"I'll keep that in mind," I say. But neither of us have the kind of money for me to see a therapist. I don't even want to know how Grandma afforded it back then.

"You could move into the other bedroom if you think that would help."

"I think I just need to get used to being back," I say. Besides, if things are still the same as when I left, the other bedroom is mostly storage. It probably doesn't even have a bed in it, and Grandma and I can't move the bed in there ourselves. But most importantly, it would be losing to something that doesn't even exist.

We don't talk while Grandma is cooking; I'm too preoccupied with my own thoughts to start a conversation, but I snap back to attention at every clattering pan or utensil, worried that she dropped it or hurt herself. If she knew I had those thoughts, she'd stab me with her cooking knife. She'd probably also stab me if I offered to help one more time, so I stay quiet. I try to play on my phone only to find that the signal here's awful. Thankfully, Grandma does let me help her bring the plates and serving dishes to the table. We eat in silence until I get the nerve to ask a question I've been wondering.

"Why have you decided to stay?" I ask. "You could probably get a decent price for the land, and you could move somewhere closer to civilization."

"This is my house, and I intend to die in it," she says. "And not," she adds, "in a nursing home. Besides, I never wanted to live near civilization. That was the point of coming out here in the first place." The hand holding her fork twitches, and rice flies all over the table. I jump up, and she waves me off with her other hand.

"I can clean up my own damn messes," she snaps, grabbing her napkin. I sit back down.

"I would have come sooner, if you had told me," I say.

"I didn't want to bother you. I figured you didn't have the time to come moon over me since you can barely come up with time to call."

"It's not like you called me that often in the last seven years either," I retort.

"I didn't want to bother you!" she snaps.

"Well, I would have wanted to be bothered about this." I take a sip of iced tea. "How bad did the doctor say it was?" I ask.

"Just that I might need someone around for a little while. He said it can be tricky. It could come or go with no warning. And no paid help would want to drive all the way down here to check in on me. You shouldn't have to be down here too long, and then you can go back to your life," she says.

"Because you'll get better?" I ask, even though we both know the answer. "Grandma—"

"Pass the rice, please," she says, cutting me off. I do, and we fall into sullen silence.

I let some time pass, and then risk a question about a different subject.

"So, did I ever talk about what happened in the nightmares I had when I was younger?" I ask. Grandma rubs her chin and looks at me shrewdly.

"It was hard to tell. You always made up so many stories. Usually about monsters in the woods or imaginary friends telling you to do things. You never knew when it was time to stop playing. Why do you ask?" She eyes me suspiciously.

"Being back is just reminding me of how weird I was as a kid. I'm sorry. I know I was a problem." After all, she didn't sign up to raise me. Still, she scoffs at my apology.

"What kid isn't weird? I just wish you channeled that imagination into more constructive things. You spent so much effort on the world in your head that you never paid attention to the real one," Grandma says.

"I guess so." Because back then, I thought it was all real. I push the remains of my dinner around my plate. Grandma lets me put the leftovers away and wash the dishes; I'm relieved she lets me help with something.

After cleanup, she sends me out to fill the bowl of cat food she leaves on the back porch. Tansy is waiting in the yard when I step outside. She flops on her back and rolls in the grass, but when I move to pet her, she darts off and bounds a few strides toward the tree line, mewing playfully.

"The food's over here, dummy," I say, dumping the wet food from the can into a ceramic bowl on the porch. The cat meows again and then darts closer to the trees before turning around and staring at me. "Do you want me to follow you?" I ask, then I facepalm. "No. That's in my head. You're just an animal. You better come eat before the raccoons get it." I turn to go back inside, and at that moment I see something move—just a hint of a shadow—beyond the tree line out of the corner of my eye. I whirl around, but there's nothing there out of the ordinary.

"Nope. Nothing there. Didn't see anything," I whisper to myself. The cat's still there, halfway between the house and the tree line, staring at me.

"Damn it," I say. "Fine." It will bother me all night if I don't, so I step off the porch into the grass and follow the cat. Predictably, she jumps up before I can reach her and runs into the trees, staying just out of my reach. I stop at the edge of the yard and look back at the house pensively. As long as I stay within sight of the lights in the windows, I should be fine, so I take a deep breath, let it out slowly. One more step and I'll cross the tree line.

But then the back of my neck prickles; I'm being watched.

Chapter Two

"Tamsin?" Grandma calls out sharply from the porch. "What are you doing?"

Being an idiot, apparently. Her voice snaps me out of it. Of course she would wonder why it would take me more than twenty seconds to fill up a bowl.

"The cat. She's over there," I say, pointing further into the woods. When I turn back to Grandma, I see the tiny man from under the porch sitting by the cat food bowl, scooping gravy and chicken chunks into his mouth. He waves at me. I ignore him. Grandma clearly doesn't see him.

"The cat knows where the food is. Come back inside." There's an edge to her voice. Fear? Once I'm back through the door, Grandma lets out a sigh. She shuts and locks the door behind me—a change from her previous attitude.

"Are you going to say the cat told you to follow her?" Grandma asks.

"I was not going to say that," I say.

"You're an adult. I was hoping you would start acting like one. You can't just go off on your own and say it was because animals talked to you or you saw tiny people in the trees. You need to start taking responsibility for things you do. I don't want to keep hearing the same excuses you had as a child."

"I was ... I was trying to make sure *your* cat was okay, Grandma," I whine. A few hours in this house, and I'm back to acting like a teenage girl.

"And the cat didn't say anything to you, she didn't ask you to follow her?" she asks.

"No!" I say, like I'm offended she would even ask. "I don't ... You're right. I'm an adult. Why would you even ask something like that?" She squeezes the bridge of her nose. My indignant denial does not seem convincing.

"If you're having problems, you can go talk to Dr. Webster again," Grandma says.

"I'll see him if I need to," I say.

"And just so we're clear, Tamsin, the cat does not talk. If you think it is, that's just your imagination."

"I know. Tansy's never spoken to me," I say. At least, I don't think she has.

"Well," Grandma sniffs, "it was always hard to tell what you think did and didn't talk to you."

"Maybe it's because of all the drugs you had me on as a kid," I snap.

"It isn't my fault you couldn't act like a normal human being without them," Grandma says. "I was always thinking you were going to run off and get yourself killed!"

"And that would have just been *such* an inconvenience for you!" I respond. I regret it immediately after saying it, but at the same time I'm still fuming and I'm not going to back down first. Grandma looks at me with stony eyes. I do my best to match her expression.

"Grow up, Tamsin," she says.

"You know, maybe the reason I haven't is that I was too drugged out to remember my own childhood," I say as a parting jab as I start up the stairs.

"Count your blessings for that. It wasn't a good time for anyone," she says. Grandma was always better at parting jabs. I stop and take a breath.

"Look, I'm sorry," I say. "I'm going to unpack, take a shower, and crash for the night. I'll leave in the morning if you want me to." Saying the words twists my stomach and my heart. I shouldn't even bother to unpack. I'll be ready to go tomorrow. I'll go back to Boston, beg my old roommates for my room back, and pretend this was all a dream. Grandma doesn't say a word as I stomp up the stairs and into my room. It's done. I don't know what I thought coming here would accomplish.

I've been back here for less than a day and I'm already seeing tiny people and projecting onto cats. Grandma can already tell there's problems. Maybe this is just what being around her does to me. My pulse quickens, and I start my breathing exercises and try to calm down. I'm the one in control of my own head. I'm in control of how I behave. I just need to remember that.

I can't allow myself to do nothing but dwell on possibilities, so I try to be productive instead and take a shower.

I grab a pair of flannel pajama pants and a tank top, along with my specialty soap and shampoo; I break out in rashes and acne if I use anything else.

I haven't had my own bathroom since the last time I lived here. For the last several years I've either lived in a dorm or a tiny space with several roommates. But now I have a bathroom of my own just across the hall. Everything in it is done up in shades of pink and cream, the toilet and bathtub included. Next to the sink is a dish of shell-shaped soaps and a basket of potpourri sits on the toilet tank, giving the entire room a citrusy smell.

The room is very clean, as is my bedroom. I guess Grandma was just being modest when she said she couldn't clean upstairs as often as she'd like. There is a pristine bar of soap in a dish built into the bathtub, but no scattering of random beauty products and toiletries that show a bathroom to be used. It's a room in perfect stasis, and I feel bad that I'm messing it up by using it, but the water is hot and I don't have anyone banging on the door demanding I hurry up.

After doing all my washing, I take a moment and just relax under the running water, eyes closed. Then behind my lids I swear I see a flash of movement. I open my eyes and peek around the shower curtain but see nothing. Maybe a bug is stuck in here somewhere. Something about it unsettles me, and I keep an eye out for the remainder of my shower. When I get out, I wrap the towel tight and hurry to my bedroom.

Back in my room, I lay down on my bed and look up at the fake stars on the ceiling. I try to concentrate on them and nothing else, certainly not on my own thoughts.

The exhaustion from traveling and arguing makes me want to sink into the mattress and disappear. I relax and let the blankets envelop me until I realize I actually *am* sinking into the mattress. I try to sit up, but the blankets and pillows hold me like glue, wrapping themselves around me and pulling me deeper. Crushing weight on all sides keeps me from moving, and I'm helpless as fabric starts to close over my face, filling my mouth and eyes. I fall through the bed and into a vast dark nothingness that stretches out forever.

The sound of a dog barking wakes me up. I roll off the bed in a frenzied panic and hit the floor in a tangle of blankets and sheets. It takes me a moment to free myself and jump to my feet, sweaty and shaking with adrenaline. My trembling fingers fumble to find the light switch, but as soon as the light comes on, everything is normal once more. Everything is fine. No monsters.

It was a nightmare, one of many I've had under this roof. I creep back to my mattress and poke it apprehensively, still worried it might attack. It doesn't. I even check under the bed. The night light is dead; I should have replaced the battery before I went to sleep.

The dog barks again. I didn't know any dogs lived close enough for me to hear. Maybe it's lost and needs help. I cautiously climb back onto the bed and crawl across it to get to the window. With the light on, I can't see anything, so after a moment of deliberation that makes me feel like a true coward, I switch the lamp back off. Even after my eyes adjust to the dark, there's no dog in sight, but I can make out the shape of the cat sitting in the yard, in perfect view from my window, eyes glinting as she stares directly at me.

For what seems like an eternity, the cat and I just stare at each other, rarely blinking. I get up, walk around the room, and come back to the window. She hasn't moved. What if the loose dog gets her?

"Damn it," I whisper. If I do nothing, it will drive me crazy all night and I won't get any sleep. Maybe if I go downstairs, I can at least spook her into leaving, or coax her inside if I'm lucky.

Outside my room, the house is dark. Grandma must have gone to bed. I'm surprised she's slept through the noise the dog and I have made, but maybe she's used to sleeping through strange noises since she lives so close to the woods. I carefully unlock the back door and go outside. The cat is still sitting in the same spot. The food bowl is empty. I remember seeing the little man eating the cat food after I put it out, but it must have actually been the cat. It must have.

"You have to wait until morning for breakfast," I whisper to Tansy. In response, she stands and takes a few steps toward the trees before looking over her shoulder at me. I look back at the house. Grandma's asleep, so if I just get this out of the way before she wakes up, maybe I can put it to rest. I turn on my phone's flashlight and follow the cat.

"Alright. Lead on. Did someone fall down a well or something?" I ask. Predictably, she doesn't answer. I cross the boundary between yard and forest without any more hesitation.

With the flashlight on, it's easy to follow the glint of the cat's eyes when she turns back to make sure I'm behind her. I try to mentally keep track of our direction. After what seems like no time at all, I'm surrounded by nothing but trees. The house is gone. I take a breath. Grandma's property sits right up against federally protected land. The woods go on and on, eventually turning into mountains. If I get lost, I could be out there for days and never find my way out, especially if the phone service is as bad everywhere else as it is on the property. I check my phone; signal might as well not exist. But I played in these woods as a kid and never died; I must know my way around well enough.

As we walk, it gets easier to see. I don't know if it's from my eyes adjusting or the moon casting more light as it moves higher up in the sky. At points where it peeks through the canopy, the moon seems bigger than it did back at the house, and the stars seem brighter. The deeper we head in, the bigger and older the trees get. My footsteps become cushioned by growth on the forest floor, and the sounds of life vanish so completely that all I can hear is my own breathing. Occasionally I see lights in the distance, which I want to believe are from the house, but the hue seems too cool, and I think I see one of the lights move.

A twig snaps somewhere next to me and I whirl, brandishing my phone as if it's a weapon. But what comes out from behind a tree trunk is a little girl, about seven years old. Her blond hair is long and loose almost down to her waist, and she wears a lacy white nightgown that ends just above her bare feet.

"Hey," I say softly, "what are you doing out here? Where are your parents?" The girl ignores me and keeps walking deeper into the woods. I follow and reach out to gently take her shoulder, but my hand passes straight through her body and the girl's form briefly ripples like disturbed water at the contact point before reforming. I gasp in surprise and draw my hand back as if she burned me.

"Okay. This isn't real. What am I even doing out here?" I ask myself. The cat has paused and seems to be staring quizzically at me a short distance away as if she too can't believe how weird I'm being.

Then I recognize the nightgown. My mother is wearing it in a few of her childhood photos in Grandma's album. And then it was passed down to me. The girl herself looks identical to my old first grade school photo. It's me. I wonder if this is an out-of-body memory, but if I ever wandered around in the woods at night, I don't have any concrete memories of doing so. Whatever the case is, I can't resist following her.

At every rustle of leaves and branches, Young Tamsin pauses and looks around. She seems to be looking for something specific, though I have no idea what. I get my answer when something buzzes down from the branches of a tree, stopping just out of the girl's reach and clinging to the trunk.

The creature is about two feet tall. On its back are insectoid wings that fold to lay flat on either side of its spine. It has a humanoid head and torso, but its forelimbs are insectoid as well, ending in delicate claws. I initially think it's wearing bulky goggles, but then I realize it has bulging compound eyes like that of a fly. It simply watches her inquisitively.

"Hello," she says to the creature. Its antennae twitch.

"You can see me?" the creature asks. Its voice is high-pitched.

"Yes. And I brought a present." At that, the creature gets a little closer, and I hear more buzzing and rustling up in the trees as more of these creatures peek through the leaves to watch what's going on.

"What kind of present?" the creature asks.

"Chocolate chip cookies my grandma made," she says. She takes out a parcel wrapped in a paper towel and lays it down on the ground. It contains several cookies. Grandma would not have been happy to see those missing. "You can have them if you want." The creature flits down to the ground, grabs the cookies, and flies back up into the tree branches, where the other creatures converge.

After the creatures whisper amongst one another between bites of cookie, the first one then flies back down to talk to Young Tamsin.

"We like your gift," it says. "Come and play with us." The other creatures fly down and surround the girl, and she looks at them with joy and wonder in her eyes.

"How many other faeries live here?" she asks.

"Lots and lots," the lead creature says, "but we're the loveliest."

"What should I call you?" she asks. The creature studies its surroundings for a moment.

"Ivy," the creature—the faerie—says, "now catch us!" With that, they all take off flying in different directions. Young Tamsin follows the closest one, and I chase as quickly as I dare, worried about tripping in the dark.

The faeries lead us until we're both panting from exertion, dancing just close enough to Young Tamsin to keep her thinking she has a chance before speeding back off into the night. At one point, I nearly hit my head as we chase the faeries past a low-hanging branch. It's soon after that I realize I've lost track of the faeries and Young Tamsin and am alone in the woods.

But I'm not alone for long. Tansy silently comes into sight a short distance away and glares at me. I almost imagine she's upset I suddenly ran off.

"So where is it you wanted to go, then?" I ask. I move to follow the cat, and then there's an explosion of sound somewhere nearby. A screeching, buzzing cacophony flares up somewhere beyond my sight and then fades as the source seems to move away. It sounds like the faeries Young Tamsin was chasing, but angrier, and strangely discordant.

Quickly following that commotion, I hear something between a bark and a howl—baying, that's what it's called. What hunting dogs do when they've found prey. At that, the cat puffs up her tail and is gone in a flash.

"Wait!" I call out. She's really just a cat, doing what a normal cat would do and fleeing from predators. I'm surprised and disappointed in the part of myself that hoped there was something waiting for me at the end of this walk. I almost let out a laugh at my own silliness when a large dark shape barrels through the undergrowth in the direction the cat fled.

"Hey! Stop! Heel! Cats aren't food!" I yell, to no effect. I've never had a dog. I don't know how to deal with them.

There's a crunching of undergrowth to my left, followed by an eruption of baying very close to me. A second dog emerges from the darkness and sniffs the ground. It looks at me, eyes shining, ears angled forward. The animal is almost as big as a pony; it has shaggy black fur, floppy ears, and a tail that curls up just slightly at the end.

"Hey, doggy." My voice is small. I have no idea how to handle dogs. Every nerve in my body screams at me to run, but I remember hearing somewhere that running is the worst thing you can do when confronted with a predator. Or maybe that was just about bears.

"It's okay. I'm friendly. Are you lost?" I say, trying my best to sound calm. Very slowly, I extend my hand for it to smell, worried I'm going to pull back a stump. The dog comes forward and sniffs my hand, and then leans back and howls.

The noise taps into a primal part of my brain that overrides all rational thought. I run. I can't tell if the dog gives chase; I can't hear anything over the sounds of my own breathing and the crunching of the forest floor beneath my feet.

Just ahead of me, there's a tree with low branches. I run for it and surprise myself with how quickly I swing up and weave through the branches to get to a decent height. Not a moment later, the dog lopes into my sight and gazes up at me with bright green eyes. The creature's so big it looks like it could easily reach me if it stood on its hind legs. But it doesn't try. It just bays once more and starts to circle the tree. It's calling someone, I realize. Maybe the other dog, maybe their owner. I strain my eyes to see if it has a collar, but I can't tell.

Since I seem safe for the time being, the adrenaline starts to bleed out of my muscles. My arms shake as sudden weakness overcomes me, but I adjust my position in the tree so I won't fall just from losing my grip. I breathe out deeply. Maybe the owner is out looking for their dogs right now, and they'll find me and help me get home.

"You seem to have a problem," says a familiar voice. The strange dark-haired man I saw in my room is now reclining on a branch to my right and a few feet above, looking down his nose at me. I have no idea how he got there or where he came from. As soon as we make eye contact, I look away and back down to the dog.

"Don't ignore me," he says. He sounds almost comically offended. I ignore him and aggressively focus on the dog.

It looks up at me and wags its tail, which doesn't make it any less terrifying.

"I might be able to help you out of this," the man continues.

"I don't need help. The dog's owner is going to come and then I'll be able to get home," I say. Damn. I shouldn't have let him get me talking. I have to remember he's not real, but maybe talking to him will help me work out a solution for myself.

"Why do you think their master will help you? How do you know you're not what they're hunting?" he asks.

"Because people don't hunt other people like that!" But thinking about it, I realize it's not hunting season for any game. There's no animal anyone should be hunting right now.

"But those are faerie hounds, and the Fae *adore* hunting trespassing mortals. And by the look of things, you've trespassed."

"You're telling me the dogs are faeries? Where's their little butterfly wings, then?" I ask.

He quirks an eyebrow. "I have no idea what leap in reasoning you've just attempted. But let me reiterate, you're trapped. If the dogs' master even comes. It won't be to save you."

"And do you, as a figment of my imagination, have a way to help me?" I ask. "Because I'm more and more sure now that *none* of this is real. Not even the dogs, and definitely not you." Maybe I should make an appointment with Dr. Webster tomorrow.

"Then jump down there and go home on your own," he challenges. The dog doesn't currently look aggressive, but it looks threatening simply by virtue of existing. I can't bring myself to climb down, even if it would prove once and for all that this is happening inside my head.

"So what have you been waiting to offer me?" I ask. He laughs, probably because he knows he just won this battle of wills.

"I can offer you a deal," he says.

"What? You think this is the right time to talk about deals? Just help me if you can!" I snap. Another dog howls somewhere nearby, and the one under the tree responds in kind.

"This is one of the best times. It sounds like you'll have company soon," the man muses. "I can guide you to safety, and in exchange I want you to free me."

"Free you from what?"

"I don't know. I think this is just a fragment of me. The rest is somewhere else, but I don't know where. That's why you need to find it." He says the words slowly, like I'm an idiot.

"Fine. But not just 'safety.' That's too vague. You need to guide me back to my Grandma's house," I say.

"Ah. Smart addition. In exchange for you freeing my body, I will guide you safely to your grandmother's house to the best of my ability."

"Does that mean anything? 'The best of your ability' might not be worth much, since you're trapped or something," I say. The other dog arrives and circles the tree, looking up at me. It looks identical to the first one.

"Of your options, I'd say I'm the best," he says, gesturing to the dogs.

"Fine, deal," I say. "Just help me."

"Say, 'I promise to hold faithful to this bargain or else forfeit my last drop of blood,'" he says.

"Wait," I say, a thought occurring to me. "You must be pretty desperate to be making deals with random people in the woods." This isn't real, right? I don't have to worry. I might as well go for the most that I can get, if just for fun, or to prove a point to myself.

"That is the same thing you are doing right now," he says, scowling.

"Sure. But who do you think is more desperate?" I ask. "Best time, right? Just like you said."

"What else do you want?" he asks.

"I don't know, but it seems like a waste to just wish to get home safely this once. I mean, if I agree to help you, you then have a vested interest in helping me right now no matter what my actual reward is," I say. As I speak, his face darkens, and I get a sort of perverse joy from irritating him, even if he is just a figment of my imagination.

"There are countless gifts I could give you once I'm free. Do you want wealth? Power? The love of beautiful people? I could make you my consort and bring you with me to Faerie when I return, but I cannot make you my wife, as I am engaged."

"Ew. No. Um. I want a wish to be determined after you're freed," I say.

His mouth twists up in annoyance, but he sighs. "Fine. I accept. I promise to hold faithful to this bargain or else forfeit my last drop of blood."

"I promise to hold faithful to this bargain or else forfeit my last drop of blood," I repeat. I hope playing along is the best way to get out of this.

"Smart choice," the man says, grinning. I don't like his expression. It's both smug and vaguely predatory. Something tells me I should have been smarter. "To start. We're in Faerie right now. You need to go through a door to get back to your world."

"What's *Faerie*? And I didn't go through any doors to end up here, unless you mean the back door of the house."

"You must have, or you wouldn't be here. It doesn't have to look like the door to a house, which is what you might be thinking of. Any passage or threshold would work. The older or more permanent the better."

"A threshold ... The back door of the house? The tree line?" I suggest.

"One of those might work," he says. Great, but I can't get back to either of those without climbing out of the tree. Instead, I carefully stand up on the branch I'm perching on, using a branch higher up to grip and stabilize myself. Carefully, I shimmy out to where the main branch splits into thinner ones. Finding one that looks fragile enough, I bring my foot down on it as hard as I can. The main branch wobbles, and the thin branch bows slightly. I stomp on it again and again, until it finally partially snaps and the very end swings down and brushes across the ground. I look at the man, who's been watching me quizzically the entire time.

"So that makes a door, right? It's kind of an arch now," I say. He nods.

"Now go through it," he says. I look down. The dogs are circling the area again, looking agitated by the commotion.

"You better be right about this."

"I am. Trust me. I have far more at stake than you. If I'm wrong, you will just be dead. I'll still be imprisoned and no one will know of my plight," he says.

"Fine," I say. I take a breath, crouch, and swing down on the branch and use my momentum to launch myself through the arch I created. I land on my feet but immediately collapse and go rolling across the forest floor.

I roll up into a ball and wait for the dogs to maul me, but nothing happens. When I look up, I'm alone. The dogs are nowhere to be seen. I guess they were just figments of my imagination, and playing along with the scenario made it go away. I'll have to remember that.

"Okay, imaginary guy. How do I get home from here?" I ask. But it doesn't look like he's around anymore. For a moment I'm almost disappointed, but then I realize it's probably a good thing there are no more imaginary people to talk to.

I check my pocket for my phone but find that it's gone. I've run so far through the woods it could have fallen out anywhere. Checking the ground near the tree I was climbing in turns up nothing. So I'm on my own. I pick my best guess at the direction to Grandma's house and start walking. If I can at least find a road, I'll be able to get home.

It's not too long before I hear the steps of something bigger than a squirrel nearby. And then I see her. Young Tamsin is walking around clumsily, weakly. So much for no more imaginary friends. I walk over to her and see that she looks exhausted, and her bare feet are bloody, though I can't do anything to help her. I follow her as she walks, hoping someone finds her or she finds a road that leads me back to the house.

It turns out somebody finds her. She doesn't get much further before she curls up against a tree to rest. Soon after, a strange-looking creature arrives. She looks human, but she's about the size of Young Tamsin but with adult proportions, and her eyes are enormous and doe-like. Her arms are long and inhumanly thin and spindly, and her hair is wild and tied off and braided in several places. The tips of large pointed ears peek out from her hair. She catches sight of Young Tamsin and rushes over.

"My dear, wake up," she says. Her voice is soothing. Young Tamsin grumbles and rubs her eyes.

"Hello," she says. "I'm lost and I'd really like to go home."

"Are you hungry, child? Let me bring you to my home and feed you cakes and jelly."

"Um ..." Young Tamsin thinks hard, pursing her lips. "Grandma will be worried if I'm out for too long. If you help me go home now I can give you some cookies and visit you another time," she says. She seems proud of herself, as if she recited the words from memory.

"You're a very polite girl," the creature says. "But you need not fear offending me. I will take you to your home." The creature offers Young Tamsin a hand, and she takes it.

"What should I call you, ma'am?" Young Tamsin asks.

"You can call me Thistledown. Who taught you to talk so nicely?" she asks. The two start to walk, and I follow.

"Cheeps told me faerie rules. He lives under our house and let me pick what I wanted to call him, so I picked mouse sounds because he eats them. He's nice. He cleans my room for me but sometimes he takes things Grandma cooks, but he says it's not stealing because he helps out a lot."

"And how did you end up out here all alone?"

"Cheeps told me there were little faeries in the woods and I wanted to meet them. I gave them some cookies and they were nice for a while, but then I don't know what happened. They started screaming and there was lots of noise."

"Well, my dear. There are evil things in these woods, things that don't like the good folk here," Thistledown says. "But today, the evil things did not catch you. Here's your house." She takes out a round, vibrant purple flower from her hair and places it in Young Tamsin's hand. "Use this if you would like to visit. I'll make you tea and cakes."

"I will," Young Tamsin says. She runs off, and I follow back into the yard and then the house.

Chapter Three

I CREEP THROUGH THE back door, up the stairs, and into my room without alerting Grandma. Once I'm collapsed on my bed, it seems like everything that happened could have just been a dream. A dream would be the most obvious explanation since I can't trust my senses.

Now that I have a chance to lay still and reflect, I realize my senses are telling me I'm in pain. My hands feel peeled raw and my legs and arms shake like I've run and climbed miles. My throat and lungs burn from exertion as well. I shimmy out of my clothes while laying down and curl up under the blanket. Maybe things will make more sense when the sun comes up.

I leave the bedside lamp on.

When I wake up, it feels like I barely slept. Watery, early morning sunlight peeks in through the window. I reach for my phone to check the time, but it's not on the bedside table. I recall reaching for it and not finding it in my dream as well. As I think, I realize the events of last night's dream are still crystal clear in my mind. They didn't fade like dreams usually do.

The pain didn't fade, either. My limbs still ache. Hopefully a shower will make me feel better. I run my fingers through my hair and they catch on something rough. A twig. My first thought is to check the window to see if something had blown in during the night, but the window is closed fast and looks like it hasn't been opened in years.

I place the twig on the bedside table. Maybe I sleepwalked. Whether I used to do that when I lived here, I can't remember.

My clothes from last night are crumpled and dirty. My jeans have dirt and grass stains that look as if I took a few spills. And I did. I jumped out of a tree and went rolling.

I get out of bed and make my way to the bathroom; the movement brings pain to my back and limbs. My palm stings when I grab my bedroom doorknob.

In the bright, harsh bathroom light, I see that my palms are scraped raw and covered in a sticky residue. Tree sap, along with a fair mix of blood and dirt. I wash my hands as gently as possible, but I still wince as the soap and warm water stings my damaged skin.

The motion causes pain in my arms and back as well; after I dry my hands, I look over the rest of my body. Bruises are starting to form on my arms, shoulders, and legs.

I lean against the wall and slide to the floor. There are two bad options for what happened last night: either I sleepwalked and hurt myself without realizing it, or I had a hallucinatory adventure in the woods.

Or maybe faeries are real but I'm the only one who can see them.

Please. Even if it were true, it wouldn't matter. To everyone else in the world, I'd still be the crazy one.

But I can't mention any of this to Grandma. If she knew what was going on, she'd make me leave. The thought reminds me of the important thing that happened last night—the thing all the imaginary nonsense made me forget: Grandma and I got into a fight and I told her I'd leave today if that's what she wanted. And I don't see why she wouldn't. She didn't want me to come in the first place, and I haven't been useful at all. I should be taking care of her, not the other way around. The last time I lived here, I was a child, but now I should know what reality is. I don't need to tell her what's going on, I just need to be more aware.

That reminds me. I pull myself to my feet and scan the bathroom for my phone, hoping I left it here after my shower last night. It's not here; the fact doesn't even surprise me. The way my life is going right now, it's probably somewhere in the woods.

After a shower to soak my sore feet and new bruises, I get dressed and go downstairs. The kitchen clock reads 6:32. It seems like Grandma's still sleeping, so I make myself some coffee and take stock of the fridge and pantry. Maybe I can make breakfast before Grandma gets up, just to show her I'm capable of cooking, though she'd certainly find something to critique. She'd probably complain if she woke up and saw I was awake and *hadn't* made breakfast. So after I finish my first cup of coffee, I pull out eggs, peppers, cheese, and ham, and start making omelets. If she still gets up around eight, I'll have timed things perfectly.

I line the peppers up on a cutting board and pull a knife out of the knife block. The handle is made of dark wood that's faded with age. A tiny nick in the blade catches my eye, and suddenly my mind is sent back over a decade ago: I'm walking through the woods, this knife in one hand, Grandma's cast iron skillet in the other, muscles tensed against every shadow and cracking twig. Was I looking for something, running from something? The memory is unclear.

"What are you doing?" Grandma demands. She stands at the edge of the kitchen, wrapped in a robe older than me.

"Making omelets," I say. That seems fairly obvious. Though maybe her real question is what I'm still doing in her house.

"I'll do that. I'm the one who does the cooking in my house." She takes a step closer, hand held out for the knife.

"It's fine. I'm a good cook. Believe it or not, I've been feeding myself for a few years now."

"Just put down the knife," she says, voiced raised a hair. It finally clicks and my heart twists.

"Do you think I'm going to do … something with this?" I wave the knife in the air. Grandma flinches. I gently set the knife down on the counter and take a step away from it, crossing my arms. "Are you serious?" I ask.

"You don't remember how you liked to steal my kitchen knives when you were younger?" she asks, taking the knife and starting on the omelets where I left off. I study her hands as she works. Her grip on the handle looks strong; her hands aren't trembling.

"Even if I did, I never *hurt* anyone," I say.

Grandma guts a pepper with more force than necessary. "Still," she says. "I had to replace a lot of them. You would take them to go hunting with your 'friends.' Sometimes you came home bleeding. You're just not careful."

"Grandma," I scoff. "I'm an adult. And like I said, I've been cooking for years and haven't cut myself." Never mind the fact that I came home bleeding last night.

"You may be an adult, but this is still my house. Now go turn the TV on. I like to watch it while I work." I obey and turn on the news.

"Even if it's not me, you're going to have to let someone else start cooking for you eventually," I say. I get nervous just bringing it up.

"Not now. Not while I can still do it myself. Understand? I'm not just giving up and handing the reins over now."

We sit in silence for a while. Her cooking, me waiting for her to tell me she wants me out. But she doesn't say anything. Maybe she forgot it even came up.

Most of breakfast goes by without either of us speaking. We eat to the sound of the local news punctuated by forks scraping across plates.

"So, should I leave, then?" I ask once the plates are in the sink.

"Yes. I need you to go to the grocery store. I have a list, but I didn't sleep well so I don't feel like doing it myself today." She knows what I was really asking, but if she wants to pretend nothing happened last night, I'll go along with it.

"Bad dreams or something?"

"I think my mattress is just old and lumpy," she says. "Anyway. Take my card. Get the things on the list on the fridge and then whatever else you want to eat. Oh, and feed the cat before you go. The keys are on the hook by the door."

When I open the pantry, the little man from under the porch is inside, polishing the canned goods. Young Tamsin said she called him Cheeps.

"Hello Young Miss!" he says. "I would love salmon today." Without thinking, I reach for a can of salmon cat food, then hesitate and place my hand on a can of chicken instead. But then I groan and grab the salmon. Even though these creatures are all in my head, I can't bring myself to be mean for the sake of being contrary. Cheeps squeals in delight and follows me as I take the food outside.

Tansy is laying on the back porch next to the food bowl when I get out there, and surprisingly, so is my phone. When I approach, the cat predictably jumps up and darts a few feet away. I ignore her for the moment and dump the food in the bowl, picking up my phone while I'm crouched down. There's a thin crack running across the upper right part of the screen, but the phone still works. I have a thought, and I check the phone's photo library, but the last picture taken was of my bus ticket.

I must have dropped the phone without realizing it while filling up the food bowl last night. That's what would make the most sense. But I'm fairly sure I used it last night in my room before bed.

When I come back inside, Grandma is watching the news and doesn't acknowledge my presence. I collect the grocery list from the fridge and the car keys from their hook and give Grandma a quick goodbye as I walk out the front door.

The Ford's handle sticks slightly when I open it and I have to turn the key twice before it starts, but otherwise the truck seems to be in decent condition. It's old, but at least it's clean. It doesn't look like it gets used very often.

The truck bounces violently down the driveway; maybe Grandma should get the suspension looked at. Still, I'm glad for a chance to get off the property.

Getting to town is a straight shot down the one main road. It's fifteen minutes before I pass anything but easy-to-miss driveways. Then comes the town high school I attended for less than a year before Grandma decided that changing my environment might be good for me. Then it was a boarding school two hours away and various camps or other arrangements during the summer months so I never had to come back to this place. I can't imagine how much that all cost, and I've never built up the nerve to ask Grandma how far she had to go into debt because of me.

I pass a few aging mom-and-pop stores on the way to the town center, which consists of a diner that's gone unchanged for thirty years, two dueling strip malls, one office park, and, surprisingly, a small apartment block that wasn't there before.

The grocery is one of the bigger stores in town, and when I arrive I wander aimlessly for a while. Grandma's list is pretty easy: milk, eggs, bread, and the other basics. As for what I want, I'm not sure. She'd probably be mad if I didn't come home with anything for myself, so I throw in some grapes and oranges. But she'd probably also complain that I'm not taking advantage of her generosity if I don't get any sweets, so I grab a tub of mint chocolate chip ice cream.

"Tamsin!" a man calls out as I'm double-checking Grandma's list. I jump and look around, expecting to see a new mythical creature waving at me, but instead it's a normal-looking man abandoning his shopping cart to run over to me, nearly bumping into other customers on the way.

"... Hi?" I say. He looks at me expectantly, a crooked smile on his face. He has a nice face; tanned, lots of freckles, a tiny white scar across his eyebrow. He looks vaguely familiar, but I can't place him. For some reason, looking at him makes my heart race and anxiety simmer in the pit of my stomach. Is it just because he's cute? *Do* I think he's cute?

After a moment, his face falls. Oh, no. I should know him and I don't. "*Oh*. Heeey," I say. My voice is not convincing. I'm a terrible person.

"You have no idea who I am, do you?" he says.

"Absolutely none. I'm so sorry."

"Zach?" he offers.

"Zach ..." I still have nothing. I'm awful.

"Your grandma's neighbor. We played together when we were kids," he says.

"Zach!" I shout. It's coming back to me. "Really, I'm so sorry."

"It's cool. I just have one of those forgettable faces. And names," he laughs. He doesn't seem offended, thankfully. "You looked like you were about to either punch me or run for the hills when I came over here. I'm sorry if I creeped you out. My bad."

"It's fine, really. I should have recognized you. You must look really different since the last time we met." I think hard about it, but all I can come up with are vague associations. The name "Zach" in my memories conjures up a scrawny, gap-toothed kid with a bowl cut. This Zach is well-muscled, and his brown hair is short on the sides and long and a little floppy on the top. He still has a gap in his smile; it's cute. All of him is cute.

"It's what it is; people change," he says. "Hey. Do you want to go somewhere and catch up? Get lunch maybe?

You know, instead of just standing around in the pet stuff aisle."

"I'd love to," I say. Since I'm here, I buy a toy mouse for the cat. Zach and I check out and meet each other at a diner a few minutes away called Carol's Kitchen. The parking lot is cracked asphalt lacking any lines delineating parking spots. The diner's red and white exterior would be at home in the 1950s.

Zach holds the door open for me on the way in. The inside is decorated in similar colors to the outside, save that the tables are bright yellow. There's a refrigerated display case showing off an array of pies, cakes, and other sweets. A host quickly greets us and leads us to a table.

"I love the Reuben here," Zach says. "And they just started letting you switch out for sweet potato fries a few years ago. Those are good. Get whatever you want; I'm treating."

"I thought ... sauerkraut was cruel and unusual punishment." The memory feels right when I say it. In my mind's eye a younger Zach and I are in a dining room that must be his, boycotting our dinner plates.

"People change." Zach shrugs and offers me another lopsided smile. "Here, they've added some new desserts, too." He pushes the menu in front of me and launches into a commentary on each item. I listen politely, comfortable not having to lead the conversation. Instead, I study Zach's face, taking in every blemish that marks him as real, human. He has a few stray hairs on his cheek he must have missed while shaving, a tiny scar above his right eyebrow, a bit of acne along his jaw. And dimples that make his smile infectious. Everything about him is different from the creepy smooth perfection of that strange man I imagined last night. Maybe my imagination is just horrible at faces.

"... like?" he says, the sudden pause forces me to zone back in. I realize our waiter is here, pen and pad out expectantly. I haven't even glanced at the menu.

"Just water, please," I say automatically.

"And to eat?" the waiter asks. I must have been zoned out for a while.

"A Reuben with sweet potato fries?" I say. That was the only thing I remember being said. He writes that down and leaves.

"So how have you been?" Zach asks once we're alone again. I can't tell if there's anything hidden in his tone, such as, *'so are you still super weird?'* I don't recall having many friends here. Any friends, really. Except the imaginary ones.

"I've been fine. I just moved back here from Boston."

"Wow. I've never been there. What's that like?" He seems genuinely interested.

"Uh, loud," I say. "And busy."

"Is that why you decided to come back?"

"I wasn't really happy there." Grandma certainly wouldn't want me to tell anyone about her health issues. She'd never forgive me. And probably also murder me.

"I'm sure Miss Mary is happy you're back. She really missed you," he says. I laugh at that, but he just looks confused.

"It's funny that you said she missed me. You know her that well?" I ask.

"Yeah. I go over there every so often to mow her grass and do anything else she needs done. She'd talk about you sometimes." Now my interest is piqued.

"What did she say?"

"That she hoped you were happy, and that she hoped you had a boyfriend and would get married and settle down and all that."

"That sounds like her."

"So I guess all that didn't happen?"

"Obviously not."

"Ah, cool. I mean, I'm sorry," he stammers. "That's not cool."

"It's fine. Don't worry about it. I'm glad you're around to help Grandma out," I say.

"It's not a problem. She's a really nice lady. Whenever I go over there, she always makes me stay for dinner and then sends me home with the leftovers," he says. I have never, in my life, thought to use 'nice' as a descriptor for Grandma. Maybe she's just different when I'm not around.

"You okay?" Zach asks, and I realize I've been staring off into space brooding. For a change, I decide to try honesty; maybe Zach will have some insight into the situation.

"I guess this will sound silly to you, but I just don't think my grandma even likes me," I say. Zach looks at me thoughtfully for a few moments.

"I do think that's silly. She raised you. She can't not like you. I mean, I always thought you were pretty likable," he laughs and fiddles with his napkin.

"But I wasn't exactly pleasant to raise," I counter. Likable? Like, *likable*? I'm not sure exactly what he means, so I say nothing about it.

"Is any kid? My mom still reminds me about the secret bug zoo I kept under my bed until I was fifteen," he laughs. "Everyone's got problems. That doesn't make you what you think it makes you. Sometimes we all just need a little push to realize it, right?"

"Thanks," is all I say in response. I have to pull back from this conversation. It's not one I'm ready to have, so for a while we sit in awkward silence.

"So how's Cheeps?" Zach asks. I almost choke on my sandwich.

"Cheeps?" I say between sips of water.

"Yeah, the house brownie," Zach says. I try to see if he's mocking me, or if this is some kind of inside joke we might have had, but he looks completely sincere.

"Oh, so I guess I told you all about my magic forest friends?" I try to laugh it off, but the noise that comes out of my throat is more of a nervous whine.

"Yeah. You introduced me to a bunch of them. We should go see how they're doing some time," he says. He still sounds completely serious. I feel like I must have hidden cameras watching me. Maybe he's humoring me. Maybe we're not having this conversation right now. Maybe Zach isn't even here and I'm eating alone. I lean in close to Zach over the table.

"I really can't tell if you're joking or not," I say.

"Why would I be joking?" he asks. I lose my nerve.

"I don't know. Sorry. But that sounds like a good idea. You should come over sometime," I say.

"I can come over right now."

That was unexpected. "Wow. That would be fun but I don't think Grandma wants company today." And neither would I, not on such short notice. His eagerness threatens to be overwhelming.

"Okay, well just text me when she does, or you do," he says, and I realize I've been seen through. He gives me his number and doesn't ask for mine.

I think about Zach's words on the drive back to Grandma's. He seemed so sure of everything he said. As children, we could have both had overactive imaginations, or he was impressionable enough to be drawn into mine. Still, I'm grateful to have someone else to talk to here—someone who isn't either Grandma or a figment of my imagination.

The drives goes swiftly until I'm rounding the final curve of Grandma's driveway; as soon as the trees part to reveal the house, I slam on the brakes. Laying on the porch is a large dog. It lifts its head to watch me inch forward the rest of the way to the house.

Very slowly, I open the cab door and get out, ready to jump back in and slam the door if the dog makes any sudden movements. It stays where it is and stares at me. Somehow, that's scarier than if it barked.

"Hey, there," I say softly. It doesn't react. It looks exactly like the animals from my dream. It just looks like a normal—if terrifying—dog. Still, I don't approach the house. The dog's tail wags once, thumping back down onto the porch.

After an intense staring contest, the dog's ears angle back, and a moment later I hear a flurry of activity from inside the house. The door opens and Grandma accompanies a fair-haired stranger to the door. At his presence, the dog stands and heels.

"I'm grateful for your help," the stranger says to Grandma. "We had a pleasant conversation." There's an edge to his voice that I don't like. Something that makes my inner ear tingle.

"Of course. I'm always glad for company," Grandma says. "I'm just glad you found him." She leans down and pats the dog on the head. I flinch, but it doesn't react aggressively. Then, Grandma notices me. "Oh. This is Tamsin, my granddaughter," she says. The man turns to face me. At the sight of his face, my vision is replaced with red, my heart pounds, my head spins, and I go stumbling toward the ground.

Chapter Four

I FALL INTO THE cab door and catch myself before I hit the ground.

"Tamsin!" Grandma yells. I hear footsteps and feel a cold shadow settle over me. When I look up, it's into the face of the stranger. The dog at his side approaches to sniff me but backs off when I flinch. Grandma is slower than they are, but she makes her way over as well.

"What's wrong? Are you feeling sick?" she asks. She sounds scared.

"I ... Maybe I stood up too fast," I say. "I'm fine now. It's okay." Grandma looks unconvinced. The man hasn't spoken and looks unsure of what he should be doing. He's only a bit taller than me, perhaps five-eight or five-nine, and has nondescript clothes—no Renaissance faire garb. He looks normal: honey-colored hair that falls to his shoulders and rich brown eyes. But there's a sense of tenseness about him, and he stares at me like I'm the source. The force of his gaze makes me want to curl up in a ball. I can't place this man, but something about him fills me with a combination of fear, sadness, and revulsion. Looking at him makes the back of my head prickle and threatens enough vertigo to send me wobbling against the truck again.

"Go inside. I'll bring the groceries in," Grandma says, pulling my attention away from the man.

"I'm fine," I insist. "I can do it." I open the back door to grab the bags off the seat.

Instead, Grandma turns to the man. "Would you mind carrying these groceries for my granddaughter?" she asks.

"Of course," he says. His voice is low and growly.

"Great. I'll go pour you some more tea," she says, and makes her way back into the house, cane wobbling slightly. She probably doesn't want to admit she needs to sit down. I'm surprised she asked the man for help at all.

I scrutinize the man as if he's planning on doing something suspicious with the groceries.

"Hello, Tamsin," he says. He says my name carefully, the word clipped.

"Hi," I say. "Uh, thanks for helping with the groceries. Do you know my grandma?"

He stares at me like he's waiting for something else. "Not well. I came to collect my dog and she invited me inside."

"Well, I'm glad you found it. How long was your dog loose?" I ask. If his dog got out and he's been looking for it, then that could explain me running into it last night. Maybe it followed me back here and I didn't realize it.

"Not long," he says.

"How did you know it was here?"

"I followed it here."

"From where? This is the middle of nowhere. Where do you live?" I say. I probably shouldn't be interrogating him like this, but something about his presence bothers me.

"I live nearby," he says. He sounds extremely annoyed. He looks off into the distance for a moment, as if thinking.

Then his gaze returns to me. "*Move away. You don't belong here.*" He says it forcefully. He's right. I really don't belong here. Grandma doesn't want me here. I should pack up and get out as soon as possible before something terrible happens.

Those thoughts fly through my head. But before I can act on any of them, a new thought occurs to me.

"Did my grandmother tell you that?" I ask. He glares at me but doesn't immediately answer. "No? Then it's really none of your fucking business."

"Then just stay out of the woods. There's bears. And other dangerous things."

"Like your dogs?" I ask.

"Worse," he says.

"You sound like you're threatening me."

"I'm warning you," he says. I open my mouth to respond but then bite my tongue. Maybe this guy is doing something criminal and I stumbled into it. What if he threatens Grandma? His even coming here is threatening Grandma. I shouldn't have been baiting him. We stare at each other.

"You're standing in front of the bags," he finally says, gesturing behind me. I move, and he gathers up the groceries and carries them toward the house.

"So should I ask what your name is, or is that also a secret?" I ask, following him.

"You may call me Hunter," he says.

"And you like hunting in the middle of the night?"

"You're too nosy for your own good," he says.

"I'm just trying to understand what's going on," I counter. We walk through the front door and into the kitchen, ceasing our conversation in Grandma's presence.

"Would you like some more iced tea?" Grandma asks Hunter as he places the grocery bags on the counter.

"That's very hospitable of you, but it's time for me to leave," he says.

"Well, feel free to stop by another time. Tamsin, walk him out, will you?" Grandma says. I walk him to the door in silence. There are many questions I want to ask, but I'm afraid I'll anger him by asking the wrong one.

"Bye," is all I say when I reach the door and hold it open for him. I'm a coward. He stops at the threshold and looks at me.

"If you remember anything I said, make it this: do not let sweet words and tempting promises draw you so far from home you cannot find your way back," he says.

"If you're actually trying to be helpful, you should just say what you mean," I say. He sighs in a very condescending, strangely familiar way.

"Farewell. I truly hope we don't meet again," he says, and leaves.

"Me too!" I whisper with as much hostility as I can muster without alerting Grandma. I shut the door, and then watch him until he vanishes down the driveway, walking. I didn't see any cars parked on the side of the road or the driveway, and it's a long walk to even the closest neighboring house, so I have no idea where he could be going.

When I'm sure he's gone, I go back into the kitchen and help Grandma put away the groceries.

"That nice man said we should move," Grandma says, shutting the fridge. "Where do you want to live? It should probably be far away. Change will be good for your health and mine." The words come out of her mouth oddly stilt-ed.

"What?" I stop short, clutching a tub of melted ice cream—I probably shouldn't have gone to lunch with Zach with this in the truck. "Just yesterday you said you never wanted to move." I lower my voice and step closer to Grandma, like Hunter could somehow be listening. "Did he threaten you? Do you want to call the police?"

"Why would you think that?" she asks, sounding genuinely surprised. "Now that I've thought about it, it seems like a good idea. How would you like to live in Washington State? After dinner, you should go on the computer and figure out how to look at houses for sale. I suppose we'll need to go get some boxes for packing."

"Maybe you should think about this a little longer before we go get boxes," I say. Even though moving is what I suggested she do, her sudden attitude shift is suspicious. I put the ice cream in the freezer before Grandma sees that I ruined it.

"Isn't this what you wanted me to do?" she snaps. "Why are you arguing now?"

"Do you even know that guy?" I ask.

"That's the first time I've met him, but I can't be expected to know all my neighbors in the area. And that doesn't mean he can't make good points," she says.

"And you didn't think there was anything weird about him?"

"He was a bit odd. I assume he's a bachelor, but there's nothing wrong with that." She thinks for a moment and then looks concerned. "Do you know him? Did he do or say something to you?"

"He told me not to go into the woods because of the bears," I say. "But the way he said it was weird." Even as I say it I know it's a weak argument.

"How was it weird?" Grandma asks.

"Because it was like, just threatening ..." I trail off.

"Did he threaten you?"

"Not exactly, but he was, like, creepy."

"I didn't think I raised you to judge people like that. Maybe he meant well but has poor social skills. In any case, he's right. You do need to keep an eye out for bears."

"Okay, but I'm pretty sure he either lets his dogs run loose at night, or was stalking around our house with them," I say. This is something I hoped I wouldn't have to bring up.

"How do you know that?" Grandma asks.

"I saw the dogs. There's at least two of them. One chased your cat," I say. Grandma scowls at that.

"So they were in the yard, and you saw them through the window?" she asks. Damn. I was hoping I'd be able to leave that part vague.

"No. I heard a dog barking last night so I went outside to check it out."

"So," Grandma says, her words slow and measured, "you went outside in the middle of the night, saw the dogs, and then he came here today and told you that you need to be careful wandering around the woods in the middle of the night?"

"Basically," I say. She folds her arms.

"He's not wrong, Tamsin. You shouldn't be doing that." She pauses, thinking. "And you only left the house because you heard a dog barking? There wasn't anything else ... strange?" she asks.

"I was not lured from the house by faeries, if that's what you're asking me," I say.

"Do you want me to make you an appointment with Dr. Webster?" she asks. I hate the voice she's using, how it makes me feel like I'm fragile and could shatter at the slightest touch.

"I just said I'm fine!" I snap. I didn't mean to raise my voice.

"You don't need to have an attitude about it," Grandma says. "I've only ever tried my best to help you."

"And you've seen how that turned out," I say, gesturing to myself. As soon as I say it, I grab my head in my hands in embarrassment. "I'm sorry. I shouldn't have said that." Grandma sighs and pinches the bridge of her nose.

"I'm starving. I wanted to make a nice lunch, but then you took so long getting home I almost called the cops," she says. This time, I'm grateful for the deflection.

"Fine. I should have texted to let you know I would be back a little later, but you could have also texted," I point out. "I just ... I think I'm going to take a glass of iced tea and sit on the porch. Don't worry. I'll stay in the yard," I add before she can protest. She doesn't say anything as I pour the tea out of the pitcher and go outside.

It's pleasantly warm outside, and I curl up in a wicker armchair and look out over the back yard. The cat is outside waiting for me. She looks unharmed, which is a relief. I was worried one of Hunter's dogs might have caught her.

She jumps up when I come outside and takes a few steps toward the woods. I feel the urge to follow her again, the desire to know what's at the end of that path. But at the same time, I want to know that I'm in control of myself, that I'm the one making my own decisions.

"Nope. Not today. You're going to get me in trouble," I say to her. She makes a sound in the back of her throat. Not quite a growl, but definitely expressing annoyance.

"Here," I say, pulling the toy mouse I bought at the grocery store out from my pocket. "I got you this." I toss it at her. It's a nice shot, and it lands only a few inches away from her. Without breaking off eye contact with me, she bats it away with a paw.

"Now I think you're just being petty," I say. She takes a few more strides toward the trees. "I'll pet you if you come over here." She ignores me, so I ignore her.

Alone outside, I analyze every moment of my interaction with Hunter. He was ridiculously suspicious. Unless I imagined our entire conversation, he knows something he won't say, and the way he apparently convinced Grandma she should move with a single conversation is strange. Come to think of it, when he told me to my face I should leave, I wanted to do just that for a second. He also mentioned sweet words and tempting promises, as if he overheard my conversation with that strange dark-haired man that keeps appearing and disappearing.

Hunter is suspicious, but Grandma also saw him and talked to him, so he isn't just in my head. All of this comes together to mean that I need to talk to him again, as much as I'm wary of him as a person. Unfortunately, I have no idea how to find him, aside from running around in the woods and waiting for him to find me. Which, honestly, is an option. A bad option, but an option nonetheless.

My thoughts are interrupted by the sound of the shed door opening and closing. I jump to attention to see Young Tamsin—wearing jeans embroidered with flowers and a flouncy blouse—leaving the shed carrying a hammer.

From there, she walks around and disappears behind the shed.

Intrigued, I get up and investigate. As I approach, my surroundings change. The fresh greens of spring become darker and tinged with orange, while the air gains a crisp chill. It's fall, maybe September or October.

Voices come from behind the shed, interspersed by the sound of hammering. When I round the side of the building, I see Young Tamsin and a boy sitting together, hammering rusty nails into a wooden plank. The boy looks about her age, with a bowl-cut and gap-toothed smile. Zach.

"It's good the shed has all this stuff," Young Tamsin says. "We're gonna win. We just gotta finish making our swords."

"And the traps," Zach says. He holds the nail while she swings the hammer with both hands. The entire scene is so ludicrously dangerous for children that I suddenly understand far better why Grandma is so paranoid with me.

"You should put that down," I say, but they don't react to seeing me at all. I didn't expect them to, but I wanted to try.

"What else can we use? We got to use iron that's been made into other stuff," Young Tamsin says. "They're scared of it." Her hammer very nearly comes down on Zach's thumb and I wince.

"Who says?" he asks, setting up another nail. She looks up from her work at him and grins in a conspiratorial manner.

"Thistledown," she says.

"Well, she does know a lot of stuff," Zach says. "Hey. Are knives made of iron? Your grandma has some in the kitchen."

"Good idea!" she says. "We'll get those next." The children continue to hammer away, no fear or doubt in what they're doing. After they hammer a line of nails down the length of a thin board, Young Tamsin takes it and partially buries it in the grass.

"That's not gonna work on the sprites. They can fly," Zach points out.

"There's gnomes and goblins and trolls too. They might come if the bad things get them too," Young Tamsin says. She comes back and hefts a sturdier board with nails hammered through the end and gives it an experimental swing. "We should make armor too. Like knights."

"How?" Zach asks.

"I don't know. But you need swords *and* armor for quests," Young Tamsin says.

"What's a quest?" he asks.

"A thing we have to do to save all the faeries," she says. "We'll take our swords with us and make armor and maybe get some of Grandma's knives."

"So what do we have to do?" Zach asks. Before she can answer, a buzzing noise fills the surrounding air.

"Sprites are here," Young Tamsin says. I can see them peeking out from between the leaves and hear them chittering and whispering to one another. There's a tense moment where everyone seems frozen, and then one sprite launches out of the tree line straight at Young Tamsin. I flinch, but she doesn't. She bats the sprite out of the air with her 'sword.' The faerie goes bouncing and rolling in the grass for several feet before coming to a stop, screeching in pain and rage. It has several oozing puncture wounds that hiss and smoke as if burning.

Before I have time to be proud of Young Tamsin's aim and courage, the rest of the sprites descend on the children and swarm them like a cloud of two-foot-tall hornets. The kids take a few more swings and make contact, but there are always more sprites to replace the injured. It doesn't take long for both kids to drop their weapons in favor of shielding their faces. The sprites bear down on them with barbed claws, tearing at skin and hair.

Then an arrow streaks through the air and pins a sprite to the shed through one of its bulbous eyes. From the same direction, a massive black dog bounds out of the trees and scatters the sprites tormenting the children before crouching down on top of them to shield them from further harm.

Another dog arrives and starts nabbing sprites out of the air as they scatter, shaking them like ragdolls and discarding them. Some manage to fly away, some limp off with damaged wings, and some lay unmoving where they fall.

Several more arrows fly, each striking at least one sprite, before Hunter enters the scene, dropping his bow and drawing a pale spear instead. But by the time he arrives, most of the sprites have fled, screeching back into the trees, howling noises that might be words.

When the sprites are gone, Hunter's dog moves from where it crouches over the children. They sit up shakily, looking stunned but not too hurt. They have a few bleeding cuts each, and Young Tamsin's hair is a mess, but nothing deadly. One of the dogs nuzzles and licks Young Tamsin's face, and she wraps her arms around its neck, as if desperate for something to hold.

Hunter approaches the kids and kneels to get eye level with Young Tamsin.

"Are you hurt?" he asks. His voice is surprisingly gentle.

"Only a little bit," she says, voice muffled from speaking into the dog's fur. Hunter picks up one of the abandoned 'swords' and examines it.

"These creatures are deadly. They're not like the ones you're used to playing with. Look." He uses the sword to gesture at one of the sprite corpses on the ground. I follow his gaze as well. The creature is actually composed of the partial remains of two other sprites, twisted together like something out of a mad scientist's lab.

"These are fae that have died. Their bodies are being used by other creatures," Hunter says.

"Zombie faeries exist?" Zach asks.

"I ... suppose," Hunter says, studying Young Tamsin. "You have Sight, yes?" he asks.

"I can see," she says.

"I mean special sight. You can see faeries even when they don't want you to. You've been playing with the sprites and the others in the woods."

"Yes," she says.

"Then you need to be very careful. The Fae can be very cruel, and some don't like it when humans can see them. The sprites might play nice with you now, but even the living ones can hurt you. There are things in the woods worse than these dead things—things that seem nice but aren't. They might hurt you, and it might be worse than today. You should pretend you don't see them, and just play with your human friends."

"Okay," she says, fidgeting with nervous energy. Something about Hunter seems to bother her. Maybe she doesn't like being lectured.

"I'm going to go now. Do you want the dog to stay with you for a while?" he asks. Young Tamsin releases the dog's neck, though she seems to do so reluctantly.

"No, he can go," she says.

"Remember, you should stay in your yard," he says.

"Okay," she says. And then he and the dogs vanish into the woods.

"Isn't he the one—" Zach starts, but Young Tamsin turns and violently shushes him.

"Let's go inside," she says, jumping up and stomping away. Zach follows.

I wait until this strange dream fades and I'm back in reality. There's something I want to check before I go back inside. Before the vision fades completely, I turn my attention to the shed. One spot in particular is covered in thick ropes of ivy, and when I peel enough away I find something lodged deep in the wood. I can't pry it out with my fingers, so I go around to the front of the shed, hoping to find something inside I can use. Instead, I see the door is padlocked. The metal is rusted. It's been here for a while, though it wasn't on the shed during that memory. I can guess that incident was probably the source of the padlock. Grandma would not have been pleased when she found out what we'd been doing.

The lock needs a key rather than a combination. I could ask Grandma for the key, but I doubt she'd give it over unless I gave her a good reason, which I don't have. I don't want to tell her I want to dig what I think is an arrow out of the side of the shed so I can get one step closer to proving faeries are real. Hopefully the key is somewhere obvious.

My next thought is to meet with Zach to ask if he remembers this happening. That would tell me for sure if these things I've been seeing are memories or completely imaginary. They feel true to me, but that could just be my mind playing tricks.

I go inside. Grandma wouldn't need to be clever; she'd just need to put the key where a seven-year old couldn't reach it. But it would also be somewhere convenient for use.

The key is in the first place I check—on top of the back door frame. But before I can go back outside, Grandma calls out from the kitchen.

"How are you feeling?" she asks.

"Better," I say. I go to the kitchen and leave the key where it is for now. It's not unlikely Grandma would be worried if she caught me going into the shed and hide the key somewhere harder to find. I'll deal with that later.

"That smells good," I say. Soup is simmering on the stove as Grandma finishes up a second grilled cheese sandwich. "Can I help with anything?"

"I suppose you could set the table," she says. As I do so, I try to think of conversation topics that won't make her worry about my mental wellbeing.

"I ran into Zach today," I say. "We had lunch and caught up." I grab silverware and ladle soup into bowls.

"Well, you could have mentioned you had lunch before I made it," Grandma says reproachfully, bringing the sandwiches to the table.

"Sorry. I'll eat the leftovers for dinner," I say.

"Zach's a very nice boy. I swear he only got cuter as he grew up," she says.

"I think he might be a little young for you, Grandma." I dip the corner of my grilled-cheese into the soup and take a bite. It's a token effort to eat something, just to keep Grandma happy. I'm still full from lunch with Zach.

"Don't worry about me. I'd never steal your little boyfriend," she says, laughing.

"I *just* got here. Don't assume I'm romantically interested in any man I talk to," I say. Grandma just laughs again.

"You weren't sneaky, missy. I remember you tip-toeing out at night dressed all cute, boobs falling out of your shirt."

"Grandma!" I say, feeling my face turn red and covering my chest instinctively. "I do *not* remember that happening."

"Oh, it did. I'll never know how many times you snuck out. Sometimes you were sneaky, sometimes you weren't. Sometimes you just ran off while I threatened to ground you. The only way to keep you in the house would have been to handcuff you. But you know what? It was a relief to know you were meeting Zach, at least that's a normal thing for teenagers to do. If you weren't alone, it was easier to believe you'd come back home safe."

"I really don't remember dating him. I feel bad," I say. It's weird he didn't mention that at lunch; maybe he was embarrassed I didn't seem to remember.

"I'm sure it will come back," she says. "You've been away for a while. You just need to readjust."

"Help me remember. Did I have any other friends?"

"Friends from school, I'm sure. But none you ever had over more than once," she says. "I wish you would have spent time with more people. I tried to sign you up for so many afterschool things. You never liked anything enough to stick with it." I stir my soup and study the bright orange liquid trails chasing my spoon until I get the courage to ask another question, this one a little more risky.

"So ... Were there any imaginary friends I mentioned more than once?" I ask.

"Why are you interested?" Grandma demands, her tone suddenly becoming irritated.

"Well, Zach mentioned some stuff we'd talk about as kids, so I was curious, and I wanted to be able to talk about it with him now," I say. Her expression softens. It looks like Zach is the key to keeping her from worrying too much.

"There were all sorts in the woods. The ones I remember were the ones you said lived in the house. There was a little elf that stole snacks and did chores. That one came up a lot when you needed someone to blame for things. Sometimes the elf got mad and did things like cutting up the bedsheets or egging the television," she says, eyeing me over her glasses pointedly. "But kids lie to cover their own butts. It's like they start and realize they have a new superpower, so that one didn't bother me as much as the other one.

"The other one you mentioned frequently was just downright disturbing. You talked about a man that was stuck in your shadow, and would sometimes walk around your room at night. I'm not going to lie, it had me so spooked at times I would check on you at night to make sure there was no one in there," Grandma says.

"You're right," I say. "That's disturbing."

"There was another thing that bothered me as well. You were so sure there were monsters in the woods, you'd set traps for them. One time I stepped on one—a board with nails sticking out of it—and needed stitches. I figured maybe you might have seen a bear and gotten spooked, but you'd never believe me when I told you they didn't want to hurt you. It made me sad that you were always so scared," she says.

Grandma and I watch TV for most of the evening; any attempt at conversation quickly fizzles out into awkward silence. It's well past midnight when I look over and realize she's asleep. I'm worried she'll be annoyed if I wake her up, so I turn the TV off and leave her where she is.

The past me mentioned worked iron, and the kitchen knives. I pick up one of the knives and examine it. Of course steel would be protective. Stabbing would hurt anyone. After a moment, I put it back. I don't know how to fight with a knife, and if I tried I'd likely do more damage to myself than an assailant. But that's not the only reason. It's not even the biggest reason. What if I do hurt someone by accident? I don't trust myself with it. I probably won't need it just going out to the shed, even in the dark.

Chapter Five

When I go outside, Tansy is waiting for me. As I approach, she sits up and flicks her tail back and forth.

"Here to whisk me away?" I ask. In response, the cat rises to her feet and stalks toward the woods, tail held high. "I'm not going with you right now. I'm doing something else." Her eyes seem to glitter in indignation as I make my way to the shed, swiped key in hand. While I'm curious to know where it is the cat is trying to take me, a different answer might be closer at hand.

Since the padlock is old and rusty, I have to hold my phone between my teeth while I fiddle with the lock with both hands before it finally clicks and I can yank it open.

The inside of the shed smells musty. The weak cone of light from my phone illuminates tool racks lining the walls, covered in a fine layer of dust and cobwebs. Among the most interesting finds are a power drill, hand saw, sledgehammer; things that could be used as weapons. The thought of needing such a weapon puts a tinge in my stomach, but regardless I file the knowledge away for later. The sprites were vicious and I wouldn't want to encounter them empty handed. A manual lawn mower sits close to the door; it looks like the only thing in here that gets used with any frequency.

I scan the tool racks until I find a thin wood chisel. This might work. Back outside, I chip away around the object lodged in the side of the shed until it's better exposed. When I try again to pull it out; it wiggles slightly, but I only withdraw a cut finger. I chip away more wood—it's thankfully old and soft—and finally I can pull the object free.

It's an arrowhead made out of a pale material, perhaps bone. The back is uneven, as if it had broken off when someone pulled out the arrow shaft—when Hunter pulled out the arrow shaft, most likely, if what I've seen is true. This arrowhead, its sharp edges and point digging into my palm, the pain from my bleeding finger, the physical sensations give my vision—my memory—substance. Asking Hunter about it directly would give it more substance.

The cat is still hovering around, watching me. I take a step toward her and she waits, the tip of her tail twitching.

"Alright. I'll go with you," I say. She obliges with a swish of her tail and darts off, though never straying too far from me. We walk for a while with no sign of Hunter or his pets, and I start to get impatient. I take a breath and exhale loudly. If Hunter doesn't show up, I might find out where the cat wants me to go, but I can't ask the cat questions and actually get answers. There's still the fact that Hunter acted threatening to me today, but he seemed kind, or at least not malevolent, in the past. Even so, my past self didn't seem to trust him, so I probably shouldn't be looking for him now.

The cat leads me past a large, ancient tree. It stands on its own in a small clearing. A broken branch hangs to the ground. The door that I made last night. The cat pauses, looks back at me, and then walks through the makeshift arch. After she passes through, she looks back at me expectantly. I pause at the threshold. Passing through means I'll be at risk again, based on what that strange man said when I promised to help him escape, whatever that entails.

"Okay, okay. I'm coming," I say. I've already come this far. Turning and going home now would mean I'll never know if this path really goes somewhere. I walk through the arch.

Nothing seems to change. It doesn't seem like I've been transported into Faerieland. As I walk, though, I do get the sense my surroundings are a bit *off* compared to what I'm used to. The moonlight is brighter; the trees taller.

"Do you think Hunter is going to show up?" I ask the cat. "I want to talk to him. I think he knows things I've forgotten." The cat doesn't answer. I'm slightly disappointed because I halfheartedly expect her to start talking. It would make the same amount of sense as everything else that's been happening.

Hunter's dogs seemed to find me pretty easily last night, but maybe he'll show up faster if I make a ruckus. I pull out my phone, intending to play songs at max volume, but I don't have any service, so instead I start whistling; the sound seems to carry well through the trees, at least well enough for a well-trained hound to pick it up. Maybe Hunter will show up, maybe he won't. I'll leave that up to the universe, but making noise might help push the universe in the direction I want it to go. He was apparently running around in the woods last night, so there's a chance he could be out here now, hunting faeries or whatever it is he does.

Looking for Hunter doesn't seem like a wise decision. I could talk to Zach, or the little man who lives under the porch who is apparently named Cheeps. But Hunter acts like he really *knows* things. And Hunter seems real. Grandma saw him, and I'm currently holding an arrowhead of his in my hand. Zach is real as well, but I worry if I question him further I'll find out he only remembers our adventures as the imaginary games of children, and he'll think there's something seriously wrong with me that I'm entertaining them as reality. If that happened, I'd have to face the likelihood that he's right.

The crunching of undergrowth behind me draws me back out of my own head. I turn, hoping to see Hunter, but instead it's seven-year-old me wearing a knitted autumn hat and sweater. Young Zach walks behind Young Tamsin. The browns and oranges of fall overlay the greens of the present like a translucent sheet, allowing me to see the surroundings in the past and present simultaneously.

The cat stalks a few paces ahead of Young Tamsin; she also stalks a few paces ahead of the present me. Even though the memory would have taken place almost fifteen years ago, the cat looks the same, with no signs of age in the present. The cat the children are following leads them into a hollow formed by curling tree roots. The cat slips in easily; I expect the children to have trouble if they even fit at all, but the gap seems to grow as they get closer until they barely need to duck their heads. They disappear from view as soon as they enter.

As I stand in front of the hollow, the present-day cat pauses and looks back at me.

"Why aren't you trying to take me in here? We've apparently gone that way before," I say. She doesn't respond.

"Well, you can wait, because I want to know what's in here," I say, crouching down. While the hollow was large enough for the kids, I have to squeeze and then crawl on my hands and knees through the dirt for several seconds before I suddenly find myself dumped out in a spacious room of sorts. It appears to be under the tree; the walls and ceiling are threaded through with thick roots. Softly-glowing lanterns hang from several roots, casting a dim glow over the space. Woven rugs cover the dirt floor, upon which sit Young Tamsin and Young Zach, along with an old woman. She's dressed in piles of billowing fabric and her white hair falls to the floor. She's in the process of passing pastries to the children when I tumble in. The cat is curled up next to her.

Young Tamsin takes a bite of the pastry, and Zach follows suit after observing her.

"It's yummy," Young Tamsin says. "Is that your cat?" she asks.

The old woman smiles. "She does what I tell her to."

"Why did you have her bring us here?" Young Tamsin asks.

"Maybe I'm just a lonely old woman who wants some company," the woman says.

"Are you a witch?" Zach asks.

"She might get mad if you call her that!" Young Tamsin hisses to Zach, though certainly loud enough for the woman to hear.

"I've been called a witch before. You can call me that if you must call me something," she says. She doesn't seem bothered.

"Do you have an oven?" Zach asks, looking around the room and then suspiciously at the pastry in his hands.

"Not one big enough for little boys," she says. There's a bit of wistfulness to her tone, but I suspect she's joking.

"But she could chop us up," Zach says sagely to Young Tamsin.

"Are you going to hurt us?" Young Tamsin asks.

"No," says the witch.

"There," Young Tamsin says to Zach. "She's a faerie. She can't lie. So it's fine."

"I have an offer for you," the witch says. "If you answer my question. I'll give you something you want. How does that sound?"

"What happens if I don't answer right?" Young Tamsin asks.

"Then you don't get what you want," the witch says.

"Okay," Young Tamsin says. "What's your question?"

"What do you want?" the witch asks. Young Tamsin eyes the witch suspiciously, as if searching for the trick in the question.

"I want something to make me invisible to Hunter, like the guy has in that wizard book Grandma read me," she finally says.

"Very well," the witch says.

"Why didn't you just ask her to do our quest for us?" Zach cuts in. Young Tamsin slaps her forehead.

"Can I change my answer?" she asks.

"Not today," the witch cackles. "Come outside. I shall show you how to hide yourselves." She rises more grace-fully than I expected and moves past the children with a flourish of her robes and flowing hair.

"You're very kind!" Young Tamsin says. She and Zach scurry out of the burrow on the witch's heels and the three of them vanish. As soon as they exit, the burrow gets dark and starts to close in around me. I scrape my way out, feeling as if any moment I'll be trapped underground forever. But that doesn't happen. I pull myself out and then spread out on the ground to catch my breath. The kids are gone, as is the autumn. I'm fully back in the present. That's frustrating. The power to turn invisible would be helpful to know.

"What are you doing?" the strange, dark-haired man asks. I crane my neck to look and see he's standing nearby in the shade.

"What are *you* doing?" I ask.

He crosses his arms. "Watching you nap, from what I can tell," he says. "Time you spend laying around is time you could be fulfilling your end of our bargain."

"How come you just randomly appear in places?" I ask, sitting up and crossing my legs under me.

He looks off into the distance thoughtfully, then frowns. "... I don't know. I don't know what I'm doing here, or where I was before this. I'm just here."

"Maybe my subconscious just hasn't made up a backstory for you yet, even though it's done a really good job with everything else." I sigh. "So, do you at least have a name?" I ask. His eyes flash back to mine, narrowed and sharp.

"Yes," he says.

"... And do you feel like telling me what it is?" I ask.

"How presumptuous. Would you simply tell me *your* name?" he snaps.

"Uh, it's Tamsin? Chill," I say. "Are you just stalling because my brain hasn't come up with a good name for you yet?" I laugh.

He gives me a look I can't place. "It's arrogant of you to assume your mind controls this world."

"No, it's just realistic," I say. "You're a figment of my imagination, just like everything else. No matter how much I chase it and hope it's otherwise, I'll have to realize it's a fantasy and adjust to the real world eventually. God, I really don't know why I'm out here." I laugh again, this time at myself, at this ridiculousness. I turn over the arrowhead between my fingers. There's probably a logical explanation for it, one that doesn't involve it being shot from a faerie's bow.

"Your human mind doesn't have the capacity to dream me up," he says, sounding miffed.

"If you don't give me something I can call you, I'll just come up with something on my own," I threaten.

"I will not give you my Name, but you may call me Leithe if you must call me something."

"Leithe. Alright, then," I say. "Why won't you tell me your 'Name'?" I place the same emphasis on the otherwise mundane word that he does.

He hesitates before answering. "There are Names and there are words one chooses to be called. All fae have a Name. If I gave you my Name, you would own me, and I'm not yet so desperate to barter away everything I am." He offers me a smile with no effort to make it appear genuine. "Though I'm not offended you didn't know. I forgot human names don't work the same way."

"Our names aren't magical," I say. "Okay, Leithe. This is a lot, but doesn't prove I'm not just talking to myself right now. I'm so tired of second-guessing my every thought."

"I'm standing right here, and I'm not you, so you're not talking to yourself," he says, in a voice like he's addressing a small child. "Let me ask you a question, because I don't understand your thoughts," he continues, "why don't you believe the things you experience are real?"

"Because ... everyone's always told me they're not."

"And they'd know better than you?" he asks. I feel my mouth open and close like a fish, but I can't make myself respond. I don't know how to answer that question. *Of course they do,* I could say, *because that's what I've always been told.* Grandma and the rest of the adults know best. But I'm an adult, too, right? Scared to continue this conversation, I change the subject.

"Apparently I used to tell my Grandma there was a guy who walked around in my shadow. Was that you?" I ask.

He gives me a smug look, as if an unanswered question is my loss and his victory; that he's *allowing* me to turn away from unpleasant answers. But he does allow it without argument. "Perhaps," he muses. "You seem familiar. As I said, my memory is unreliable, but I recall the impression of a thing a bit like you. Though smaller, perhaps. We may have spoken before."

"You mean like me, but as a kid?" I ask.

He shrugs. "I have no interest in the mortal life cycle."

"That's weird, you know, hanging out in a kid's room."

"None of this is my first choice," he says, eyes narrowed. "I am trapped and—unfortunately for both of us—it seems to only be around *you* I can draw close enough to the rest of the world to make myself known."

"I'm beginning to doubt your ability to grant my wish. You don't really seem to have it together," I say.

"I have the power to grant any wish your mortal mind could dream up. I'm diminished now, but at my true power I'm beyond what you humans call gods," he huffs.

Shadows by his feet flare around ineffectually like a bag of baby snakes. "Not that it matters; you already made the deal."

"That deal was made under duress. That wouldn't hold up in most courts," I say, more to irritate him than anything else.

"And yet you still had time to extort me for a wish, I remind you," he tosses back, and then continues, "besides, it would certainly hold up in *my* court."

"I recall you extorting me first," I say.

He snorts in indignation. "You're either clever or lucky to have survived unscathed for this long," he says, "I'm going to guess lucky."

"Are you threatening me?" It does occur to me that I'm alone with him.

"I'm simply pointing out the dangers of playing with things you don't understand." Despite his words, I get the sense he relishes my unease.

"I want to understand. Either someone helps me understand or you all need to leave me alone. I can't take this for much longer. I just want to live my life." The sudden heartfelt confession seems to surprise the both of us. His eyes even soften very slightly.

"You're dabbling with the Fae," he finally says, after a dramatic pause.

"I already knew that. Do you have anything else?" I ask. He opens his mouth to speak, but his words are drowned out by the baying of a hound close by. I turn to look in the direction of the sound, and when I look back, Leithe is gone. Damn it.

A few moments later, one of Hunter's hounds makes its way out of the trees and stops a short distance away, watching me. I wanted Hunter to show up, but naturally he has to do it at the least opportune time, right when I may have gotten some information from someone.

"Hey, doggy," I say, waggling my fingers at it. It responds to the invitation and trots over to where I sit on the ground. Its wet nose pushes into my hand, and I scratch its ears. It's not nearly as scary now that I've seen how gentle it was with me and Zach in the past.

Hunter soon follows it from out of the trees. I didn't hear a single footstep from him as he approached. He doesn't say anything, just looks at me with an unreadable expression. He's dressed as he was in my memories, in a dark green tunic with a leather vest over it, a cloak, a spear and bow crossed over his back.

"Hi. I wanted to talk to you," I say.

He raises an eyebrow. "A stark change from the last time we spoke. Why are you on the ground?"

"I was resting," I say. The fact that he's so heavily armed reminds me I'm alone in the woods with a man I don't know. I stand up slowly.

"Go home," he says. He sounds tired and already deeply annoyed with wherever this conversation is about to go.

"No. These woods are public property. You have no right to tell me to leave."

"It's dangerous."

"Then why are you out here?"

"I'm dangerous." His voice is completely serious, with no irony at all. I actually have to laugh, but I stifle it quickly since he doesn't seem amused.

"Why?" I ask, hoping rapid fire questions will break him down.

"Go home," he says again, with slightly more force than last time. He takes a breath. "I will send one of my hounds to walk you home if you would feel safer."

"Is this yours?" I ask, holding out the broken arrowhead. He glares at it.

"Yes," he says.

"I dug this out of the side of my shed," I say. "How did it get there?"

"I shot it there."

"About fifteen years ago? When you were shooting at a sprite?"

"Yes."

"So that actually happened."

"Yes."

"Are all the things I've been seeing real memories? They all happened?"

"I don't know what things you're referring to. And I've answered your questions about the arrowhead. Go home now," he says.

"But we met before, when I was a kid, right? Please just tell me what's going on. Tell me about the things I've been seeing. I'll leave, I just want to understand first. Then I'll be satisfied, and I won't come back."

"Would it make you happy to stop seeing them?" he asks.

I almost say yes, but I can't bring myself to. It's not exactly true. "I don't think that would answer my question. Just tell me: are they real? Are you real? Are you a faerie? If I stopped seeing them, would they still be real?"

Hunter sighs and pinches the bridge of his nose. "Yes, to all of your questions," he says, sounding defeated. I can't help but let out a delighted squeal.

"So what are you doing out here?"

"I keep watch over this place, and deal with any threats to it."

"What kind of threats do you deal with?" I ask.

"Have I not given you the answer you wanted? Go home," he says.

"I'll go home when I'm satisfied. What are the threats in the woods?"

"You will never be satisfied. Go home."

"Why did you come to my grandma's house today?"

"To tell you to stay home."

"Why do you care so much about what I do?" I demand. He says nothing for a long time.

"Perhaps I don't want silly children to die preventable deaths," he says.

"You might have known me when I was a kid, but I'm an adult now. If I get hurt because of my decisions, that's my fault."

"Spoken like a true child," he says. He takes several steps closer, closing the distance between us. I take a step back, afraid I've finally pushed him too far.

"Look me in the eye," he says, standing in front of me. I'm conscious of the fact he's probably fast enough to grab me if I tried to run.

"Why?" I ask, though I obey.

"*Forget about all of it, go home, and go to sleep. In the morning, you will believe this was all a dream*," he says. His voice is more forceful, but there's also a lyrical element to it. It's strange.

"Um," I mumble, trying to find the right words. My head feels funny. I'm tired. I want my bed, my pillow, to curl up under an old quilt. It's not comfy out here. I take a wobbly step away, toward where I think home is, and then I stop and shake my head clear.

"You can make me do and think things with magic!" I gasp. "You tried to do it to me at the house, and you did it to Grandma to make her want to move!" At my outburst, Hunter closes his eyes, mumbles something I can't make out, and takes a breath.

Before he can speak, I interrupt him with another sudden realization. "Did you make me forget stuff before? Like meeting you and other faeries when I was a kid?"

"... Yes," he says.

"You—Do you even care what you've done to me? I've spent my entire life thinking I can't tell fantasy and reality apart. Unless—I mean—maybe I really can't and ... this is a way for my mind to process that? God, I just don't know what to trust," I ramble, leaning back against a tree. I want to sink to the ground and curl up in a ball, but Hunter is still here.

"I believe you know what's real," Hunter says. "You're a human born with Faerie Sight. It happens sometimes. It can be the result of mixed births, stray blessings, and sometimes random happenstance. Most often, Sight fades as children grow, until they lose it completely. In the rare instances a human keeps it until adulthood, it serves more as a curse than a gift. Fae despise humans who can see them even when they don't wish to be seen. The luckiest humans get their eyes plucked out or simply killed. Others get dragged into Faerie. Even in cases where fae never lay a finger on the Sighted human, they often end up locked away by their own kind." His voice is calm and measured, like he's trying to be soothing now. Maybe I made him feel bad.

"Why do you care that some people can see you?"

"Old contracts and such. There are decrees by the courts that state humans and fae shall exist apart. No human can be brought into Faerie against their will. But that doesn't apply to Sighted. They can't easily be controlled and they often find their way into Faerie, so the decrees don't offer them the same protection," he says.

"What is Faerie, exactly?" I ask. Since Hunter has suddenly become more talkative, I decide to push my luck further. It occurs to me he might answer even more questions if I start crying. Just the thought of trying that card makes me feel a little guilty.

"The realm of the Fae," he responds. "It exists alongside your world. It is ... like a spider web, perhaps? There are strands of Faerie where it connects to your world. Those parts are very similar; you may not even realize you've crossed over. But the further away you go, the more alien it will become."

"And what are the Fae?" I ask.

"The natives of Faerie," he says. I roll my eyes, and he continues. "That's the simplest explanation. If you're asking about the differences between fae and humans, in general terms, fae never grow sick or old and have what you would consider strange and magical powers."

"Can you do some magic right now? Just not mind control magic," I add quickly. Hunter rolls his eyes and draws an arrow from a quiver hanging from his belt. He holds it in his hand, balanced vertically across his palm, and then it shimmers and becomes a small black snake. It curls around Hunter's hand, and when I reach out and touch it; I feel cool smooth scales against my fingertips. The snake slithers from Hunter's hand to mine. I stare hard at it, and my vision starts to split if I squint. It feels like I'm simultaneously feeling scales and wood. It makes my head hurt. The feeling doesn't last for long, ending when the snake shimmers again and reverts back to an arrow.

"Wow," I whisper. My tone of wonder makes him smile slightly. It's amazing and I want more than anything for it to be real, but in the back of my mind I still worry my subconscious came up with all of this. Everything has just gotten so bizarre. But even so, I don't want it to stop.

"That's just common glamour. It's far easier than glamour on the mind. Many fae are far better at it than me," Hunter says.

"So do you refer to one another as faeries, or do you have a different name you use?" I ask.

"Fae are the people, the way you're humans, but we have our own groupings we use to differentiate among one another. The courts are the most important of those," he says.

"Can you tell me about those?" I ask. Then a hound bays in the distance. The one with us perks up its ears. Hunter looks up at the sky and seems to be calculating something, and then looks back at me. The smile is gone, and he seems sad.

"Later. My duty is to patrol this area and search for threats. My other hound has found something."

"Alright. I should get home before my grandma realizes I left. Can I come back tomorrow?" I ask. He looks at me for a long moment. He still looks sad.

"You can't leave," he says. "No human who knows of us can be allowed to return to their own people." My stomach turns, and suddenly I realize it might be better if this *is* all in my head.

"Are you going to kill me?" I ask. I try to laugh, but it comes off more as a squeak.

"No. You'll just stay here until I return. There are two options for you to think about while I'm gone. You can stay in Faerie forever, or you can consent to have your memories of this time removed, and then you may go home. You wandered into Faerie of your own accord; this can't be an unexpected result. I've just told you what tends to happen to those with your curse."

"I'm still practically in my own back yard," I protest.

"You're not. They may look similar, but you passed through a gateway and entered Faerie, and are therefore subject to the laws of its people. Now, I have to go, but the hound will stay and protect you while I'm gone." He says.

"Wait! I won't tell anyone about this!" I call out, but he simply steps into the shadows and is gone. The dog looks up at me, ears down and wagging its tail slightly. It almost looks apologetic on its master's behalf.

"Asshole!" I yell. I hope he hears me. The dog whines.

Everything I've ever been told indicates this isn't actually happening. I hoped my fantasy would just work itself out, or that confronting it head-on would make it all magically go away, but now I just feel like I'm in deeper. But it's my fantasy—it *has* to be—and I can walk away whenever I want. So that's what I'll do. Grandma was probably right. I saw the real man Hunter in passing at some point and constructed some crazy narrative about him. I want to think I'm important so I imagine my grandmother's cat wants to take me on an adventure. But none of it is real. There are no monsters in the woods.

"Later," I say to the dog, spinning on my heel and walking away. At least, I try to. My ankle catches on something and I trip and fall on my face. I sit up and turn around to see what happened, only to discover that there's a rope now tied around my ankle that's attached to a tree at the center of the clearing. The dog whines again.

The rope feels solid and very real under my fingers. There's no knot where it's been tied off. It's just somehow around my ankle. I try to tear it with my hands, and then by bracing it with my feet and pulling, but it's strong. I even try to bite it, but all I get for that is a bitter taste ground into my teeth. The entire time, the dog just watches me.

I could try to make my own gate the way I did last night, but there are no branches low enough for me to try the same trick.

After tiring myself out, I lean against the tree and close my eyes. If I'm dreaming, or hallucinating, or whatever, maybe going to sleep will actually wake me up or snap me out of it. I just have to remember it's not real. The bed of moss I'm sitting on isn't real. The knobs and whorls on this ancient tree trunk pressing uncomfortably into my back aren't real. My stinging, scraped palms from my fall last night aren't real.

Eventually I'm too tired to keep my mantra going, and I welcome oblivion.

Chapter Six

THERE'S CHAOS ALL AROUND me. With every inch of ground we take, countless companions are cut down. My limbs are heavy as if I'm fighting to move underwater. I can't save myself.

I can't save anyone.

I wake up screaming, launching myself to a sitting position with all the force I wasn't able to use while helpless in the dream. I'm still in the woods. The rope is still tight around my ankle. My nap did nothing but give me a headache and a sore back.

I hear a noise, a rustling in the undergrowth that seems to be coming from several places around me at once. I can't see anything other than a hint of movement or vague shape in the corner of my eye.

The hound Hunter left with me is standing nearby, watching our surroundings silently, ears perked up, body leaning slightly forward. It's on alert, and that only makes my sense of unease stronger. What's in these woods that would scare a dog the size of a baby horse? I want to believe it's just Hunter returning, but he's never made noise when he walks.

I could try to retreat from this and take refuge in the thought that maybe this really is somehow all in my imagination. But this all feels so real. Every sore muscle in my body is telling me it's real. But there's an entire part of my brain devoted to parroting back other peoples' voices, voices from the real world. They all say the same thing, but Grandma's voice overpowers the rest of the cacophony. *The things you see are not real. The things you hear are not real. The things you feel are not real.*

Another rustle pulls my attention back to my situation. This sound is closer and more distinct than the previous ones, like a slithering or sliding of something through the undergrowth.

I wait, hoping more and more that Hunter will be what steps into view, but the dog doesn't look like it's preparing to welcome its master. The entire animal looks like a single, tensed muscle, its legs bent slightly, preparing to lunge toward whatever's approaching. Maybe Hunter wasn't exaggerating when he said the forest is dangerous. Maybe I'm about to find out what it is he's out here guarding against.

For countless ear-ringing heartbeats, I stare into the trees, wanting to call out a question, but afraid of what might answer. I don't even realize I'm holding my breath until my lungs start to burn. I allow myself to breathe, and then the underbrush explodes.

Several shapes burst out from the trees, screaming and hissing. They're just a blur to my panicked eyes, but they look like animals—maybe people—covered in twigs and leaves. The hound clamps its jaws around one and shakes it viciously before flinging it away, teeth crunching into sticks and other vegetation. Drops of a potent-smelling liquid—sap—splatter across my face and hands.

Another creature veers around the hound and comes straight toward me. It looks like a person—well, it's person-shaped, but made up of roots and supple branches save for its head: a deer skull with a single intact antler. Roots and vines wrap around discolored bones in an imitation of muscle. A claw-tipped skeletal arm juts out from the creature at an awkward angle as it lunges—it looks like the limb of a bear or other large carnivore rather than a deer. I press my back against the tree and kick at the thing, but it catches my leg. The creature's plantlike body opens up and lets my foot sink into it, and then vines wrap around my ankle until I'm stuck fast, thorns digging into my flesh and drawing blood. I gasp in pain.

It might just be the play of shadows across the empty skull, but the creature looks like it's leering at me as it yanks hard on my captured leg, dragging me toward it. It crouches over me and twists its claws into my hair, and then the hound rears down and grabs it by the neck, ripping it away from me. I howl in pain as the monster takes a chunk of my hair and flesh along with it.

While the hound is focused on savaging that creature, another monster of plant and bone—this one shaped almost like a large cat but with too many limbs sticking out of too many places—leaps onto its back and tears at its fur with myriad hooked, thorny extremities. The hound cries out, sounding like any animal in pain would, faerie or not.

This dog got hurt because it had to guard me. The fear I had of these monsters is now intermingled with rage.

I have no weapon, but I rush forward anyway, grabbing hold of the branches that make up the many-legged creature's form. I try to pull it off the hound, but before I can, vines start wrapping around my hands. I yank them free before they're stuck. Before I can think of a new strategy, I'm pulled off my feet by a root that lashes around my already injured ankle. I land hard on my forearms and am immediately dragged away from the hound and toward the tree line. I claw at the dirt for a handhold but only succeed in tearing up patches of the moss that covers the clearing. It's now that I realize the rope connecting me to the tree is gone. It must have snapped when the first monster grabbed my foot. Not long ago being free would have made me happy, but now it makes everything worse.

The hound tears off the skull of the creature that first attacked me, and it collapses into an inert pile of bones and vegetation. The dog then twists and manages to get a solid hold on the catlike monster on its back, yanks it loose, and launches it into a tree, where it sounds like several of the bones and branches making up its form crunch on impact. The hound then notices my problem and takes a step toward me, only to be hindered by another monster latching onto its hind legs and holding it in place.

I think I'm going to die. And then the force pulling me back suddenly vanishes with a *snap*. I look up to see Hunter raising his spear for a second strike at the monster that had been dragging me. He brings the spear point down into the creature's torso and twists while it's still reeling from the first strike. While the creature is pinned to the ground by the spear, writhing but steadily weakening, Hunter stomps on its head for good measure.

I think for a moment he's going to say something to me, but he doesn't even look in my direction. He just steps over me and impales one of the monsters attacking his hound. He brings the spear up at an angle to fling the monster's body into the trees.

The spear itself is barely visible as Hunter swings it through the air, with the tip looking more like an arc of light than a physical object. I've seen plenty of films with choreographed fighting, but the way Hunter moves makes those actors look like awkward toddlers.

Hunter and his hound are facing away from me, and the remaining monsters seem to be focused on him. He may not have noticed that the cord holding me to the tree snapped. This could be my chance to get away. If I just sit around and wait for Hunter to clean up the rest of the monsters, I'll just end up tied to a tree again, either to be trapped here forever or lose a part of my mind. If I run, I have to take my chances with the monsters, but I've passed through the forest more than once now and survived.

Without thinking more about it, I crawl into the trees. Hunter doesn't seem to notice. I pull myself to my feet and hiss in pain. This day has done a number on my ankle. Walking hurts, but I can manage. I take it step by step, and eventually the sound of fighting fades, and I'm alone.

Except that I'm not. I get a few moments of silence, and then the rustling starts, first from my left, then behind me. I can't tell if the monsters are near or far, chasing me or something else, but I run anyway. I only hope I'm going toward the house. Several times a sound or a hint of movement makes me change my course, until I'm not sure where I'm going at all. My surroundings are completely unfamiliar.

A rustle behind me catches my attention. The monsters must have followed me. I whirl around, but it isn't a zombie plant monster that emerges from the dark, but a creature the size of a young child, with spindly limbs and huge, doe-like eyes.

"Thistledown," I say. She smiles when I say her name.

"Come, my dear," she says, gesturing for me to follow her. I look behind me on the chance this is another memory and she's actually talking to my past self.

"Yes, you," she says, noticing my hesitance. I follow.

Thistledown leads me swiftly and quietly through the woods until we reach a fallen tree that's left a huge hollow in the earth where it once stood. She moves aside a hanging woven grass sheet and ushers me inside before turning back to secure the curtain properly over the entrance behind her.

I have to squeeze because inside is a home sized for a human child. I bump a small table and chairs aside so I can sit, and even with my legs pulled close to my chest, I take up a lot of space. It looks like I'm inside of a dollhouse. The table and chairs in the center of the room look like they were made by hand out of wicker. There's a mud-brick fireplace in one corner, near which sit many earthenware containers and hanging bundles of herbs and flowers. The entire place has a homey, comforting smell.

"Thank you," I say. She smiles at me again, and then carefully goes around me to get to the kitchen.

"No need to thank me, my dear. Be careful with your thanks. Do not accidentally place yourself in someone else's debt," she says, taking down a ceramic kettle and filling it with water. "It warms my heart that you still remember me."

"You helped me before when I was younger. But I don't remember much anymore. My memories were taken," I say. Thistledown places the kettle on a hook in the fireplace and bends down to stoke the fire.

"Yes. The hunter took them away from you," she says. Her voice has a hard edge to it, like this angers her.

"Why did it matter so much what a little girl knew? It shouldn't even matter what I know now, it's not like anyone would believe me if I told them faeries lived in my backyard. And—wait, is his name Hunter, or is that just his job description?" I ask.

"It is what he goes by here. I do not know if he goes by any other names," she says. She walks over, picks up a chair I knocked over on my way in, and sits next to me while the water heats up. "But I do know that he is very dangerous, and he will kill to keep his secrets."

"Are we safe here now? I don't want to bring trouble to you," I say. She places her hand on mine reassuringly. She has very long, sharp nails, almost claws. They dig into my skin even at her gentle touch.

"I have a smidge of magic—enough to keep the wraiths out if we don't make too much of a commotion, and the hunter will likely be too busy with them to look for you right now," she says, sighing. "It is sad. So many nights the wraiths borrow physical forms and wreak havoc on this land."

"Why do they do that?" I ask.

"Do you remember anything you learned of the courts, my dear?" she asks.

"Hunter mentioned them, I think, but I don't remember any specifics."

"The courts are the lords of Faerie. And the Gentry are the lords of the courts. They are deathless beings, eternal. They care not for the courtless—for us," she says. The kettle screeches, and she jumps up to tend to it.

"So the courts are sending them here to harass you?" I ask. Thistledown pours the hot water into two cups and brings them to the table on a tray. The one she places in front of me is the bottom half of a glass beer bottle, the sharp edges where it was broken having been worn smooth.

"Wait for it to steep," she says, taking her seat once again. "The courts have no regard for anything but their own amusement. They discard their rejects and exiles here to rot and taint the land with no concern for those who live here, fae or human."

"And Hunter fights them, so he's protecting the rest of you?" I ask. She laughs with no amusement whatsoever.

"No, dear. He's court fae. The ones corrupting the land are being kept prisoner, and the hunter keeps any from approaching the cage. Any 'protecting' he does for those that live here is incidental." A prisoner. A cage. It could be Leithe.

"Who's being kept prisoner?" I ask, trying not to sound too desperate to know.

"Powerful court fae, victims of some political scheme, as I understand," Thistledown says, taking a sip of tea and gesturing for me to do the same. It smells and tastes flowery and extremely sweet.

"There's more than one?" I ask. Leithe didn't mention that.

"So I have heard," Thistledown says. "Though I have not seen for myself." The warmth from the tea is soothing, but the sudden sensation reminds me I have a body, and that that body is in pain. I touch my head where the monster—wraith—pulled out a bunch of hair. There's a tiny bit of blood, but not much. I hope Grandma won't notice.

"Oh, poor thing," Thistledown says. "I've neglected you." She jumps up and grabs a collection of tiny jars and scraps of fabric. "Let's see what we can do about all this." She opens one of the jars, sniffs the contents, and then applies a paste gently to my scalp. It stings and has a strong herbal scent.

"Thank you," I say. "You said Hunter would kill to protect his secrets, but he didn't kill me when he could have, and in the past, he only took my memories, right?" I ask as she applies the paste to a cut on my face I didn't know I had.

"My dear," she says, pausing her work to look me in the eye. She looks sad. "I fear you may be looking for goodwill in him that does not exist," she says. "It is generous of you to see 'not killing you' as a reason to offer him sympathy, even when he's so greatly wronged you by stealing the memories right out of your head."

"It does sound naive hearing it out loud," I say.

"It is a sign of your kind nature, my dear. You want to trust everyone, because you want everyone to like you. But that kindness makes you vulnerable. Others will use it to take advantage of you." She brushes a lock of hair out of my face.

"I have no idea who to trust," I say.

"It is so very hard to discern who has your best interests at heart, my dear. But when in doubt, trust those who have cared for you during your life. Your family, your friends who've been at your side," she says.

"If I trusted Grandma, I wouldn't be out here in the first place—maybe that would be for the best." I let out a hollow laugh and rub my eyes.

"You've spoken of your grandmother, but never in kind terms. Are you certain she has your best interests at heart?"

Thistledown asks. Her large eyes reflect the flickering candlelight that illuminates the room.

"I guess … I don't know. You're right. She doesn't even really want me around," I say.

"But I am here to help you, my dear," she says, setting her teacup down and stepping behind me to braid a lock of my hair.

"Thank you, Thistledown," I say.

"Have you remembered your quest?" she asks.

"I don't remember what it was," I say. But I saw my past self mention one. Thistledown finishes her first braid and starts a new one. Her nails tap the back of my neck as she works.

"That's alright. I told you in the past and I can do so again. As I said, the prison in these woods spills forth vile monsters." She finishes her second braid and returns to her seat across from me. "The fae here are too weak or unwilling to oppose the hunter that guards the prison. We need help." Her large dark eyes look into mine. "We need someone to free the prisoners and save everyone."

"But why would you ask a child to do this quest?" I ask.

"We have no one else to ask. We are desperate. But you are not a child anymore, are you?"

"Well, no. But how am I supposed to free them? Do you know where they are?" I ask.

Thistledown hangs her head. "No," she admits. "I do not know. That is why we must beg for help."

"Okay," I say. "I'll look. I'll do my best. But right now I should probably go back home, if that's possible."

"You do not have to return to your mortal life if you do not wish to," Thistledown says. "You are always welcome in my home." That's something Grandma has never said to me.

"But I do need to leave. For now, at least," I say.

"Very well. I can guide you out. The hunter has probably forgotten about you for now. When you leave Faerie, you'll likely be safe," Thistledown says.

When she finishes tending to my cuts and scrapes, Thistledown leads me outside. As we walk, I'm alert to every noise.

"Here we are," Thistledown says. I look around. There doesn't seem to be anything door-shaped.

"Where do I go?" I ask. Thistledown gestures toward a small stream nearby. "I thought I needed to find a door," I say.

"Any threshold will do, dear. Cross, and you'll be on your way home."

Before I go, I turn to face her. "This ... prison. Where would I start?"

Thistledown smiles at me and takes my hand in both of hers. "You are so kind, my dear. The prison is hidden, but you'll find it. You must trust in yourself. And trust no one else, for they will seek to trick you with pretty words. And please, if you must speak to the hunter again, don't tell him what I've told you. He'll surely kill me."

"Of course. I would never," I say. "I'll be back. I—" I'm about to say 'I promise,' but I remember my dealings with Leithe. "I'll definitely be back," is what I say instead.

With that, I hurry across the stream. When I turn around, Thistledown isn't on the opposite bank. What now surrounds me are the normal sounds of early summer, no shrieking wraiths or baying hounds.

With no real indication of the way I should go, I head downstream. Eventually, the ground turns marshy, and the mud sucks at my feet as I walk. I remember there's a bridge over a stream about a mile from Grandma's house. If this is the right stream, I only need to keep following it, and then I'll be able to follow the road home, as long as I don't miss her driveway in the dark.

I walk in the water instead of along the bank. It's silly, but I think there was a movie where someone walked in a stream to avoid being tracked by dogs. Thistledown said Hunter wouldn't follow me out here, but the possibility haunts me.

My ankle still hurts, but the water is cool and soothes it a little. I want to stop and sit down on the bank, but I worry it would make me easier to track. I hope the water washes away any trace of my footprints in this direction.

The tree line finally breaks, and I can see the bridge as a dark outline cut against the sky, though the water shines even in this dim, partially blocked moonlight. For a moment I just stop to take in the scene. I'm out of the woods. Everything looks and sounds like a normal night. There's no howling dogs or creeping plant monsters. I'm still muddy, sore, and bruised, but that can be taken care of.

Now that I'm out, I search for my phone. It occurs to me I may have dropped it at any point during the night, but I find it in my back pocket. Surprisingly, it still works, even after I got dragged on my ass all over the place. After I wake my phone up, I look at the lock screen in confusion. It was almost exactly eleven p.m. when I left the house, but my phone screen currently reads 11:07. It's physically impossible for me to travel from the house to this bridge in seven minutes, much less through the woods after having a conversation with someone and taking a nap. There's physically no way. Maybe something magical did happen to me. Or maybe there's some kind of freak but rational explanation.

I'm about to climb up the rocky incline to the road, but something stops me. Something about the bridge tickles the back of my brain. I played under this bridge with Zach. But there's something else about this place. I take a few steps forward until I'm nearly under the bridge and take a seat on one of the boulders.

I stare at the water and try to conjure up another memory from childhood, something to show me what I'm missing here. I look for a younger version of myself or Zach, but there's no sign of them or anyone, just darkness and the sound of trickling water. The entire scene is soothing, save for the rough rock I'm sitting on and my general soreness. If I were a little more comfortable, I could drift off to sleep where I am.

And then the rock beneath me shifts and suddenly starts to rise into the air. I roll off and land on my ass in the water. The rock—or what I took for a rock—fractures and falls away in a shower of dirt and stone, revealing a large and gnarled gray-skinned hand, pieces of stone and plant matter still clinging to the flesh. An arm follows the hand, pulling itself free from the earth. In what I took to be a rock formation under the bridge, I now see the emerging outline of a humanoid shape. Another arm breaks free with a resounding crack and brushes rocks from the creature's face. It exhales deeply, rumbling like a rockslide and filling the air with the smell of rotting swamp water.

I take a step back, and with a noise like a landslide, the creature slowly turns its head to look at me. It says something in a voice like rocks grinding together that I can't make out.

The troll. The words force their way to the forefront of my brain. My past self mentioned this creature.

"Hello," I say. The words refuse to come out with any strength. The troll is sitting down, but I guess it must be at least ten feet tall. As I take the creature in, it reaches out its hand toward my head. Its palm is at least the size of my entire face, and its gnarled, clawed fingers are disproportionately long. It moves slowly and awkwardly, so I'm able to duck and shuffle backward as its hand closes in the air where my head was a moment ago.

I run a few more steps away and launch myself painfully up the rocky slope to the road. I risk a look behind me and see that the creature hasn't moved. Its hand still hangs in the same space, stretched out and searching.

With a final brief burst of adrenaline, I pull myself over the lip of the ravine and roll into the grass on the side of the road. I lay there for just a moment to catch my breath, but then I hear another rumbling breath from beneath the bridge. Worried it might chase me, even slow as it appears to be, I stumble to my feet and limp down the road until I have to stop and rest my ankle.

There's no more noise out of the ordinary, and I'm sure I'd hear a rock monster if it was chasing me, so I allow myself to relax and make the rest of the walk back to Grandma's at a pace my ankle agrees with. I almost wish I had someone I could call to come get me, but I don't have a reasonable explanation for what I'm doing out here.

But maybe I wouldn't need to explain anything to Zach. We explored these woods as kids and apparently encountered all sorts of strange things. If these things were real, maybe he'd be able to tell me. If someone else could confirm it, maybe I'm not crazy. But the fear of rejection tugs at my mind. I'm scared of admitting to anyone that everything's not completely normal. I'm afraid of what they might say. Afraid of how they might look at me.

Lost in thought, I almost walk straight past Grandma's driveway, but my phone flashlight catches the reflective plate on her mailbox.

Walking down her driveway is a little more daunting than walking down the road since the trees suddenly come far closer around me. A wraith could still jump me, or Hunter could appear and drag me off. I move my phone back and forth as I walk, trying to keep an eye on all my surroundings at once. I face the flashlight toward every noise and movement in the corners of my eyes.

Nothing aggressive jumps out at me until the flashlight illuminates one of Hunter's hounds watching from the trees, making me gasp. The dog doesn't move; it just watches me. I flash my phone around, looking for Hunter or the other dog, but I don't see any sign of them. I look back where the dog was, expecting it to be mysteriously gone, but it's still there.

"Go away," I whisper. One of its ears twitches, and it cocks its head to the side.

"Leave me alone," I try. The dog whines, and its tail wags once and then stops. It doesn't look like it's going to do anything, but I'm reluctant to turn away from it.

"What do you want?" I ask. The hound emerges from the trees and I take a step back, but it doesn't behave aggressively. It comes to a stop in front of me and looks like it's waiting for something. The thing is huge. It's almost as tall as my hips at the shoulder. I step around it to continue toward the house, partially expecting to try and impede my progress, but to my surprise it just moves to walk alongside me.

I let it walk with me back to the house, not that I could stop it if I wanted to. I reach the house without incident and circle around to the back door. The hound follows me until I step up onto the porch. There, it stops and sits down.

"Were you just walking me home?" I ask. It wags its tail. I look around again for Hunter, imagining he's somewhere out there, watching. But I know that even if he was around, I probably wouldn't see him unless he wanted to be seen.

"Okay. I'm home. Uh, thanks?" I say. I carefully reach out and pet the dog on the head. We stare at each other for a moment, and then it turns and trots away, into the dark. For a while I watch, wondering if Hunter's still out there, until the back door violently slamming makes me jump in fright and whirl around.

My first thought is that Grandma has discovered me and that I am in serious trouble, but the person slamming the door and stomping to the edge of the porch is me. Not a young child version of myself, but a teenager, about fourteen. She sits on the edge of the porch with a *humph* and crosses her arms. The slamming, the stomping, even the sitting—every movement she's made since she left the house seems to have been calculated to make as much noise as possible. She must be in a fight with Grandma.

I walk around and sit next to her, so I can see her face. Sure enough, she's fighting back tears.

"I know you can't see or hear me because this has all already happened, but whatever it is, it'll be okay," I say. She sniffs, fumbles around in her jacket pocket, and pulls out a cigarette and matches.

"Oh, no. Don't do that," I say, though I know it won't do anything. I'm starting to regain vague memories of this night. I know a bit about what happens. After scrutinizing the cigarette for a while as if it might bite her, she lights it and takes a drag. Immediately, she starts choking and coughing. She drops the cigarette and doubles over, coughing and gagging until I think she's about to vomit.

She recovers and wipes spit from her mouth. She looks thoughtful for a moment, and then her eyes go wide.

"Shoot!" she says, jumping up and stomping on the cigarette where she'd thrown it on the ground. Fire averted, she sits back on the porch and holds her head in her hands.

"Young Miss, what troubles you?" a voice asks. I turn to see Cheeps, approaching cautiously. She rubs her eyes and turns to look at him.

"I ... You seem familiar," she says.

"Your Sight has returned! I worried I would never again be able to speak with you," Cheeps squeaks excitedly. He scampers over and places a tiny hand on her arm. His hands look like those of a rat—four-fingered, pinkish, and slender with rounded pads.

Teen Tamsin rubs her eyes and looks at him again as if that might make him vanish.

"I think I knew you when I was younger," she says, gently placing a finger over his hand.

"Yes, Young Miss. Until you came home one day and couldn't see me. It seemed you forgot about the Fae. But you can see again!" He wraps his tiny arms around her torso as far as he can. "But that isn't what troubles you now, is it?"

"My grandma's being a *bitch*," she snarls. "I told her. I keep telling her I think there's someone else in the house. I sometimes see someone in my room at night. But she told me I was too old to make jokes like that and then just started yelling when I told her I wasn't joking."

"Oh yes. The shadow man. You once told me of your epic quest to save him. Has he been saved yet, Young Miss? I should love to hear the story," Cheeps says.

"A quest ..." Teen Tamsin stares intently into the trees. She carefully detaches from Cheeps and stands.

Before they can talk more, the memory fades, as quickly as it arrived. With nothing more keeping me out here, I go inside, lock the door, and peer out the window, just to see if Hunter shows himself now, but I see nothing out of place.

I sigh and lean against the door. I'm home. Everything is fine. My adventure will go unnoticed. All I want to do now is go to bed, but I'm probably filthy. I need to take a shower.

"Hello?" Grandma calls out from the living room. "Is someone there?"

Chapter Seven

"*Fuck*," I whisper under my breath. Now I notice the flickering lights and colors emanating from the living room. The light isn't on, but the television is, though the volume must be very low.

I don't respond to her, hoping she'll decide she imagined the sound, but then I hear the laborious squeaking of Grandma's easy chair as she stands up.

"Hey, Grandma, just me," I say, deciding I'm not getting out of this.

"Tamsin? I thought you went to bed," she says. I hear her start walking toward the hall.

"I'm going to bed now," I say, fast-walking to the stairs. I don't make it there before Grandma reaches the hall light switch and turns it on. She takes in my appearance without expression. I must be dirty and bloody.

"What did you do?" she asks.

"Went for a walk. Slipped a few times," I say. "I thought you were asleep."

"Then I woke up," she says. "Don't change the subject. Did you think someone told you to go do something outside? Did the cat? Did you hurt yourself?"

"I didn't hurt myself, and no one told me to go for a walk. I just felt like it, okay? Am I not allowed to go for walks, Grandma?" I ask.

"What exactly am I supposed to do about this? Should I just keep my opinions to myself until you just don't come home at all? Until you *die*? Are you seeing Zach out there? You're a grown woman, you can bring him to the house if that's the case. I'd rather you bring him to the house, at least I'd know where you are."

"I'm not screwing Zach!" I say, louder than I intend.

"Then what are you doing? Why can't you just tell me?" she yells back.

"I'm hanging out with faeries, Grandma. Is that what you want to hear?"

"Are you asking me to admit you to the hospital, to schedule an appointment with a psychiatrist?"

"You don't have to do anything. It's not your problem."

"It's always been my problem. You've always made it my problem. You've done this so many times, sneaking out on your own and refusing to say what you're doing. You've gotten hurt before. Why do you have to make me the bad guy because I don't want it to happen again?" she says.

"Stop making it about you!" I shout. "You don't want to listen to me, you just want to be mad. I'm sorry I chased your daughter away, okay? Can I please just go to bed?" She silently moves aside to let me get to the stairs. She doesn't say another word to me. That wasn't something I meant to say. It just came out because, in that moment, I knew it would hurt her.

When I get upstairs, I go to the bathroom to take stock of myself. The harsh fluorescent lights reveal how dirty I am. My shirt and jeans are stained green and brown from being dragged through the dirt and leaf litter. My arms don't look much better. In my hair and across my face from my jaw to my cheek are dried smears of light brown mud. The mud comes off in chunks when I pick at it, revealing a large but healing cut on my face. The cut looks days, maybe even a week old now. This must be Thistledown's medicine. When I wipe away the stuff on my head, I see new hair already growing back. Amazing.

I strip off my boots, socks, and pants to get a look at my ankle. My left boot is pierced straight through in several places, but it looks like it protected my ankle from the worst of the monster's thorny bite. There are still several shallow puncture wounds that are now crusted with sweat and dried blood and sting when I touch them. Thistledown didn't get to those. The scrapes on my palms and knees from my adventures last night are now even worse from the repeated irritation.

The next order of business is the mud, sweat, and blood. I turn on the shower, finish undressing, and crawl into the tub when the water gets warm. The soap and water stings all over, but it feels refreshing regardless. I curl up in a ball on the floor of the tub and just sit under the water and let my eyes close.

Now that I have a moment of calm, I realize how utterly exhausted I am. I could easily just fall asleep right here in the tub. The events of the forest feel far away, now. I want to believe that nothing from out there can touch me inside the house. But I'm here in the house, still bearing the marks of what happened in the woods. Besides, Leithe *has* appeared in the house before, on the day I arrived.

"If you've found time to bathe I hope you've made progress on fulfilling your end of our bargain." Leithe's voice drifts from the other side of the shower curtain and startles me to alertness. I peek around the curtain to see him examining himself in the mirror.

"Go away!" I say, holding the side of the shower curtain to my chest.

"Why? Last time we spoke you seemed eager to get information out of me," he says, turning from the mirror to face me.

"I'm naked!" I hiss.

"And?"

"And I don't want you to see me naked!" I say.

He looks at me quizzically for a moment. "Oh," he says, as if reaching an answer. "I remember. Humans are odd about their bodies." He turns around and faces the door. "I'll take my clothes off if that would put you at ease."

"*It would not!*"

"I don't understand you things."

"I'm not asking you to understand, just to listen," I say. "I don't know what it's like for faeries, but *I* grew up not wanting people I don't like or even know very well to see me naked." I make sure the curtain is completely closed and quickly rinse myself off.

"Why, are you ashamed?" he asks.

"No. It's just that what my body looks like is no one else's business. You talk like faeries just walk around naked all the time, but you're wearing clothes now. Are *you* ashamed?" I shut off the water, grab the towel hanging on the rack, and wrap it around my torso.

"I am not. And we do not 'run around naked,' we're simply not terrified of one another's skin."

"And you think that makes you more enlightened than us or something?" I ask, stepping out of the tub and sitting down on the toilet seat. "Okay. Whatever. You came to badger me about the bargain, right? I actually do have news about that. There's a prison in the woods somewhere where court fae prisoners are being held. Do you think one of them might be you?" He's silent for a moment, and I wish I could see his face.

"Prisoners?" he asks. His voice has a tense edge to it.

"Plural, yeah. That's what I was told. Who else would be there? And what did you all do to get locked up?" I ask.

Leithe crosses his arms. "That's irrelevant to our bargain," he snaps. Seems like I've struck a nerve.

"It *is* relevant. I don't want to help you if you're locked up for doing something horrible," I say.

"Then perhaps back in the woods when you needed my help, you should have remembered to make sure I met your standards first," he says.

"Maybe you shouldn't have been a criminal," I say. It's not a good comeback. At all.

"I'm not a criminal!" he spits. He starts to whirl to face me but stops short. The outburst makes me flinch. "I've done nothing wrong. I–" He sighs and reaches up to press a hand to his forehead, but stops short of that as well. "I don't know why this has happened. I can't remember. My last memory is being with my betrothed. And then I was somewhere dark. And sometimes I'm here. And sometimes I'm other places. I can't keep track of my own mind."

"I'm sorry," I say before I can stop myself. It's too familiar.

"I don't want your sorrow," Leithe says. "If you must offer me something. Make it something useful. What else do you know about the prison?" Whatever vulnerability I saw in him is gone as quickly as it came.

"It's being guarded by a faerie hunter and his hounds, and I don't know how to get there," I say.

"He'll likely have the advantage of intelligence and overall ability, but since you're human, you'll be able to utilize human weapons against him," he says.

"Like steel and iron?" I ask.

"Yes. Iron warped by humans does us exceptional harm."

"Does that mean faeries can't live among humans?"

"Some fae engage with and live among your kind in your world, those that don't mind living in the bile and rot humans produce daily. That never interested me, so I don't know much about them."

"You're not being particularly helpful with this, so maybe you should stop having such an attitude," I say.

"Perhaps if you succeed in making me whole again," he says.

"Well, how come you keep disappearing and reappearing?"

"I don't know any more than you do about that. I'm fractured, as I said. I lack memories. I suspect there's a connection that waxes and wanes."

"Where are you when you're not talking to me?"

"I don't know," he begrudgingly admits.

"Are you here physically? Can you touch things?" I ask.

"May I turn around?" he asks. He's still facing the door.

"Yeah, I guess," I say. He turns around and reaches out his hand toward the mirror; the moment I expect him and his reflection to touch, his hand goes straight through the glass. He pulls his hand back out, and all that's there is a translucent shape of a hand bleeding tendrils of smoke. The tendrils quickly pull back and reform into what looks like solid flesh.

"You see?" he says, holding the hand out as if to show me. "I'm not physical. The physical part of me is somewhere else."

Unable to suppress my curiosity, I reach out to touch his hand, and my fingers pass straight through his skin, causing it to disperse into smoke for a moment before reforming when I pull my hand back. There's no resistance, and only a slight drop in temperature to show I passed through anything.

"I don't know how we can speak, but being able to talk to a human is better than nothing. You might be capable of freeing me, as unlikely as that may be," he says. He sounds like he thinks he's giving me a grand compliment.

"This evening I got tied to a tree, mauled by wraiths, and almost had my head crushed by a person made out of rocks. I'm not in a hurry to go back there to search for your prison cell. By the way, are you making those wraiths? They're hurting people. You need to stop."

"If I had control over my powers, I wouldn't need you," he says, crossing his arms. "Do you know anything else about this prison? Perhaps what it looks like, or what the key is?"

"Not yet," I say.

"There may be another way. If you could find my betrothed, you could tell her what happened to me, and she would come for me. Though that would require you to travel deep into Faerie, through the Dreaming Court's domain all the way to the City at the Edge ..." he muses.

"Um, Leithe," I say. "You said the last thing you remember was being with her. So do you think ..." I take a deep breath. He won't like me asking this, but it seems like important ground to cover. "Do you think she might have had something to do with it?"

"Absolutely not," Leithe says, nostrils flaring. He responds immediately, but afterward his face freezes in an enraged expression, but his eyes seem to ponder something.

"Do you think she might also be imprisoned?" I ask. Maybe that possibility would be more palatable.

"That's ridiculous," he scoffs. "She would never be captured by something like this. She could never be imprisoned. There is no cage in creation that could hold her." His voice gets animated, passionate. His eyes light up when he talks about her. But if she's too tough to get captured, and would never turn on him, then what are the alternatives? That she doesn't know where he is, that she doesn't care? I don't think antagonizing him will make him change his answer.

"You know, in the beginning, I was just trying to play along." I change the subject and start rambling before I can hold myself back. "I hoped that, you know, everything would play itself out and I would realize this is all silly and fake, but I've found things that made me think maybe this is more than that, but I guess I shouldn't be surprised playing along got me in deeper."

"It's amazing how far in denial you are," he says, rolling his eyes. "I've told you so many times that this is happening, but you're not listening."

"Listening to you means not listening to a lot of other people," I say.

"And you listen to other humans instead of me? I have wisdom that can't be gained in a thousand human lifetimes," he says.

"Okay, well, now you're in jail and can't even open doors on your own," I say.

He bristles. "Be careful not to run your mouth to fae with the power to chastise you."

"I'll keep that in mind. Now get out of here so I can get dressed," I say.

"I don't know how to leave," he complains.

"Fine, then just stay in here," I say. With the towel still wrapped around me, I go to my room. After looking around and making sure Leithe isn't in the room, I let the towel fall and pull on a tank top and flannel pants. After I'm dressed, I check the bathroom, but Leithe is gone.

My bed feels amazing, and my brain starts shutting down the moment my head hits the pillow, pulling me into a hopefully dreamless sleep. But before that happens, I hear someone rummaging through my drawers.

"Leithe?" I ask, brushing the hair out of my face. It's not Leithe. It's Teen Tamsin tossing the room and throwing things into a backpack sitting in the middle of the floor. She looks upset. She stuffs some clothes into the bag, but before she does, I see a toothbrush and an opaque spray bottle. After double-checking the bag's contents, she carries it to the window and tosses it out onto the ground. For a second, I think she plans on following it, but after scanning the yard for a moment she instead heads to the door and exits the room.

I blink and rub my eyes, and my room is back to normal; all the drawers are neatly shut. Still, I look out the window just in case there's a backpack in Grandma's garden. There isn't. Sleep comes soon after that.

In my nightmares, I'm spinning amidst a swirling cacophony of bright colors and discordant song. Hands reach for me—stroking and grabbing and pulling—as I whirl across the floor in the arms of someone whose face I can't see.

I wake up at dawn, sweaty and disgusting even though I'd just showered. There's no way I'm getting back to sleep, so instead I get up and go downstairs.

The kitchen has been destroyed. The cabinets have been thrown open and their contents emptied over the floor. The refrigerator has been as well. Milk and flour spatter the walls and mix on the floor to form a white slurry. Dry spaghetti and pieces of cereal crunch under my feet as I approach to survey the damage. Was Grandma so mad last night that she did this?

I start by picking up containers on the floor to salvage what food I can, but it looks like they've been intentionally emptied. It's then that I notice there's tiny footprints in the flour and milk. I abandon the mess for now, grab a can of salmon cat food off the floor and take it outside to Tansy's bowl. And then I wait.

Cheeps doesn't take long to arrive, and his legs from the knee down are caked with flour.

"I think we need to talk," I say as he's reaching his tiny hands into the bowl.

"Ah, so Young Miss can see me after all," he says, scooping a chunk of pâté into his mouth. I try not to gag. The stuff smells awful; I can't imagine eating it.

"Did you wreck the kitchen?" I ask. He pauses his breakfast and suddenly looks sheepish.

"When my family is mad at one another, I get so distraught. You fight and fight and sometimes I just can't take it anymore," he says.

"You did this because Grandma and I yelled at each other?"

"Yes, Young Miss," he says.

"Well, Grandma doesn't know about you, so she's going to think I made that mess and get even angrier with me. And she might yell more, and when I tell her the truth she won't believe me."

"I suppose I could clean it. I don't want you to be mad at one another."

"Or you could show yourself to her and explain what you did," I say.

"You know I can't. I told you before. We cannot allow unsighted humans to know us for what we are. The courts will be angered. I am very small; I can't glamour myself up into looking like a human person," he says sadly. Damn. For a moment I thought I was about to solve one of my biggest problems.

"Oh. well, I wouldn't want you to get in trouble," I say. "Um. This might sound bad, but I don't have all of my memories. You said we're your family. Are we related?"

"It's quite alright. You forget a lot, Young Miss. The first Mistress and Mister built the house. I came to warm myself by the hearth and eat the food Mistress left out for me. To thank her I cleaned and kept the mice away. The Mister and Mistress had many children, and they grew and left. When the Mister and Mistress died, the house was empty, and then the new Mistress and Mister came, and they had a Young Miss, and then that Young Miss left, and then she came back, and then she had you, Younger Miss, but then she left again, so now you're the Young Miss. You live in my house, so you're my family." He cleans the bowl remarkably fast. "Now, stay outside until someone comes to get you," he says, before vanishing under the porch stairs.

"Okay," I say to empty air.

For a while, I stare into the trees. Nothing remarkable happens. I listen for a sign of whatever Cheeps is doing, but I hear nothing but the sounds of birds going about their morning business. While I'm tempted to go back into the house, Cheeps has already proven himself to be destructive when irritated. So I wait until the back screen door swings open.

"What are you doing out here?" Grandma asks.

"Listening to the birds," I say. I wait for her to continue our argument from last night.

"Have you eaten?" she asks.

"Not yet," I say.

"I feel like making French toast this morning. Come in if you want some." With that, she retreats back inside and shuts the door. I quickly get up and follow, bracing myself to get blamed for the wrecked kitchen. That will have to be the last straw; there's no way she'll want me around if she thinks I throw tantrums like a toddler when I'm upset.

But when we reach the kitchen, it's perfectly clean. There's no sign of the mess that was there. Cheeps is also nowhere to be seen. Grandma opens the fridge and looks around. She removes the carton of milk and scrutinizes it.

"Didn't you just buy milk?" she asks. The carton is almost empty. It was full last night. I guess there was only so much Cheeps could salvage. I shrug noncommittally. She then removes the egg carton, tests the weight in her hand, and gives it a disgusted look.

"Did I raise you to be the kind of person who puts egg cartons back even when they're empty?" she asks. Her tone is more dry than overtly hostile. "Eggs were on the shopping list. Did you forget to check it?"

"I'm sorry," I say.

"I guess we're just having regular toast this morning," she says.

We don't speak during breakfast. The atmosphere is heavy with the possibilities of what Grandma might say, but every time I sneak a peek at her she's focused on the TV. Finally, I get brave enough to ask a question.

"That guy with the dog from yesterday, he said he was your neighbor, right?" I ask.

"He did. Why?" she says.

"So where did he say he lived?"

"He didn't," she says.

"Who's the closest house on your left?" Even the closest house was a bit of a drive.

"Still the Smiths."

"And your right?"

"Gary and Margaret."

"Okay, so where could that guy possibly live, then?" I ask. She thinks hard.

"I'm sure there's an easy explanation," she says, but she doesn't sound sure. "There's the Randall Place past

Gary and Margaret. It's just been sitting since the Randalls passed away. Maybe he bought it."

"When you introduce yourself to your neighbors, isn't it a normal thing to tell them which house you live in?"

"I suppose so."

"And you didn't find it weird or scary at all that a strange man just showed up at your door?" I ask. She looks like she's thinking hard about it.

"He ... was very polite ... or ... Well, when you put it that way, I suppose it does seem kind of strange, but none of that occurred to me at the time," she says. "Maybe I'll call Margaret and see if she knows."

"Good idea," I say.

"You're asking because you're still suspicious of that man," she says.

"Yeah. I still think he's weird." She rolls her eyes.

"Complain all you want to me," she says, "but don't go being rude to our neighbors."

"I'll try," I say. Grandma *hmphs* in response.

My phone chirps. It's Zach, asking if I want to hang out.

"Is there anything you need me to do today?" I ask Grandma.

"Spare my peace of mind," she says. "Oh, and if you feel like it, you can go into the attic and look through Skye's old clothes up there. The pants might all be too short, but some of the shirts, skirts, and dresses might fit you."

"I will. And does it do your mind any good to know that Zach wants to hang out with me today?"

"You two ran around like hooligans when you were younger, but he's grown up. I hope spending time with him will make you do the same," she says.

"I'm sure it will be good for me to talk to a real person rather than an imaginary one," I say.

"That reminds me," she says, after a thoughtful silence. "I'm making you an appointment with Dr. Webster. You're going as soon as he can see you."

"I can't afford him, and you probably can't either. And he's like an hour away, that's a lot of gas money—"

"Don't you dare talk about money to me," she snaps. "You don't need to worry about that kind of thing. You remember Gary and Margaret's youngest son?"

"No."

"Well, Margaret told me he started seeing Dr. Webster after he left the army and had an incident. He takes some pills and goes to meetings, and Margaret says he's doing wonderful now."

"That's really great for him, but—"

"You're going. And you're going to take whatever he tells you to take," she says. I don't respond. There's no point.

After washing the dishes, I tell Zach he can pick me up in an hour and go to the attic to retrieve the bags of clothes. The attic is accessed by pulling down a ladder in the ceiling of the upstairs hallway. As soon as I climb up, I'm engulfed in a stagnant, sweltering heat. The attic is sharply slanted on two sides, leaving a narrow space down the center where I can walk without crouching. Pushed to the low-ceilinged sides are large trash bags and cardboard boxes covered with dust. Unfortunately, none of them are labeled.

I open one box at random, and at the top of a stack of clothes is a carefully folded button-down made of tan heavy cotton. I unfold it and hold it out; it's a well-worn man's shirt. This must be a box of my grandfather's clothes. Grandma doesn't like to talk about him, but it appears she can't bring herself to get rid of his things.

The next box I open is full of clothes I wore as a young girl. There are many frilly and floral-patterned dresses that Grandma originally made for my mother that then got passed down to me. A quick look tells me I'll only find children's clothes in this one, though I check all of the pockets anyway, in case I left anything useful in them.

"Young Miss," Cheeps says, peeking around a wood support beam as I'm setting aside the box of children's clothes.

"Hi, Cheeps," I say. "I appreciate you cleaning the kitchen."

"I have something for you. As thanks for the salmon," he says, scurrying over and holding out a flower to me. It's enormous in his hands.

"Well, that's very nice of you," I say.

"You gave it to me for safekeeping, Young Miss, to give back to you when you could see once again," he says. Now I recognize the flower. It's the one Thistledown gave me when I was younger. She told me I could use it to find her.

"That's kind of you, Cheeps. You know about my quest, right? Is there anything else you can tell me about it?" He scratches his ears and thinks.

"I do not know, Young Miss. There was a hunter, and perhaps a thistlewitch? And the shadow man, of course," he says.

"Can you think of anyone else who might help me with Hunter? I can probably leave out some salmon tonight ..." I trail off. Cheeps' ears perk forward.

"Well, I think I recall Young Miss mentioning the river," he says.

"What about the river? Are you talking about the troll?" I ask.

"Could Young Miss perhaps leave out a saucer of milk tonight as well?" he asks hopefully.

"Oh, yeah. I'll do that," I say. He claps his hands in delight.

"Not the troll," he says. "Young Miss told me the very scariest and strongest fae is from the river."

"Thank you, Cheeps. I'll have that salmon and milk for you tonight," I say. He pumps his tiny fists in the air.

"I shall go. It has been too long since I cleaned Young Miss's bathroom." He starts to leave, but then stops and turns to face me. "Young Miss, it is not cleanly to leave your towels on the floor after your bath. They are heavy and hard for me to hang up."

"I'll hang them up next time," I say. That explains how the upstairs has stayed so clean, even when Grandma has trouble with the stairs.

It's getting close to the time I told Zach he could pick me up, so I bring the two boxes I found with women's clothes back down to my room and close up the attic.

I need to decide what to wear. Anything too nice and Grandma will get more confident that there's something going on between me and Zach, but I want to look put-to-gether. The clothes I brought with me mostly consist of jeans, t-shirts, and sweaters found in various thrift shops.

The first box has a few pairs of overalls and baggy, high-waisted jeans, all faded and worn-soft with age. Most of the tops are supposed to be tight, but for a woman a little larger than me. There are a few sweaters, though most of them are short enough to leave the navel showing. These look like they belonged to my mother. The other box has my clothes from the last time I lived here. Most of the blouses are brightly colored and might still fit.

There's a knock on the front door and I quickly throw on a yellow shirt fringed with lace and a pair of skinny jeans and start for the stairs, but then pause. Before I leave, I pop my phone out of its case, gently smooth down Thistledown's flower, and put it between the phone and the case before putting them back together. I'll keep the flower with me, just in case. When I get downstairs, Grandma is letting Zach in. He waves at me.

"Are you ready?" he asks. "I have something I want to show you."

"Sounds exciting," Grandma says. "You two have fun." Her tone implies a specific kind of fun. I roll my eyes. Her implication seems to go over Zach's head.

"Goodbye, Grandma," I say, leading Zach out the door.

The truck ride to his house is bumpy and the vehicle fumes and curving road give me a stomachache. His house is much closer to the road than Grandma's. It's old, but well cared for, and next to it is a large barn that's been converted to a workshop. Several old cars sit in various states of repair.

"Sorry the yard is a mess. Dad still brings work home, you know?" Zach says sheepishly.

"He works at the auto shop, right?" I ask.

"He owns it. 'Foster's Auto Repair.' It's got our name," he says.

"Right. Sorry." Memories stir and start to languidly flow around my brain. "You used to work there when we were kids. You still doing that?"

"Yeah. I work there full time now," he says. "Dad says the shop will be mine one day." We go up the wooden front steps and he opens the door for me. The house smells so overwhelmingly of cigarette smoke that immediately upon entering I feel nauseous.

Zach leads me up the stairs and to the end of the hall. The path is familiar. It leads to his bedroom. There's a twin bed and an AC unit in the window. He shuts the door behind me and then smiles eagerly. Maybe Grandma was right.

"So ... what did you want to show me?" I ask. I think he's stepping forward to embrace me and I tense, but then he moves around me and crouches to pull something out from under the bed. It's a black canvas bag that curves along one edge. He unzips it and pulls out a wicked-looking compound bow.

"Cool," I say. He holds it out to me, and I carefully take it. It's heavy, and I'm unsure if I could even draw it. "Uh, do you hunt with this?"

"I practiced some, but I thought you'd be able to use that," he says. He reaches under the bed again and retrieves another black canvas bag, this one rectangular. Unzipping that one reveals a rifle.

"Do you hunt with that one, then?" I ask, still not understanding exactly why he's showing me these. If I concentrate, I can recall some vague memories. Zach's dad would take him hunting. I was invited, but Grandma forbade me from going. It led to a nasty blowout that was made worse by every plant in the garden getting uprooted and tossed into the grass. Grandma assumed I did it to get back at her and I suspected it was a herd of hungry deer, but now I realize it was probably Cheeps throwing a tantrum in response to our fight. I never understood

Grandma's refusal to let me go. After all, she was the one who originally taught me to handle a gun.

"No, I was waiting for you to get back," Zach says.

"So we could go hunting together?" Maybe he remembered how badly I wanted to go with him and his dad back then.

"Kind of. I wanted to make sure that when you came back, we were ready."

"Ready to do what, Zach?"

"To get you to where you need to go. You have a quest, remember what Thistledown told us? You're special, and you can't let anyone stop you from saving everyone. And I'm here to help you," he says.

"You really believe what Thistledown said? Back up, you really believe Thistledown exists?" I ask, utterly bewildered by this declaration.

"Well, yeah. We saw her all the time," he says.

"But ... you don't think it was all just silly kid stuff?" I ask.

"Of course not. I could never think that," he says, looking at me intensely. I shy away from his gaze and look for something to veer the conversation in a different direction.

"So these will hurt the wraiths? I know Hunter's weapons did, but it might be like, magic or something," I say, looking over the bow.

"I assume so. If anything, they'll definitely work on the hunter," he says.

"Wait, what?" I ask. I suddenly can't have the bow in my hands; I gingerly set it down on the bed.

"What? He's going to try and stop us, maybe even kill us."

"So you want to bring weapons and just *shoot* him? You'd be okay with killing someone?"

"If it's what needs to be done," he says. The conviction in his voice was almost inspiring moments ago, but now it's growing terrifying. I can't hold the bow anymore, not while thinking about why Zach got it. I carefully put it back in the bag.

"It's not. We don't really know what's going on. We were kids the last time we interacted with these people. We're not just going to run in all ... guns blazing now. I mean, I appreciate that you care this much, but ..." He looks at me sadly and puts the gun back in its bag.

The weapons are gone, but the feeling of the bow in my hands, the thought of blood, and the lingering stench of cigarette smoke makes me feel like I need to puke. I excuse myself and make my way to the bathroom where I lean over the toilet for a perilous few minutes. I can't shake the terror at the thought of such violence. The image of myself covered in blood—of Zach covered in blood—comes to mind despite my best efforts.

When I calm down, I exit the bathroom and see a woman looking up from the base of the stairs quizzically. Zach's mother. She has long brown hair streaked with gray held back with a bandana and a face creased with laugh lines. She's wearing greasy work clothes. She's also a mechanic, I recall. With both his parents there, the shop was where Zach grew up.

"Are you okay, sweetie?" she asks.

"I'll be fine. Sorry if I worried you," I say. She comes up the stairs.

"Don't tell Zach I told you, but he's so happy you moved back. He missed you so much. When you left, he wasn't himself for weeks."

"Oh. I didn't realize," I say. Maybe all of this is him trying to reconnect with me after so long.

"Well, just remember you're welcome to come over anytime, alright?" she says, squeezing my shoulder.

Zach has put the weapons away by the time I return. I hope that's the end of it, but it isn't.

"I get it," he says, "but just remember that whatever you have to do, I'm with you."

"Zach, I will never ask you to hurt anyone," I say. He nods, but something about his expression makes me think he doesn't believe me. "But what I will ask you to do right now is tell me *everything* you remember about the faeries," I continue, sitting down next to him on the bed.

His face lights up. "We have a quest," he says. "We have to free the prisoners at the center of the fog. But the hunter doesn't want us to go there, because that's what he's guarding."

"You don't need to help me with this," I say.

"Yes, I do."

Chapter Eight

"So how was Boston?" Doctor Webster asks. We're sitting in his office, which is actually his living room since he runs his practice out of his house. It hasn't changed much in the seven years since I've been here. The walls are a soft cream color; the couch I'm sitting on is blue and plush. On reflex, my hand searches the arm of the couch for a stray thread to tug on, but finds nothing. Maybe he had a different couch the last time I was here. He sits across a dark wooden coffee table in an aged brown leather chair, legal pad close at hand on an end table.

Dr. Webster himself is vaguely familiar to me, though I don't remember the glasses and streaks of gray hair by his temples. His sense of style is the same—a large, comfortable-looking sweater, loose pants, and slip-ons. He has a nice face, a kind face, but as I look at him I can't help but feel he must be silently laughing at me.

"Boston was a lot," I say. It's been a week since any incidents. Grandma's been keeping a very close eye on me and having me do all sorts of chores that keep me in the house, and I've been careful not to get into any arguments with her that might upset Cheeps.

I still frequently see the cat outside. She still tries to lead me away, but even just going outside to fill up her food bowl I can feel Grandma's eyes boring into the back of my head. She doesn't let me out of her sight.

"I'm sure moving there was quite an adjustment, and coming back here must have been an adjustment as well," Dr. Webster says.

"Yep," I say. Zach has asked to hang out several times since the day he brought me to his house, but I've been finding excuses to decline. His intensity about the faeries and me and my quest was frightening.

"How do you feel about those changes?" Dr. Webster asks.

"The air is nice." I know I'm supposed to open up to him or this is a waste of Grandma's money, but I can't bring myself to do it yet. While I don't have any specific memories of our sessions, Dr. Webster was my therapist when I was younger. I probably told him some pretty wild stuff and I'm sure he'll be disappointed to find out I haven't changed at all. For a while, neither of us speaks, and then Webster breaks the silence.

"Just so you know, you don't have to talk if you don't want to," he says. "If you want to talk, it doesn't have to be about anything heavy. We can also just sit, or you can write or draw on one of the pads in the drawer there." He gestures to the coffee table. "But I think I'll be most useful to you if I know what you want to work on."

"I'm sure my grandma has already told you everything that's going on," I say. "She made me come. No offense."

"None taken. And your grandmother didn't give me many details. I was hoping to hear them from you, if that's okay. But if not, we can do whatever you want. This is your time. The garden looks pretty good this year, if I do say so myself, so if you want to move around a bit we could always go outside," he says.

"It's all the same stuff as the last time I was here," I finally say.

"I took notes on it back then, but do you want to refresh me?" he asks. I might as well get this over with. I take a deep breath to steady myself before speaking.

"Well, there's faeries in the woods and one of them wants me to free him from his magic prison and the other one wants me to stay away and Grandma's cat keeps trying to lure me somewhere and also there's a troll under a bridge that wants to murder me. Oh, and there's a tiny man in my house that I just found out was responsible for all the messes I got blamed for as a kid but didn't do. And my crazy has spread to my friend and he thinks I'm the chosen one and wants to charge in there guns blazing." I laugh at the end, trying to sound flippant but it comes off more as nervous.

Dr. Webster thinks for a moment and makes a note on his pad. "Leithe, Hunter, and Cheeps?"

"Wow. You took good notes."

"You were very descriptive." I scrutinize his face for mockery, but he seems sincere.

"Wait. Can I read those notes?"

"That's typically against my policy. Why do you want to see them?"

"I feel like there's a lot of holes in my memories of living here. I was hoping reading the notes would help me fill them."

"I think it might be more helpful to talk around those holes and see if we can't fill them in. Why do you feel like you have lost memories?"

"Because I've been watching them happen outside my head, like a movie. I see things that happened to me when I was younger. I know it's weird, but when I see these things, they just make sense, like they fit like puzzle pieces into spots where there was nothing.

"And the thing is, the more memory fragments I get back, the more it seems like there's some wild conspiracy going on, and I was involved—and there are people that still want me to be. All of it seems really dangerous, with magic and swords and monsters and stuff, so I don't know how to proceed." I look hard at Dr. Webster the entire time I'm speaking, looking for a change in expression, a sign that he's inwardly laughing at me, but his expression remains neutral.

"How do you think you should proceed?" he asks.

"You're just humoring me," I scoff.

"I'm not. I want to know what you think."

"But you don't think anything I've said is real," I say.

"I think it's real to you, and that means it doesn't matter if it's real to me," he says.

"I just want to know the truth," I say.

"What do you want the truth to be?" he asks.

"I don't know. I guess it would be nice if this was all actually happening, because that would mean there's nothing wrong with my brain. But I want to go back to the promise and the guy. If someone was locked up and offered you a wish if you saved them, would you do it?"

"Well, I can only say what I would do if I were in your position, but I doubt I have all the information that you do. Personally, I suppose I would do my best to help him if I thought he was unjustly imprisoned. But that's just me.

Someone else might have a different response, and that's okay." He checks his watch.

"That's a good point. I think out of everyone involved, I have the least amount of information about what's going on. Maybe it's a metaphor for real life," I jokingly suggest.

"Maybe so. Would you like to discuss that next week?" he asks.

"No promises. Grandma only insisted on one session. I'll call you," I say, getting up and heading out the door.

I stop in the middle of the gravel driveway. Dr. Webster really likes flowers. His front yard is full of yellow and orange daylilies that shine in the sunlight. A path leads around back, where I know there's an even bigger garden full of butterfly bushes, lavender, and other eye-catching blooms. I wonder if it's really a hobby, or if he just does it for his patients. I think I came here many times as a child. I should have memories of this place, but I feel nothing. I concentrate to see if I can summon up a vision like I've been having closer to the house—something that might be enlightening. All I conjure up is a headache.

I get through half of the hour-long drive pondering my discussion with Dr. Webster before giving in and calling Zach. He picks up quickly.

"Hey. You want to go on an adventure? No guns. Or bows." I say. That's all he needs to hear. At his suggestion we meet up by the bridge between our houses; I text Grandma to let her know I'll be home later than planned.

There's a dirt shoulder across the bridge large enough for a car or two to park. Zach is there when I arrive, leaning against the hood of his pickup truck. He waves as I pull up and park. I'm relieved to see he listened to my request and didn't bring any weapons.

"So," I say, getting out of the cab, "where do I need to go to fulfill my destiny and stuff?"

"I have no idea; I was hoping you did, honestly," he laughs. "Oh, and I know you said no guns or bows, but ..." He pulls a folding knife out of his pocket. "I brought you something just in case. You never know what can happen. I brought one for me too, but I can leave them both in the truck if you're that worried."

"Well, I guess that would be fine," I say, taking the knife from him and experimentally opening it. The blade springs open, making me jump and almost drop it. Embarrassed, I carefully close it and shove it in my back pocket. Zach has the grace to say nothing regarding my incompetence.

"Cheeps mentioned a strong and scary fae near the river. Do you think he meant the creek here?" I ask. It could be a river to Cheeps, considering his size.

"Maybe," Zach says, and we head into the woods along the creek.

"Hey," I ask, looking back at the bridge once there's a safe distance between it and us. "Do you remember anything living there?"

"A troll. I think we used to mess with it, but I don't know if that's a good idea anymore," he says.

"I'm amazed you can remember so much that I can't."

"It's not because I'm special or anything. Thistledown told me your memories were taken. I just wasn't important enough for that." He laughs.

"That's a horrible thing to say. Thistledown told you that?" I ask.

"She didn't say it like that, but I know what's going on. I get it. I'm not you."

"Yeah. You seem to be handling all of this way better than I am, for one."

"Like I said, I knew you were going to come back, and I wanted to be ready."

"I'm sorry I don't remember more about what we did together," I say. He reaches over and gives my shoulder a reassuring squeeze.

"Don't apologize. It's not your fault," he says.

"So, do you remember anything about this mysterious, river-dwelling fae?" I say to change the subject. It was getting too emotional. Zach thinks hard.

"Well, I don't know. Why do you want to look for this thing? We should just find the prison. The hunter will probably notice we've entered Faerie as soon as we do."

"I thought it might be good to look for someone who might help us. Do you know how to get to the prison? " I ask.

Zach shrugs. "You were always the one who knew where to go. Maybe if we cross over in the right place, we might be able to get there before the hunter could stop us?"

"I don't think that's an option," I say. Engrossed in our conversation and my own thoughts, I failed to realize we must have already passed into Faerie, because now the creek we've been following is a fast-flowing river at least thirty feet across. The colors around us are deeper and more vibrant; the trees greener, the sky the shade of a robin's egg, and the river a blue seen only in paintings. We walk with our feet in the water. Maybe it will make it harder for Hunter to track us, or maybe it won't.

While I take in the sights, a dark creature approaches along the river's edge. It looks like a pitch-black horse. As it gets closer, I can see it's a beautiful creature. Its coat shines in the sunlight and its long mane and tail drip with water and hold bits of aquatic plants. At first I think it's carrying something in its mouth, but when it's nearly close enough for me to touch I realize it actually has an arrow piercing the side of its face, right at the hinge of its jaw.

I move to the side as it approaches, not wanting to risk angering this faerie creature, but it stops in front of me. It's at least six feet tall at the shoulder, and I have to crane my head up to look it in its eyes; they're pure white, no pupil or iris. It lowers its head, presenting the arrow to me. The arrow looks similar to the one Hunter shot the sprites with. The flesh around the wound looks burned and ragged. The creature must be in great pain. Its ribs and hip bones protrude, as if it can't open its mouth to eat.

Zach looks tense and has his hand in his pocket, presumably on his knife, though he hasn't done anything yet. Gently, I reach out and place my hand on the side of the horse's face. Its skin is cold. With my other hand, I grip the arrow shaft and pull as hard as I can. The wood is slick with moisture and slimy with algae and difficult to keep a good hold on. It shifts slightly but doesn't come out.

"Sorry. This will hurt, probably," I whisper, and I wiggle the arrow to loosen it. The creature flinches and snorts but lets me work. Finally, I pull it free; unlike the bone arrowhead I found in the shed, this one is a modern steel triple-bladed broadhead.

Freed, the horse seems to grin at me, and for a moment I swear I see large canines peek out from behind its lips. We lock eyes, and it seems to ponder something while a feeling of dread builds in my gut as I realize how easily this thing could bite my head off if it chose to.

But it doesn't. Instead, it flicks its tail and walks into the river until it vanishes beneath the surface.

"I may have just done something stupid," I say.

"You're a good person," Zach says. "There's no shame in that."

We continue walking, and I hold onto the arrow where a small piece of the shaft is still attached. It isn't long before we encounter more faeries. Brightly colored sprites dance over the water, skimming the surface and laughing. Remembering my previous encounters with them, I consider heading into the trees to avoid them completely, but their senses are better than mine, and they notice us and stop their playing to stare with their insectile eyes.

"Hey," I say. There's no point in trying to avoid them now. One of them flits over and hovers in front of my face, wings vibrating to the point of invisibility. The others follow, but stay a little further away, hovering over the water.

"Poor poor humans, so far from home," the sprite says. "Did you bring any candy?"

"Not today, but I could bring you some," the sprite cocks her head and studies me thoughtfully. Eventually her eyes reach the arrow still clutched in my hand.

"Where did you get that?" she asks.

"I pulled it out of a horse-thing," I say. Her naturally bulbous eyes somehow widen even further. She turns to her companions, still playing in the water while watching our conversation, but before she can speak, a dark shape bursts from the water's surface and grabs a sprite in a toothy maw that opens far further than a horse's mouth should be able to open. The sprite's bones crunch as the horse creature chews once and then swallows it mostly whole as it wails feebly.

The other sprites scream and flee. The horse snaps at another and barely misses its legs.

"Let's go," I say, grabbing Zach's hand and running after the howling sprites. We run until my lungs ache and I struggle to catch my breath. There's no way we could outrun a horse, so I hope it chooses not to chase us. When I finally have to stop, it's quiet. There's no sound of thundering hooves that would indicate we're being pursued.

I barely have time to find relief in the silence around us—broken only by Zach's and my own panting—before a swarm of sprites descend upon us.

"You gave him back his mouth!" The lead sprite snarls as she whips past my face and scrapes a barbed claw across my cheek. More slam into me as I hold my arms up to protect my face. One hits the back of my knee, and another my shoulder, sending me stumbling backward.

"Now we can't play in the river!" The sprite shouts, continuing her assault. Zach draws his knife, but the sprites are as hard to strike as houseflies. A sprite grabs my hair and pulls me backward again.

"Unless maybe if we give him a big old *human* to eat!" Another sprite says. Several sprites grab my hair and shirt and drag me backward until I swing the arrow I'm still holding over my head. From the feeling of resistant flesh and a sudden hiss of pain, I gather I struck at least one.

The assault resumes quickly, and it's all I can do to protect my face with one arm and swing the arrow with the other. I can't tell where Zach is, but I don't dare uncover my eyes to look for him for fear the sprites will gouge them out.

"Where's Ivy?" I cry out. "She might remember me. I brought you treats before!"

"Ivy's rotten wraith-food, like you'll be kelpie food!" a sprite screeches. Dead. Maybe even one of the dead sprites that attacked Grandma's house when I was a child.

"What if I give you something else?" I cry out. To my surprise, the offer works. The sprites halt their attack. In the reprieve, I look around for Zach, but he's gone.

"Like what?" The lead sprite asks, hovering just out of reach.

"Human sweets. Cookies, candy, whatever. But I can't bring them if I'm eaten by a horse," I say.

She ponders this. "Bring things with chocolate. Bring your weight in chocolate treats," she finally says reluctantly, as if disappointed not to be feeding me to the monster instead, though she's unable to resist the allure of sugar.

"That's a lot to get at once. I could bring stuff once a week starting tomorrow," I say. The sprite kicks her legs in the air petulantly.

"No. Tomorrow. Before the sun reaches its zenith," she demands. "Swear on your very last drop of blood."

What is it with faeries and blood? I don't have a choice. It's this or get eaten by a horse. "I swear, on my very last drop of blood."

"Then the deal is sealed," she says. The sprites seem satisfied and flit away into the canopy, leaving me sitting in the dirt trying to catch my breath.

"Wait!" I call out. "Where's Zach?" But no one answers. I have no idea where he went, but since the sprites seemed intent on feeding me to the creature they called the kelpie, I fear they dragged Zach off in that direction as well.

I've only taken a few cautious steps back toward the river when I hear the sound of twigs snapping underfoot. I turn, hoping to see Zach, but I'm faced instead with myself, at about fourteen years old. Teenage Zach follows close behind her. I follow them as they head toward the river, keeping an eye out for my own Zach or the kelpie as I walk.

The kelpie does appear, walking along the riverbank. At first I fear it's coming for me, but then Teen Tamsin points it out.

"There's a horse," she says.

"It's going to try to kill us, I'm calling it now," Teen Zach says.

"Probably only if we offend it," she counters.

"These things decide what to be offended by on the spot," he shoots back.

"They have rules. They just aren't always the same as ours," she says. She steps out of the approaching creature's way and gestures for Zach to do the same.

"Greetings," Teen Tamsin says to the kelpie when it reaches her and stops. It looks at her with white, corpselike eyes and snorts softly. She seems to take this as encouragement, and slowly reaches her hand up to stroke the creature's neck, eyes overflowing with wonder.

The kelpie allows Teen Tamsin to place her hand on its neck, but as soon as she does so, she looks confused. She tugs at her hand, but it seems to be stuck fast to the creature's skin.

"I can't let go," she says to Zach. The kelpie, its eyes now glittering with malicious intent, turns and starts walking casually into the river, Teen Tamsin stuck fast and dragged after it. On reflex, she places her other hand on the kelpie's flank to brace and pull herself free, but she only succeeds in getting both of her hands stuck.

Zach grabs her around the waist and pulls, but only succeeds in getting dragged along as well, his shoes leaving ruts in the sandy bank.

"Don't touch it. You'll get stuck too!" Teen Tamsin cries out. I can hear the panic and terror building within her. It makes my heart beat fast as well, though I know if I didn't survive this encounter I wouldn't be here now.

"I'm sorry I touched you. I didn't realize I offended you. Please let me fix this," she says. To my surprise, her pleading seems to get through to the creature, and it stops and tilts its head to look back at her. I hope for a moment, and then it seems to smirk and takes off running along the riverbank, Tamsin and Zach dragged screaming along behind it.

Zach loses his grip on Tamsin after a few dozen feet and goes rolling into the trees. I leave him for now and chase after Teen Tamsin and the kelpie, though I've barely recovered from fleeing the riverbank just a short while earlier. Tamsin's feet barely touch the ground even hanging off the kelpie's flank given the creature's speed and height. It veers in and out of the water, as if taunting her with the threat of drowning. To my surprise, she manages to awkwardly swing herself partially onto the kelpie's back, at least enough so that she's no longer at risk of being battered along the ground. She tries in vain to steer it away from the water, but with both hands still stuck, there's little she can do.

A hound bays nearby. At the sound, the kelpie dives into the river, submerging itself and Teen Tamsin completely. Not a second after it vanishes, an arrow arcs through the sky and into the water. Hunter and his hounds quickly follow, splashing into the river and diving where the kelpie submerged.

For several painfully silent moments, nothing happens. And then Hunter surfaces carrying Tamsin, who is coughing and sputtering. He pulls her to the shore and deposits her there, where she collapses and chokes up more water onto the ground. As I get closer, I see that her palms are raw and bloody, and the fabric of her jeans has been torn away where it must have had contact with the kelpie's skin, leaving much of her thighs exposed.

"Are you okay?" Teen Zach asks as he runs past me to Tamsin's side.

"Alive," Tamsin chokes out before having another coughing fit.

"Be gone from here," Hunter says, voice laden with pure hostility. I assume he's talking to the kids, but then I realize he's facing toward the river. Following his gaze, I see the kelpie's head poking out of the water. Hunter's arrow is lodged in its jaw, in the same spot from which I removed it today. The kelpie tries to open its mouth to snarl, or maybe speak, but the arrow in the hinge of its jaw seems to keep it from opening its mouth at all, and all that comes out is a guttural growl and a stream of bubbling, ichorous blood.

"Go starve. Since death would be too good for you, my next arrow will take your eye," Hunter says. The kelpie snorts and vanishes under the surface.

Teen Tamsin wipes her mouth and looks up at Hunter standing over her. She's soaking wet and shaking. From cold, adrenaline, fear, or probably all three.

"Th-thank you," she says to Hunter. Her eyes are wide and sparkling. His expression is more difficult to read. It's a slight frown, just a downward twitch of the corner of his mouth. I imagine he's annoyed at having to rescue her. It makes sense, given that this is at least the second time he's done so.

"You shouldn't be here. This place is dangerous for humans," he says.

"The horse seemed like it wanted me to pet it. I didn't know what would be ruder there—petting it or ignoring it," she says.

"Seeming is a tool the Fae love to weaponize, but many creatures will torment you whether you're respectful or not, if they happen to be in a tormenting mood," Hunter says. Tamsin stands up on still-shaky legs. She looks like she might buckle, and Zach offers his shoulder, which she takes.

"Well, you didn't have to save me, but you did. So I want to pay you back in some way. Is there something I can call you?" she asks. This must be the first time I met Hunter as a teen, after my childhood memories had been taken.

"... You may call me Hunter," he says. He seems reluctant to speak the name, and after he does so there's a tense pause. The name seems to almost trigger something in Tamsin's head; her eyes crinkle, and she studies his face as if trying to draw something buried in her head to the surface, but the moment passes and she says nothing about it.

"Thank you for helping us," Zach says, breaking the awkward silence. He seems wary, eying Hunter's array of weapons. The weapons seem to catch Tamsin's eye as well.

"If you want to pay me back, leave and do not return. This is no place for humans," Hunter says. The words are stale and rote. I'm beginning to gather just how often he's told me this.

"But people come hunting out here all the time," Zach protests.

"Then you still believe yourselves to be in the mortal realm? Look around. You passed into the realm of the Fae some time ago, otherwise I would not have needed to save you in the first place," Hunter says. Again, it sounds like he's reciting a speech from pure muscle memory.

"If you don't want to have to bother saving us, why not teach us how to fight like you do?" Tamsin asks, still eying the bow in his hands.

"You would never be able to fight like me," he says. "Now, come. I will take you back to your world. Do not argue with me," he adds preemptively, as Tamsin begins to open her mouth. She shuts it again. They start walking. I follow.

"Back so soon?" says a voice. I turn and see a humanoid head peeking above the water. What skin I can see is dark—the same black as the kelpie's coat; his long black hair dances in the current, braided with strands of aquatic plants. Gray, ropy scar tissue radiates from a healing puncture wound on the left side of his jaw. His eyes are the same corpse-white as they were when he looked like a horse.

"You're the kelpie. Is your real form the horse or the person?" I ask, rambling out of fear. I consider bolting then and there, but I doubt I could outrun a horse creature if it really wanted to catch me, though I might have a chance if he's reluctant to travel too far from the river.

"Breathe. I have lacked the ability to speak for some time due to the cursed arrow, and now I want to indulge myself. Besides, you removed the arrow, so as thanks I will not devour you until our next meeting," the kelpie says. I wonder if the last part is intended as a joke, but the creature seems serious.

"Do you mean you will do me no harm until our next meeting?" I ask. Otherwise there's nothing stopping him from chopping off my legs now and coming back to eat me later. The kelpie grins; even in a humanoid form, he still has very large, very sharp teeth.

"Very well," he says.

"If you wanted someone to chat with, you could have talked to the sprites," I say.

"I was hungry, then. And they enjoyed mocking me while I lacked the use of my mouth. The hunter enjoys his petty punishments." He moves its jaw side to side and winces.

"You *were* trying to eat me, weren't you?" I ask.

"You're a trespassing human. How was I to know he'd take such offense? He never stopped me from eating anything else," the kelpie shrugs. "Now word of his obsession with his special humans has gotten around. What would you say about someone so willing to kill and maim their own kind for a stranger?"

"If my own kind had a habit of tormenting and killing kids, I probably wouldn't mind so much. Speaking of my own kind, have you by chance seen my human friend, Zach? I lost him."

"He came by, fighting with some sprites. Ran off, though, into the woods somewhere," the kelpie says.

"Thank you for not eating him," I say. It's a relief.

"It was no trouble to me. He looks quite unappetizing," the kelpie says drily.

"I came here because I was told a very powerful fae lives in this river. I bet that's you," I say. The knotted scar coils and twists as the kelpie smiles.

"Probably," he says. "Though I don't think you came all this way just to tell me something I already know."

"I was hoping to get your help," I say. "I need to find a prison that's somewhere around here." The kelpie waits expectantly for a moment before speaking with a hint of annoyance.

"And? What will you offer me in exchange?" he asks.

"Chocolate treats?" I say. Maybe that's a universal fae delicacy. The kelpie snorts.

"Flesh. Human. The younger the better. Preferably still moving. Bring me a gift the next time you come asking for a boon and perhaps I will consider it."

"I'm not feeding you *people*," I say incredulously before I can stop myself.

"How boring," the kelpie says. "Then it appears you have nothing interesting to offer."

"I'll find something more interesting than eating people," I say. "I'll be back, but I need to go find Zach before he gets hurt."

"Very well. Do come back soon," the kelpie says, vanishing under the water. I run. It seems like a good idea to be out of sight before he decides this meeting is formally over and I'm back on the menu.

The kelpie's conversation made me lose track of my past self, but at least it doesn't take me long to find Zach's trail in the present. Large boot prints in the dirt and leaf litter mark his passing. I follow those a short way, but eventually I'm stumped trying to figure out if a mark on the ground is a print or if the pattern is just my imagination. The question is rendered moot by the sound of footsteps nearby. Zach soon follows.

"You alright?" I ask. He looks frazzled and has a few superficial-looking cuts, but otherwise seems unharmed.

"Are *you* alright?" he asks. He runs over and puts a hand on my shoulder, though seems unsure if he should do anything else.

"Yeah. I talked to the kelpie. We should stay away from the water from here on."

Zach and I agree we've had enough of faeries for the day. We can't cross the creek to get home the way we came, but eventually we find an arch formed by two trees that works well enough as a threshold, though that means we return to our world in a different part of the forest. Zach, with his experience in these parts, figures out where we are after not too long, though we still have to walk for over an hour to get back to the truck. Our adventure in Faerie took far more time than we thought, and it's dark by the time Zach drops me off.

"Hi. I'm back," I say as I walk through the front door. I hear a muffled groan from the kitchen in response. I rush into the kitchen, where I see Grandma sitting awkwardly on the floor against the counter, a shattered coffee mug and puddle of coffee beside her.

"Are you okay? Are you hurt?" I say, rushing to her side.

"I'm fine. I dropped a mug and leaned down to clean it up, then realized I wasn't getting up on my own. I didn't fall. Stop panicking and just help me up," she says. She's far more calm than I am. She puts one arm around my shoulders and in the course of several tries I haul her to her feet. After she's standing and leaning on the counter for support, I retrieve her cane and start checking her over.

"Are you sure you aren't hurt? Should I take you to the hospital, just in case?" I ask.

"No, for God's sake. I'm fine." She waves my arms away with clumsy, trembling hands. I try to help her back to her regular armchair, but she shakes me off and walks there by herself.

"I don't need that much help. I can do this much by myself," she snaps.

"I'm sorry. I shouldn't have left." I bend down to pick up the pieces of the shattered mug. The coffee is cold.

"I don't need constant supervision. It only just happened. I was down there for a minute at most," she says.

"Grandma—"

"No. Don't you dare coddle me. I'm an adult. I don't need you around all the time. This was just a freak accident. I don't need someone hovering over me twenty-four seven."

"Why did you even let me come here, then?" I say to the coffee puddle.

"What?" Grandma asks.

"Nothing." I throw the pieces of the mug away. "Are you hungry? Can I get you anything?"

"No," she says with a child's petulance.

"Why were you drinking coffee this late?" I ask. The time on my phone is closing in on nine p.m.

"It's decaf," she snaps, her tone putting an end to the conversation. I fill up a coffee mug from the pot and add a splash of cream and set it down on the side table next to Grandma's chair without a word. She mumbles a thank you and I mumble in acknowledgment.

In the silence, I wipe up the spilled coffee. The puddle has made its way into the gap between the fridge and the counter, so I do my best to get as much as I can with a rag. While I'm down there, I notice something odd. There appears to be a folded piece of paper taped to the side of the fridge. Curious, I carefully pull it free and unfold it, smoothing the creases with the tips of my fingers. It's a piece of notebook paper stained and worn thin with age. On it are a few lines of my handwriting.

The key is a kiss, like all the stories. A kiss from captive to captive frees them both.

Chapter Nine

"I cleaned up the spill. I'm pretty tired. I think I'll go lay down," I say, refolding the piece of paper and slipping it into my back pocket.

"Zach wear you out?" she asks.

"*Grandma!*" I whine, rushing up the stairs, leaving her cackling in her armchair. It's embarrassing, but I don't go out of my way to correct her. It's better for her to believe that than be worried about me and Zach running from monsters in the woods.

When I get to my room, I plop down on the mattress and stare at the note.

"How does this work, Leithe?" I murmur. "Do you just show up if I want you to, or ..."

"Who can say?" Leithe says. I look up to see him leaning against the bedroom door, arms crossed. The hem of his robes blends into the shadows cast by the lamp; it seems like there's dark shapes coiling on the floor around him. "Your injuries are fading. How much time has passed?"

"Since we spoke in the bathroom? A week. Is that the last thing you remember?"

"The last thing with any clarity. Between now and then is simply ... fog; an awareness of something that constantly slips out of my grasp." He shakes his head. "But that doesn't matter. Have you made any progress?"

"I think so. Look at this." I pull out the paper from my pocket and hold it out so he can read it. "It's my handwriting, but I can't remember how I learned it." Leithe scrunches up his brow and glares at the words.

"It's probably the key," he says.

"What do you mean?" I ask. He sighs dramatically, as if I've asked the purpose of a doorknob.

"Spells of binding are always more effective when there's an escape clause woven in. That, and punishments for my kind are never meant to last forever. The punishment is deemed complete when the escape clause is fulfilled."

"If this is your escape clause, wouldn't you know?"

"Not if the details of the prison were woven after I was thrown inside," he sighs. "I don't know how I'm supposed to kiss someone when I lack a solid form, though. But that's where the weavers of such curses derive their amusement—by making the key something seemingly impossible to achieve from within the confines of the punishment. You'll have to look between the lines; stretch and bend the words as far as they will go without shattering completely. These things can be tricky."

"At least now we know there's only you and one other prisoner. Maybe you could blow the other prisoner a kiss," I offer.

"If I knew where they were, I would try it," he points out.

"Yeah, yeah. Adding 'find other prisoner' to the plan," I say.

Leithe stares at the paper thoughtfully, resting his chin on his hand. "I don't know who this other prisoner could be."

"Did you and anyone else have any mutual enemies?" I ask.

"I only had one ally," he says, more to himself than to me.

"Your betrothed?" I ask.

"But it's as I said: she could never be held by something like this. It can't be her. She's a *queen*. That note must be wrong. Either you didn't write it down correctly or you were deceived. Go find the real key. This farce must have been orchestrated to make me lose faith in her. I wasn't originally of her court but she chose me anyway. Many of her subjects were jealous of me, especially those who thought *they* deserved her instead. It must have been one of them that did this. Lelit, maybe. She always hated me." Around us, the room gets darker. Long shadows crawl up the walls and dance in the waning lamplight. His yellow eyes shine with feverish intensity in the darkness.

"Leithe, it's okay," I say, reaching out as if I could touch him. He lashes out to swipe my hand away, though his arm passes harmlessly through me.

"Are you one of Lelit's children? Or are you Lelit herself, here to make me believe I have a chance at freedom?" His expression is crazed; I don't think he knows where he is anymore.

"Stop it!" I demand.

"Release my mind, creature!" The slithering shadows on the floor lash out at me like lunging snakes. I recoil and shield my face, though the shadows pass over me harmlessly; when I look again, Leithe is gone.

"Figures," I say, resting my head in my hands in frustration.

I'm stuck. I'm suffocating. When I try to breathe, my nose and throat fill with spider webs.

And then I wake up, face pressing into my pillow. I lay there in the dark for a moment, waiting for my pulse to slow, and then I hear one of my dresser drawers slide shut. Rolling over and forcing my sleep-crusted eyes open, I see a vision of my teen self hurriedly shoving things into a backpack. It's the same vision I saw once before. Like last time, she pulls the backpack shut and then carefully drops it out the window into the garden below. And then she walks out of the room, closing the door as quietly as she can.

This time I'm going to follow her. I get up and open the bedroom door only to see no signs of life. I curse myself. I shouldn't have let her out of my sight, seeing how fickle these glimpses of memories are. The sound of someone going down the stairs gives me hope, but by the time I make it to the upper landing, there's nothing there. I sneak down the stairs in time to see the front door shut behind a figure.

I worry there's not much time to catch up, but I still pause long enough to grab a steak knife from the kitchen before following the memory through the front door. There's no one outside, and by the time I come around to the side of the house, the backpack is missing from the flowerbed, leaving behind a patch of flattened tulips.

I head toward the trees, assuming she could only be headed toward the woods. Soon I see a light flicker on ahead of me. It illuminates Teen Tamsin as well as Grandma's cat, eyes shining in the sudden light. The girl nods at the cat as if they have some understanding, and then pulls a kitchen knife and an opaque spray bottle from the bag. She juggles the two of them indecisively for a moment before carefully sliding the knife into a side pouch on the backpack meant for a water bottle.

"I'm ready," she says. "Let's go." It's strange hearing my own voice come from another figure. The cat turns and heads into the woods, and the girl follows, casting one last glance at Grandma's house. She looks sad, scared, but also determined. She sets her mouth in the same hard line that Grandma does when she's preparing for an argument.

I follow them, wishing I could take her hand or offer words of support, or ask what it is she's so determined to do. As we walk, I try to parse my moth-eaten memory for the reason I planned this outing, with a backpack full of tools to harm faeries. The younger me walks with purpose, but also with an eye on her surroundings, as if she expects trouble.

After a while, she juggles the flashlight and spray bottle in the same hand so she can pull out her phone and type something rapidly before snapping it shut and shoving it back into her pocket. I'm momentarily distracted by the flashlight waving all over the place like a concert spotlight, so I'm late peering over her shoulder at the text. All I catch is that it was to Zach. After that, we walk some more, with Teen Tamsin checking her phone every few minutes. It's a little flip phone. I remember Grandma giving it to me so I would have no excuse for avoiding her.

It doesn't happen immediately, but trouble inevitably arrives. The cat's ears twitch and she suddenly bolts; a dark shape—one of Hunter's dogs—bounds out of the night and follows in pursuit, leaving the girl alone.

"Shoot," she curses, brandishing the spray bottle like a gun against the shadows.

"I suppose there's no point in asking you what you're doing." I recognize Hunter's voice as it drifts from the shadows. He sounds tired and irritated.

"I'm trying to help!" she says, eyes searching the shadows for any sign of Hunter. "Why can't you let me help?"

"I'm sworn to act, as I've told you," he says.

"This is water and iron shavings. It'll straight-up melt you," Teen Tamsin says. "Just go away and let me do this!" From the shadows, his hand shoots out and grabs her wrist, twisting it and forcing her to drop the bottle.

"You know very well that I can't," he says, kicking the bottle beyond the trees. She drops the flashlight. I think she did it by accident until Hunter grunts in surprise and pain, releasing Teen Tamsin to pull the kitchen knife from his stomach. While he's distracted, she scoops up the flashlight once more and runs headlong into the trees. He yanks the knife out and throws it into the distance with a noise like anger or disgust, pressing his other hand against his stomach. The wound is sizzling and giving off wisps of smoke. With a labored breath, Hunter takes a few steps and vanishes behind a tree trunk; when I follow, he's gone. He didn't go in the same direction as my past self did. She went deeper into the woods. He went toward the road.

I follow Hunter, hoping maybe I might learn something he refused to share with me in the past. I cross the road when I reach it. After that I lose his trail. I wander for a while before stopping and leaning my forehead against a tree trunk in frustration. I'm tired. And this is stupid. I shouldn't have thought I'd be able to track Hunter in the first place.

It's then that I hear footsteps partially muffled by leaf litter. There's a shape in the darkness that's moving away from me. It can't be Hunter. He doesn't make noise when he walks, so I follow curiously.

Before I can get close enough to see who it is, the trees part to make a large clearing. The waning moonlight outlines a three-story house. A wide path of slightly thinned grass marks the place a gravel driveway must have once run. Ivy climbs up the porch columns and hangs down in sheets. A tiny sapling has forced its way through one of the wooden front steps.

This is the Randall Place. The old couple that used to live here died when I was very young, and the house has sat empty ever since. I can't recall a specific time I came here, but I must have with Zach at some point in order to recognize it. Grandma told me to stay away, that the ceiling would collapse, or I'd get tetanus from an exposed nail.

There's something strange hanging in the air as I approach. It's as if there's a pane of distorted glass between me and the house. I think I can make out my reflection—merely a faint outline—in the air in front of me. I reach out and touch it and feel resistance against my fingertips. I press harder, pushing the barrier inward until the surface tension gives way and it feels like I've plunged my hand into a bowl of gelatin. My skin prickles from the contact. I push forward, fighting against the pressure, until I pass through the barrier completely. And then I'm standing in front of the decrepit house, not far from the front porch steps.

The barrier must be some fae nonsense, though I haven't noticed anything else out of the ordinary. I place one foot on the first step and it seems stable enough to hold my weight. The boards creak on my way to the front door. I expect it to be locked, but the knob turns and the door swings open easily.

Inside is dark save for the faint rays of moonlight coming in through the door; the windows are opaque with grime. One pane has been broken by an intruding tree branch, but the tree blocks out any light that might have come through. My phone doesn't provide much light, but it lets me see that moldering carpet has been ripped up and piled against the wall. Several carpet nails have been pulled out as well, but there are still enough to force me to watch my step.

A dirty sofa sits in front of a brick fireplace. A small pile of sticks, twigs, and dried leaves and grasses sits neatly on the hearth.

"I'm not surprised the barrier didn't stop you," Hunter says from behind me. He's standing in the doorway, the shadows of his hounds falling across the threshold.

"Do you live here?" I ask. I try to sound casual, like my heart isn't pounding. I'm cornered in this house. This was not a smart plan.

"I sleep here sometimes," he says.

"And you made a barrier to keep people away?"

"Not well, as you can see. I can keep rowdy children away, save for one," he says pointedly.

"We're not in Faerie, which means I'm not trespassing," I say. He nods slightly. I resist the urge to sigh in relief. I wasn't sure whether I was correct or not.

"Even so, you have trespassed, and undoubtedly will again. But I'm tired, so we can leave that confrontation for a later day," he says, carefully removing his weapons and placing them by the door.

"Do you frequently menace children in the woods?"

"You'll have to be more specific." Hunter walks into the living room and jerks his head to beckon the dogs in. They trot into the living room, smell me, and settle down. One lays on the floor and the other hops up on the sofa and sprawls nearly across its entire length.

"I remember when I was younger, and you grabbed me."

"Was this the time you stabbed me?" He asks. "I'd assumed you felt vengeance was yours." He walks to the fireplace; I edge around the sofa to keep it between us. I'm conscious that I'm gripping the hilt of the kitchen knife tightly. Hunter either doesn't care or doesn't notice. He kneels by the hearth and starts preparing a fire.

"Can't you just do that with magic?" I ask.

"I could, but I enjoy the motions," he says, not looking at me.

"Just because you left your weapons at the door doesn't mean you've given me any sense of security," I say. "You're probably twice my size." Even though we're about the same height, he has much more muscle.

"Keep clutching the knife, then. Give yourself a hand cramp. You've already stabbed me once, so I can't see the damage a few more times might do," he says. "But during this meeting between us, I promise on my life and my sworn duty that I won't attempt to do you harm."

"What, do we pinky promise and then I just believe you?"

"I thought you were wise to our secrets now. Fae cannot lie. Any promise made will be kept to the word," he says. That sounds right. I think it's been told to me before, a long time ago. But by whom, I can't recall.

"Okay, then add that you won't keep me captive, and promise for the dogs, too," I say.

"You're starting to think like one of us. I also promise not to hold you against your will, or allow my hounds to do so or to do you harm," he says.

"Why are you so ready to chat today?" I ask, perching on the arm of the sofa.

"The dogs aren't much for conversation," he says. He seems satisfied with the arrangement of the kindling, so he pulls out a pack of matches, lights one, and tosses it into the fireplace. As he leans forward to coax the flames to life, the dim reddish light catches the angles of his face and hair.

"I was expecting you to use two rocks to make a spark or something," I say.

"Matches are useful," he says.

"If you want to have a conversation, maybe we can talk about what happened to my memories."

"There's nothing to say about them." The fire burns brighter, and Hunter rises and moves to the couch. His hound shifts to put its head on his knee, and he places his hand on its back.

"If you just gave them back, I wouldn't have any more business with you."

"I doubt that."

"They're my memories, aren't they? I think I have a right to have them."

"No one in the world cares about your rights," he says.

"If you knew you were missing something that you used to have, wouldn't you want it back?" He doesn't answer immediately, instead only stares into the fire with an unreadable expression.

"I would. But what I want is just as irrelevant as what you want," he finally says. His fingers dig and twist into his hound's fur. "What would your life be like if you simply stopped looking and lived out your human life in peace?"

"I don't know," I say. "But knowing there's more out there, I can't even imagine what it would be like to ignore that."

Hunter closes his eyes and leans his head against the back of the sofa. "Why did you come back?" he asks after a moment.

"I just told you, I want the rest of my memories back."

"That's not what I meant. Why did you come back to live in that house? You were gone for several years."

"To take care of my grandmother."

"Then you should take her far away and not come back. Eventually, you might forget everything again."

"Believe me, I've suggested it, but Grandma would never move," I say. Though now that he suggested it I want to stay simply out of spite. "But I think you know that. You've tried to magic her into leaving, haven't you?"

"You're both stubborn," he says. "It never holds very long on her, and repeated glamouring is dangerous to a human's mind."

"And you care about the wellbeing of my grandmother's mind?" I ask. He doesn't answer. "I might be able to convince her to leave, but it would help if I knew more about what was going on," I continue.

Hunter closes his eyes. "Prisoners are being kept here. My sworn duty is to guard them and make sure they don't escape. I am, essentially, magically compelled to guard this prison at all costs, including preventing anyone from coming into contact with it."

"So you don't have a choice?" I ask.

"Don't pity me. If it came to it, I would kill you. Regardless of any personal feelings I may have."

"Why do you care? Why don't you just kill me if I'm a nuisance?"

"Why do you think?" he asks. His tone isn't rhetorical or sarcastic. It's a genuine question.

"... Because you're a nice person?" He snorts with what sounds like a laugh.

"Perhaps," he says. He doesn't seem interested in continuing the conversation. For a while we just sit while the fire crackles.

"So what did these prisoners do to get locked up here?" I ask. I need to guide the conversation back to Leithe; maybe I'll learn something Leithe can't tell me.

"There was a court power squabble. They lost."

"What kind of people are they?"

"The same as any other Gentry. Endlessly engaging in caprice and petty scheming to stave off the boredom of eternity, utterly incapable of compassion or self-reflection," Hunter spits.

"You don't seem to have a high opinion of your own people," I say. He laughs, but without any perceivable joy.

"My own people ..." He muses over the words. "The Gentry aren't my people. They see themselves as above all other fae since they're incapable of true death." Hunter bends forward and reaches under the sofa. He pulls out a plastic liquor bottle half-filled with something brown, unscrews the cap and takes a swig.

"Where did you get that?" I ask.

"I walked into a store and bought it. The bills were leaves and the glamour wore off after a few hours." He studies the bottle for a moment and then holds it out to me. "You're of age for humans now, right?"

"Yeah," I say. I take the offered bottle and take a sip. It's strong whiskey that burns its way down my throat and makes me cough a little. Hunter snorts. I hand the bottle back and he drinks again.

"Is this what you do when you're not patrolling the woods, sit in front of a fire and get drunk?"

"Sometimes I drink in the woods, too."

"You sound like an alcoholic," I say. I look around the room for something else to talk about. I accidentally make eye contact with one of the dogs and it wags its tail and seems to look at me hopefully.

"Can I maybe pet your dog?" I ask. He nods, and I press my hand into the fur on the dog's haunch. The fur is coarse to the touch and the dog is warm. Solid. At my touch, the dog wags its tail more and puts its head on my lap. I scratch it some more and its leg bounces in place.

"Can I make a weird request?" I say.

"I can't stop you from asking," he says.

"Well, it's just that I'm still worried this is somehow all in my head. That I'm dreaming, or talking to myself, or something like that. So could I, um, touch you, just to convince myself that you're really real?" My face gets warm. I wonder if there was any possible way for me to phrase that question without making it so awkward.

"The entire time we've been talking you've thought I'm not real?" he asks.

"I have a hard time telling, probably because you've all been messing with my head." I probe for any signs of guilt on his face, but he's unreadable.

"Fine, then," he says. With a gesture, he dismisses the dog from the couch; it jumps off and instead curls up closer to the fire. Leaving my kitchen knife sitting on the arm of the sofa, I get up and sit closer to him. For an awkward moment, neither of us move, and then he holds up his hand to me.

I carefully touch my fingers to his, half expecting them to dissipate into smoke like Leithe's did, but they don't. His skin is warm and calloused, and definitely solid. I trace my fingertips down to his palm and over the lines and creases. I graze over a vein in his wrist that looks green. I wonder if his blood is green.

"Satisfied?" Hunter asks, and I realize I probably don't need to still be touching him. I quickly pull my hand back.

"Yep. Seems real," I mumble, avoiding eye contact.

"I have a favor to ask you as well, then," he says.

"Is it to stay out of the woods?" I ask.

"No. Because I know you wouldn't keep that promise. I'll just ask you to be careful who you trust. The fae in these woods don't always intend you harm, but anything attempting to entice you to go deeper does not have your wellbeing at heart."

"And you do have my wellbeing at heart?"

"As much as I can, given the circumstances."

"Why?"

"Do I need a reason not to want to see a girl suffer preventable harm? Other fae you might meet here aren't going to be like me. Even those who wouldn't intentionally do you harm don't always understand the limitations of a human body. So once again, when we part ways, I advise you to leave and live out your life far from here."

"I would do that if you would just give me back my memories," I say.

"Somehow, I don't think you would," he sighs. "I'm no longer going to speak of this. Now," he begins. "I must resume my patrol. Remember, if you continue trying to force yourself into my court's domain, I will take action against you the next time we meet. You do know how to get back to your home from here?" He starts to stand, but on impulse I reach out to grab his arm.

"Wait," I say. To my surprise, my hand closes on air and his hand closes around my wrist. He looks surprised as well, and quickly releases me.

"What?" he asks.

"Could you at least walk me back to my yard?" I should try to get as much information out of him as I can while he's in a talkative mood. Besides, it keeps him from getting the chance to change his mind before I make it somewhere safe. He looks at me for a moment.

"If you wish," he says. I'm surprised he consented so easily, but pleased as well.

"Thanks."

"If you want to thank me, don't come back here." He stands up and offers me a hand, which I accept. The hounds rise when their master does.

"Hey, real quick," I say, still holding onto him. "Tell me faeries are real and that I'm not crazy."

"Faeries are real, and I don't believe you're crazy, though you lack a fundamental sense of self-preservation," he says. And he's still there. It still seems real.

"Okay. Let's go." I release him. He puts out the dwindling fire, and we leave the old house and pass through the barrier. Hunter concentrates for a moment and dismisses part of it so that I don't have to push my way through it.

"So why do you live in an old house in the human world instead of in Faerie?" I ask as we walk down the overgrown driveway. The dogs take off once we exit the house, scouting the area and looking for interesting smells.

"It's more peaceful, I suppose. I'm left alone. Usually."

"Well, as long as I stay out of Faerie, can I come visit you here again?" I ask. There's another long pause. Hunter's face is mostly unreadable, though he unsurprisingly seems irritated by the question.

"If you must," he says.

We make our way back to my house, walking in silence until we reach the edge of the yard. I had several questions I wanted to ask, but with permission to come see him again I decide to wait rather than risk irritating him more than I already have tonight. He doesn't seem so bad, despite what Thistledown said about him.

"Do you remember what I told you?" he asks, stopping at the edge of the tree line.

"About what?" I ask.

"The important things. Don't trust anyone. Stay out of the woods. Assume everyone and everything is out to deceive you. This once, please listen. The memories you lost are not worth this," he says. His tone changes from the usual low and vaguely annoyed to something that could almost be called pleading.

"You can't just *do* this," I say. "You tell me not to trust anyone, and that what, you're the only one actually looking out for my best interests? How am I supposed to believe that when you won't tell me anything important? I'm sorry you don't have a choice in what you're doing, but I feel like I don't either. I can't just take your word for it. I guess you've given me what help you're capable of giving, but I need to find my own answers. And I'm not going to stop looking. I just wanted to give you the courtesy of saying that."

"I hoped it would be different," he says. He seems like he wants to say more, but nothing else comes out.

"Well, goodbye, then," I say, taking a step into the yard.

"Goodbye," Hunter says, closing his eyes. He always looks so tired.

I'm halfway to the house when I hear a sharp whistle cut through the night air. An instant later, a huge weight slams into my back and knocks me to the ground, barely giving me time to cry out and cover my face. The ground knocks the wind out of me, and there's massive paws pressing painfully into my back. I try to sit up, but the dog adjusts its weight to keep me down.

With what visibility I have, I watch Hunter walk around and kneel next to me. He has his spear out and plants the point into the ground near my face.

"I shall reiterate," he says. "We are not on the same side. You are a nuisance. I tried to speak with you and explained as much as I can to satisfy your curiosity. If you make yourself too much of my problem, I will kill you. Don't think that you're safe if you're on this side of the tree line. There is nothing stopping me from walking into that house and killing you in your bed. I'm not human. I could kill you at any time, and it would be easy. Would you prefer I just did it now to save us both the trouble? I would no longer have to worry about you, and you would no longer fret about a past you don't need." His voice is low and unaffected, even while making threats.

"N-no," I gasp. A light inside the house comes on.

"Would that be your grandmother? Which do you care about more, her or your memories?" he asks. "Well?" he goads when I don't immediately answer.

"... her," I say, mustering more force as the air returns to my lungs.

"Then act like it. And remember that you—and she—are alive solely by my kindness, a resource you are about to exhaust." The porch lights come on, bathing most of the yard in watery light. I shut my eyes on reflex, and the weight vanishes from my back. I lurch upright and run on shaking legs back to the house, stumbling my way onto the porch. Grandma is standing by the back door in a nightgown, looking at me in shock.

"Wh—" she begins, but stops when I throw my arms around her and let out a sob.

"I went outside. I'm sorry," I say, voice strangled as I fight to keep from breaking out into tears completely.

"Tamsin, please let go," Grandma says. Of course she wouldn't want anything to do with me. I'm just a problem for her. I pull back.

"I'm sorry," I say again. Then I notice she's holding a rifle, which she gently props against the doorframe before pulling me back into a hug.

"Why do you have a gun?" I ask.

"Bears," she says. I laugh weakly. "Do you ... want to talk about it?" she asks. I release her and look back toward the trees, but I can't see anything past the harsh glare of the porch light.

"There isn't anything to talk about. I was just dumb. I won't do it again," I say. "Let's just go back inside. I just want to go lay down."

I lead her inside, make sure the door is shut and locked, for all the good I expect it to do, and then I make my way to the stairs.

"You have a paw print on your back," Grandma says.

"What?" I try to twist around to see it, but can't manage.

"For a second, it looked like there was someone else outside with you," she says, just as much to herself as to me.

"Did it look like anyone you know?" I ask.

"I ... no. I couldn't make them out," she says.

"Okay. Never mind. Goodnight." I rush upstairs to my bathroom and twist around to look at my back in the mirror. Sure enough, there's a large dirty paw print on my shirt between my shoulder blades, and the remnants of another near the hem. And Grandma saw them. And Grandma saw someone else outside with me. It all actually happened. I want to feel joy, or smugness in the knowledge that I've been right the whole time, but my mind is assaulted by fear and revulsion.

I rush to the toilet and vomit bile and the partially digested remains of my dinner until I'm shaking uncontrollably. I push myself away from the toilet and lean against the opposite wall. I've been an idiot. I've been approaching this like a game when it's not, and that could get the people around me killed. I didn't stop to consider what it would mean if this wasn't a fantasy I constructed for myself, but now I see it means I've waltzed into an arena

I'm not prepared for. Should I call the police? Is there a faerie protocol, or would I just be sending people to their deaths at Hunter's hands or some other monster's?

I pull myself to a standing position in front of the sink and scrub my mouth out. I don't have the strength to shower even though my forearms bear grass stains, and I'm sure the rest of me isn't much better.

I drag myself to my bedroom and collapse onto the bed, pausing only to strip off my dirty clothes. Hunter's right. It was one thing when I thought it was all in my head, or even when I thought it might be real but that there wouldn't be any consequences for anyone but myself. But I could get other people hurt. Still ...

I roll onto my side and look down at the paw print on my stained shirt. It's real. But perhaps the memory of whatever happened to me years ago is better off lost. As long as I stay out of the woods, I won't come into contact with Hunter. I can just ignore the stupid cat and move on with my life. The thing that will be difficult to ignore is Leithe, and his promise.

"You look awful," Leithe says. Of course he would appear now.

"What do you want?" I ask. I don't have the energy to be witty or biting.

"Have you learned anything useful?" he asks. Useful. I learned that any step I take toward helping Leithe or finding my memories will do nothing but get Grandma killed. I try to hold it back, but it takes only seconds for a wave of tears to well up and burst forth. I let out a sob. Leithe looks startled and then perplexed by my outburst.

"I'm sorry," I choke out. "I can't help you anymore."

"You made a binding deal," he says. His tone is patronizing, reminiscent of an adult explaining a simple concept to a child.

"I know. But I shouldn't have. He's going to kill my grandma if I do anything."

"Figure out something else. Kill him first," Leithe suggests, as if the solution was simple.

"Can you keep my grandma safe while I do that?" I ask.

"Once I'm free—"

"No. Right now—can you keep her safe right now?" I ask, cutting him off. He doesn't answer, just glares at me in silence.

"You can't," I continue. "You can't do anything right now. I can't do anything. And your wish isn't worth anything if I'm dead. Our deal is off. I'm sorry. You'll have to find someone else to help you."

"The deal is *not* off. I'm not releasing you from it."

"I don't care. I'm done. Just … please leave me alone."

"You don't understand—"

"*Leave me alone,*" I shout, squeezing my eyes shut and putting my hands over my ears. I sit like that against the wall, knees pulled tight to my chest, for a very long time. That's where I am when Grandma knocks on my bedroom door. I open my eyes; Leithe is gone.

"Tamsin?" Grandma calls from behind the door. "What's wrong? Who's talking to you?" Several potential answers zip through my head.

"I'm …" *I'm fine,* is what I want to say, but I can't. My room is silent.

"No one's in here. I just … thought I saw something, but it's gone," I say.

"Can I do anything?" Grandma asks after a tense pause.

"No. I don't think so." I think that's the end of it, but a few minutes later Grandma knocks on the door again, this time to offer me a mug of steaming chamomile tea. She mumbles something about wanting to make a mug for herself but boiling too much water before turning and going back downstairs. I take a sip. It's delicious—loaded with honey like how she made it for me when I was a kid.

I sit on my bed and bathe in the silence, clutching the hot ceramic mug in my hands. The honey-sweet tea sticks in my throat. When I can't bring myself to drink any more, I crawl under the blankets and fall into a dreamless sleep.

Chapter Ten

WHEN I WAKE UP, there's no mysterious childhood vision or angry Leithe. Just my room, as it has been for the last several days. Tepid sunlight leaks in from the window. I've slept through the night, nightmare free. Even so, fatigue weighs on my eyelids and all I want is to roll over and go back to sleep—for an hour, for the rest of the day, I don't care.

There are no monsters in the woods. There are no monsters in the house. I've seen nothing of Leithe, Hunter, or anything else supernatural since the night I broke off my deal with Leithe. The cat has been around. Grandma has only spoken to me when necessary.

I get up because I have to pee. A sudden wave of dizziness washes over me when I stand, making me buckle and brace my hand on the mattress to keep from collapsing. The feeling quickly passes but leaves behind a twinge of nausea in the pit of my stomach. The stress of what I've been doing must have finally caught up to me.

My dirty clothes from that night are still strewn across my floor, dirty paw prints clearly visible on the back of my shirt. I haven't been able to bring myself to wash the marks away. I kick the shirt under my bed on the way to the bathroom. I don't want to look at it. I don't want to think about it.

I force myself to shower since I haven't done so in days and probably smell. Traces of the ugly bruise along my cheekbone and the big ones on my back and knees linger from Hunter's ultimatum. Grandma didn't ask about them. She hasn't asked me any questions about that night.

Grandma is awake when I go downstairs, watching the news in her bathrobe and pajamas, cup of coffee clutched in her hands. She's been getting up before me and staying up after I go to bed. My grandfather's rifle always sits leaning against the living room wall where it's within her reach.

"Good morning," she says as I enter the kitchen. "How are you feeling?" There's trepidation in her voice, blanketed by false cheerfulness.

"Fine," I say. I feel fine, neutral. I can't muster the energy to feel any other way.

"Good," Grandma says, apparently satisfied.

Grandma makes breakfast, and we eat while exchanging small talk about nothing in particular. There's something about the texture of the scrambled eggs that turns my stomach, so I slide them around the plate until I don't think Grandma's paying attention, and then take my plate to the kitchen.

I go out on the back porch and fill the cat's food bowl. She does exactly what I expect—bounds up and struts toward the tree line, but I dump the food in its bowl and go back inside. I just don't care about whatever she's doing. I come back and sit down on the couch in the absence of anything better to do.

The TV is playing a drama I struggle to concentrate on. It feels as though there's a fog over my brain; the man and woman on the screen are having an argument and the woman slaps him across the face and he responds by pulling her into a kiss. My mind drifts back to my final argument with Leithe. Then I get annoyed he's still in my head, so I force myself to think about something else—Zach. Zach has nice eyes, doesn't he? Try as I might, I can't remember what color his eyes are. Leithe's are yellow. Hunter's are brown.

I don't realize until her second or third try that Grandma has been talking to me.

"What?" I ask, pulled back out of my head.

"I said we have to leave for my appointment soon. Do you remember?" she asks.

"Yeah, of course. When is it?"

"One-fifteen. I told you yesterday," she says reproachfully. "We can get some lunch while we're out, if you want." My brain isn't so foggy that I can't see how carefully she's treating me. But maybe it's a treatment I deserve.

"Sure, if you want," I say.

The specialist Grandma sees turns out to be almost forty minutes away. During the drive, I find my mind drifting frequently, and have difficulty focusing on the road. The movement also makes my nausea worse. At one point I don't realize a light ahead of me turned red and I have to slam the brakes, jostling Grandma. She grimaces but doesn't say anything. I stifle a laugh. I can't take care of myself; why did I think I might possibly be able to take care of her?

The doctor's office is done up in shades of beige. They seem to be going for a homey feel, but the sharp, sterile edge in the air reminds me where we are. It makes me uncomfortable for a reason I can't put my finger on. It makes my stomach churn.

When Grandma is called back, I stand to go with her, but she puts a hand out.

"You can wait out here," she says.

"Okay," I say, sitting back down. "Let me know if you need anything." She grunts in acknowledgment and follows the nurse into the back. I realize that sounds stupid. We're at a doctor's office. There's no reason for her to need me.

I go through the pile of magazines on the table next to me while I wait, but I struggle to concentrate on the words so I put them down in frustration. After fiddling around with my phone for a few minutes, I have to put it down. I've gotten more and more nauseous since Grandma and I left the house, and now the pain is too distracting for me to focus on anything else. All I can do is take deep breaths and hope it goes away.

And then I know I'm going to vomit. I bolt up and run to the bathroom, which is thankfully vacant. As soon as I get my head over the toilet bowl, I'm retching up my breakfast, along with streaks of bright red. Eventually I expel the last of the bloody bile. My eyes water and my vision blurs, but when I wipe my eyes my fingers come back red. I sit up and look in the mirror and see that what I thought were tears are actually drops of blood. A tiny trickle of blood drips from my nose as well.

"No, no, no ..." I whisper as I grab handfuls of paper towels to clean my face. I wipe blood on everything I touch. I'll have to clean those as well. While I scrub my skin raw, someone knocks on the door.

"Ma'am, do you need help?" says a woman from the other side of the door.

"I'll be right out!" I say. My throat burns when I speak.

I examine my face in the mirror. After cleaning the blood off, it looks like my eyes and nose aren't still bleeding, so I wipe up the rest of my mess and carefully hide the bloody paper towels underneath some other trash in the hopes no one will notice.

A nurse stands outside the bathroom when I emerge.

"Do you know if you're contagious, ma'am?" she asks.

"I ... I think it's more likely I just ate something bad," I say. I should probably tell the nurse what just happened or go to the hospital, but I don't have the money, and neither does Grandma. And besides, it seems like it stopped for now.

The nurse goes into the bathroom, presumably to sanitize it, while I sit back down in the waiting room, as far away from other people as possible. They politely don't say anything, though I'm sure they could hear me puking through the walls.

After Grandma's appointment, we drive to the diner back in town. Nausea slowly builds in the pit of my stomach as I drive.

"I think I'd rather just go home," I say.

"Why?" Grandma asks.

"I feel a little sick," I say.

"It's probably because you haven't been doing anything. You didn't eat any breakfast. You can get whatever you want at Carol's," she says. I don't feel like arguing further. By the time we slide into a diner booth, I just want to lie down.

"How did your appointment go?" I ask Grandma. She waves a hand at me dismissively.

"It went about the same as every other appointment. Nothing interesting to report," she says.

"Can I get you something to drink?" our waiter asks, handing us menus.

"I'll have one of your strawberry limeades. I haven't had one of those in ages," Grandma says.

"Just water, please," I say. The thought of drinking anything else makes my stomach gurgle.

"We have water at home. Stop worrying about running up the bill. It's my treat," Grandma snaps.

"My stomach—"

"Then she'll have a ginger ale," Grandma tells the waiter. She turns back to me. "The fizz will settle your stomach. Honestly, you probably feel bad because all you've been doing this week is sleeping. Have you talked to Zach lately? Does this mood have something to do with him?"

"Not really," I say. He'd texted me a few times, but I either gave him the briefest of responses or didn't text back at all. It's wrong. He's my only friend and I owe him more than that.

"Is everything okay between you two?" she asks.

"I just don't feel well. It's not about him," I snap. Grandma frowns but doesn't respond.

We peruse the menus in awkward silence until the waiter returns with our drinks and asks for our orders.

"Oh. I'm going to be bad today. I want a Philly cheese-steak, please," Grandma says.

"I guess ... just a cup of chicken noodle soup, please," I say. After the waiter leaves, Grandma glowers at me.

"We came all the way out here, and that's all you want? You were always so picky. You'd hardly eat anything when I'd take you out for special occasions and you always complained it gave you a stomachache. Honestly, I didn't think I'd ever meet a child that didn't like Twinkies. But no, you'd rather eat radishes straight from the garden, still covered with dirt," Grandma says.

"If you already knew I wouldn't want to eat anything here, why did you bring me? Did you just want to complain?" I snap.

"Well, it was funny when you were younger, but now I'm worried you'll disappear if you turn sideways. Did you eat anything at all in Boston?" she asks.

"Yes. I ate." My head is starting to hurt. I take a sip of ginger ale. It irritates my still-raw throat. Something about it tastes bad, as if ginger ale could be rotten. Maybe they need to clean out the drink machine.

When the food comes, my soup also has a foul edge to it. It just makes my stomach roil more, so I eat only a few spoonfuls. Grandma eats her sub with gusto, and eyes my bowl more and more intensely with each minute I don't eat.

"Are you still working on that?" the waiter asks, gesturing to my bowl. Grandma's plate is empty.

"I think I'm done," I say.

"You want a box?" he asks.

"No, thanks," I say.

"We *will* take a box. She needs more meat on her bones," Grandma interjects. "I don't know why I take you anywhere. Do you need to see someone about an eating disorder? I'll make an appointment for you," she says.

"Would you just *stop for a second*!" I snap, louder than I intended. "I can't think straight. I can't eat. All I want to do all the time is lie down and sleep. But I'm trying, okay? I'm sorry it's not enough." It all spills out before I can stop it. Grandma just stares at me in silence. There are a few times when she looks as if she's about to speak and then changes her mind.

"Your nose is bleeding," she finally says. It's so unexpected that it takes a moment for me to process the words, then I hurriedly press a napkin to my nose and run to the bathroom. I lean over a toilet for a few minutes just in case, but it looks like I'll be alright. My nose only bled a little and stopped by the time I reached the bathroom. Maybe it was just left over from the incident at the doctor's office. Grandma doesn't say anything when I return to the table.

When the check comes, she drops her wallet on the floor and I lean over and pick it up without a word; she accepts it without a word. She doesn't say anything during the drive home, either. I probably embarrassed her by freaking out in public. She did opt to send the to-go box back, though. So I take that as a sign that she heard at least some of what I said.

After we get home, Grandma finally turns to look at me. "Tamsin, I don't know how to help you. I have never known how to help you."

"I don't know either," I say.

"I think I'm going to lay down for a little while. I'll be back up to make dinner later." She sounds tired, deflated.

I sit on the couch and stare at the television. Grandma left it on when we left earlier. There's another made-for-TV movie playing now. I sit and do nothing until the buzzing of the screen makes my headache worse;

then I go outside and sit on the front porch. The late afternoon air has started to cool off, and it's pleasant in the shade.

I feel like I shouldn't be here, that I'm invading Grandma's space, but I don't have anywhere else to go. I'm still scared of the woods because that's where Hunter's lurking.

My phone chirps and the noise pulls me out of my brooding. It's another message from Zach, asking how I'm doing and if I want to hang out. I've been avoiding him because of his interest in exploring the very places Hunter is willing to violently defend. But I can't just avoid him forever. Plus, I desperately want to get out of this suffocating house for a while.

I tell Zach to come pick me up and go inside to leave a note for Grandma on her armchair, and by the time I come back outside I hear Zach's truck rumble down the driveway. He must have already been close by.

"So where are we going today?" I ask as I pull the door open and hop into the cab.

"Anywhere you want. I brought supplies. Maybe we can find what we're looking for this time," he says, but then he takes a second look at me. "You don't look so good."

"Honestly, I feel like shit, but I need to get out of that house." I wait with trepidation, wondering if he'll suggest something completely mundane.

"If you're not feeling well, we should go look for Thistledown for help," he says. There is no note of irony in his voice.

"So faeries are still real?" I ask. Bouncing down the driveway makes my stomach turn.

"Yes?" Zach says. "Why wouldn't they be?"

"I don't know. It went away for a while, so I started wondering if any of it really happened. I don't know if I should be hoping it did or not."

"Why would you hope it's not real?" he asks, concern in his voice.

"Because ..." Because I want to be normal? No. That isn't true. These past few weeks I've felt more alive than I ever have. "Because I don't want Grandma to be embarrassed of me. And besides, the faerie stuff is dangerous."

"I don't think there's anything wrong with you. And who cares what your grandma thinks?"

"I do. You were around when I was a kid. I would see and do weird things, right? I made everyone's lives harder."

"Not mine. There's nothing wrong with anything you do. Ever." During this conversation, Zach's voice has grown steadily louder. His expression is intense and im-passioned.

"I appreciate the support, Zach, but you're not the one who decides that."

"Because your grandma is."

"No!" I rub my temples. "She isn't either. I am. I haven't figured it out yet but I'm trying." I mull over a thought that's been creeping around in the back of my head. "Why is this so important to you?"

"Why is what important to me?" he asks.

"Me. What I'm doing. What I believe. Do you know something I don't?" I ask.

"Yeah. I know what it's like hanging out with you. I actually listen to you. I think you're pretty cool. So yeah, I feel like I know something other people don't. I think you should do what makes you happy, and you don't seem very happy right now, just what I think." Zach gets bright and impassioned again. I suddenly feel horrible.

"I'm sorry I snapped at you," I say.

"It's okay. I know you're under a lot of pressure." Zach pulls off the road and stops. We're next to the old bridge. The late afternoon light hangs heavily over the area.

"Why did we stop here?" I ask.

"This used to be our big hangout spot, away from the adults and stuff. It's where we would go when we wanted to go nowhere in particular, you know?"

"Right," I say. I don't recall that in any detail, but it sounds reasonable.

"You want to get out?" he asks. I nod and climb out. He follows, and we walk out to the middle of the bridge and watch the stream wind slowly beneath us. The late afternoon scene is pretty until I notice an empty beer bottle stuck in the mud. After that, I notice the other trash lying on the bank, or partially buried in the stream bed. I'm conscious of the massive creature—the troll—I encountered beneath this bridge.

"Was there so much trash back then?" I ask, trying to picture the scene as it would have been when we were children.

"More or less. Probably washes down from the park trail if it didn't come from drivers tossing their trash out the window."

"What did we do here?"

"Just, y'know, be kids."

"I wish I remembered more. I'm sorry."

"It's okay. You don't have to apologize to me," he says.

A thought comes to mind. "What about the troll?" The last time I ran into it, it didn't seem friendly.

"Yeah," Zach laughs. "We'd throw rocks and run before he got up. You remember?"

"Not really. But I remember Hunter," I say. Zach's face darkens.

"I'll do anything to make sure he can't hurt you," he says.

"Did he ever hurt us?"

"We were always a thorn in his side. I can't imagine he would have just let us go if he caught us," he says.

"Weren't there times when he saved us?" I ask. I've witnessed him do it more than once, now.

"And there's times when he didn't. He took your memories, didn't he?"

"You're right," I say. The memory of the last night I saw Hunter, of the fear and helplessness, shoots ice through my veins. I grip the bridge railing so hard my knuckles turn white. He told me himself not to sympathize with him.

"But we have Thistledown, and the witch. We're not alone in this," Zach says. He squeezes my shoulder reassuringly. I smile at him.

"We visited the witch before," I say, recalling one of my visions. The words aren't phrased as a question, but I still ask them with uncertainty.

I glare down at the water again, trying to force memories to the forefront of my mind. I've coaxed visions to life before, but I can't do it this time. The memories I try to bring to the surface are too slippery and only fall back into the depths. For a moment, I think I see two tween kids sitting by the bank throwing pebbles and laughing, but it's just as quickly gone. It could have just as easily been wishful thinking.

I sneak a look over at Zach; he's staring ahead. His eyes look far away, and I wonder if he's absorbed in a memory I've since lost. He has a nice profile. His hands rest on the weathered wooden railing. I wonder if I should reach out and grab one. I wonder what we had in the past that's been lost.

I lift my hand and move it hesitantly toward Zach's. I never learn if I would have had the courage to take his hand because before I reach it I have to turn and violently vomit over the railing.

In the middle of shuddering and heaving, I feel Zach pull my hair away from my face. When I finish, I lean on the railing until my limbs stop shaking.

"Are you okay?" Zach asks. He lets my hair go and takes my face in his hands so he can look at me. His eyes widen.

"You're bleeding," he says.

"God. I'm so sorry." I wipe my mouth with the back of my hand. It comes back red. "I don't know what's happening to me. I think I might need to go to the hospital." My throat burns and the words come out as a shaky croak.

"I don't think so," Zach says. "We should go see Thistledown. I bet she'll know what to do."

"I can't," I say. Tears spill out of my eyes despite my best efforts—or perhaps it's blood. "Hunter told me he'll kill my grandma if I make trouble for him, and trouble always happens if I go into the woods. I can't." Zach's mouth tightens, and he looks around and turns back to me.

"Wait right here. I'll be back." Without waiting for an answer. He runs the rest of the way across the bridge and disappears into the woods.

Zach took his car keys, so it's not like I could leave if I wanted to. After a minute I sink to a sitting position and pull my knees up to my chest. My legs shake too much to keep standing.

The sun sinks while I wait, leaving my surroundings in colorless twilight. My nausea starts steadily building again as I see two watery shapes pass the tree line and approach. One is Zach, and the other is about half his size. When they get closer, I can tell it's Thistledown. Her wide eyes are full of concern.

"My dear, look at you," she says, hurrying the rest of the distance and cradling my head in her hands. Her skin is covered in very short, downy fur. "What has happened?"

"I don't know. I'm sick," I say. She wipes my eye and her finger comes away red. She scrutinizes the blood.

"Have you broken an oath made to one of the Fae, my dear?" she asks. "An oath sworn on your own blood?"

"What would that have to do with this?" I gesture weakly to my bloody face.

"Break a faerie oath, and you forfeit that which you swore upon. You may lose it gradually or all at once, but by the look of your oathsickness, it will soon take your life," she says, slowly and patiently. Cold realization spreads through my chest and I groan.

"I bailed on a promise," I mumble.

"With whom?" Thistledown asks. "You know you can trust Thistledown to take care of you." She pats my shoulder reassuringly.

"... I promised to bring the sprites sweets," I say. Shame makes me reluctant to mention Leithe to Thistledown. It was a foolish deal.

"Hmm." She purses her lips. "Sprites aren't particularly powerful fae. It is unlikely a broken oath made with them would affect you so rapidly," she says pointedly. Hiding the truth was useless; she saw through me immediately.

"I made a deal with the prisoner here to release him, a man called Leithe," I admit.

Thistledown *tut-tuts* at me. "Poor girl. You've gotten yourself into quite a predicament, allowing yourself to be taken in by such creatures. But it's quite alright. Thistledown shall help." She squeezes my cheek. "First, let's fulfill your promise to the sprites to offer you a reprieve. And then you can begin searching for the means to free this Leithe." I groan. I have to bring the sprites my weight in chocolate. Last time I weighed myself I was about 125 pounds. This is going to be expensive.

Zach drives me to the grocery store while Thistledown promises to wait for us by the bridge. As soon as we begin our errand, the twisting pain in my stomach slightly abates.

I don't have a lot of money, so Zach and I stand in the junk food aisle and compare prices for a while. As I'm weighing the value of candy bars versus chocolate chip cookies, a thought comes to me. I put the cookies down and go to the dairy aisle. Chocolate milk is four dollars a gallon, and a gallon is about eight-and-a-half pounds. Fifteen gallons for about seventy dollars will cover my debt to the sprites in full. Chocolate milk should technically count as a chocolate treat. I hope the sprites agree.

Zach shrugs when I offer my suggestion and helps me push a cart full of chocolate milk to the register, where the cashier raises an eyebrow and begins to scan our items.

"Having a party?" she asks.

"Lots of hungry little mouths to feed, you know," I laugh. She laughs back and starts talking about the shopping she had to do for her daughter's birthday party and doesn't ask me any more direct questions.

Thistledown is waiting for us when we pull up to the small dirt shoulder in front of the bridge.

"Where's our chocolate?" The lead sprite demands, flitting out of the tree branches and hovering nearby.

"I brought her here to collect her due," Thistledown explains.

"Good idea," I say. Not having to go into the woods and risk crossing paths with Hunter suits me fine. I gesture toward the truck bed full of chocolate milk.

"Here's my weight in chocolate treats, as promised," I say. The sprite inspects the plastic jugs suspiciously, then tries to pull one's lid off. I rip the tab and pop the lid off for her. She sticks her arm into the jug and scoops a handful of chocolate milk to taste.

"It's milk," she says.

"With chocolate," I point out nervously. I see no reason why this wouldn't count based on the wording of the deal, though maybe I should have asked an expert how flexible these deals are.

"I did not know that milk could have chocolate," the lead sprite says with a voice full of wonder. "We accept this." She giggles and hiccups. I let out a breath of relief.

The sprites have nothing more to say to me as they ferry away their chocolate milk. As they depart, they chat in high-pitched voices about how surprising it is that humans could come up with such a delightful creation.

With one promise taken care of, I sit on the edge of the open truck bed and allow myself to relax.

"I shall go now," Thistledown says, coming over and patting my knee. "You will need to take on your other promise soon. But I know you will find a solution." I smile at that, and she slips off into the woods.

On the drive back to Grandma's house, I don't have much to say to Zach other than thanking him for his help. While fulfilling my promise with the sprites offered me some peace, that relief is tainted by an anxious pit created by the knowledge that I'm truly trapped; Leithe's promise is a matter of life and death for not only him, but myself and my only family.

Chapter Eleven

"How was your week?" Dr. Webster asks. My stomach twists as I recall the events of the last several days. The oathsickness abated when Zach and I brought the chocolate milk to the sprites, but I think that has more to do with my newfound intention to fulfill my promise to Leithe. Now the pain in my gut comes from nervousness at the fact I'll have to start looking again soon, or else die.

"Not that great," I say. "Been on a bit of a downswing, I guess." Dr. Webster frowns and checks his notes.

"Those weren't uncommon when you were younger. You haven't taken any medications in the last three years. Is that something you'd be interested in resuming?"

"Not yet," I say, picking at the couch upholstery.

"That might be a route to consider at some point, but we don't have to talk about that right now. Besides that, anything you want to talk about?" he asks.

"I met back up with Zach. We were friends when I was a kid, and I guess we're friends again, so that's nice," I say.

"That is nice."

"Yeah. We played in the woods. He was great for enabling my delusions in my youth," I say, with no idea of what I'm even trying to bait him into.

"Engaging with your imagination doesn't equate to delusion."

"So when does it equate to delusion?"

"Where would you draw that line?"

"When you don't know the difference, I guess. When you're not playing anymore."

"Many children don't know the difference. Many adults live their lives according to rules that could be considered imaginary. Even imaginary rules can serve to provide structure in one's life."

"I'm not a kid anymore. I should be able to tell the difference." I've picked a thread loose, now I feel guilty and cover the evidence with my hand.

"I think the fact that you're able to take a step back and analyze the things that are going on around you is something children don't always think to do. That's something that comes from being an adult. Though, that does bring up something we should discuss. Since my practice specializes in children and families, someone more specialized might be able to better help you. I can always write you a referral to someone with more experience in this area."

"No." The answer comes out desperate and whiny, and I immediately feel embarrassed. "I mean, if I'm inconveniencing you, I'll go somewhere else, but you're the only one I want to talk to. It wouldn't be the same with anyone else."

"You're not an inconvenience, and I'm always happy to talk to you. I just want to make sure you're getting the best help possible."

"I appreciate it. Talking to you does help," I say.

"That reminds me. If you're interested in drawing, I have pencils and paper. When you were younger, you drew frequently, whenever you didn't want to talk. It seemed to help you mull things over in your head," he says.

"Sure. I'll give it a shot." He pulls an art pad and pencil out of a drawer and hands them to me. Pages have been removed. I start doodling.

"So what did I used to draw here?" I ask as I press the pencil tip into paper.

"Lots of different things you and Zach got up to in the woods," he says. "And the things you saw there."

"Do you still have the drawings?" I try to sound casual, but I'm getting excited. They might have something useful in them.

"I don't. I gave them to your grandmother after I stopped seeing you," he says. Damn. She probably threw them away. I can't imagine she would have wanted to keep them.

"Ah," is all I say. I focus more on my drawing to hide my disappointment. I'm just drawing lines; I don't yet know what I'm going for. "Do you remember details about what I drew?"

"They were all very creative. Did you ever think about being an artist?"

"Because I doodled as a kid? No," I scoff. "I can't make anything special. I mean, I was an art major for a semester, but then I saw what some of my classmates could do. There wasn't anything there for me."

"No one starts out good at anything. So what did you end up studying instead? Did you find something you liked?" he asks. I grip the pencil hard.

"I dropped out two years ago. Grandma must think I'm a total failure."

"Why do you think she'd think that?" he asks.

"Because ... I've failed at everything else, I guess. Chased my mother away, couldn't be a normal granddaughter, that kind of thing."

"Why would you think you chased your mother away?"

"Well, I was born and then she left, so. Correlation, causation, I don't know." I scribble intensely on the paper to avoid looking at Dr. Webster.

"It can be natural for people to want something tangible to blame so that their world makes sense, but I promise you: nothing relating to your mother was your fault. From what you and your grandmother told me, she had a complicated life with problems that had nothing to do with you. But," he pauses, checking his watch, "we're about to go over our time, so we shouldn't get into this until we have plenty of time to have a good discussion." I nod, taking a moment to examine what I drew before returning the pad to him—a horse, dripping with water and with a mouth of razor teeth. I carefully rip it out and put it in my pocket.

When I get home, Grandma is watching TV while reading a book. I wonder if she's actually paying attention to either of them.

"Hey, did Dr. Webster give you drawings I did when I was a kid?" I ask.

She looks up and glares at me. "Why?"

"... because I want to see them?" I say, though it comes out as a question. "It might be therapeutic."

She ponders my answer for a moment. "I probably threw them out. If I did happen to keep them, I have no idea where they would be."

"Do you mind if I look in Grandpa's office?" I ask. It's always been Grandpa's office, even though I've never met the man.

"Go ahead," Grandma says, sighing. Surprised she gave in, I go to the office. The door is usually kept closed; Grandma doesn't come in here except for tax season, and while I was never directly punished for doing so, I'd be the victim of admonishing stares whenever she caught me playing in here.

Checking the desk drawers reveals nothing but organized files of insurance and tax documents. One of the drawers has a cardboard box labeled 'letters' in Grandma's handwriting, but when I open it I see an aged, handwritten letter addressed to 'Dear Mary,' and realize I have no right to look in this box, and quickly shut it again.

I slump onto the floor in frustration; it feels like blasphemy to sit in the leather desk chair. I don't know why I expected to find anything in here. But as the aged fabric of the rug scratches against my palms, I recall the sensation of lying on the floor in this room, of seeing everything from an ant's eye view. Since no one is watching me, I follow the instinct and lay on the floor.

At first I see nothing, but then when I run my fingertips over the underside of the desk, I feel the faintest hint of tape residue. There was something stuck here, but it was removed some time ago. Still, something—a tingle in the back of my head—keeps me from getting up. There must be something else here. Finally, after checking every nook and cranny, I pull out the drawers and find a piece of notebook paper taped to the underside of one.

On the paper, as I suspected, is a drawing, one that wasn't made by a small child. I must have been older, a teen. It's a lovingly detailed profile of a fair-haired man. It's not perfect, but I can identify it as Hunter even before I see the name "Hunter" written in stylized bubble letters at the bottom of the page, alongside a quickly abandoned attempt at one of his dogs. I wonder if he posed for it or if I spent enough time staring at him to draw it from memory. There must be more notes and pictures around the house. I search inside books and behind the bookshelves, but I don't find anything new.

When I exit the office, Grandma is still reading, her back to me. She doesn't seem to notice I've left the room. Her bedroom is directly across from the office. I'm doing something horribly invasive, but I have to know. Before she turns around, I tiptoe across the hall and silently open Grandma's bedroom door wide enough for me to squeeze in.

Grandma's room is jam-packed full of odds and ends she's collected over the years, but still manages to be tidy. One of the pillows on her bed is a quilted monstrosity made out of my old clothes. The patches don't quite fit together. I made it the last time she tried to teach me how to quilt. I'm surprised she still has it.

I check her nightstand and dressers and find nothing, but under her bed is a black document safe. It's strange, because she keeps all of her important documents in an unsecured drawer in Grandpa's office, which I know be-cause I just sifted through them. I try the safe; it's locked. I listen to see if Grandma has called me or gotten up, but I don't hear anything.

I go back through her drawers, now looking for the safe key, praying she doesn't keep it with her. After what feels like way too long, I find the key in her jewelry box.

I drag the safe out from under the bed and unlock it; my drawings are there, held down by a box of bullets for the rifle. There are several folded together and many of them still have remnants of old tape stuck to them.

"Tamsin?" Grandma calls from the living room.

Shit.

I grab several of the papers—too few for her to notice if she checks, I hope—and shove them into my back pocket before shutting the safe and pushing it back under the bed. I start for the door, and then I hear the armchair creak, so instead I go to the window. The window is stuck fast from age and paint and I have to try twice to push it open. I climb out into the flowerbed and pull the window down behind me, then try as best I can to casually walk around the side of the house and come in through the back door. Grandma is looking into Grandpa's office when I come in, and at the sound of the door opening she turns and frowns at me.

"I thought you were in the office," she says accusingly.

"I needed some fresh air," I say.

"I didn't hear you go outside," she continues to accuse.

"I was quiet so I wouldn't bother you."

"Didn't find anything in there?" Grandma asks. By her tone, she didn't expect me to. Of course not. She knew the drawings weren't hidden in that room.

"Nothing from Dr. Webster's office," I say.

"Shame," she says. She looks closer at me. "Are you okay?"

"No worse than usual," I say. I'm flushed and sweaty from nervousness and sudden exertion.

"Alright. Next time tell me if you're going outside." She turns to go back to her chair. I sidle up the stairs, a wad of papers still sticking extremely obtrusively from my back pocket. I realize I still have the safe key in my hand as well, having forgotten to return it to the jewelry box in my hurry to escape. I'll have to try and sneak it back later. I'm just relieved Grandma ignored my warnings to keep the doors and windows locked.

When I get to my room, I pull the wad of papers out of my pocket and lay them out on the bed. The unfolded pages are named and dated on the back in Dr. Webster's handwriting. I carefully unfold them and lay them out on the comforter. I'm disappointed I only managed to grab three in total.

Looking over the drawings, I can see that they're all mine from different times in my childhood, and they're all deeply disturbing. The first appears to be a bleeding tree with human arms instead of branches. I unfold the next one; It's a picture of monsters made of tangling vines and branches reaching toward the viewer with wicked claws. It's simply captioned "run."

I unfold the last one. it's a symbol that might represent a closed eye, but it's sloppy and hard to tell. There's a note in a scrawling child's script that reads "they hide you." It seems my past self tried to leave instructions. This might be what the witch taught her when she asked for the ability to hide from Hunter, though I don't know how I'm supposed to use this information now. Keeping the paper with me might be a good start; I fold it up and put it inside my phone case with Thistledown's flower. Maybe carrying it around will hide me, maybe it won't.

I fold up the papers and ponder a good hiding place. Grandma probably won't come upstairs, but I don't want her to find out I found them. Under the mattress might be a good spot. As soon as I think that thought, I know I've hidden things under it before. I lift the mattress with some effort, and find the paper taped to the top of the frame. I pull it free and drop the mattress. It's a picture of a knife captioned "iron hurts them and steel hurts them more."

The rest of the evening passes as I stare at the drawings laid out on my bed, only broken up by the brief time I'm downstairs for dinner. The sketches didn't tell me much I hadn't learned: iron and steel hurt fae, and I should stay away from any horrifying monsters I come across. The eye-like symbol is the most curious, and perhaps the most useful, if my younger self had left more detailed instructions. These thoughts circulate until a drawer sliding shut behind me catches my attention.

There's a girl—teenage me—modeling different shirts in the mirror. After trying on a few different ones and putting on a second bra, she settles on a low-cut blouse and checks out her unsubstantial cleavage from different angles, adjusting the shirt in order to show the most off. I don't remember doing this, but just watching it makes me cringe.

After touching up her makeup—heavy-handed pink lips and dark blue eyeshadow by a child's hand—and hair—choppily flat-ironed, she turns off the light and sneaks out of the room. I lose sight of her when she leaves the room, but follow hints of movement and sound out the front door, where I see her vanish between the trees. Maybe she's meeting Zach. I still don't recall being romantically involved with Zach as a teen.

Teen Tamsin walks down the driveway and crosses the road, illuminated only by moonlight. Before long, one of Hunter's dogs emerges from the dark. I jump, but she simply reaches out, scratches its ears, and hands it a piece of ham.

"I want to see Hunter. Is he at the house?" she asks. The dog wags its tail and starts trotting back the way it came. We both follow it to the Randall Place. Hunter has been using it for a long time, apparently.

The dog leads us up the front steps and noses the door open. I follow my younger self inside. I see the back of Hunter's head where he sits on the musty couch.

"Go home, Tamsin," he says without looking in her direction.

"Go home, Tamsin," she says at the same time, lowering her pitch to match his voice. Then she giggles. Hunter's other dog, which had been lying by his feet, rises and bounds over to her. She gives it a piece of ham.

"Must you bribe my traitorous sentries?" he asks, though he doesn't sound particularly annoyed about it.

"Don't be jealous; I brought something for you too," she says, walking around the couch and plopping down next to him.

"And you came on the off-chance I'd be here?" he asks.

"You come back here for a break most nights around two," she says cheerily. She removes two ice cream pints from her backpack and hands him one. "I didn't know what you'd like because you wouldn't tell me, so I brought chocolate because it's a classic. It's going to melt, so you have to eat it fast. Oh!" She digs through the backpack and pulls out a wooden stirring spoon. "This was the only non-metal spoon I could find."

After a moment, Hunter lets out a resigned sigh and takes the offered ice cream and spoon. Pleased, Teen Tamsin pops the lid on her own pint and digs in, pausing every so often to watch Hunter eat and gauge his reaction.

"It's very sweet," Hunter says. Teen Tamsin looks up, worried.

"Too sweet?" she asks.

"No ... it's good," he says.

"Good. I'll bring other flavors soon so you can decide which one you like best."

"You should not," he says.

"But I'm going to," she says. Hunter takes another bite of ice cream on the comically large spoon. The way Teen Tamsin looks at him, with a small smile and slight blush and how quickly she looks away if he looks in her direction, makes me want to hide my face in my hands. Having an embarrassing crush on Hunter is something I don't think I needed to remember.

"What do you want today?" he asks.

"A story," she says.

"What kind?"

"It's dark, so a scary story. Do your best to scare me," she says. And I know exactly what she's doing. If he tells her the story, she'll ask him to walk her back to the house because she's scared. Or God, even worse, try to stay there for the night.

Hunter takes another bite of ice cream and rubs his chin as he thinks. Finally, he clears his throat, tosses the mostly empty ice cream container to his dogs, and begins.

"There was once a boy who was in all regards normal save for one thing—one of his eyes was dark brown and the other was pale green. He thought he was very smart, and he often liked to stick his head out to look at his unique reflection in the lake by his home, even though the wise old hermit told him it was dangerous. One day while the boy was admiring his reflection in the lake despite the hermit's warnings, a kelpie jumped out and ate his face and the boy died. The end." Teen Tamsin sticks her tongue out at him.

"That is *not* a real story. You're just being mean. Start over and tell the real one," she says.

"Fine. There was once a boy who was in all regards normal save for one thing—one of his eyes was dark brown and the other was pale green."

"What was his name?" she asks.

"For the sake of the story his name was 'the boy.' Do you want to hear it or not?" Hunter demands. Teen Tamsin mimes locking her mouth and tossing the key over her shoulder. Satisfied, Hunter continues.

"Because of his eyes, the boy caught the attention of a beautiful fae maiden who was one day riding by his family's cottage. His eyes captivated her, and so she sent her knight to spirit him away from his home and bring the boy to live with her in her grand palace in Faerie. She showered him with gifts. He wore only the finest spider silk garments dripping with multicolored pearls from the bottom of the sea. He rode a fine fae steed by her side when she took her morning rides across the skies of the mortal world. She wrote him odes and ballads of her love for him. He was always at her side. She showed him off to all the other lords and ladies of her court, and they were all very jealous."

"It isn't scary yet," Tamsin cuts in. Hunter just stares at her until she covers her mouth with her hand.

"*Unfortunately,*" Hunter begins once more, "the fae maiden had one rule that the boy was not allowed to break. When they went on their rides through the mortal world, he was not allowed to get off his steed. The boy always obeyed this rule, because he adored the maiden even more than the mother of his birth. But one day during his ride, he caught sight of some beautiful flowers. He wanted to give them to her and thought she would not mind so much if he broke her rule just for a moment, just to bring her something beautiful, so he got off his steed. But the moment he was out of the saddle, the steed bolted, and the boy was left alone, for the fae maiden did not realize he had diverted from their course.

"All alone, the boy wandered a world he had long since left behind. Thieves saw his beautiful clothes and jewels and took them, leaving the boy in rags. Finally, he saw a familiar road and followed it to his family's cottage. He remembered it, and cried tears of joy to be reunited with his family again.

"But when he got there, he saw that there was another boy living with his parents, eating his share of food and sleeping in his bed. For the boy did not know this, not only do fae have a habit of leaving their own kind in place of human children—such as is the case of a changeling—but they can also leave behind a creature called a fetch—a magicked doll combined with a strand of hair or drop of blood— to conceal their thieving. This is what the fae maiden had done so the boy's family would not notice his absence, for a well-made fetch can mimic a human so well not even its own mother would discover the deception. Therefore, when the boy's mother caught sight of the raggedy child at her door, she thought *him* the faerie, and believed he was there to do her son harm, so she chased him away with a pair of garden shears."

"That's horrible," says Teen Tamsin. Hunter graciously ignores her interruption this time.

"The boy fled, and wandered the woods calling for the fae maiden to come for him and bring him back to her palace. After many long and harrowing trials, the boy found his way back to the maiden's palace, and he presented himself to her. She was overjoyed to have him back, and this time was determined to not lose her treasure again, so she had her knight pluck the boy's eyes out and had them made into a lovely bracelet so she could admire his eyes whenever she wished and would never have to worry about him getting into trouble, for a bracelet cannot disobey rules.

"In her opinion, the pain and terror in his eyes as they gazed helplessly at her only made them more beautiful. To this day, his eyes are still adorning her wrist, and sometimes they shed a single tear." There's a pause. At some point during the story, Teen Tamsin had pulled her knees close to her chest and wrapped her arms around them.

"If the maiden loved the boy, why would she do that to him?" she asks.

"Because the love one of the Fae can have for a human is rarely more than that for a favored toy or ornament, no matter what it may seem," Hunter says.

"Oh," she says. They sit in silence for some time while she pets the dog by her feet. "That's so sad."

"It's also true. What is the life of a butterfly to you? It's pretty, and if that pleases you then you might keep it in a jar to look upon it, but when it dies and shrivels up you'll throw it out in the garden and move on with your life, no?" Hunter says.

"I don't trap bugs in jars," she argues.

"Fine," Hunter says. "But you do understand that you're the insect in this metaphor? That's the difference between your existence and that of the Gentry. At best a human can be a pretty curiosity, at worst a cockroach to be crushed for the crime of existing."

"*You're* not like that," she says. "You're nice."

"I am not nice," he says.

"You are!" she insists. "You're nice, and you're really cool, and I like your dogs ..." she trails off. "So ... you know ... I guess you must have had a lot of hot faerie girlfriends and stuff," she continues. Her face is turning red, and I feel mine doing the same, even if I'm separated from this mortifying situation by years. Hunter stares at her, though she avoids eye contact with him. His expression is difficult to read, but I think I detect a hint of pity.

"That's not something I'm interested in discussing. Perhaps you should go back home now. You've been out long and your grandmother might wake and worry." His words are measured, as though he's trying not to come off as too harsh.

"But I'm not tired yet, and I still want to talk," she says with a playful whine in her voice.

"I gave you your story," he says.

"Yeah, but, well ... I like a boy, and I don't know how to tell him," she says. I think she thinks she's being sneaky and subtle. Hunter clearly does not.

"Then you should ask your grandmother or your school friends for advice. Though I find it quite likely that Zach reciprocates your feelings," Hunter says. Very cold, but effective. Teen Tamsin's face falls. She looks like she wants to say something more, but loses her nerve.

"Okay," she says.

"Go home. One of the hounds will take you," he says.

"Fine," she says, clearly upset and having lost the will to argue.

"Take the trash," Hunter says, gesturing at the ice cream pints. She snatches them up and stalks away, one of the dogs following close behind. She slams the door shut, and as the vision fades, I watch Hunter rub his temples and sigh.

When my attention returns fully to the present, I'm alone in the abandoned house. I hurry home, not wanting to run into Hunter coming for his break. I feel—or imagine—at least one pair of eyes watching me until I shut Grandma's front door and the deadbolt clicks into place.

Chapter Twelve

I wake up breathless from fleeing half-remembered beasts in my dreams, creatures that frightened me in and out of sleep for the few hours I had until sunrise after my late-night stroll. Sometimes Hunter was pursuing them; sometimes he was leading them.

Exhausted, I pull the blanket and pillow over my head to remain in the dark for a bit longer before I have to get up and dedicate my waking moments to finding Leithe. It's for this reason I don't hear Grandma calling for me or climbing the stairs until she knocks on the door.

"Tamsin?" she calls from the other side.

"Uh-huh," I mumble into the mattress. Grandma must take that as an invitation because she opens the door.

"You've been sleeping for a while. I'm just checking on you," she says. I push the covers off my head and stare bleary-eyed at her.

"Well, I'm here," I say. "I'll be down in a minute." She doesn't respond, instead just stares at the floor. I follow her gaze and see the drawings I stole from her bedroom safe, swept off the bed last night before I went to sleep. I forgot to hide them.

"Where did you get those?" she demands, gesturing with her cane. I stare at her silently; she stares back. We both know where I got them.

"I found them," I say lamely.

"Why were you in my room?"

"Why did you lie about throwing my pictures away?" I attempt to change the subject.

"That is not what we're discussing right now. You went into my room without asking. You invaded my privacy."

"Well that's what *I* want to discuss right now!" I snap, louder than I expected. "Yes. I went through your things. I shouldn't have, but I'm not sorry. Why did you lie? Why do you have to keep everything from me?"

"You're making a big deal out of nothing. Those pictures are absolutely *disturbing*. You didn't need to see them. Now, stop trying to turn this around on me."

"Why do you get to decide that? You don't get to decide what I need anymore."

"Because you've done such a great job on your own," Grandma says, voice dripping with venomous sarcasm.

"I was, actually, until I came back here. Maybe being around you just drives me insane."

"Then go away. You shouldn't have come back in the first place," Grandma says.

"Fine. I'll pack my shit and get out. But I can't be here right now. I'm going for a walk first. I'll come get my things later if you haven't thrown them out into the yard by then," I say. Before she can respond, I squeeze around her and through the door.

I run until a frustrated sob bubbles out of my chest, and then I stop to lean against a tree and compose myself. I squeeze the trunk and press my forehead against it until the bark makes winding divots in my flesh. I do my best to swallow my tears in case Grandma happens to come looking for me. I've been screwing everything up since I got here. I might be able to stay with Zach until I've figured out how to save my own life, but that would just be putting him and his entire family in danger instead of Grandma. My options are to solve this today, or leave and die.

I slide to the ground and take a deep breath.

"Leithe?" I whisper, hoping to call him from whatever void he's waiting in. "I don't want to die, so I'm going to help you, but I need you to help me help you." I wait for a response, for him to appear out of nowhere and snark at me, but nothing happens. Maybe after our last talk, he's decided he'd rather me just die. If he doesn't want to talk to me, then at least I won't have to grovel at his feet for help like he wasn't the one who put me into this situation in the first place.

Thistledown is another person I could ask for help, but if she lives in Faerie, she faces an even greater risk from Hunter than I do. There's the witch, but I have no idea how to find her on my own.

As if on command, the cat weaves into view through the greenery and heads toward me.

"Hey, you," I say. "You wouldn't by chance have any answers, would you?" The cat doesn't acknowledge my presence, and I quickly realize why. Following a little way behind are two children, me and Zach at about age seven. They're wearing hats and jackets, and as they approach, reds and browns bleed like watercolors across the present-day's spring vegetation. I'm once again viewing the past. The cat makes a circle around me before continuing deeper into the woods.

"The kitty says that tree," Young Tamsin says, pointing through me to the tree at my back. Zach scrutinizes the tree until his eyes light up and he points to something by my knee.

"I see it!" he shouts. Young Tamsin shushes him.

"They won't work if you're too loud, remember?" she says. "And then the hunter will come get mad at us." Following Zach's gaze, I see what looks like a symbol carved into a tree. A closed eye, like what was drawn in the picture I found.

They hide you. The children stand near the tree while the cat darts to a different one several yards away and circles that one. The children follow the cat, and I follow the children. This must be what the witch taught them, to stay close to the marked trees. But did the kids mark the trees themselves? Can I replicate it now? Will the piece of paper work or does it have to be a tree? I don't think I have the freedom to experiment with this.

This goes on for several trees. Each one is marked with the same symbol. I wonder where this path goes.

"Do you think trees and flowers dream?" Young Tamsin asks as they walk. She keeps her voice down, looking at the trees suspiciously.

"They're alive so I guess so," Young Zach says.

"The troll says that the whole world dreams, even the dirt and the rocks," she says, bending down to pick up a pebble.

"Is that why he likes to sleep so much?" Zach asks. Young Tamsin shrugs and tosses the pebble into the undergrowth.

There's a period of silence broken only by crunching leaves as Young Tamsin seems to think hard about something. "Hey. When we get our wishes, what are you going to ask for?"

"For lots of money, I guess, because then I could buy anything else I wanted and I could give my mom and dad an allowance so they could buy anything they want. What are you going to wish for?"

"For my mom to love me and come back. Then Grandma would be happy and not hate me." Young Tamsin says this matter-of-factly. The words sting me.

"Okay. Well, if you're still poor then I'll give you an allowance, too," Zach says.

"You don't need her," I say, knowing neither of them can hear me.

The kids keep going until they reach a large tree with a jagged open scar from a lightning strike. The cat takes one last look at the kids and then slinks inside.

"It'll be okay," Young Tamsin says to Zach as she takes his hand. "Are you ready?" He nods, and the two of them slip into the crack as well. It looks barely wide enough to let in a child, let alone an adult, but when I try to make my way through, the gap seems to widen to make room for me.

When I emerge, the children are gone. I'm in an immense, cylindrical building with a winding staircase along the side that travels toward a ceiling so far above me that I can't make it out. The area is pleasantly warm, bathed in soft light from no discernable source. Fine silks hanging from the walls flutter without a breeze. There's a table and chairs that look as if they were grown organically from wood.

The silks sway, and between one flutter and the next there's now a Teen Tamsin and Zach sitting at the table across from a girl, perhaps fifteen or sixteen. She's wearing the same billowing fabrics the ancient witch wore when I met her as a young child, though her hair is now auburn and falls loose and free to pile beneath her chair. Teen Tamsin takes a sip of tea while she seems to gather her thoughts.

"What I want is to save Hunter," Teen Tamsin says, setting the teacup back on its saucer with a soft *clink.*

"Save him from what, exactly?" the witch asks, raising an eyebrow.

"From his boss, from his duty. He's miserable here. I want him to be free," she says. Her voice is full of passion.

"Why does his fate matter to you so?" the witch asks.

"Because I love him. He's a good person and he doesn't deserve this," Teen Tamsin says. As she speaks, her cheeks get red as if she only just realized what she's saying. The witch listens to Tamsin's confession with a neutral expression.

"You don't even know him that well," Zach protests.

"I know enough," Teen Tamsin says, with glorious teenage confidence.

"Freeing him from his charge in this forest won't free him from his knight's oath," the witch says.

"Then how can I free him from his oath completely?" Teen Tamsin asks.

"Do you think if you free him he's going to come live at your grandma's house with you so you can have a bunch of half-faerie babies?" Zach snaps.

"Oh my god. Shut up," Teen Tamsin says. "Why do you have to be so rude?"

"Because you're being dumb." he retorts.

"His lord would have to free him," the witch says, ignoring the children's squabbling.

"Then I want to go talk to his lord. Will you tell me how to find him?" Teen Tamsin asks, turning her attention away from Zach.

"You think he'll do what you want just because you ask nicely?" Zach says. Teen Tamsin glowers at Zach but says nothing. The witch smiles just slightly with the corner of her mouth.

"He makes a good point," the witch says. "If you want Hunter's oath, you will need to have something to offer in exchange."

"Like what?" Teen Tamsin asks.

"Perhaps your eternal service in exchange for Hunter's freedom?" the witch suggests. Teen Tamsin's face pales and she presses her lips together in a thin line.

"No," Zach says before Teen Tamsin can respond. She seems so distracted by the prospect of servitude that she doesn't bother chastising Zach for answering for her.

"Are there any other ways?" she asks.

"Another way might be to align yourself with one of the lord's rivals and hope they're grateful enough to grant you a boon once Hunter's lord has been trounced," says the witch.

"What would I even have to offer someone like that?" Teen Tamsin asks. Her previous enthusiasm seems quelled.

"As it so happens, the prisoners Hunter guards likely have the power you'd need," the witch says. "And they might be inclined to take up your cause, assuming you help free them."

"Who are they?" Teen Tamsin asks. The witch scrutinizes Teen Tamsin over the rim of her teacup.

"You may have encountered one of them before," the witch says. Teen Tamsin thinks for a moment and then her eyes widen.

"Sometimes I think I see a man—in dreams or in dark places. He seems ... stuck." The witch nods.

"The prisoners here are held in a cage forged from their own minds. Just as their bodies are trapped, their minds are trapped in an endless dream, yet unaware of it. Sometimes you catch glimpses within the prison, or he catches glimpses of the world without, as your worlds pass each other by."

"Why would that happen?" Teen Tamsin asks.

"Is that answer what you want as your gift today?" the witch asks.

"No," Teen Tamsin says. "That probably doesn't matter. It's more important to know how to free them."

"Very well. That is what I will give you today," the witch says. "When weaving enchantments and curses, they will always be stronger if the key to freedom is woven in with intention. When those trapped souls walked free, they were betrothed to each other, and to some, that is their transgression. The key to waking them is a kiss, from one of these poor captives to another."

"But they can't kiss, because they're locked up?" Teen Tamsin asks.

"I believe that is the intention," the witch says.

"That's so cruel," Teen Tamsin says. "How am I supposed to get that done?"

The witch shrugs. "That's for you to discover." Before Teen Tamsin can argue, the witch turns to Zach. "Is there anything you'd ask of me?"

"No. I don't need anything," Zach says.

"It's okay to ask," Teen Tamsin says, seeming surprised by his answer.

"There's nothing I want," Zach insists.

"Fine. Then let's go. She's not going to tell us anything else." Teen Tamsin leaves through the jagged crevice; Zach follows close behind but pauses at the last moment.

"I'm sorry. I lied. There is something I want," he says to the witch.

"I suspected as much," she says.

"I want to keep Tamsin safe."

"Then lock her in a cage far from here, otherwise she'll always come back," the witch says. "I can give you a cage spun from faerie gold that only you can open."

"No. I don't want that," Zach says immediately, and then he pauses and looks unsure of himself, stopping and starting several times before finding the courage to speak.

"You want her to free the prisoners. You and Thistle-down both suggest that as the solution to all of her problems. Is it because it's true, or because you'll somehow benefit?" he asks.

"You think my assistance somehow tainted?" she asks, smiling slightly.

"Yes," Zach says, without needing to think about it.

"Then listen. Or don't. It makes no difference. Fae cannot lie, as you know, so I will tell you this. I believe my wish for your friend is truly in her best interests. Does that satisfy you?" the witch asks.

"I guess so. For now," he says, though he still sounds suspicious. When he leaves, the vision fades away, and I'm alone, though not for long.

"It is about the right time for your next visit," a voice says. I jump in surprise and turn to see a woman coming down the stairs. She's the most beautiful woman I've ever seen. Her auburn hair is braided and piled and would surely drag on the floor if loose. Her green dress is simple in cut but shimmers in the light as she moves. Her green eyes seem fathomless. She looks older than me, though she could be anywhere from thirty to fifty. She holds herself with far more easy confidence than I ever could.

"You look different than I recall," I say.

The witch smiles. "My preferences change from moment to moment. Sit. I'll start the tea." I sit where my teenage self once sat. The witch disappears behind the silks and returns a moment later with a ceramic teapot, two cups, and a tray of pastries. She places a cup in front of me and fills it before filling her own and taking a seat across from me.

"How many times have I visited you?" I glance at my tea. It smells good, great even, but something in the back of my head—a resurfacing memory or simply instinct—makes me hesitant to partake.

"This is the third. And, I suspect, the last. These things do tend to go in threes." The witch sips her tea and seems to notice my reluctance. "You are my welcome guest and have permission to partake of my hospitality. No harm will come to you by my hand on this day." She pushes the tray of pastries closer, along with a jar of honey I didn't notice earlier.

"Does that mean you're planning to harm me tomorrow?" I ask, but I do take a sip of tea. It's delicious.

"It's impossible to say without doubt what tomorrow will bring," she says.

"Is there another name I should call you, besides 'the witch'?" I ask, taking a pastry. It's amazing.

"That epithet serves our purposes for now."

"Okay, well, I have a lot of questions."

"I may have answers, depending," she says. "Do you remember the rules of our visits?"

"No. That's kind of the problem. I can't remember anything about what I've done here in the past."

"You may ask me for one gift," she says. There are so many things I could ask for—freedom from Leithe, my memories, but I fear there's a single right answer here.

"Okay. Well, before I know what to ask for I need to know what the *fuck* is going on. I've gotten bits and pieces, but I want the whole story."

"I don't have the whole story, just my part," the witch says. "What I can tell you is that you slip in and out of Faerie as Faerie slips in and out of your world. What you've experienced is a byproduct. You have an awareness humans normally do not, and so you can pass through borders humans shouldn't be able to touch."

"I feel like I've been going crazy. I don't know what's real and what isn't."

"You do. You always have. I suspect your inability to accept it arises from attempting to fit your world into the mold that has been laid out for you."

"But if I'm the only one who doesn't fit, that seems to be a problem with me."

"If I told you there was an invisible bear rearing up behind you right now, would you believe me?" she asks. I look behind me but see nothing.

"I've heard faeries can't lie, so I guess I would," I say.

"So you would trust me, even if my world does not match yours. It is not your fault others in your life aren't able to extend the same trust to you. Use all your senses. Look at me, feel the wood of the table, smell the tea, listen to my voice. You try so hard to doubt the truth of your own life, your own experience, in favor of those who haven't lived it."

"But what if I'm wrong?"

"How can you be wrong if there is no perfect, right answer? Your world is yours; their world is theirs. Those worlds can overlap in places, but they don't need to be perfectly aligned at all times to both be true."

"And if I've been in a mental ward this entire time, hallucinating everything?"

"If you can't tell, does it really matter? Such questions go in never-ending loops. The question ultimately becomes whether you'd rather be there or here," the witch says.

"Actually, I think the question is why *you* want me here. What's your angle?"

"Good. You don't trust blindly," she says. "My helping you benefits me in ways you need not concern yourself with right now."

"I'm concerned anyway," I say.

"I'm not going to tell you," the witch says, taking a prim sip of tea.

"And you won't have anything to say if I walk out of here right now?"

"No. You'll be back eventually," she says. She's probably right.

"So you want me to release the prisoners Hunter is guarding, right?"

"I want you to do what you want." She looks at me evenly, her face betraying nothing.

"As long as I release the prisoners?" I say.

"I suspect you'll want to do that sooner or later."

"It would be a lot easier to do if I had all of my memories," I point out.

"I don't have them. And before you ask, they will likely come back on their own in time. Asking me to restore them would be a waste of a gift." she says.

"Then I want …" I'm about to ask for a way out of Leithe's deal, but I trail off. She's probably right. Even if I wish away my mistake now—if she can even help me with that—I'll just end up here again, maybe tomorrow, maybe in a few more years. And besides, a way out isn't what I want. I couldn't live my life far away from here knowing what goes on right beyond human perception.

"My grandmother is ill. She at best probably has a year or two left. If you'll give me a gift, I want you to heal her," I say. The witch seems genuinely surprised by my request. But she doesn't argue or suggest something else. Instead, she stands and begins rummaging through her things.

"I cannot completely eradicate an illness without turning a human into a fae, body and soul. However—" she opens a ceramic jar and takes out a tiny object. "This will help her live out the extent of a human life, unless you'd prefer me to make her fae?" the witch asks.

"I don't think she'd want that," I say.

"Then have her eat this." The witch places a small oval seed in my hand.

"Thank you," I say.

"Do not thank me. After all, I give you these gifts with only the highest of expectations."

"Alright, so I have a riddle to figure out, but how do I even find the prison?" I ask.

"You carved a hidden path when you were younger. It will get you close, but after that it's up to you," she says, waving a hand dismissively, as if that wouldn't be the hard part. "Only by freeing the prisoners can you free yourself. Our meeting is concluded for today." With those words, she climbs the staircase and is soon gone. I think about snooping through her things, but I worry she wouldn't take that well.

When I emerge from the witch's home, it's spring again; the autumn colors of the past are gone. A meandering line of marked trees forms the path back toward Grandma's house, but there's another path going deeper into the woods. That must be the way to the prison the witch mentioned. The sun is much lower in the sky than it was when I entered the witch's home; it's probably nearing mid-afternoon. I was in there longer than I realized. I don't know what's waiting for me at home, if my meager belongings will be strewn across the porch, so I move forward. I can ponder the riddle as I walk.

The further I go, the more claustrophobic the path gets. The trees cluster closer together, with sheets of lichen hanging from the boughs and thorny undergrowth sprouting violently from every available patch of earth. The tangle gets worse and worse until I'm fighting for every step. Even worse, opaque fog crawls up from the ground and gets thicker as I go. First it consumes my ankles, then my knees, waist, and then I'm completely engulfed. My surroundings only become visible right before I would run into them.

The fog physically resists me as if I'm walking through syrup; it oozes into my nose and down my throat, making my entire body feel heavy. And then I step out into an open glade, and the pressure is gone. In the center of the otherwise clear glade sit two enormous trees twisting away from one another. Their canopies cover the entire area, save for a line between them where they refuse to touch. What's visible of the sky between the boughs is a soft, ethereal purple twilight. A hazy mist drifts along the ground. The path doesn't seem to continue, but I don't see anything here that looks like a prison.

A sniffle interrupts the moment, and I look to see seven-year-old Tamsin and Zach emerge from the fog from the center of the glade, holding onto one another for support. Young Tamsin has a cut going up from the side of her chin through the corner of her mouth. Tears are cutting paths through her dirty cheeks, but she looks forward determinedly. Zach has tears welling in his eyes.

"You came back for me," he says.

"You're my teammate. I'll always save you," she says.

"But that means you're not going to get your wish," he says. Before she can answer, the baying of hounds rings out over the glade. I jump, but I relax when I realize the children jump as well. Hunter isn't actually here.

"He said if he caught us back here again, he'd make us forget about everything," Zach says frantically. "I don't want to forget all the stuff we did."

"It's okay. I made clues for myself and hid them in lots of different places where Grandma won't find them and get mad. When I remember, I'll come over and help you remember," she says.

"Promise?" Zach asks.

"Promise," Tamsin says. Hunter's dogs barrel through the mist and encircle the children. Young Tamsin glares at them defiantly as the vision fades and I'm alone once more.

There's a force—a strengthening magnetic force—pulling me toward the trees at the center. At the same time, the air gets heavier, closing in around me, making it difficult to walk, and buzzing in my ears. Shapes dance in the fog, some humanlike and some definitely not. Strange whispers reverberate through my head. Whether they're coming from outside or inside my brain, I can't say. But they need me to keep going.

I take a step forward and an arrow plants itself in the ground in front of my foot. Hunter's here. I try to run forward, to get to the end of this before Hunter can stop me. The hounds bay, one on either side of me and closing in quickly. I force my way a few more feet through the pressure bearing down on me, and then a sudden, horrific pain blooms in the back of my calf, and I collapse onto my knees. I turn, grasping blindly for a way to make the pain go away, and I feel a wooden shaft sticking out of my leg; just brushing my fingers against it sends shockwaves of pain up my body.

"Fuck *you*, Hunter!" I scream. The hounds enter my field of vision and block my path forward, as if I could even move now.

"I warned you. I warned you!" Hunter snaps, his words harsher and louder than I've ever heard him speak. "Don't pull it out!" he says as I make to grab the arrow shaft. I open my mouth to spit obscenities, but I'm drowned out by a sudden bout of howling from the hounds. Hunter's eyes widen as his gaze moves from me to something beyond me.

I turn to see the fog roiling and bubbling like a mass of cancerous flesh. The magnetic pull strengthens, causing the very ground to buck and break apart; clods of dirt and stone fly into the fog. High-pitched keening fills the glade around us, coming from the forest beyond, along with the hissing, slithering sounds that marked the arrival of the wraiths the last time I witnessed an attack.

Several creatures made up of old bones and plant matter swarm into the glade and vanish into the fog. There's a cracking, grinding sound, and then a hand-like appendage made of an entire twisted and warped bear skeleton bound together by thick roots rises out of the fog, falls hard onto the ground, and strains to drag what must be the rest of the creature's massive body forward. Seeing this, I fall back in surprise, landing on my ass and forcing the arrow deeper into my leg, making me scream in pain. At the sound, the creature shifts directions, one of its arms coming down toward me.

Hunter's dogs spring into action. They circle the creature and snap at it, distracting it from me. Three arrows sink into the creature's arm with hardly a breath between them just as the creature sweeps a glacially slow arm toward one of the dogs, which swiftly dodges.

A hand grabs the back of my shirt and yanks me back, dragging the arrow shaft across the ground and causing it to twist into my leg and making me scream out again. At the sound, the creature turns its attention back to me.

Hunter releases my shirt collar and instead grabs me around the waist and lifts me up against him. The dogs dart in and snap at the creature to distract it, but the creature swings its arm down and strikes the ground as Hunter carries me back. I think we're in the clear, but the moment the creature's hand makes contact with the ground, it splatters into a barrage of disgusting root tendrils, one of which latches onto Hunter's arm.

Hunter throws me hard away from the creature and draws his spear with his free hand.

"Go! The further it gets from the trees, the weaker it will get," he says. He cuts his arm free and takes a step back. I start to crawl away, but then I hear a sharp, pained whine. I turn to see that the creature has one of the dogs gripped firmly in one hand, while Hunter prepares to grapple with the other as it reforms.

At the dog's pained cry, Hunter whirls and darts in to free it, while the other dog harries the creature from the opposite side. The creature begins to slowly retract its arm, pulling the dog toward its center; at the same time, a large mouth ringed with sharp teeth opens up at the center of its body, preparing to close around the struggling animal.

I can't just leave it. I rise on unsteady legs and take a breath. I grab a stick off the ground, hoping to do whatever I can to help. With the first step I take, the pain from the arrow becomes so excruciating my body won't obey me, and I collapse into the dirt.

Chapter Thirteen

IT'S DARK. I CAN'T tell if my eyes are open or closed. It makes no difference. I'm floating, and the temperature is neither warm nor cool. The only thing I can feel is my own skin as I clench my hands into weak fists.

The absolute lack of sound is a sound in and of itself; it vibrates against my eardrums and makes me want to curl into a fetal position and clutch my head. Silhouettes dance across my vision as they might against my closed eyelids, but even if I call out and reach for them, nothing responds.

I don't know how much time passes while I explore the darkness for something—anything. I don't know how to move. There's no ground to walk on, and no resistance to push against as if I was swimming. I move my legs anyway, as if the act of miming walking would move me through this void.

And then I bump into something solid and gasp in surprise. I can barely make out the outline of the shape in front of me. I can't tell if there's a light source or if even the outline is my imagination.

"Hello?" I call out. The darkness swallows up my words as soon as they leave my lips.

"You found me," a frail voice says. I recognize it. It's Leithe's. Though there's still no discernible light source,

I begin to make out his form. His face is hollow and his robes hang off his frame like a shed skin. He looks as if he could disintegrate like wet paper at any moment. "Are you truly here, or is this another way to taunt me?" He reaches his hand out toward my face, and I recoil in surprise.

"Where are we? Is this your prison? How do I get you out of here?" I ask. As he listens to my words, his face falls.

"No. You're that human girl," he says. He blinks several times, as if to clear his head.

"Tamsin," I remind him. "Who did you think I was?"

"Never you mind. This is the dark place. Sometimes there's light, such as when you call me, and just as quickly I return here. I heard you calling me a short while ago. But I don't know where we are. I don't know where the rest of me is. But," he reaches out quickly and grabs my hand. His grip feels so fragile I wonder if his hand would simply shatter if I yanked my hand away too hard.

"You're closer than before, or we couldn't touch, or you couldn't be in this place with me." Having made his point, he releases me and pulls his hand away.

"Then I'm pretty sure I know where you are," I say, remembering the drawing I made as a child. "I think you're in a tree. I found a clearing surrounded by fog, there's two trees and—" Memories rush back to me. The trees. Hunter. The monster. The arrow. I check the back of my leg. There's no injury.

"If you know where I am, why haven't you released me yet?" he asks.

"Because the glade is full of monsters and guarded by a guy who doesn't want me there. I don't know what you expect me to do about that."

"Figure it out," he says. "Though, honestly, I'm impressed you've done this much as a human."

"I can't believe a compliment just came out of your mouth, even a backhanded one," I say. He opens his mouth to respond, but suddenly seems fainter and farther away than before. White spots appear in my vision as Leithe becomes a speck in the distance, then all I see is light.

The pain tells me I've returned to my physical body. Aside from the general ache of exertion and from getting tossed around, there's a dull but persistent pain in my calf where Hunter shot me. I'm lying on something soft that smells faintly of mold. I'm in the Randall Place, laying on the living room couch in front of the fireplace. One of Hunter's dogs lies sleeping in front of the couch, wrapped in ragged bandages. Hunter sits on the floor next to the fireplace, making arrows. As he finishes each one, he holds the arrowhead to his lips and whispers something.

"Why are you talking to your arrows?" I ask. My throat is dry and it hurts to speak. Hunter doesn't look at me, and for a moment it seems like he either didn't hear me or doesn't care.

"It's a minor spell, to help them hit what I aim at," he finally says.

"Oh. Like me. Why am I still alive?" I ask. After Hunter's threats, I'm surprised I woke up at all. "What was that thing?"

"That was what one of the prisoners is capable of inflicting upon the world, even caged," Hunter says, keeping his eyes on his work. "Now, be quiet and don't go anywhere."

"Yeah, if I run, you'll catch me. Or whatever," I say. "Good thing for you it'll be hard for me to run with an arrow wound." As I mention it, I examine my leg. The arrow has been removed and the wound has been bandaged.

"How do you make steel arrows if steel hurts faeries?" I ask.

"I don't. I just pick them up when human hunters lose them," he says.

"Oh." I gesture toward my bandaged leg. "Is this your way of apologizing?" I ask.

"If you move too much, you might start bleeding again," he says.

The front door creaks open, and I prop myself up to see over the back of the couch, wincing as the shifting irritates my wound. Thistledown stands at the threshold, clutching a bundle of leaves in her hands. She smiles kindly at me. I'm unsure if I should acknowledge I recognize her in front of Hunter.

"I brought food, as you requested," she says. Hunter nods at her and she scurries into the living room and places her leaf-wrapped bundle on the hearth. I sit up, slowly and stiffly, as she unwraps the bundle to reveal a stack of small brown cakes and a plastic fast food container repurposed to hold a dark, sweet-smelling jelly. From around her waist she detaches an old beer bottle sealed with leather and twine tied around the top.

"You must be hungry and thirsty. Please partake," she says, handing me cakes topped with jelly and the beer bottle, which turns out to be full of water. I eat and drink gratefully. The cakes are slightly bitter, but the sweetness of the jelly balances them. The taste is nostalgic. It brings to mind cozy evenings in Thistledown's tiny home, sipping tea and listening to her crooning voice as she tells Zach and me stories of Faerie.

"Thank you," I say to Thistledown. She smiles and places her slender hand over my own.

"You need not give me thanks. The hunter has already paid me for my service," she says.

"Oh. Sorry," I say. She laughs again.

"Offering sorrow is just another way to be tricked into debt," she says. "The court fae know many tricks and will use all of them to keep us at their mercy." Her gaze flickers in Hunter's direction, but he doesn't seem to notice.

"Th—That's interesting," I say. I almost thank her, but stop myself. She pulls my hand close to her chest, forcing me to lean forward.

"You will be alright, my dear," she whispers to me, tucking a strand of my hair behind my ear. "Thistledown knows it."

"Thistledown, you can go," Hunter says. Her expression sours, but she switches to one of deference before she lets go of me and turns around.

"Perhaps it would be wise to let her regain her strength for a time, sir knight," Thistledown says to Hunter.

"I said you can go," he says, without looking at her. She bows to him and departs, offering me one last smile on her way out.

"She acts like you're a really big deal," I say.

Hunter says nothing, and I worry he's just going to ignore me, but then he speaks. "I'm court fae, Thistledown is courtless. The courtless don't owe fealty to the courts, but they know they live and die at the courts' whims."

"That sounds like a terrible way to live," I say.

He looks up at me. "I don't care if fae kill and abuse each other. They bring it upon themselves."

"But you do care if they hurt humans," I say. "You've protected me and Zach before. And you just saved me again when you could have just left me to die."

"These are not things with which you need concern yourself."

"Then let's talk about what *does* concern me: what are you going to do with me now?" I ask.

"You may remember this or not, but this is the third time you've nearly entered the prison. I suspect someone has been manipulating your actions, whether you know it or not. So tell me, right now, who it is that is guiding you there," he says. Leithe, Thistledown, Zach, the witch. The real question would be who doesn't want me going to the prison.

"I found my way there on my own," I say, after some thought. It's technically the truth. No one gave me specific directions. "I wanted to know what's inside."

Hunter rubs his forehead. "I don't know why I even asked. Humans have the freedom to lie."

"I'm sorry I've caused you so much trouble. I never wanted to. Please just let me go home to my grandma. She's sick," I say. I hate using Grandma's circumstances like that, but I desperately need to play on his sympathies.

"And you'll go and you'll never come back into these woods?" he asks. I want to say no, but I know that would be a lie, and I know he can see it on my face as well.

"Then leaving you free to do as you wish would be failing at my duty," he says after a tense silence. "My mental glamours have little effect on you, so I am going to take you to someone stronger. He will remove your memories and give you the desire to go somewhere far away. If it fades and you return, I'll do it again."

"No. Don't do that. Please don't do that. You don't know what it's like to have to fight with your own mind. I don't know what thoughts are even really mine," I beg, and I hate myself for the desperation I can't keep out of my voice. Without my memories, will I die for reneging on Leithe's deal, withering away without ever knowing why?

"If that's unbearable to you, I can kill you now instead," he says.

"What about Faerie? Last time you said one of my options was to live in Faerie forever?" I ask.

"You can't stay here. You'll just cause more problems. So what would you have me do? Sell you into slavery to some fae lord far away? You think that would be better than living the rest of your life ignorant of this world?" he says. Anything that doesn't result in losing my memories gives me a chance to somehow get back here. But Hunter makes a good point. Throwing myself at the mercy of some other fae doesn't seem wise.

"... Okay. I'll go to the memory guy," I say. Traveling, at least, might give me a chance to escape. "But before that, I really have to use the bathroom. Like, really bad. Can I do that before we go? I'm not going to go anywhere; I know you're faster than me and know the woods better, but I'm going to go a little farther away because I know you have good hearing and it would be like, really embarrassing if you heard me."

"Oh. Yes. Go," he says. "I … let me know if you need help walking." Though his tone is begging me not to.

I can't put much weight on my bad leg, but it seems far more healed than an arrow wound should be after a few hours. I make sure to limp for good measure, in case it makes Hunter feel bad.

Outside, I immediately look for hiding runes on trees, but find none. That was my Plan A, and I'm still putting together a Plan B. First, I do actually need to go. I take care of the that order of business and then take a few more steps away and sit down. Hunter's other dog is lying on the porch. It eyes me, but doesn't seem particularly alert to what I'm doing.

I try to reach out with my mind to call Leithe. For what seems like too long, nothing happens, and I worry that Hunter is going to get suspicious and come looking for me.

"Come on. Please. Show up when I actually need you," I whisper. I glance back at Hunter's dog. It hasn't seemed to notice my whispering, or doesn't consider it important enough to report. I don't know how smart the hounds are, but they seem more aware and in-tune with Hunter than normal dogs would be.

"Leithe. I need you. Right now," I try again, this time I try to be commanding instead of pleading.

"For what?" he asks. I want to cry out of relief, but I swallow the feeling. I'm not saved yet.

"Are you the one making the wraiths that have been leaking out of the prison?" I hiss.

Leithe gives me a perplexed look. "There's no one else it could be."

"Then send some wraiths over here, now. A while ago, you created a giant monster. I need you to do it again if you want me to be able to free you," I whisper, glancing furtively at the dog lounging on the porch. Leithe stares off into the distance, frowning, before eventually returning his gaze to me.

"No. I will not. Solve this yourself," he says. I gape at him, at his apparent apathy.

"Are you *serious*?" I say. "Do you want to stay there forever?"

He crosses his arms. "I suppose I'll have to get a more competent servant next time," he says.

I stare at him in silence, wishing Hunter wasn't around so I could scream and shout. But I close my eyes, take a deep breath, and exhale slowly. "Is it because you can't do it?"

"How dare you," Leithe growls.

"That would make the most sense," I continue, ignoring his anger. "It would be stupid of you to offer me no help when I'm the only one even possibly willing and able to free you right now. So if you could help me, it would be in your best interests. But you can't. You can't consciously do anything to affect the world outside your prison, but you don't want to admit how powerless you really are; you'd rather me think you *won't*, rather than *can't*. Tell me I'm wrong."

"You must think you're such a clever little human. You—"

"Tell. Me. I'm. Wrong," I cut him off. He glares at me. I hold his gaze.

"You are wrong to think you have the right to assume anything about me or my methods," he finally says. He's fuming.

"That's not a direct answer, so I'm going to assume I'm right," I say. "How painful is it for you to have to beg a human for help?"

"I have no desire to listen to this drivel. Send me away."

"But I have a desire to say it, especially because this will probably be the last time we get to speak because I'm going to get my memories ripped out of my head and then die a painful death because of a deal I won't remember. And there's something I've been wondering: when we were in that dark place, was it your betrothed you initially mistook me for?" He says nothing; he seems to be pointedly ignoring me now, but with every word that comes out of my mouth, the lines of his face harden further.

"How long have you been waiting for her? Do you really think she's going to come save you?" I ask. "Maybe she's trapped and as powerless as you are; maybe she got free years ago and moved on with her life with some other faerie; or maybe she's the one who did this to you in the first place. Do you ever wonder about that?"

"Do not say another word about her," Leithe says. His tone stops me short. I'm used to hearing him sound haughty or irritated, but now his words are soft and measured, and they send a chill up my spine. I've finally crossed a line.

"Oh?" I say, trying to sound confident, to mimic his haughtiness. "And what are you going to do about it?" For emphasis, I reach out and pass my hand straight through Leithe's head. He stands straight and tries to tower over me, but we both know that's a hollow threat.

"I think I might enjoy thinking about you drowning in your own lifeblood, helpless and unable to understand what you've done to deserve such a fate." His yellow eyes burn into me. I try to meet them defiantly.

Before I can come up with a retort, one of Hunter's dogs howls, making me jump. Leithe vanishes in the moment my attention is pulled away from him.

"Tamsin," Hunter calls from just inside the door; maybe he's worried I'm still not decent. I limp back to the house.

"What?" I say.

"We need to go now," he says. The dog that was lying on the porch is now at Hunter's heel, staring warily into the trees.

"We can't wait for my leg to get a little better?" I ask.

"No. There are more wraiths. I need to go deal with them, and I fully expect that if I leave you here you'll be gone when I get back. So we go now," he says. "I'll carry you if you cannot walk."

"I'll walk," I say. Even if it hurts, I want to drag this out for as long as possible. If antagonizing Leithe actually managed to create more wraiths, I hope they're smart enough to beeline for me. If Hunter's distracted, I have a chance at getting away.

We walk for a while. I'm not sure exactly where we're going. Sometimes I see something familiar and sometimes I don't, so my best guess is that we're weaving in and out of the human world and Faerie. Maybe that's how Hunter usually gets around so fast.

"So, I remembered a few more things," I say, trying to strike up a conversation. Maybe to guilt him more, maybe to needle him for information since he expects me to forget about it all soon anyway, maybe just to fill the silence.

"A shame," he says.

"I remember when I got to the glade when I was about seven or eight. I got a cut on my face. I'm surprised it didn't scar."

"Thistledown's work. She tended to your leg as well."

"And you took my memories away after that?"

"Yes," he says. For a while he doesn't elaborate, but as I'm about to say something else, he finally speaks. "It didn't stick. Around that time was when I realized how resistant you are to glamour. After that, I had to take you to someone better at glamour than I am."

"Why'd you let a kid get so close to the prison anyway? Couldn't you have tossed me out sooner?"

"I regret it," he says, to my surprise. "I should have done more to scare you off when you were young. But you enjoyed playing with the fae that live here, like Thistledown. And they enjoyed entertaining you, so I let it go on for too long. I expected you to lose your Sight as you aged, so I believed you would stop visiting before any real harm had been done."

"Why didn't you just tell me where I wasn't allowed to go?" I ask.

"I did. Many times," he says reproachfully. "Telling you not to do something only makes you more determined to do it. And you had a gift for sneaking away from whatever fae was supposed to be watching you."

"What about when I was a teenager?"

"You tended to behave so long as I let you visit sometimes," he says.

"Yeah. I guess I had a pretty big crush on you back then," I muse. He seems to flinch a little bit.

"Again, I regret giving you an inch. I realize it's not my place to say, but you seemed very lonely back then. It was hard to turn you away."

Before I can answer, the trees shift and rustle as if in a nonexistent wind. Something hisses and skitters through the undergrowth. A screech from my left alerts me to the presence of a wraith a split second before it bursts into sight and leaps at me, only to be shot through the head with an arrow in midair. It crashes into me and I fall on my ass before shoving its writhing remains away.

Hunter and his dog are distracted and looking away from me, in the process of dealing with several other wraiths. This is probably my best chance. I heave to my feet and run, streaks of pain shooting up my bad leg with each step. Hunter shouts my name, but it doesn't sound like he's following me.

I break through the tree line and trip and stumble into the road. I must be in the human world, and I'm pretty sure I'm only a short distance from Grandma's house.

As soon as I take a moment to catch my breath, I hear movement behind me. I start running again, praying on the adrenaline keeping me going just a bit farther. Risking a glance behind me, I see that my pursuer isn't Hunter or his dog. It's a wraith with a deer skull as a head and centipede-like body composed of spines and branches and supported by countless limbs taken from different animals. Its gait is lopsided due to its uneven legs, but that doesn't do much to slow it down. It makes sense that they're chasing me. I'm the one Leithe is mad at.

Grandma's house finally comes into view. I cross the last stretch with renewed strength and slam hard into the front door. I fumble for the handle with shaking hands, but manage to open it and slam it behind me just as the skittering monster crests the porch steps. I hear it ram into the door and begin testing it for weaknesses, its skeletal limbs clicking against the wood.

"Grandma?" I call out. There's no answer. Then I notice the house is an absolute wreck. The contents of the pantry are strewn across the kitchen floor. The couch has been shredded and the stuffing ripped out.

"Grandma!" I shout, opening her bedroom door. She isn't inside. I hear the wraith crawling around on the porch as I grab Grandma's gun and sift through the safe for bullets, glad I forgot to return the key. I load the gun clumsily. I've only handled it a few times, enough to gain a healthy respect for it.

I check upstairs next, panic mounting. Her truck is in the driveway, so I don't know where she would be. I consider calling her, and the thought reminds me that I left my phone in my room when I stormed out. It's still on my bedside table. There are several messages from an unknown caller, as well as a few from Zach and weirdly, Dr. Webster. But it's the date on the lock screen that catches my attention first. I've been gone for almost two days.

"Oh, no. No," I whisper. The most recent text I received was from Dr. Webster: *We are worried about you. Your grandmother is in the hospital. Please reach out.*

Shoving the phone in my pocket, I race back downstairs to the front door. Peeking out the window, I see the monster is where it was, still trying to get in through the door. However, it notices me through the glass and switches tactics, slamming into the window instead.

Taking a deep breath, I pull the front door open with one hand and swing it the rest of the way with my foot so that I can level the gun with both hands. The wraith abandons the window and comes straight toward me. At least they aren't smart. I pull the trigger and wood and bone shards go flying, and what's left of the creature lies unmoving on the ground, for now. I'm not staying long enough to discover if these things can put themselves back together. I grab the keys, get in the truck, and peel down the driveway as fast as I can.

Chapter Fourteen

THE HOSPITAL HAS A chemical smell that makes my nose itch. When I get there, the receptionist asks if perhaps I meant to go to the emergency entrance; when I catch sight of myself in the elevator mirror, I understand why. I'm absolutely filthy, not to mention limping. And my left pant leg has been sliced up the back to the knee, presumably to give Thistledown access to the arrow wound. My pants and the cloth wrapped around my calf are stained with blood. I get lost twice trying to find Grandma's room. When I finally find it, Grandma is asleep. A TV in the upper corner is playing an old rom-com.

I collapse into a chair next to the bed. I must fall asleep, because I wake up to a doctor standing over me and gently trying to get my attention.

"I'm sorry. What did you say?" I ask, rubbing my eyes.

"I said, are you the granddaughter?" she asks.

"Yes. What happened? Is she going to be okay?" I ask. The doctor checks her clipboard.

"Your grandmother had a fall. Other than bruising, she has a fractured ankle and rib. She's on some heavy painkillers right now, but she'll be okay with rest. What about you, are you okay?" She looks me over pointedly, gaze pausing at my leg.

"Mostly just dirt. I'll be fine," I say.

"Right. Well, push that button if you need help," she says, waving her clipboard at a red button on the side of Grandma's bed. I don't like being here, but I have a feeling neither Hunter nor Leithe's wraiths will pursue me this far. It's forty minutes away by car and has metal everywhere.

While I wait for Grandma to wake up, I go to the bathroom to clean myself up as best I can, which amounts mostly to scrubbing my face and arms with paper towels. In doing so I discover several tiny scratches I've accumulated over the past few days. I'm afraid to unwrap my leg, but gently poking at it leads me to believe it healed up more while I was sleeping. Thistledown's medicine is no joke.

When I return to my seat by Grandma's bed, I sit for a while and just watch her breathing. It's faint but consistent, and occasionally she makes a tiny whistle sound when she exhales. Her face looks slack and more vulnerable than she's let herself be seen as in my entire life.

I wonder if I should even be here. If I had been doing my job and helping her, this wouldn't have happened. I doubt she'd want the first thing she sees when she wakes up to be me. Even so, I should at least offer to stay until she's healed up, though I'd probably just make everything more difficult. I had a chance to reconnect with the woman who was more a mother to me than my biological mother ever was, and I ruined it. A sob bubbles out of me before I can stop it, and I bite my knuckles to keep anything else from escaping.

"I'm sorry. I'm sorry. I'm sorry," I whisper. I guess I'm only capable of apologizing when I know she can't hear me. Carefully, worried she'll wake up and snatch it away,

I take one of her hands in both of mine, wishing I had anything to offer here.

I'm awoken by Grandma's hand squeezing mine. She's awake and looking at me.

"I'm sorry," I say immediately.

"Did you chew through the porch boards?" she asks. Her speech is a little slow. She's probably still feeling the painkillers.

"No, but I shouldn't have left. I shouldn't have gone in your room."

"You're not my mother." She doesn't whine it like a petulant teenager—like I would have. She says it patiently, like a statement of fact rather than a complaint. "I'm *your* mother—grandmother. I'm supposed to be taking care of you. This is because I couldn't do that. I shouldn't have hidden your things from you."

"No," I protest, but she cuts me off with a shake of her head.

"I chased your mother away; took that connection away from you."

"What do you mean?" I ask slowly. Part of me thinks we shouldn't have this conversation right now, that she wouldn't be saying these things if she wasn't on drugs, but this might be my only chance to hear them.

"Skye was very sick, and I didn't get her the help she needed. Because of that, she left."

"What was wrong with her?"

"Her boyfriend at the time was abusive, so she was in a bad place emotionally when she came home. And having a baby can be physically and emotionally traumatic. It's painful, your hormones fluctuate. It can have an effect on your brain," she says.

"She had postpartum depression?"

"She ... was convinced you weren't her baby, that her 'real' baby had been stolen when she wasn't looking and you were left behind instead." At those words, every vein in my body becomes filled with ice.

"But ... there was no evidence of that? It was completely crazy?" I ask. Grandma looks me in the eye, and I see the moment of hesitation and watch as it morphs into defensive irritation.

"Obviously. I was there when you were born," she says.

"What aren't you telling me?" I ask. When I push, Grandma sighs with resignation.

"It *was* very strange," she admits. "I delivered you, and I was sure you were dead. I didn't feel a heartbeat. You were blue. I tried to explain to Skye she lost her baby, and she insisted on holding you. I gave you to her and left the room to get more towels, and when I came back, you were alive and well, whimpering and crying, even. I was overjoyed. It was a miracle, but then I saw the look on Skye's face. She was confused. She said she was so exhausted she closed her eyes for just a moment and when she opened them, you were different. Not hers. I told her there was no realistic way you weren't her baby, but she insisted. I tried to ignore it, telling myself she just needed time to bond with you, but she never did. She left before your first birthday. She never accepted you were hers."

"... Thank you for telling me," I say, my entire body numb.

"It was so strange," Grandma continues. "I was sure you weren't breathing. I don't know how I could have gotten that wrong,"

"It must have been hard for you to carry that around with you for so long," I say. "But I think you and Skye were right, Grandma."

"It wouldn't make any *sense*," she insists.

"But you saw it, right? She believed she saw it, and I think you won't let yourself believe you saw it, but you *know* you did. I know it doesn't make sense right now, but I think it will, eventually." At least, I hope it will. I take out the seed the witch gave me from my pocket.

"Someone gave this to me. She said it would make you healthy." I turn over Grandma's hand and press the seed into her palm. "You can take it or not. It's up to you."

She looks at the seed. "I wish I knew what went on in your head."

"I've been telling you for years. I wish you could give believing me a chance," I say.

She studies me in silence for a while. "Did you wreck the house before you left? Toss the kitchen and rip up the couch and such?"

"No," I say. I ready myself to be further accused.

"No," she says, "Cheeps did, right? He's the one you always blamed."

"He probably did it. He throws tantrums when we fight," I say, waiting for the anger and disbelief.

"The porch had been chewed up. It looked like some kind of animal. The boards were weakened. My foot went right through one when I went out to look for you after you ran off. There's no way you could have done that. There's no way that kind of damage could have accumulated in a few hours. I don't know what I'm supposed to believe, but I can try to believe you. We can try to do this over again," she says, closing her hand around the seed.

"Thank you," I say. I sit with Grandma for a while. We watch television in silence until she speaks again.

"I have something that I need to ask you," she says. Her words are measured, as if she's been building herself up for this moment.

"What?" I ask.

"Do you remember what happened the day before I drove us to Chesapeake to set you up at that boarding school?" she asks.

"No." I think hard, but I can't remember the specifics. She took me to that city. I started attending the school. I didn't go back to her house again. "It was in the middle of the semester, so it took a while to get everything settled, right?" Grandma stares at me for a long time before speaking again. She takes a deep breath.

"The night before that ... you ... I got a call from your phone telling me to pick you up at the old bridge. When I got there, I found you covered in blood and completely insensible." She waits, watching me. I rack my brain.

"I don't remember," I whisper in answer to her unasked question.

"I checked you all over, but you weren't injured. But you were hysterical. I couldn't get the story out of you. I asked you again and again where the blood came from, but it was like you were sleepwalking. So I took you home, washed you up, washed all the clothes, and scrubbed the inside of the truck. I cleaned everything. I was ... afraid." Grandma takes a rattling breath to steady herself. "I didn't know what happened to you, and the only thing I could think of was that if you stayed in that house, it could happen again.

"So I put you in the truck and got you out. I've wondered why I did that for a long time. I've been so afraid to ask you what happened that night, but this—" She gestures at the hospital room. "This made me think about a lot of things. I didn't want to go without asking you."

My stomach twists; I want to vomit. For just a second, I see my hands covered in blood, then I blink and they're clean. "I really don't remember what happened."

"It's okay. Trauma can do that. Don't force yourself," she says. "I wanted to tell you that I'm sorry. I know you must have felt like I abandoned you by sending you to that school. I'm sorry I couldn't give you what you needed here."

"I never thought that," I say.

Grandma drifts back off to sleep soon after. Then, as I told her I would, I go back to the house to clean everything up before she gets discharged. I didn't specify exactly what kind of messes need cleaning.

My mind is so distracted that I barely remember the drive back to the house, only snapping to attention when I turn onto the winding driveway and park. There are no strange sights or noises; no sign of Hunter, the dogs, or any wraiths. Hopefully, Hunter assumes I wouldn't be stupid enough to come back so soon and has better things to do than case my house. He seems to prefer always having at least one hound at his side, and since one of them is injured and recuperating, I doubt he left one to keep watch here. Still, I grab the gun from where I hid it under the back seat and bring it with me when I get out of the truck.

The door is still ajar from when I left. I didn't waste time shutting it. Grandma is right—much of the porch wood looks like it's been savaged by some kind of rodent nonstop for years. I must have missed that detail earlier. I'm glad I didn't break through the boards while running from that wraith. Cheeps could have gotten me killed.

When I go inside, I hear soft sobbing coming from under the couch.

"Cheeps?" I say in what I hope is a soothing tone.

"Young Miss?" Cheeps says. He crawls out from under the couch, clutching wads of couch stuffing. "You forgot my milk! And then you left, and then Mistress left too!"

"She got hurt because of your tantrum." And mine, but I leave that out for now. "I thought we talked about this."

"You said you would give me milk, but you didn't! I even waited so patiently, but you said you would leave forever!" he says.

"You did this because I forgot to leave milk for you?" I ask.

"Yes! You broke your word, Young Miss. We're family, and you broke your word!" he cries.

"I'm very sorry, Cheeps. I'll leave a bowl of milk out for you every night for a week, okay? But you should start cleaning this place up, or the Mistress could get hurt again and have to leave forever. Do you want that?" I ask.

Cheeps' large eyes widen even more. "No!" He scampers off, hopefully to clean.

With one problem taken care of, I march up to my room and sit down in the middle of the floor. It seems my room was spared Cheeps' wrath. Come to think of it, he never trashed my room—probably to make it more convincingly look like I was the one responsible for his messes.

I haven't been able to consciously guide these visions in the past, so I don't know where exactly to start if I want to do so. I try to let my mind drift while holding onto the details I know from Grandma's retelling: a cold winter day, snow everywhere. I focus on my breathing, perhaps somewhat like meditation, though I worry I might just fall asleep on the floor. I don't know the last time I slept in a bed.

I'm thinking about my bed, about how it's only a few feet away and I could definitely meditate while laying down, when I realize the room has gotten considerably colder. I open my eyes to see Skye—my mother—lying on the bed, clutching a bundle of blankets. She looks exhausted, hair sticking to her face from sweat and cheeks shining from tears. She gently strokes her baby's tiny cheek. Grandma stands over the bed, looking at her grief-stricken daughter clutching her grandchild. Its skin is gray and tinged with purple.

"Honey, I'm going to get you more blankets and try the phone again. I'll be right back," she says. She speaks carefully, as if the wrong words could shatter Skye like dropped porcelain. Skye barely nods at Grandma's words. After Grandma leaves, Skye presses her lips to her child's forehead and stifles a sob.

As she clutches the baby to her chest, eventually Skye's head lolls to the side and her eyes close. That's when it happens. The window slides open and Thistledown is there, clutching a bundle wrapped in fine silk. A gust of winter wind rushes in and causes Skye to stir and open her eyes.

"Shh, now," Thistledown croons, placing a slender finger over Skye's lips. "Everything will be just fine." At the words, ripples of glamour radiate from Thistledown's mouth, though calming Skye seems to take a lot of effort from her.

As Skye drifts back off into sleep, Thistledown gently takes the baby from Skye's arms and replaces it with the one she carries, tucking the new one tightly into the blanket. The new baby is a healthy pink and its gray eyes dart curiously around the room.

"Poor dear. Poor, poor dear," Thistledown says, looking down at Skye's baby. She looks back to Skye and wipes a tear from her sleeping face. "You've been given a wonderful gift, dear. A wonderful gift." Looking now to my infant self, she says, "Soon, very soon, we will meet again. Auntie Thistledown will make you so many lovely cakes." She pokes the baby's tiny nose playfully, and it giggles.

Thistledown, alerted by the sound of Grandma coming back up the stairs, quickly and soundlessly slips back out the window and closes it once more, vanishing just as Grandma opens the door.

"Honey, do you want me to—" she starts, but stops when she sees a healthy infant looking wide-eyed back at her. "Oh, Jesus," she says, rushing over to check the baby. I can see the confusion in her eyes, but she jumps into action quickly. "Skye, honey. Wake up, look," she says, softly shaking her daughter's shoulder. "Look, she's okay. Your baby's okay." Skye wakes and looks down at the child in her arms. She immediately jumps back and might have even dropped it if Grandma hadn't been there.

"No," she says. Her expression becomes a mix of fear and disgust. "No. That isn't—No. No. That isn't mine." She pushes the baby away into Grandma's arms as Grandma watches her daughter, horrified. For me, for Skye, it's hard to say.

I've seen enough. I snap the thread and return to the present. I want to sit down to take all of this in, but I can't sit on my bed—Skye's bed. This room has very suddenly ceased to feel like it was ever mine. I'm a changeling. One of the things Hunter told me about in his stories. That's how I've been able to do the things I've done; I was never human in the first place.

I look over my hands, as if expecting them to morph into claws, or my skin to grow fur or scales. But none of that happens. I take out the pocketknife Zach gave me and run my finger down the flat of the blade. The steel is cold, but nothing remarkable happens. It doesn't burn or melt my flesh.

The next question I need to answer is what happened that night Grandma told me about, so going to the bridge and trying to dig up another vision seems like my best option. After that, I'll look for Thistledown, but unless I can lure her out of the woods, I'd risk running into Hunter.

Before opening the front door, I check the window; there's still no sign of Hunter or his dogs. Still, I run all the way to the truck, knife in hand. The roar of the engine is a relief; it makes me feel protected by this metal monster.

Partway to the bridge, I round a corner and see Hunter standing in the middle of the road. He doesn't gesture or shout anything, just stands there. I see no sign of the dogs, but I slow to a stop about thirty feet away from him. Far enough that I could react before he gets to me, I hope. I suspect the dogs might be lying in wait in the trees, but I still don't see them. I honk the horn pointedly. He scowls. I roll the window down an inch and keep my finger on the button, just in case.

"I'm trying to drive," I shout through the window. Hunter takes a step forward. "No! You can stay over there. If you yell I'll hear you." He stops at my command, thankfully.

"My goodwill is spent. Get out of the car and come with me now," he says. I've heard him sound annoyed before—he's pretty much always annoyed with me. But by the tone in his voice, I can tell he's truly done playing nice.

"I'm sorry!" I shout, and I floor the gas pedal. An instant before the truck moves, Hunter raises his bow and the trees to my left explode with action as one of his hounds launches itself out of hiding and charges the truck. Thankfully, the truck gets a few feet before the hound impacts, and it slams into the back door instead of the driver's door. Still, it slams into the truck with a force no normal dog could muster. Metal crunches inward and glass cracks. But then the truck is moving, closing quickly with Hunter, who hasn't moved.

He draws his bow back, and for a moment I think he's going to try to shoot me through the windshield, but then he angles the arrow down and to the side and shoots my left tire. I still tear by him. I shut my eyes on reflex as it seems like I'm about to hit him, but there's no impact. Regardless, I pick up speed and hope I can put plenty of distance between him and me before I reach the bridge. The tire light comes on, and I can smell burning rubber through the window. It's going to be so much money to fix this thing; I'll have to do a lot of groveling to Grandma after this, but that's a problem to deal with if I even make it to tomorrow.

There's still the problem of Hunter's other dog. Thistledown's treatment healed my leg rapidly; it's now only a minor irritant. His other dog could be fully back in action by this point. Only one charged me back there, so I worry the other one will jump from out of nowhere. In the rearview mirror, I think I see a glint of something—sunlight off an arrowhead or tooth, maybe.

But I focus on the mirror for too long. When I turn back to look at the road, I'm going too fast to make the curve I should have remembered was there. I slam the brakes and twist the wheel, but that doesn't stop me from flying off the road and slamming into a tree.

Before I recover from the shock of impact, the cab door is wrenched open and Hunter drags me out of the driver's seat. I flail ineffectually at him with my fists; I might as well be doing nothing for all he seems to care. Hunter is monstrously strong, though I'm skinny so he doesn't necessarily need supernatural strength to toss me around.

"Ow!" I yell as he starts dragging me down the road. He ignores me, not even offering some platitude that he's only doing this because he has to. He's really mad, and I don't hold it personally against him.

Hunter walks me to the bridge and down the slope, ignoring my every attempt to goad him into conversation. His dog follows behind us. We finally come to a stop in front of the giant rock pile that makes up the sleeping troll.

"Elder," he says. "I beg of you to forgive my rudeness in waking you. I need a boon from you." Nothing happens; we wait in awkward silence as I steadily lose feeling in my arm.

"So the troll is the one who took my memories the second time," I say. Hunter ignores me.

"Would you mind loosening your grip before my arm falls off?" I ask. He doesn't respond, but he does let up a little. "So you *can* hear me," I continue. Again, he doesn't respond.

Before I can say anything else, the rocks shudder and shift. Loose pebbles roll off the troll's body as it raises its head. It slowly blinks gravel out of a pair of small shiny black eyes. It leans down and I can't help but take a step back, though I'm stopped short by Hunter's grip on me.

The troll raises one of its huge arms and reaches toward me, hand outstretched. I hold my breath as the troll's hand comes to rest on the top of my head. I wait for its fingers to close and turn my head into mush, but it doesn't.

"Little one … Good to see you … again," it says. It speaks almost in slow motion, like it has no reason to hurry and no concern with keeping up with anyone else. Its voice is low and heavy, like something that's bubbled up from deep within the earth.

"Elder," Hunter says before I can say anything. "This human is a threat to the Folk. "She's no longer a child and resists the glamour I'm capable of. I beseech you to once again weave a glamour that will remove all knowledge of us from her mind and compulse her to live out her life far from here," he says. I could try stabbing Hunter, but he has my good arm and I wouldn't make it far before the dog got me. After everything, I guess I've failed. I'm going to once again lose who I am, and then I'm going to die. My biggest regret is that I've just now managed a real connection with Grandma, and I'm about to lose that too.

"You wish to lose … your painful memories?" it asks, lowering its head to stare at me intently. For a second, I'm just confused. I didn't think it would care about my opinion.

"It's for the best," Hunter says.

"No," I say. "I don't want to lose my memories." Will it really be that easy?

"It doesn't matter what she wants. She's being manipulated by something. She's going to get herself killed or do something to my ward," Hunter says.

"I care not ... for your mission ..." the troll says. "I will not ... steal the girl's memories unasked ... she can die or live ... by her own choice."

"If that is your decision, elder," Hunter says. He takes a deep breath and releases my arm, turning to face me.

"This is it," he says. "The last of my patience is spent on this warning. There will be no more words between us. If you enter the glade again, I will kill you." He suddenly stops and coughs into his hand. As he brings his hand away from his mouth, I catch sight of a spattering of something dark, though he tries to hide it. I look back at his face, taking it in anew. He looks paler than I recall, and there's a tiny droplet of greenish blood dripping from his nose.

"Are you oathsick?" I ask. For a moment, I think he might respond, but instead he walks away into the trees. No more words. He meant it. Of course he had to mean it. He can't lie.

"You're very kind," I say to the troll, remembering the warning about giving direct thanks.

"I am tired ... now," it says, leaning back against the slope and closing its eyes.

"Wait, please. Before you go. You took my memories away once before, right? Can you give them back to me?" I ask. For a moment I'm worried it's already sleeping again, but then one of its eyes creaks open.

"Yes ... I took them because you asked ... But now you do not know ... what you ask be returned to you ... I will not return them ... You can find ... them yourself."

"How? I've seen some snippets, but I don't know how it works."

"You see … yourself as … the world around you … dreams of times passed," the troll says. It lets loose an enormous yawn and a large millipede skitters out between its stony teeth and away into the twilight.

"Wait. Please don't fall asleep yet. There's something else. I think I'm a faerie. Am I a faerie? Can you tell?" I ask. My only answer is a rumbling snore that seems to shake the ground and make the stream pebbles vibrate in place.

Chapter Fifteen

AFTER A BRIEF REST on the stream bank, I trudge back up the slope to Grandma's truck to get the gun, though having a weapon in my hands does nothing to make a plan materialize. My only choice is to what—hope I can get all the way to the glade by following the hiding runes, and then what? Shoot Hunter when he tries to stop me? I don't want to shoot anyone; I just want to rest.

A pair of headlights materialize out of the dark and slow down as they approach the bridge, coming to a stop next to where I'm sitting. I prepare to wave the good Samaritan away and insist I don't need help and then realize I recognize the truck.

"Tamsin!" Zach calls out as he rolls down the window. "Are you okay?"

"Mostly. What are you doing here?" I ask.

"I was heading to your house, actually. I wanted to check on you."

"I got into it with Hunter, but he's going to leave me alone for now," I say.

"Well, I brought my stash, just in case. It looks like we're going on an adventure," he says brightly.

"Zach, I appreciate how much you believe in me, but I don't want to ask you to do something that could get you hurt. I shouldn't have involved you," I say.

"If you're going, I'm going. Whatever you need to do, I'll make sure you do it," he says without hesitation.

"Well ... thank you, really. I think what I need to do is reach the center of the glade. Hopefully I'll figure out more by the time I get there. But Hunter told me in no uncertain terms that he'll kill me the second I set foot in there."

"Not if we get him first," Zach says.

"I don't want to kill him," I say. "He doesn't want to be doing this."

"He'd still kill you," Zach points out. "But I'll handle it however you want."

"And you could do it? You could just kill someone like that?"

"To protect you, yeah." The quickness and certainty of his reply is almost scary. Still, I'm glad I have a friend like him, though I still feel guilty bringing him with me.

Zach's weapon stash is spread out across the back seat of his truck. I go through it and consider taking a hunting knife, but I have nowhere to keep it and I need both hands to use Grandma's rifle. But something else catches my eye—the arrow that was lodged in the kelpie's jaw is lying on the floor of the cab. I must have left it there. That, I pick up, the beginnings of a plan—a truly stupid plan—swirling around in my mind. But that's something to deal with after dealing with the reason I came here. In all the commotion, I forgot it.

"Hey, do you think trees dream?" I ask Zach. I remember a conversation about that so long ago.

"I don't know," he says. He doesn't seem interested in the question, but the idea is stirring around in my mind. *You see yourself as the world around you dreams of times passed*. The trees' dreams. Maybe that's what I've been seeing this entire time.

"Grandma mentioned something happened here. I'm going to see if I can find out what it was," I say. Zach only looks confused. I let my mind drift, looking for a space between waking and sleeping, as I did in my bedroom while searching for that winter day. If I can tap into these dreams on purpose, maybe I can find out what happened here, even if there's no guarantee it will help me now.

I feel like I'm holding onto a slippery thread with just my mind, following it down into a swirl of images and sensations. Seasons pass in seconds, the wind ripples through my branches and my roots dig deep into the earth. For a moment, I'm lost in the vastness of this ancient life's memory, but I pull my consciousness back together and focus on tracing a single thread: me. Tamsin.

When I open my eyes, an adult, gun-toting Zach is still standing next to me, but as I concentrate and refocus my vision, I can also watch the sun rise and set impossibly fast as I encourage the trees around us to dream further and further into the past. I see images of Young and Teen Tamsin accompanied by Young and Teen Zach running in and out of the woods, sometimes escorted by Hunter or a hound and sometimes alone. I watch the images fly by, but none of them stand out to me.

And then, one night long ago, I see Hunter walking out of the woods carrying my bloody, unconscious teenage body. I focus on that, pulling that night around me like a blanket, but he doesn't say or do anything that gives me any information. Seeing it makes my heart and stomach lurch. I feel phantom, forgotten pains in my body as my mind fights to remember what happened that night. Whatever happened to me, it didn't start here. Grandma told me more or less how it ended; I need to get to the beginning.

"I need to follow this," I say.

"Follow what?" Zach asks.

"A memory. You can stay here and wait if you want," I say.

"I'll go with you, but I think we should be going to Thistledown and then straight to the glade," Zach says.

"That won't help us if I don't know what to do once I get there," I say. "Maybe one of these memories will tell me what I need to know. I've certainly forgotten plenty." Zach grunts what sounds like a disapproval but follows anyway.

The dream moves backward in a blur of images as Zach and I move further toward the beginning. It's disorienting to keep one eye in the present and one in the past, but I want to keep track of where I'm walking.

Finally, I reach a point where I can allow the dream to play forward and it might make sense. At this point, I'm relieved to see that we've come back to the safe path. Teen Zach and Tamsin are leaning on each other, both bloodied. Zach is far worse off, however. He has something that looks like a tree branch—or perhaps a large fang or claw—sticking out of his abdomen.

"It's okay. Thistledown can patch you up. It's just a little further to her house," Teen Tamsin says, struggling to pull Zach along. He grunts in response, seeming to be in too much pain to respond with words. I'm surprised by how strong I was, since it looks like Zach's feet aren't supporting much of his weight at all. The two of them make progress until Teen Tamsin's foot catches on a fallen branch and she stumbles, losing the tenuous stability that was keeping the two of them standing.

Teen Zach and Tamsin tumble to the ground, Tamsin almost landing on top of him. Zach cries out in pain as he lands, and the sound squeezes my heart. Whatever happened back then, I'm responsible for it. I resist the urge to help my past self pull him to his feet. I can't change any of this now.

"Hey, c'mon. I know it hurts, but you need to get up," Teen Tamsin says, trying to pull him to his feet.

"I'm scared," Teen Zach says. He's not trying to help her stand him up.

"I know. Please stand up. We're teammates, remember? We have to keep moving together." Zach looks at her sadly, as if he doesn't believe her. I tell myself that no matter how bad this looks, Zach survives, because he's standing right next to me in the present.

There's movement to the side as something scuttles out from between the trees. I start, but it ends up being Thistledown, and she focuses her attention on the children; she's not here in the present. At her approach, Teen Tamsin looks up.

"Thistledown!" she says. "Zach's hurt. Please help him." Thistledown comes to Zach's side and looks down at him, taking stock of his injuries.

"How did this come about?" she asks.

"We tried to get to the prison again, but Zach got hurt so we had to come back out," Teen Tamsin says. "Please help him."

"This happened before, yes? The last time you tried, you turned back in order to care for the boy?" Thistledown asks.

"Yeah. He was hurt. That was more important," Teen Tamsin says.

"I see," Thistledown says. "I shall help."

"Oh, thank you!" Teen Tamsin says. "Zach, Thistledown will patch you up. You can rest here. It's going to be okay." Zach noticeably relaxes a bit, though he's still obviously in extreme pain. Teen Tamsin sits back on her heels to give Thistledown room. Thistledown examines the thing—as I look at it closer I think it's either a pale tree branch or a bone—sticking out of him, and then she caresses his cheek with a finger.

"It will be alright, little dear," she says. And then with a single swift motion, she slits his throat with her nail.

Both my present and past selves scream in unison, though I somehow have the presence of mind to muffle myself with my hands. Teen Tamsin shoves Thistledown back with surprising savagery and throws herself over Teen Zach's body, trying to stop the blood flow from his neck with her hands. The initial spray covered her face with his blood.

The present Zach levels his rifle in the direction I'm looking. "What is it?" he asks. I ignore him.

"Why?" Teen Tamsin sobs. "You said you would help him!" While this unfolds, Thistledown looks on silently, irritation at Teen Tamsin's outburst twisting her features.

"I am helping, dear. I'm helping you. He was a fine playmate, but twice now he's held you back from what you must do, and you have so much waiting for you."

"Okay. I'll do it. I'll go back. Just save him," Teen Tamsin begs. Zach's blood leaks out from between her fingers.

"Oh, child. Listen to me. Thistledown knows what needs to be done. It will be okay. From here on it will be easier. Come to my home and I'll make you tea and cakes." Thistledown reaches out to touch Teen Tamsin's shoulder reassuringly. Tamsin bucks it off without taking her eyes off Zach.

"You're evil!" she screams. Thistledown has the gall to look hurt by that comment.

"Well," she says, "I'll just run along and start that tea, and you can join me when you've calmed yourself." With that, she scuttles back off into the shadows.

"Hunter!" Teen Tamsin screams into the darkness, "help!" Zach's panicked breathing gets weaker and weaker, his wide, terrified eyes locked on Teen Tamsin's face. He tries to speak, but all that comes out is a few bloody air bubbles. It sounds like he was trying to call for his mother.

"Everything's ... going to ..." *be okay.* That's what she wanted to say, but I know she doesn't believe it. I didn't believe it back then. And I'm a faerie. I can't lie. Instead, Teen Tamsin chokes on the words and cries harder because of her inability to offer Zach comfort. Hunter must be coming and must save him. Maybe the witch finds us. Even though I know Zach survives, this is no less horrifying to witness.

And then Zach's breathing stops; his eyes become unfocused and glassy. The only sound is Teen Tamsin's shuddering breathing as she keeps her hands pressed to Zach's neck, long after the blood stops flowing.

That's what she's doing when Hunter and his dogs arrive. Hunter's expression is unreadable as he looks at the scene. One of the dogs nudges Teen Tamsin reassuringly, and the other sniffs Zach's body.

"Don't touch him," Teen Tamsin snaps. The dog backs away obediently. "Save him," she says to Hunter, having finally noticed his presence.

"I can't bring back the dead. I don't think anyone can," Hunter says. His voice is soft, like he's trying to sound sympathetic. The words seem to make her realize Zach is dead. She sobs harder but doesn't remove her hands. Hunter kneels in front of her. Carefully, he takes her hands and lifts them away from Zach's body.

As he does this, Teen Tamsin finally seems to realize how much blood she's covered with and starts hyperventilating.

"What happened?" Hunter asks, scrutinizing Zach's wounds.

"It's my fault. It's my fault. It's my fault," is all Teen Tamsin says. She repeats the words over and over again.

"Tell him who did it!" I hiss, though I know none of them can hear me. My past self seems too hysterical to give Hunter any useful information. As Hunter tries to calm her, she grabs his tunic and cries into his shoulder. He very carefully puts an arm around her.

No words are said for a long time as Teen Tamsin cries, but she finally recovers enough to say something, it's just not the thing I was hoping to hear her say.

"I want to forget," she says. "Make me forget."

"I'm not strong enough anymore," Hunter says, "but I'll take you to the troll. He will make you forget these sad things, and we will glamour your grandmother to send you away from here, so the memories won't return." Teen Tamsin sniffles and nods.

"Will you take care of him?" she asks. She doesn't gesture to Zach's body, but the message gets across.

"Yes," Hunter says. "The dogs will stay with him until I return." He tries to help Teen Tamsin stand, but her legs buckle, so he puts a hand on her back and a hand behind her knees and picks her up like she weighs nothing. He vanishes as he walks back the way we came, toward the troll. True to their master's word, Hunter's dogs do stay and stand vigil over Zach's body.

I could allow the dream to continue to play out, but I can't look at it anymore. I let it fade and instead turn to look at the adult, alive, healthy Zach standing next to me.

"What?" he asks.

"Do you remember when I got sent to boarding school?" I ask.

"No, not really," he says.

"Do you remember any specifics about our adventures?"

"I remember we have to reach the prison. And that Thistledown was always nice to us," he says. "Are you done here? Should we head to the glade now?"

"Is that all you care about, the prison? You've been trying to push me in that direction this whole time—ever since I got back."

"Well, it's important, isn't it? That's why we kept going. I think you need to go there." With each word this person says to me I'm more and more sure Zach really has been dead for seven years.

I remove Thistledown's flower from where I hid it in my phone case and hold it in my open palm; I'm not sure how I'm supposed to use it to find her.

"Um, take me to Thistledown, please," I say to the flower. The wind catches it and takes it from my hand. But there isn't a breeze; it's drifting under its own power. I follow it, and Zach follows me.

We walk in silence from that point on, trailing the flower as it dips and rises in a nonexistent breeze. The thought of speaking to Zach creates a lump in my throat. I don't even know what I would say. Asking him if he remembers dying seems like a terrible way to bring it up. He seems like he wants me alive for now, but I don't know how he'll react if I reveal what I just learned.

I have to wonder about Thistledown's plan. Her goal seems to be that I make it to the glade, and now I assume she's the one responsible for Not-Zach since they seem to have the same goal. I also wonder about the witch. She also seems to want me to go to the glade, so I should assume she's also working with Thistledown. And all of them might be working for Leithe, maybe they'd all been tricked into making promises to him as well and were obligated on pain of death to help him. But if they were all working together, why wouldn't Leithe have told me I had allies?

It's as I mull all these questions over in my mind that we reach Thistledown's home. The flower settles on the ground in front of her door.

"Thistledown," I call, "I want to chat." I try to keep the edge out of my voice.

"Hello, darlings," Thistledown says, opening the door. "Would you like to come in for some tea?"

"Why did you kill him?" I ask her. Seeing her, I couldn't keep the question off my lips. Zach doesn't even seem bothered. Perhaps he doesn't even realize the question is about him.

"The troll's glamour is wearing off. Wonderful, wonderful," she says. "You have such a strong will."

"Thistledown," I say. "Why did you kill him?"

She sighs, giving me a look like she's preparing to indulge a child's silliness. "You weren't listening to me. You needed help focusing on what is important," she says slowly, as if that's the thing I'm having trouble understanding. "But I did realize how lonely you might be without a companion, so I asked the witch to make you a new boy, though I didn't realize until after that that the hunter and the troll conspired to send you away from here. I knew you'd be back, so I just had him wait for you." My hands tighten on the gun. The barrel twitches as I resist the urge to point it at her. I'm terrified by how much I want to shoot her right now. The fact that she doesn't seem to understand why I'm upset only infuriates me more. I take a deep, slow breath.

"So you were punishing me. And you made sure the new boy would want me to go to the glade," I say.

"Well, I suppose so. It made Thistledown so sad that you weren't listening. It was for you. You needed encouragement. I know you're strong enough to get through it, but I always worry about what the hunter and his allies do to your mind."

"Your plan is that I release the prisoner in the glade, right? Why is it me that needs to do that?"

"Because it's what you were raised for. This has been long in the making."

"And it's why you switched me with a human baby," I say. She seems surprised at the statement, but recovers quickly.

"That was to keep you safe. If the hunter knew you, he would kill you."

"He's already trying to kill me."

"Yes. You'll need to kill him sooner or later, in all likelihood."

"Why do you always default to murder?" I snap. "And where's the baby, Thistledown?"

"The poor mortal thing? It's of no consequence to this."

"It's of consequence to me!" I shout.

"Fine. Fine. There's no need to raise your voice," she chides. "I tended to the child as best I could and gave him to the witch."

"Is that where you got me? Who are my parents?"

"I've sworn oaths not to say. It was decided that you must discover that for yourself."

"*Who* decided that? I didn't." She says nothing. "Are you doing this for Leithe?" I press.

"No," she says. "I'm doing this for you. You've grown up like a human in the company of the courtless. You've known struggle, both for yourself and others. You could change it, if you choose to. That power is within your grasp. The resentment leaking out of the prison is poisoning the land and setting loose roaming monsters. But you could fix it. Everyone's lives depend on you. You'll do what needs to be done, won't you? You won't be alone. I've been helping you the whole way, holding your hand and nudging you along when you needed it."

"You killed one child and kidnapped another one, Thistledown. You killed my *friend*."

"There are more important things at hand. It will be worth it when you get where you need to be," she says insistently. "You didn't need those mortals."

"They were people; it didn't matter if I needed them or not!" I say.

She *tut-tuts* at me. "This is the problem. They were distracting you. They're gone now. You have far more important things to do. You can get new mortals when that's done," she says, as if offering me candy for a job well done. I take a deep breath and slowly exhale.

"If you won't tell me anything, I'll go get answers from someone else." Without another word, I turn to walk away. Zach immediately moves to follow.

"No," I say, turning to face him. "Don't come with me. I can't be around you right now."

"But I'm here to help you," he says, looking at me sadly. My anger quells a bit. I don't know how much of Thistledown's plan he's in on.

"Wait an hour, and then go to the glade. If I haven't made it there by then, just go home, okay?" I say. He nods, though he still looks disappointed.

"My dear," Thistledown says to my back. "I have the utmost faith in you, and what you could be. But I worry you will make no progress by yourself, not when you let yourself be distracted so easily. Don't forget that when you are lost, Thistledown's home is always open to you."

I don't answer.

I leave Thistledown's cottage and walk the path toward the witch's residence. Thistledown mentioned she "made" Not-Zach, so maybe she can tell me something Thistledown can't, or won't.

I don't get very far before I stop. The witch won't give me anything. I've already tried to get more information from her. She'll be just as useful as Thistledown. Instead, I circle back and head toward the creek.

"Leithe," I call out as soon as I'm pretty sure neither Not-Zach nor Thistledown followed me. For a moment, I think he's going to ignore me because he's still mad, but soon after I call for him, he walks out from behind one of the tree trunks. He leans on the trunk, crosses his arms, and waits for me to speak first. As I probably should.

"I said all those things to make you angry so the wraiths would attack and I could get away from Hunter," I say. "And I had to get away from Hunter so I can free you." I want to apologize, but Thistledown warned me that saying things like that could get me even more indebted to him.

"You could have just *asked*," he says.

"I did, remember? You said no."

"I'm still not pleased," he says, pushing himself off the tree to fall in step with me.

"I know. I'll admit the stuff about your betrothed was pretty bad," I say.

"Is that all you called me for?" he asks. "To say that? You're not even going to beg for my forgiveness?"

"No. I am not," I say. I think more about it. Why did I call him? Why did I care enough to explain myself? "I just found out my only friend was murdered by someone I thought was on my side," I say. That's it. I called him because I'm alone, it's dark, and I wanted someone—anyone—to talk to.

"Well? What did you do about it?" he actually sounds intrigued, like this is juicy gossip to him.

"Nothing. I'm just sad about it and you're literally the only person I could tell."

"Why did you think that person was on your side?" he asks.

"She seemed nice, and she helped me before."

"That's foolish. Unless you've exchanged Names and vows, you should never assume someone is on 'your side.'"

"Names and vows, you mean like being married?"

"Humans have a similar ceremony, yes? Something about name giving and taking? For us, the strongest of marriage vows is the exchanging of Names—true names. They have yours, and you have theirs. It is an unbreakable alliance, a promise of complete loyalty. A way to know you have one ally against the rest of the world."

"I can't tell if that's supposed to be romantic or pragmatic."

"Can it not be both? But back to your problem: perhaps you can use your wish for revenge. I'm sure we could think up something lovely," he says with relish.

"I'll have to think about it, I guess," I say. I was going to use my wish to cure Grandma, but now I hopefully won't need to do that. "Actually, I think I do have a question for you: can you tell if someone is a faerie or not?"

"Can you tell the difference between a blade of grass and an oak tree? A human like yourself and a bug?"

"Why is it always bug comparisons with you people? Yes. Fine. I get your point," I say. I hesitate. Even with the things I've seen, this seems like a foolish question. "So … I look like a human to you, right?" Leithe's face shifts through a series of expressions. First he seems to think I'm an idiot again, then he looks at me thoughtfully like I'm asking a trick question, then he seems to go back to thinking I'm an idiot.

"You look utterly human to me," he says. I feel disappointed, and Leithe seems to see it on my face. "Why ask such a question?"

"It's stupid. I thought I saw in the past that when my mother gave birth, a faerie switched her baby with a different one. But it was probably wrong, maybe just wishful thinking—that I might be special or something."

"Some glamours are powerful enough to make a faerie appear human, but even then, it's unlikely I wouldn't be able to see through it," he relents. "I can't relate to you, but I suppose it's natural to wish to be more than you are."

"It's not that. I just feel so out of place, like I don't belong here. I guess I thought this would give me the chance to fit in somewhere else," I say. He laughs at that, at me, and I feel my face get hot. "What's so funny?"

"You wouldn't fit in with us. No one would welcome you. You don't know our ways. You would feel just as suffocated and alone as you do right here. You would just be surrounded by different enemies," he says. Even though I want to argue, he's probably right.

As we walk, the night gets darker, as if the tree boughs close ranks to block out the moon and stars. I end up having to rely on my cell phone for light, which to my chagrin I realize I haven't charged in a while and it's running at eight percent. I trip while trying to keep the phone flashlight pointed ahead of me instead of at my feet.

"There's a rock," Leithe says.

"You could have said so sooner," I snap.

"I saw it. I assumed you saw it."

"If you can see in the dark, can you at least tell me before I trip on things?" I ask.

"I ..." Leithe trails off. I look over at him; he's staring off into space. "The dark. It's dark. This is another mockery. Another way to taunt me." Agitated shadows begin whipping around him.

"This is real. Calm down" I say. I reach toward him, even though I can't touch him. He snarls and lashes out at me. I recoil, and then he's gone. I sigh and keep heading toward the creek.

When the tree canopy ends, I exit onto a riverbank bathed in moonlight. Tiny motes of soft light dance against the wind. I think I've successfully made it to the right place in Faerie—the kelpie's domain. The kelpie doesn't seem to be around, however. Even when I sit on the riverbank and wait for a while, it doesn't show up. I was hoping it would sense an intruder and come investigate, but that doesn't seem to be the case.

Onto the next plan, then. I take out Zach's pocket knife and carefully cut a line vertically down my forearm and allow some blood to fall into the water. Maybe kelpies are like sharks.

It doesn't take long. Far from the bank, I see a dark shape rise just above the water's surface. As it gets closer to shore, I see that it's the kelpie's head. It rises out of the water and trods onto the shore, its hooves rising and sinking in the mud. I take a deep breath.

"Hi," I say. "I want to propose a temporary alliance. You don't like Hunter, right? Well, I want to do something that will really piss him off," I say. The kelpie's nostrils flare, and he snorts.

"Do you bring a gift?" he asks, giving me a look at his crocodile teeth.

"I can get you one. I could bring you a bunch of meat, lots of different kinds," I say.

"No gift," he muses. "How rude." And then he charges, opening his mouth wide.

I take Hunter's arrow from behind my back and bring it around. It seems to guide my hand by its own power; it knows where Hunter wanted it to go. It pierces the kelpie's flesh and sinks into the bone, once again locking the creature's jaw in place. The kelpie tries to snap his jaws shut around my neck, but bone grinds against the arrow. I fear for a moment that the steel will bend or shatter, but it doesn't.

"I'll remove it if you help me. You know that's not an offer you'll get from Hunter," I say. Slowly, with hate in his corpse-white eyes, the kelpie backs away until he's no longer bearing over me. I take this to mean he's accepted our deal.

"I need you to get me to the center of the glade before Hunter can kill me. That's all you need to do. Once I'm there, you can leave, and I'll come find you when I'm done with my business and take the arrow back out. I'll even destroy it in front of you so this can't happen again. So can you do that?" I ask. He snorts and nods.

"I'm going to get on your back, then. And I need you to turn that sticky power you have off. Can you do that?" He nods again. I reach out to grab his mane, then stop.

"Then do it now, and keep it off until I remove the arrow," I say. The kelpie rolls his eyes and nods again. I take a deep breath, and then clumsily pull myself onto the creature's back. He doesn't bend or kneel to make it easier for me, which I don't blame him for. At least he can get some joy out of watching me struggle to get on a horse for the first time in more than ten years.

Chapter Sixteen

Out of everything I've done in the past several weeks, riding a kelpie has to be the most terrifying. The creature must go out of his way to terrorize me. I think he runs under several low-hanging branches on purpose, trying to knock me off. I press myself tight against his neck, arms wrapped around it, knees pressed into his sides. I've never ridden a horse bareback before; my thigh muscles feel like they'll give out any second, and I'm bouncing against his back so much I'll have bruises everywhere when this is done, assuming I'm still alive.

We fly through the night; when the kelpie hits the fog at a full gallop it's as if we've plunged into an icy soup. We break through into the glade, and I risk a glance up to see the twin trees in the center. We're heading straight toward them. I almost let myself feel hope, and then the kelpie jerks violently to the side to avoid an arrow that just barely misses sinking into his neck.

Hunter is near the edge of the glade. By the time I locate him, he's already fired another arrow; this one grazes the kelpie. In the corner of my eye, I see Hunter's hound racing in from another direction. The dog gains on us. I try to will the kelpie to go faster, but he moves erratically, perhaps to throw Hunter's aim off.

All I can do is hold on and pray we reach the center before Hunter's hound or arrows reach us, but hope doesn't get us very far. I feel a sudden impact and the kelpie screams in pain. An arrow is sunk deep into the kelpie's front shoulder. The kelpie stumbles, but catches himself and continues running, though slower.

I brace myself for another impact, but instead I hear a gunshot. Hunter stumbles, and I see Zach run closer and ready his rifle for another shot. Hunter's dog diverts from its path and instead runs toward Zach in order to aid its master. Hunter turns to face Zach. Hopefully the opening Zach gave me will be enough.

As we get closer, the fog envelops us and time slows. The air gets heavy, and the distance between us and the trees seems to expand and distort. The edges of my vision blur and I see strange shapes dancing in my periphery. All I can hear is the sound of my own and the kelpie's breathing.

There's a gust of wind near the back of my thigh, and the kelpie screams and stumbles again. An arrow protrudes from the kelpie's side. The creature slows. He won't be able to keep this pace up. But I only need to get a little farther.

And then something hits me in the lower back, and pain explodes like a wildfire throughout my body. I slip from the kelpie's back and hit the ground.

My legs won't work; hand over hand, I drag my useless body forward. I'm almost there. I'm so close. The trees loom over me, their branches reaching forward in welcome, and darkness envelops me.

I'm pushing forward against a corporeal darkness that threatens to suffocate me. There's a dull roar in my ears that grows in intensity until it drowns out everything else—even the pain from Hunter's arrows. Each step is harder than the last. I don't know where I am, or where I'm going, only that I can't turn back. This will be my only chance.

Suddenly my ears pop from pressure, and the roar is thrown into terrifying clarity. Flashes of shapes explode into motion as the darkness is ripped from my eyes like a veil.

I'm in the middle of a battlefield. The sky is a blood-red open wound, dripping with fire. Winged things fly high above and contend with waves of arrows. Bloody feathers drift down from those that are struck.

Creatures clash all around me. Close by, two lightly armored human-sized soldiers battle a giant. It looks around fifteen feet tall, with sagging milk-white flesh like uncooked dough encased in jagged black metal armor. It swings a massive mace with both hands. The smaller combatants dance around the giant, slicing at it with delicate blades. They seem to have the upper hand until one of them dodges out of the way of the giant's mace and gets struck in the arm by an arrow shot from somewhere else on the battlefield. The arrow distracts the soldier long enough for the giant to grab their head in one pale fist and crush it with a horrible crunch. The giant drops the body on the ground and turns to the remaining soldier.

The soldier flees straight past me, and the giant lumbers after. I throw myself out of the giant's way and stagger into the path of another soldier on horseback bearing down on a different giant, spear brandished.

In my panic to get out of the horse's path I trip on something hard and fall, cradling my head in my arms. The horse flies over me and the rider's spear and giant's armored fist clash with a metallic screech.

Corpses cushion my fall. I land on the torso of a dead soldier that's been disemboweled; her lacquered wooden breastplate shattered. Instead of blood and human organs, fungal tendrils and milky liquid spill from her abdomen. Rapid decay spreads from her eyes, nose, mouth, and wounds, transforming her skin into white spores that detach and float into the chaos all around.

I cover my mouth with my shirt collar and crawl away on my hands and knees, over countless other bodies. Many have human features aside from one or two striking differences—skin of bark and hair a tangle of leaves and flowers, or the claws and fangs and mane of a beast. I wonder if these are real people, or if they're set dressing for this dream. I wonder if I die here would my body lay here with them forever? Would I wake up? I don't want to find out.

Jagged bits of armor and broken weapons poke and jab at me. I see a dagger still clutched in a body's hand, but as I'm trying to free it a giant's foot comes down close to me and shakes the ground so much that I abandon the weapon and keep going.

I don't know where I'm going. I can focus on nothing but dodging feet and praying no one pays any attention to me. I press close to the side of a fallen giant to avoid another wave of mounted cavalry as they crash into another wave of giants. For the moment, I seem to be in a relatively safe spot where I can get my bearings, and then a sudden cold breeze blows in.

The giant I thought was dead twitches, shudders, and begins to rise. I scramble away and into another corpse that's awkwardly wobbling to its feet. All over the battlefield, bodies stand up and launch themselves at the giants. This seems to turn the tide somewhat; the giants are pushed back and the other army steadily advances.

Behind me, a roiling cloud of black smoke crawls along the ground. Hands and arms reach out from the mass, grab the earth, and pull it along. Humanoid silhouettes break free from the cloud and fly into dead bodies, after which the corpses rise and join the battle.

Leading the cloud is an armored figure riding a great undead stag. The stag's flesh is sloughing off in places and its empty eye sockets ooze black smoke. The rider's armor looks like it's made of bone and includes a bear skull helmet that completely hides their face. They hold a pitch-black greatsword in one hand. They're flanked by pallid soldiers also armored in bone and equipped with spears and round shields.

Whispers and shouts ripple across the field, repeating the same words.

"The Crawling Court. The dead host has come," I hear the soldiers around me say with mixtures of awe and fear.

The figure on the stag surveys the battlefield and the bear skull's empty eye sockets settle on me. They point at me with their sword and pull the stag's reins to veer in my direction.

I run, not wanting to know what that creature wants with me. There are fewer bodies to trip over in my path, though more moving creatures to dodge. I bump into a few soldiers, but they don't pay me any attention, focused instead on their enemies.

I think I can hear the stag's hooves gaining ground behind me. And then a section of the ground in front of me opens like a trap door, revealing an underground structure and a young blond girl. Myself, I realize, at about age seven or so.

"Get in!" she orders. I obey her and jump, landing on something soft, bouncing, and rolling off onto a hard floor.

The girl—Young Tamsin, the same age she was in several of my visions—pulls the trapdoor shut behind her. With the door shut, the sounds of battle vanish.

We're in my bedroom, as it looked many years ago, which isn't that different from how it looks today. The light is dim, and primarily comes tinged blue from the whale-shaped night light by the bed. The paint on the walls is less faded and the dresser is less scuffed. The most notable difference is the drawings taped all over the walls. Some I recognize from Grandma's safe.

"You're wearing normal clothes," Young Tamsin says to me, climbing down from the dresser on which she needed to stand to reach the ceiling. "Everyone's wearing clothes from *Lord of the Rings*,"

"I came from outside here. I'm trying to free the prisoners," I say.

She crosses her arms and scrutinizes me. "If you're a grown-up, shouldn't you be better at things?"

"I don't think being a grown-up automatically makes you better at anything," I say. "Where did you come from?"

"I'm on a quest to save the forest. I had to save some people trapped somewhere, But when I got close I got stuck here instead," she says. As she speaks, she sits down on the floor, opens up a sketchbook, and starts drawing with a set of colored markers splayed across the floor.

"How long have you been here?" I ask, sitting down on the bed.

"I don't know," she shrugs. "A while. My friend Zach was here but I think he got out. Have you seen him?" She studies my face and then returns to her drawing; a humanoid figure begins to take shape on the page.

"I didn't see him on the battlefield. I think he made it out of the dream, but I'm not sure of anything these days." Who's to say Zach didn't leave something of himself behind in this dream? It appears that I did. "Do you know why this bedroom is underneath that battleground?" I ask.

She looks at me like the question is idiotic. "I made it," she says. "You just have to think about something really hard, and you make it, because this is a dream. I figured that out really fast."

"I guess you're really smart."

"My grandma says so," she says matter-of-factly. She draws my clothes. I study her other drawings; there's one of Grandma reading a book, one of Hunter's dogs, several depicting the combatants above, of giants and undead soldiers. There's one of the figure on the stag.

"Do you know what they're fighting about up there?" I ask.

"No. They fight and fight but no one ever wins. They might move around but nothing *really* changes. I guess they just hate each other." She draws the details of my face and hair. My expression on the page is sad and scared.

"The witch told me the prisoners are trapped by their own minds. I wonder if that's why no one ever makes progress," I muse, more to myself than to her. For a while, the only sound is that of markers sliding across paper.

"I think this is where the bad things come from. I got attacked by zombie sprites once. I think they came from here but didn't know they weren't still here, so they just attacked everything," Young Tamsin says.

"Do you think this is Leithe's dream, then?"

"I don't know," she says. She holds her drawing up and compares it to me. "I'm not *afraid* to go out there, by the way."

"I didn't think that. I think it's smart to gather information," I say. She nods, taping the new drawing onto the wall.

"Thank you for helping me," I continue. "But I can't stay here for too long. I'm worried I'm going to run out of time." Young Tamsin nods.

"Um, where's the door?" I ask. Young Tamsin only offers a disgusted groan.

"You have to *make* it," she says. "You're probably gonna die if you leave. Thistledown said I was the only one who could do the quest."

"Thank you for the warning, but I'm going to try anyway," I say. I have a few choice things I want to say about Thistledown, but none I should say in front of a child.

Standing on the bed, I put my hand on the ceiling and imagine the trapdoor opening back up. Lines appear in the wood as if drawn in marker, and then there's a trapdoor.

"Thank you again, for helping me," I say. She ignores me. She's already drawing a new picture.

I push the trapdoor up just a bit and peek out. The battle is still raging, but no one pays any attention to me; the figure on the stag is gone. I hoist myself out, and Young

Tamsin looks up and speaks just before I close the door behind me.

"You can make a door anywhere," she says. "If you need to run away."

"I'll remember that," I say. When the door shuts, the seam vanishes and it's like it was never there.

I turn my attention to the battlefield. There's still fighting all around me and it takes all my concentration to avoid thrashing giant limbs and wildly swinging weapons.

Young Tamsin was right—the battle doesn't seem to have made any progress in the time I was in the bedroom. The giants, smaller soldiers, and the undead—the Crawling Court—are still locked in a battle where no significant ground has been taken by either side. I strain my eyes to find something—anything—that stands out from the rest of the fight, anything that might give me a clue of how to get through this. But the land is flat and unremarkable, and the sky is unchanging.

It's because I'm scanning the horizon that I don't see the giant until it staggers into me and sends me flying. A half dozen smaller soldiers rush forward to surround it, jabbing with long spears while I cough and wheeze on the ground, failing to catch my breath. The giant raises its club and swings. The blow strikes several soldiers, crushing armor and probably bone as well. The club goes over my head, leaving a gust of wind in its wake.

The giant takes a spear in the stomach from the remaining soldier, but instead of recoiling it grabs the spear and wrenches it out of the soldier's hands, pulling the man forward and sending him off-balance just long enough for the giant to crush him as well. And then it turns to me.

I hope I'll be beneath the giant's notice so long as I don't move, but it looks at me with its bloodshot eyes and swings the club almost casually, as if knowing it doesn't need to put any effort in. I scramble backward, tripping over broken corpses.

I try to make something—a shield, a wall, a glowing barrier—like how Young Tamsin described, but I can't focus on anything but the club as it comes down.

The club impacts the ground directly in front of me, sending a shockwave radiating outward. I'm confused for a moment, and then realize the attack missed because someone has thrown an arm around my chest and is wrenching me upward and backward.

I'm pulled onto the zombie stag in front of the rider and have to twist to get a good look at my rescuer's bear skull helmet.

"You don't belong here," the figure says. I recognize the voice.

"Leithe!" I shout. The giant winds back to strike with the club again. It swings, and to my shock the stag catches the club in its antlers and twists, nearly tearing the club from the giant's grasp. Leithe leans forward and slashes at the giant with his sword; the giant recoils with just a thin bloody line marring its forearm.

"You barely nicked it!" I say, throwing one leg over the stag's neck so I'm straddling it.

"Oh, watch," he says. As he speaks, the wound begins to bleed fog that coalesces on the ground, and the giant's flesh starts withering before my eyes. It drops its club, and other combatants make quick work of it.

"Who's Leithe? Who are you? How did you come to be here?" he asks. What relief I felt is gone, replaced by confusion. I swore I recognized his voice.

"I'm Tamsin. I'm just trying to pass through. I'm not trying to cause any trouble for you or your people."

"You called me Leithe … I didn't use that name in this time; I didn't start using it until much later," he says. So it is him.

The stag moves with little direction from Leithe, avoiding the worst clusters of combat. Shadows follow in its footsteps, slipping into fallen warriors and raising them to rejoin the fight.

"I think you're dreaming about the past. Things aren't going to go exactly how you remember them."

"Right. It's coming back to me. I led my court's forces against the Deep Host long ago. And I've met you before, in the present."

"Yes. You made a deal with me to free you."

"Then do so. What are you waiting for?"

"You need to kiss your betrothed. That will break the prison and free you both."

"She isn't here. At this point in the battle she hadn't yet arrived on the field," he says.

"Who's at war? How does this battle play out?" I ask.

"This is the final battle between the Deep Host and the courts. Every court sent its armies. I led the Crawling Court's forces as my king's champion." He studies the field thoughtfully. I feel him tense behind me. "This moment is the lull before the final push."

"This is the *lull*?" Countless overlapping screams of agony and victory punctuate my question.

"The king of the Deep Host hasn't taken the field yet. That will be when the fighting is at its worst." As he speaks, there's an expanding rumble from the giants' side that rises to a cacophonous roar of countless giant voices chanting in unison.

"Sounds like he's here," Leithe says. Somewhere in the distance, I see a glint of something bright, like sunlight reflected off a piece of glass. A moment later there's a massive explosion in the same spot. The shockwave sends the surrounding soldiers flying and even causes the stag to stumble. The heat and light are so intense my eyes fill with tears that immediately sizzle away.

"How did you beat him?" I ask.

"With great difficulty," he says. "And it would be wrong to say that I beat him. It was a united effort by the monarchs, of which I am not one. He had the power to incinerate anything that fell under his gaze."

"It's your dream, can't you just turn him into a little frog or something?"

"I'm not a native of the Dreaming Court; dreamcraft isn't my specialty, but I spent enough time among dream fae to tell this dream was woven by a master. I could never unravel and re-weave it," he shouts over the explosions that ripple across the field.

"I met a kid that could do it!" I shout.

"Fine!" Leithe turns the stag toward where a figure approaches who towers even over the other giants. With how the giants fall over themselves to get out of the way, it can be no one but the king. He's encased in black armor with a crown of horns on his helmet. Bloody red points of light ooze from behind the helmet's faceplate.

Leithe raises a hand toward the giant king and seems to concentrate. All that happens is the king levels his gaze toward us and his eyes brighten to a piercing intensity, and everything is on fire—the air, my skin, everything around me must be burned to ash in a second.

But then I take a breath. My throat burns and I choke on ash but I'm still alive. Leithe and I are on the ground and he's holding the charred remains of his cloak over us as a shield. All around us, ash drifts lazily in the air and the shadows of dead soldiers are burned into the rocky ground—so is the shadow of Leithe's stag. Much of Leithe's armor is charred and falling away in large flakes. He rips off his damaged helmet and tosses it to the ground in annoyance.

The king of the Deep Host continues his advance, striking down any that approach him with a large blade. He seems distracted from us for the moment. The court soldiers regroup and surround him, but their spears bounce uselessly off his armor and he seems to enjoy slowly picking them off.

My legs buckle. I can only stay standing by holding onto Leithe's arm. My skin is untouched even though it felt like I must have been burned.

"What can we do?" I whisper, unable to raise my voice any higher.

"Nothing," Leithe says. He leans on the greatsword like it's a cane. "I fought back then, but it made no difference. It won't make any difference now."

"Who beat him originally?" I ask. "Tell me how it happened. Leithe." I shake his shoulder when he doesn't respond.

"... We lost ground. His gaze burned everything to ash so there was nothing left for my forces to puppet," he says.

"But the courts won, right? You said they won," I prod.

"They didn't arrive together. The first was the Blooming Queen." The king of the Deep Host finishes playing with the attacking soldiers and notices us still standing in the middle of the wasteland he created, and his gaze focuses on us again.

"What did the Blooming Queen do, Leithe?" I shout.

Trees explode from the earth where the giant king is standing, wrapping around his legs and climbing up to entrap him completely. The attack causes him to look down, and the inferno that would have enveloped me and Leithe instead erupts in front of us.

When I can see again, there's a figure locked in combat with the giant king. At this distance, I can't tell if she's completely made of wood, but her lower half looks like a spider formed of vines and branches. Though her torso looks around the size of a normal human, because of her lower half she almost reaches the king's height. She moves quickly, and where she strikes the king with her thorned legs, plants grow from the wound. Where she strikes him with the whip in her hands, stringing, biting insects burst from gaps in his armor. Any wounds she suffers quickly grow over with new bark or become new biting, gnashing mouths. My plan is working. This dream seems to respond to Leithe's memories, even if he can't consciously change the events.

"And she beats him?" I ask. It seems like she has the upper hand. Perhaps he's too cautious to use his gaze powers on something so close to him.

"No," Leithe says. The king of the Deep Host impales the Blooming Queen through the chest with his sword. The flesh touching the blade burns and smokes as if the blade had just come off a forge. Her body regrows as fast as the blade burns it away, and vines spread around the weapon, keeping the king from removing it. They're in a stalemate; neither of them will surrender the sword.

"The Crawling King arrives next," Leithe continues. The surrounding area seems to darken, and an indistinct mass rises from the cracked-open ground and takes a rough humanoid shape armed with a spear. It moves to impale the giant through the chest, who twists and instead takes the blow with his arm. The flesh around the wound begins to blacken and rot, but not nearly fast enough.

"And they defeat him?" I ask.

"Nearly, so he takes a gamble that might have no one win," Leithe says. The giant king's eyes flare brightly—so much so that I have to shield my eyes—and I wait for the wave of roaring heat, but it doesn't come.

"Look," Leithe says. Instead of fire, all around us are shimmering, multicolored butterflies that shed sparkling dust into the air as they flutter outward and away.

"This is the first time I witnessed the extent of her power," he says. "Her ability to exert her will on the world was unmatched. She took the king of the Deep Host's fire and made it something beautiful." He speaks with raw wonder in his voice.

"Who is she?" I ask.

"The Dreaming Queen, Queen Mab," he says reverently. The butterfly swarm clears enough for me to see the arrival of a woman in a chariot, riding over the field. The chariot looks organically shaped and is pulled by countless white moths.

The woman herself radiates an inner light. The glow is calming, like a light in the dark. She has long cream-colored hair that streams behind her as she rides, back straight and face forward, hands clasping the curved front of the chariot with calm regality. She doesn't wear armor. Instead, she wears a diaphanous gown, the train of which is so long a second group of moths flutter behind her to hold it off the ground.

The Dreaming Queen rides past us without sparing a glance. She circles the three monarchs locked in combat. The king of the Deep Host snarls with rage and forces his blade deeper into the Blooming Queen's torso, twisting it as he goes. He then relinquishes the blade to spin around and grab the Crawling King's spear in his gauntleted hand. With his other hand, he punches the Crawling King in the head, whose body collapses into rot and skittering insects, and turns back to face the Blooming Queen. She's fallen to her knees, and the giant king stands over her, apparently savoring his impending victory.

"Who shows up next?" I ask.

"No one," Leithe says. He seems strangely relaxed compared to moments ago. I'm confused until a spear pierces one of the giant king's eyes from behind. The spear seems to shatter reality around it, and the rotted mass I took for the Crawling King dissipates, replaced with him standing unharmed behind the giant king. In the same moment, the figure of the Blooming Queen on the ground vanishes as well, and instead she's standing nearby, where she places her hands on the giant king and sends cutting vines rippling through his skin. The vines travel through the king's body until they erupt through his remaining eye.

"The Dreaming Queen trapped him in a glamour long enough for the others to defeat him. She is the master of the domain of dreams. She showed him what he desired, and he embraced it to the detriment of all else."

"Then let's ask her how to get through this dream," I say. I take a step forward, but Leithe grabs my wrist and stops me.

"You can't just walk up to a *queen*. She didn't even know who I was when this took place," he says. I can't help but let out a giggle before composing myself. He glares at me.

"Sorry. You just sound so flustered, like you're a normal person. Not in a bad way. Wait." Realization dawns on me. "Is this lady the fiancée you're always talking about?" It might be my imagination, but I think his cheeks get the faintest hint of pink.

"This is long before that," he says. Something catches my eye—the lack of something, rather. The space we're in seems to be shrinking, surrounded by nothing but white.

"We're running out of time! Go kiss her!" I try to pull him forward, but he doesn't budge.

"That can't really be *her*. She would never be trapped, playing out a role like this. She wouldn't have been fooled for a moment by this dream."

"Well, go try anyway. Maybe it'll be a good enough loophole," I beg.

"I ... can't. She wouldn't accept me."

"Well, when did things change?" I ask. The wave of nothingness gets closer, and I see entire chunks of the environment get eaten away. I hope this is a sign he's waking up, though maybe in the waking world I'm finally dying from Hunter's arrow.

Leithe murmurs something in response to my question, so quietly I can't hear it.

"What?" I ask, pressing closer to his face.

"Elsewhere," he whispers. "It changed in Elsewhere. Beyond the end of Faerie." His words fade as the nothingness reaches us like a snapping rubber band. The white void is blinding, and I shield my eyes. There's a roar in my ears and I cradle my head in my hands to keep it out. I try to call for Leithe, but my words are lost as soon as they leave my mouth.

I don't know how long I cower like this. Shifting patterns dance across the inside of my eyelids; I pick apart the roaring enough to hear voices speaking a language I don't understand. Every so often I think I hear a snippet of a word I know, but no matter how hard I strain I can't tell what the voices are saying.

I peek at my surroundings through my fingers and let my hands down when it's clear the brightness is no longer an issue. I'm in a place full of colors and nothing else. There are streams of different colored fog mixing and separating in patterns that make my head hurt to watch. There's every color imaginable—every hue and shade and some I've somehow never seen before. There's no breeze—the fog moves of its own accord, as does the layer of grass under my feet. Voices speak all around me, just at the edges of my perception, but there aren't any people connected to them.

"Leithe?" I call out. My own voice echoes all around me, reverberating in my ears. *Leithe? Leithe?* The sound shifts until it doesn't sound like my voice at all, but other voices that I'm just barely unable to connect to faces. The words they speak shift until it sounds like they're calling my name. The voices sound fearful, angry, beckoning. For a moment one sounds just like Grandma, calling, coaxing me awake from a bad dream. I see her in the corner of my eye, but when I whip around there's nothing but a swirl of color mixing back into the endless fog.

Lacking any other direction, I walk. The grass cushions my footsteps, but the sound of my breathing is magnified and echoes into new whispers in the fog around me. As I walk, I see more shapes in the corners of my eyes. Some look like regular people; some look far too tall, angled or stretched-out to be human. Some don't look human at all. All of them vanish if I turn to face them.

I don't know how long I walk. The grass seems to catch around my ankles, occasionally making me stumble. Sometimes I call for Leithe; sometimes it sounds like he calls back, but even if I run full tilt in the voice's direction, I never find him.

I trip on something hard and fall forward, landing on my knees and palms. I run my fingers over warped wooden boards. It seems I fell on a short flight of steps that lead to a wooden platform. A porch, I realize, as the front wall of a house materializes out of the fog in front of me. This is the Randall Place.

Curious, I stand up and open the door. The creaking hinges sound like laughter. The fog isn't any thinner inside; I can make out the stairs up to the second floor on the right, and stripped-bare floor of the living room on the left. A few more feet, picking my way around exposed carpet nails, and I can make out the back of the couch arched like a fat cat in front of the cold fireplace.

"What is this, some horrific vision of my future?" a girl's voice says. She comes into view as I take a step around the side of the couch. She's curled up on the cushions glaring up at me defiantly. "Try again, evil fog." It's me, but with longer hair and a rounder face. Her arms are curled tightly around her knees.

"Do I really look that bad?" I ask. She tilts her head thoughtfully.

"You should have made yourself look more like my shitty Grandma, that would have been *scary*," she snaps.

"Do you mind if I sit?" I ask. She grunts and I take it as permission. The couch in the real Randall Place is more comfortable, even with the mildew.

"I have a lot of issues with my Grandma," I say. "But I think there's a chance for something good between us in the future. I hope so." I rub a tear out of my eye. Teen Tamsin stares aggressively into the empty fireplace and doesn't speak, but I see tears welling up despite her best efforts.

"Whatever, fog lady," she says.

"How did you end up at the Randall Place?" I ask. She ignores me for a moment, but the urge to talk wins out.

"We were in the middle of this battlefield, but then I ended up in this fog somehow, and this is the only building I've found," she says. "My friend was with me, but I think he might have gotten hurt. If I asked if you've seen him, would you even tell me the truth?"

"Zach?" I ask. She nods. The words want to roll up into a lump in my throat, but I force them out anyway.

"He didn't make it out," I say. "I'm sorry. I couldn't save him." A sob bubbles out of my throat and I press my mouth into my hands until I recover. Teen Tamsin watches silently.

"It's my fault," she says. "It's all my fault. I brought him here, and now I can't save anyone."

"It's not your fault," I say. "You wanted to help, and other people were willing to take advantage of that. I'm going to try to fix what I can."

"Can you save Hunter, at least?" she asks.

"I don't know. I'm going to try. Do you want to come with me?" I ask. She looks me over and for a moment I think she's going to say yes.

"No," she says. "I can't go back out there. The voices, the things in the fog ..." She stops and starts several times, but can't seem to find the right words.

"I understand, but I have to go. I don't know how much more time I have here," I say. She doesn't call out or try to stop me from leaving, but simply turns back to stare into the empty fireplace.

Walking away from the Randall Place, all I want to do is turn back so she doesn't have to wait there alone. I wonder if the house serves as a refuge or a prison for her. Is it similar to Young Tamsin's hidden bedroom—a safe, familiar place to hide? Maybe Young Tamsin's bedroom was just as much a prison as that house in the mists.

I have to keep moving or nothing will change. I have to trust that I'm moving even if I can't see what's in front of me.

I don't call out for Leithe since the words will only twist in the air and return to me as echoes, but I do keep him in my mind as I go. I imagine Leithe approaching me out of the fog. I see him in every silhouette that stalks me. And eventually I simply close my eyes and cover my ears to shut out the creeping fog and the voices that just sound like they're mimicking the idea of human speech without understanding the words.

I walk blind until I stumble over something hard. I worry it will be the front steps of the Randall Place again, but it looks like a block of stone flooring. Further on, the outline of a ruined building is visible through the fog. It's little more than the patchwork remains of a stone floor and a single wall that rises until it starts to curve in what might have once been a dome. The ruins seem to be just as empty as the rest of this place, until I see a hunched figure leaning against what's left of a raised dais.

"Hello?" I ask softly. The figure doesn't respond. I get closer until I'm in front of them, then kneel down to their level. What I thought might be a hood is actually a mass of unkempt dark hair falling over the figure's face and shoulders.

As I suspected, it's Leithe, though I didn't expect to see him in such bad shape. His skin is sallow and cheeks hollow, and he has dark circles under his eyes. His eyes themselves are glazed over and don't focus on me even when I'm right in front of him.

"Leithe," I say. "It's Tamsin. Do you remember me?" He doesn't acknowledge my presence, so I gently put a hand on his shoulder; he flinches away from my touch.

"You creatures have finally come in the flesh to claim me?" he asks. His voice cracks as if he hasn't used it in a long time.

"I came to help you," I say. Leithe laughs weakly.

"Now I know you're not real. No one would come here to help me," he says. "I failed my quest. It was doomed from the start."

"But someone does come to save you, right?" I ask. He doesn't answer, so I prod further. "I asked you about the time it all changed with the Dreaming Queen, and we ended up here. Beyond the end of Faerie, right? So that must mean you meet her somewhere in this place. What happens to you here?"

"It was a love-drunk oath," he begins, almost to himself. "If I brought my king the secrets that Queen Mab hid here, he vowed to raise me to the position of his consort. But I cannot hear what the voices tell me, or see what they show me. It's always just out of reach."

"And who finds you?" I ask, hoping I'm coaxing him along the right track.

"I'll be here forever," he says.

I shake his shoulder. "I don't think you will. I think you're dreaming about times in the past—times that troubled you, or times that meant something to you. I think you brought us to this moment. Please, show me what happened."

He finally looks at me. "She found me here," he says. Something changes. The voices seem to gasp in unison and then they fall silent. The colors in the fog fade as they become overpowered by a pale light. As we watch, the light gets closer, and at the center there's the form of a woman from which the light radiates.

I stand up as the woman approaches; Leithe only shields his eyes from the light. As expected, the woman is the Dreaming Queen. She wears a long white gown that trails behind her, drifting in a nonexistent breeze. This is the first time I've seen her up close. She has a sharp face and deep gray eyes; her expression is unreadable as she looks down at Leithe, completely ignoring me.

"You are far from the Crawling Court," she says. Her voice is low and resonant. Leithe looks up at her through the hair covering his face.

"This place isn't for you. You must know no one who crosses this threshold returns, save for me," she continues. "You thought you would be the first?"

"... Yes," Leithe says. The Dreaming Queen kneels down and cups the side of Leithe's face with her hand. Her touch seems to soothe him; he leans into it.

"So did the rest. Come with me to my court." She takes his hands and gently pulls him to his feet. "Come. These vestiges can no longer harm you." The space around us starts to fade as if we're changing scenes again.

"Leithe," I say. "Hurry up and kiss her." He just gives me a pointed *shut up* glare and keeps walking.

"Excuse me, uh, ma'am," I say. Her gaze slides to me. Even though we're about the same height, I get the sense that she's looking down at me from far above. "I know this sounds weird, but we're stuck in a dream and can only escape if you and Leithe kiss." I sound like a lunatic. Or a pervert. She turns and leads Leithe away without saying a word. Maybe I imagined that she looked at me in the first place.

"Wait!" I say, lunging forward and grabbing her wrist. The moment I touch her skin, it feels like I grabbed a live wire. There isn't pain so much as a complete overload of energy. It courses up my arm and through my body. I recoil, but I'm unable to let go.

The sensation is blinding and for a moment I can feel nothing but energy coursing through me, and when the feeling abates, I'm somewhere else. I'm resting my head on my forearms, which themselves rest on something smooth and cool. It looks like a marble window sill. Outside I see a city far below me that looks like a patchwork of civilizations from different times and places. A narrow street full of blinking signs in an Asian language butts up against a city square of sandy mud-brick buildings. Beyond the sprawling city is a white-sand desert; overhead the night sky is full of stars and shining nebulae.

"Your Grace," says a voice behind me. "Forgive me. I didn't realize you were out here."

Chapter Seventeen

WHEN I TURN, FABRIC swishes around my legs. I'm wearing a dress now—a long pleated dress tied high around the waist. It's sleeveless, with delicate clasps on the shoulders shaped like butterflies. That *are* butterflies, I realize when they slowly flutter their wings. My head is also heavy for some reason, but there's no mirror around for me to examine it.

I forgot about the person who addressed me. I look up from examining my gown to see a naked woman floating a few inches off the ground. She has long and wavy auburn hair and a large green snake draped over her shoulders. The snake eyes me lazily.

"Were you talking to me?" I ask.

The woman cocks her head. "There are no other 'Your Graces' in this palace, at least not until the wedding," she says. Her voice is low, husky, and carries a slightly sardonic tone at the mention of a wedding.

"Do you have a mirror?" I ask. The woman raises an eyebrow, but then flicks her wrist and a gilded full-length mirror melts into existence beside her. In addition to the gown, my hair is piled into an elaborate braided updo that leaves half my hair hanging down my back. Similar to the shoulder clasps, colorful butterflies that flap their wings to catch ambient light serve as living hair ornaments. My face is perfectly done up to compliment my eyes. I look like a completely different person.

"The hell …" I mutter, grabbing at my face and clothes.

"Mab?" the woman says. "Forgive me, but you seem distraught." She crosses her legs as if there's a chair underneath her and strokes her chin with a finger. "Are you perhaps second-guessing your engagement?" she asks hopefully.

Mab. She called me Mab, like Leithe's betrothed.

"Um. Speaking of which, where is my betrothed?" I ask.

The woman rolls her eyes. "I don't keep track of every place your morbid little pet goes, Your Grace," she sighs. "You are my queen, and I love and adore you, but I don't understand this choice. He's beneath you—an exile from his own court grabbing for power above his station. This union secures no alliances. It's more likely to irritate the Crawling King than anything else, marrying one of his former lovers."

"I'll take your advice into consideration," I say.

The woman raises her eyebrows. "That might be the first time I've ever heard those words," she says. "Your Grace, I suspect you don't care about what will happen to the rest of the court, but I hope you will remember your duty as queen."

"What makes you think I won't?" I ask. Maybe I can get more information out of her. But the opposite of what I intended happens. She seems to think I'm offended by what she's said.

"I'll say no more of it, Your Grace. Though while I'm here, I shall inform you Noctiva is ready for the fitting."

She hurriedly floats down the hall away from me. The mirror she made melts back into nothingness.

It looks like I've somehow been given a role in this dream. I need to find Leithe. With no other leads, I wander the area. It's a magnificent building that seems to be a patchwork construction like the city below. I pass through parts of castles, mansions, and palaces from all times and places. I try to think hard about Leithe, hoping that's enough for me to find him.

As I walk through an outdoor rock garden, I see a hint of movement in the corner of my eye.

"Is someone there?" I say. No one responds, but something makes me curious. The path curves around a boulder, hinting at a secluded space off the main walk. I follow the path, and when I clear the bend I see a boy pressing himself against the boulder in an effort to hide.

"Zach?" I ask, dumbfounded. The boy is Zach when he was a teenager. He looks just as confused as I am.

"Tamsin, I didn't realize it was you," he says. "You're all disguised and stuff."

"They think I'm the queen; I don't know why," I whisper, worried someone might overhear.

"I've been trying to find you. Do you have any idea what we're supposed to do to solve this?" he asks. I deflate.

"No," I admit. I take a deep breath to steady myself. Zach is here. I don't know if he's real. I don't care.

"Are you okay?" he asks.

That's all it takes. I burst into tears. Seeing him look at me with such concern is too much.

Zach comes to me and puts his hands on my shoulders. He's wearing the same clothes he had on in the vision where he died. Now that he's closer, I can see a splash of dull red spreading across a swatch of fabric wrapped around his abdomen.

"It's going to be okay. Okay?" He pats my shoulder reassuringly.

"You're hurt," I say. He looks down at the wound.

"I forgot it was even there. You know, lots of people in movies go around kicking ass more hurt than this," he says. Maybe the wound is only as serious as his mind thinks it should be. If so, there's no reason for me to tell him he should be worried.

"Are you really here?" I ask, wiping my face and swallowing a sob.

"Yes. I'm right here," he says.

"It's been a long time," I say.

"I know, but we're together again. We're teammates," he says. He's trying to be soothing, and it makes me let out a hiccupping laugh despite myself.

"I'm the adult here, but you're comforting me. I should be taking care of you," I say.

"I'm four months older than you," Zach says. "You're not an adult just because you look like one right now."

"No, Zach. That's not it." I take in the details of his face. He's just a kid. I don't want to tell him what happened—that the 'him' I'm speaking to might just be a dream echo of a dead boy, that I have no idea whether he'll end when this dream does. But if I was in his shoes, I think I would want to be told.

"We got out," I start, trying to steel myself. "We got out, but we left a little bit of ourselves behind, stuck in this dream. It's been seven years outside." He silently takes this information in and doesn't speak for a while.

"So there's another me out there, just living my life," he says. I take a deep breath.

"After we left, you were ... you were killed. Thistledown killed you ... because she thought you were keeping me from my 'destiny.' And she created a doll to take your place that would try to get me to come back here," I say. His face remains impassive while I explain.

"So my family doesn't know," he says.

"No. As far as they know, you're still alive."

"I guess that's good," he sighs. "You're my best friend, but it was always so frustrating how everything was always about you, and you just accepted it like that was how the world was supposed to be."

"I'm so sorry," I say.

"I know, but I would never miss the opportunity to say 'I told you so,' because I did. Many times," he says with the hint of a smile.

"I know you did. I should have listened to you."

"I'm glad old age gave you the wisdom to admit that," he says. A laugh bubbles out between the tears. "So you're what, twenty-one? What's that like, do you drink a lot?"

"Almost never. It's not as exciting when you're allowed to do it, I guess." Lost memories bubble up, perhaps reclaimed from the fragments of myself I found here: Zach and I sharing beers we snuck from the mini fridge in his dad's garage, both pretending we actually liked the taste.

"Did you go to college? Do you have a job now?" he asks. "Are you a comic book artist?" Another memory. That's right. That's what I wanted to be when I was younger.

"Nope. I'm unemployed and living with Grandma, so things aren't that different," I say. "Look. I'll do something. I don't know how faerie stuff works, but I'll talk to the witch. I'll see if she can do something to help you. I'm going to do everything I can to get you out of here, I promise. I don't want to lose you again." A thought occurs to me. "I'll get a wish from Leithe if I free him. He can do stuff with ghosts. Maybe he can bring you back to life."

"Right ..." Zach says, staring off into space. "Let's focus on doing that. We don't need to keep talking about all this." He says it lightly, like he couldn't care less, but his expression tells me he's barely begun to process it. But how do you process something like this?

"This place is wild. The first person I saw when I got to this castle place was a completely naked lady," I say, trying to distract him with the first thing that comes to mind.

"There's plenty of naked people here. I don't think faeries have a 'no shirt, no shoes, no service' policy."

"I think Leithe mentioned that the time he popped into my bathroom while I was in the shower."

"I hope you kicked his ass," Zach says.

"I don't think he meant to do it, but I'll think about getting him back later," I say.

"So you really have no idea why they think you're the queen?" he asks.

"No. I didn't do this on purpose. I've been jumping around, I think based on how Leithe's mind drifts. When I popped here from this place full of technicolor fog, I looked like this."

"Maybe Leithe missed his fiancée so much he made you look like that by accident."

"Huh. I hope not," I say.

Zach and I walk through halls, up and down staircases. We sometimes pass fae creatures, but I don't ask for directions—it would seem weird coming from the queen, and I'm worried something bad might happen if I draw too much attention to myself. What I do tell them, as imperiously as I can, is to send my betrothed to me should they find him.

"My love, I heard you were looking for me," Leithe says from behind us as we walk through another garden. He looks much healthier than the last time I saw him. His hair is tied back into a ponytail and he's wearing long robes and several pieces of eye-catching jewelry. He's watching me, waiting patiently.

"Oh, yes," I say, realizing he's waiting for me to explain. "Um ..." I was hoping he'd recognize me.

"Her Majesty was hoping you would join her for a walk," Zach cuts in, sensing my struggle.

"I don't see why you need a page to announce that," Leithe says, offering me his arm. I take it and we begin walking. Zach follows behind.

"When did you take a human boy?" Leithe asks. "Or is that a dreamling mimicking a human? It's still hard for me to tell."

"Leithe, it's me," I whisper. I worry he'll get mad if he finds out I'm not his betrothed, but stringing him along is probably worse.

"I ... know?" he says.

"It's Tamsin. Remember me? This is a dream. We were at the battlefield together, and then in the place beyond the end of Faerie. And now we're here," I whisper.

"Tamsin ..." he muses; then his eyes widen, and he takes his arm from me in annoyance. "Where's the queen, then?"

"I don't know! Don't blame me, I'm trying to help you," I hiss.

Leithe suddenly looks fearful. "This must be the day it happens."

"What happens?"

"The memories are coming back to me," he says. "The entire city is preparing for the wedding. This is the last day I remember before I came to, tossed around in a dream and only able to catch sparse moments of clarity. We're going to get attacked. I don't know by whom. They're going to imprison me. I don't know what happens to the queen."

"She's imprisoned, too. We need to find out where she is," I say. "The two of you have to kiss to break the curse. You're about to get married, right? So you won't make a stink out of kissing her like you have been?"

"We can try the throne room," Leithe says. "She spends most of her time there."

"If everyone thinks Tamsin's the queen, maybe if you kissed you'd like, trick the curse?" Zach suggests.

Leithe looks appalled. "It *isn't* her. I won't kiss someone who stole the form of my betrothed."

"It was just an idea, man," Zach says.

"It's not a bad idea," I say. "I mean, I'd rather kiss you than die, Leithe."

"Perhaps as a true last resort," he says.

Leithe leads us to the throne room. There's no ceiling; instead the night sky sits visible above us. The room is huge, with walls and floors of white marble veined with gold. A dais with a marble throne sits on one end and a set of double doors on the other. Faeries buzz about, discussing where tables will need to be placed, what decorations should go where, and other details. They bow to me when I enter.

"They're preparing for the wedding," Leithe explains.

"Do these please you, Your Grace?" the woman with the snake asks, floating over from another part of the room. "I've sent my children to collect only the most beautiful dreams from the desert. We will have a feast spun from the finest joy, love, rage, and lust. Amusements are being arranged for the citizens as well. Every soul in your domain will honor you, love you, want you, and want to be you."

"Thanks. That sounds great," I say. She cocks her head and studies me curiously.

"Lelit," Leithe says with little enthusiasm.

"Leithe," Lelit says. His name seems to put a sour taste in her mouth and she turns back to me quickly. "If Your Grace believes we have things well in hand, will you not do Noctiva the honor of attending your fitting? She has been most hard at work on your gown."

"Sure. Leithe, walk me there?" I ask.

"There has to be something to surprise the groom on his wedding day," Lelit cuts in. I look at him, desperately trying to get across my meaning.

"I will see her to her chambers for the fitting, at least," Leithe says. "And then I'll go."

"If you must," Lelit sighs.

It turns out Mab's personal chambers are at the very top of the palace. We walk up several curling staircases before entering a comfortable sitting room. The walls and ceiling are covered in mosaics and the room is furnished with low wooden couches draped with delicate white cloth.

"I told Lelit I would not accompany you further. Noctiva should be in the dressing room." He points to a doorway blocked by a hanging cloth. "Just go try the dress on and come back. It shouldn't take long, and you shouldn't be expected to do anything. Then we can be done with this and go search for the real queen."

"Zach, I guess you should wait out here?" I say. Zach nods.

I push aside the cloth and enter the room. It's large and has gowns of all kinds hanging along the walls. They're in many different styles, but most of them are white. In the center of the room is a woman—I think—sitting next to a loom. Spools of delicate fabric are strewn all over the floor. The woman herself is covered in embroidered black veils.

"Hi. I'm here to try on my wedding dress. I heard it was ready," I say.

"Yes, Your Grace. Please," The woman who must be Noctiva gestures for me to come forward with a hand. Her voice is high-pitched and youthful. Her fingers are long and as thin as needles at the points. They remind me of the limbs of an insect. As I get closer, I see the comparison is probably a valid one. There are countless spiders all over the fabric, weaving intricate designs.

Noctiva holds up what she's working on. The gown is white—fitting with Mab's previous fashion choices. It has many transparent layers embroidered with beautiful flowers and moths and butterflies. Scintillating stones are stitched into the patterns, causing them to dance as the fabric catches the light. There's so much fabric it's impossible for me to tell what the dress is supposed to look like.

"It's beautiful," I say. Something tickles my legs. I look down to see several large black spiders climbing up the dress I'm wearing. I jerk in surprise, but then freeze. These are faerie spiders, presumably acting with a purpose. They crawl up my back to my shoulders, where they undo my dress clasps so it falls to the ground.

Noctiva then stands—she's hunched over, but towers over me. She helps me into the dress, sorting and smoothing the countless layers until they're perfect. Her spiders secure the clasps that run up my spine. When that's done, she directs me to a mirror in the center of the room.

Despite the situation I'm in, I suddenly feel like a giddy princess. The neckline sits against my throat, but the fabric from there to my bust and down to my wrists is sheer save for embroidery. Hanging lacy sleeves slashed at the elbow fall to the floor. The skirt is full and layered with lace and applique. I swish the skirts and spin a little before I can stop myself.

"It looks great," I say. "But I should probably get back to Leithe."

"Of course, Your Grace. But before that, I would like to discuss your hair." Noctiva shoos the butterflies out of my hair and has her spiders undo the braids so it falls freely down my back.

"Now, we'll want everyone to see the lacework, but I still want most of your hair down." She pulls and prods at my hair with her pointy fingers for some time, arranging it this way and that and tutting when she decides she doesn't like what she's done. My neck and wrists start to itch from the gown and I resist tapping my foot out of impatience.

"Tamsin!" Zach cries from the other room. I push Noctiva aside and run out, hiking up my suddenly annoying skirts as I go. Zach is in the sitting room, as is Leithe. And Mab.

Leithe and Mab are caught in an embrace when I arrive. Leithe buckles and goes limp, and Mab releases him so he unceremoniously drops to the floor.

"For someone he claims to love, he's terrible at knowing you," Mab says. As she speaks, her form ripples and shifts until it's Lelit floating in front of me.

"Are you jealous or something?" I ask. I feel hot, feverish almost.

Lelit snorts at the question. "This isn't pettiness, Mab. You know lust and desire are tied to my Name. Even you couldn't hide your desires from me forever. I know. You chose to marry a death fae from the Crawling Court for one reason. After the wedding, you'll use his Name to command him to find a way to truly end your life. Tell me I'm wrong."

"You're wrong…" I say, but it's weak. I don't know if it's true or not. Lelit looks at me sadly.

"Perhaps you haven't yet admitted it to yourself," she says. "Whether or not he could do it, I won't let you try. Your life is too important to the court. Your power is our foundation, and other courts are jealous that we thrive while they do not."

"Okay, then. I won't do it," I say. "There's no need to do anything drastic."

Lelit crosses her arms and shakes her head. "I will not be taking chances," she says. "It took much planning and many deals, but we've arranged for a prison that will hold you for a time. Perhaps when we speak again, your mind will be changed."

"We?" I ask. The dress is starting to make my skin burn more than itch.

"Yes, Your Grace," Noctiva says, emerging from the dressing room. "It's for the court." Oh, no. I try to rip the dress off, but the fastenings are out of my reach. It burns. It feels like it's sucking the air out of my lungs.

Leithe. Our last-resort plan was for me to kiss him and hope it works. He's passed out on the floor by Lelit's feet. I stagger forward and collapse. The gown seems to be twisting itself around me to make it hard to move. That, or it's simply draining all of my strength. I crawl, trying to reach him. Lelit watches, face a mixture of anger and pity. I grab Leithe's hand, but I don't have the strength to drag the rest of my body forward.

"You will rest in the dark, Your Grace," Noctiva says. It sounds like she's trying to be soothing. Her words sound like they're coming from very far away. Lelit and Noctiva look like they're rising into the sky, or maybe I'm falling. Zach is shouting for me through a tinny speaker. He's running toward me, but it looks like he's swimming through molasses.

The floor opens. I'm sinking. At the bottom will be sleep. A nice sleep. A long sleep. The world around me starts to fade into white light. The room, Lelit, Leithe, Noctiva, all of them flake away into nothing. Zach falls to his knees next to me and takes my hand. His edges are blurry. He seems to realize what's happening.

"Am I going to disappear?" Zach asks.

No. I won't let you, I want to say. I don't have the strength to speak. I can't even make my fingers close around his.

"Tamsin, please," he says. For the first time, he sounds like a scared boy. "I don't want to die."

No, I try to say. *Please, let him stay*, I pray to anyone who might be listening. *Please.* I focus on the coolness of his hand against my burning skin until the world turns into light, until he breaks apart and scatters and I'm left clutching nothing but air. Then I fade into darkness, alone and lacking the strength to cry.

I'm alone. There's nothing around me but a black void. Light must come from somewhere since I can see my own body, though there's no obvious source. I don't have weight. Mab's wedding gown floats around me as if I'm submerged in water, though I feel no resistance if I try to move. But there's no point in moving. There's nothing here to move to; no up, down, or any other direction.

"Zach? Leithe?" I call out. My voice is small, and the noise is eaten up by the dark almost instantly. There's no response.

It's funny. I learned why Leithe and his betrothed were betrayed, but now there's nothing I can do about it. This would be a nice place to sleep. I wonder if my body will die while I'm in here—maybe it already did. Will I remain here like the echoes of Zach and my past selves, unaware that time has moved on? Would Grandma spend the rest of her life wondering what happened to me? Would my body be found? Maybe all of that has already happened while I've been here.

The thought of leaving Grandma with no answers, right when we might have a chance at a decent relationship, twists my stomach. I think about Leithe, stuck here forever reliving his memories, of Zach and my past selves, trapped here as well. It isn't fair. This isn't how it should all end.

My younger self told me that she could manipulate this dream with willpower alone. She had confidence that I must have lost over the years. But she's me, and I might still have something of hers in me.

I just want to go home. I want to see Grandma's front door again. I can see it in my head. The wood is aged and has been repainted several times over the years—once when I was a child because I drew all over it with Sharpies I found in Grandpa's office. My lost memories have come easier since I met my past selves. There's a crack near the bottom hinge that's been there longer than I can remember. Grandma used to hang festive wreaths on the door during holidays, which I always argued was pointless because no one came all the way out here to visit us. I think about it in winter, when the wreath she put out had fake holly with bunches of bright red berries. I think about the welcome mat—it's one she let me pick out, with frogs on it. I think about the heavy brass doorknob that is never locked and frequently catches and needs to be finessed just right.

That's the door I create before me. I open the door, and beyond is Grandma's living room to one side, the kitchen to the other, and straight through I can see the back screen door. Warm midmorning light bleeds into the room from behind the cream curtains. I step inside and close the door behind me. It's a snapshot of the house from no specific time, but rather a fusion of the fondest memories I could muster.

I could stay here, just like how Young Tamsin made a home for herself beneath a raging battlefield. The scent of fresh coffee reminds me of many mornings in my childhood when Grandma would be awake when I stumbled groggily down the stairs for school.

I could stay here, but I won't, not when that would be leaving things unfinished. I pass by the doors to Grandma's bedroom and Grandpa's office, and I reach the back door and push it open.

Chapter Eighteen

WHEN I STEP THROUGH the door, I'm standing on a massive tree branch as wide as a city street. The tree trunk goes down until it vanishes into the salmon-colored dawn light that suffuses the entire space. The sky is still dotted with early-morning stars that have yet to completely fade. When I look behind me, the door is gone.

"Zach? Leithe?" I call out; I receive no answer. I'm alone here. I have two options, so I decide to climb up. Maybe, like Jack's beanstalk, this tree leads to where I'm supposed to go.

They start out sparse, but the higher I climb the more spider webs I see. They span the branches with strands as thick as my fingers, glistening with morning dew. I see no spiders, thankfully.

I don't need rest in this place, and no matter how long I spend climbing, the sky doesn't change from its dawn-like stasis. On the way up, the branches are so choked with webbing I have no choice but to climb over it, but it's not sticky. Eventually, the branches appear brittle and dead; webs seem to be coming from inside the trunk.

And then I reach the top, and there's nowhere else to climb. I stand on a branch about three feet in width, and I'm not sure where to go from here. Maybe the answer is actually to take a leap of faith and jump; I don't have enough faith for that, yet. Maybe there's no answer, no key.

There's a hollow near the top of the tree where webs ooze out like a diseased blister. The mass is about as tall as me—as tall as a person. With that realization, I grab chunks of webbing and pull them away, and soon I can make out a humanoid figure inside the cocoon.

"Leithe?" I call out gently, though there's no response. Maybe this is another incident where the Dreaming Queen arrives and rescues him.

Carefully, I peel the webbing away from their face. What I reveal is Mab's face, eyes closed in sleep, or in death. It's the face I saw riding into battle against the king of the Deep Host—the face of the woman who rescued Leithe from the land beyond the edge of Faerie. But it isn't just Mab's face. It's also the face I've seen in the mirror every day of my life. It's my face. We're identical, but I hadn't seen it until this moment.

"... Your Grace?" I say, carefully poking her shoulder. She doesn't respond, and her skin is cold. I pull away more webbing. She appears nude. Her hands are crossed over her chest in a funerary pose.

"I don't know why we look the same. I don't know if this is some dream trick, but you need to wake up," I say. "Leithe misses you. This prison is doing bad things to the forest." I shake her shoulders, but she doesn't stir. Instead, the jostling causes the entire tree to shake. Mab's body falls backward into the hollow, taking me with it by my hands—stuck fast to her. She falls further and further; spider threads snap one after another until we're free-falling in darkness.

Our surroundings have the consistency of water. I try to hold Mab and swim up, but she's too heavy—heavier than a body could possibly be. She drags me down deeper and deeper. I can't breathe from the pressure on my lungs.

In the distance, deep below us, there's a spot of light that suddenly expands into an overwhelming collage of color and sound. Together they form countless moments from Mab's life. I see the rise and fall of civilizations, both human and fae. I see Mab on her throne, asleep more often than not. She's tired. The barest hint of the eternal life she's experienced makes my head feel like it's about to burst. It's too much.

I see Mab standing with the witch, who's in the form of a young girl. I don't hear the words of the conversation as the moment passes by, but I *feel* the hope it gives Mab. Hope for an ending. An ending that would lead to a beginning.

Like the fragments of myself I encountered in this dream, Mab lost me, like a branch pruned away from the whole. This fragment of hers was hidden away with a human family. Her fragment always had a connection to Leithe—her betrothed—even if he couldn't recognize her. Her fragment grew and always felt an irresistible pull back to the glade, unconsciously wanting to be whole, to take over so she could finally rest.

Gently, I press my lips to her forehead—it's a kiss between two of the captives, even though it's technically the same two. Mab's body falls away from me, deep into black depths until she vanishes from my sight; then I wake up.

I wake up by slamming face-first into grass. I'm back in the glade. Everything feels strange in a way that's hard to name. The tree above me has split open, leaving a hollow large enough to encase a person. The other tree arches away from me. There's a hollow open in that tree as well, and Leithe is lying unconscious and naked on the ground beneath it.

The breeze tickles my skin, and I realize I'm stark naked as well. I also realize my head feels heavy, and it's because I now have hair down to my hips. I position it to cover my chest, and as I fiddle with it I realize Leithe and I aren't alone. Hunter and Zach are in the glade, staring at me in shock. Zach has several arrows sticking out of him in what would surely have been lethal places on a human. Hunter is bloody from a gunshot wound to his side. The kelpie is lying some distance away, wheezing in pain. Weary, Hunter throws himself down on one knee toward me and looks at the ground. He says nothing.

"You are free, thanks to the assistance of your servant, Thistledown," Thistledown says, emerging from where she hid herself in the tall grass and kneeling before me. "If you found my service adequate, I would ask a small boon of you."

"What do you want?" I ask.

"It is but a small thing: I wish you to raise me to your court and make me one of your handmaidens, Your Majesty." So this was her plan. Help the struggling royals get back to the top so they'd take her with them. That's what Zach died for.

"Why?" I ask.

"Because I made it my mission to help you reach this point. You have offered me thanks many times. If your feelings are true, offer me this as your thanks." It's the very word trap she warned me about. But she made an error.

"No," I say. Her eyes widen. She must not have expected this.

"You said it yourself before: I was raised by humans. I don't care about *losing face*. I didn't make a blood oath. I'm not giving you *anything*. You killed my friend, and you think I'm going to reward you for that?" I shout. After realizing my anger, Thistledown doesn't waste any time; she turns and flees, but doesn't get far before an arrow arcs through the air and into the middle of her back. She collapses onto the ground without a final sound. By the time I turn to Hunter, he's dropped his bow and is once more kneeling on the ground.

"Why did you do that?" I ask.

"Your Grace," he says. His tone has changed. It's respectful. And fearful? "I long wondered who killed that boy. Please forgive me for taking justice into my own hands. If you see fit to punish me that, or for my part in your imprisonment, please at least spare my hounds." Justice. As angry as I am, I still don't know what kind of justice I would have had in me to demand from her.

"Do you recognize me?" I ask.

"Yes, Your Grace."

"It's me. Tamsin."

"I realized that when you mentioned the boy," he says, still looking at the ground. "It was not a plan I anticipated, disguising a part of yourself as a human. The Gentry are truly capable of incredible feats of magic." He can't quite keep the venom out of his voice.

"I wasn't lying to you. I really didn't know until just now," I say.

"It was a good trick, to go so far as to fool even yourself," he says. "I truly believed you were human. That was my failure."

"I ..." I want to say I'm sorry, but I've been warned never to do so. "But the imprisonment is over. You don't have to guard this place anymore. You can leave," I offer instead.

"You're giving me permission to leave safely, Your Grace?" he asks.

"I mean ... you could stay. If you want."

"If I have your leave then I must return to my lord," he says.

"Can I talk you into working for me instead of your lord?" I ask.

"Not unless you can talk her into releasing me from her service," he says. That's about what I thought.

"Okay. Then, um, wait here," I say. I don't know how to deal with this, so I turn around and walk back to Leithe. I nudge him with my foot and then kneel down next to him.

"You awake?" I ask, shaking his shoulder gently. Leithe groans and opens his eyes. They widen when he sees me kneeling over him.

"You came for me," he says. He reaches up, grabs my face, and pulls me in for a kiss. I hold up my hands to keep him at a distance.

"You don't recognize me, do you?" I ask.

He looks confused and props himself up on his elbows. "What do you mean?" he asks.

"I'm Tamsin. I'm not your betrothed. Maybe I was at one point—it's hard to tell what's real and I am *very* confused—but I don't have any memories of it and I don't feel like that person at all. Whatever the truth is, I know I'm not who you think I am," I say.

He looks at me for a long time, scrutinizing my face. "You wore an excellent glamour. You looked no different, but I couldn't see you," he finally says. "It's odd." As he says so, he waves a hand and he's suddenly wearing elaborate robes.

"Oh. I guess I can also do that now." I focus on weaving threads together to try and glamour myself into my old clothes, but all I can manage is a swampy-looking blur.

Leithe waves his hand and fixes it. "You used to be better at this."

"Because I'm not your fiancée and I've never done this before," I snap.

"So what's your wish, then?" he asks, "since I must assume that's the reason you're speaking to me." Leithe stands up, and I follow suit.

"Is it possible for you to free him from his oath of service?" I point at Hunter. Leithe thinks about it.

"I believe that's one of Lelit's pets. I can't free him without negotiating with her," he says, striding over to where Hunter is still kneeling. "His presence means she is most likely responsible for our imprisonment. We should kill him before he reports back to her that we're free."

"Absolutely not," I say, moving to stand between Leithe and Hunter.

Leithe sighs. "I understand you don't remember how these things work, so you should allow me to teach you. Lelit will discover what happened. Her betrayal has come after ages of service to Mab. The loss of your memories won't make you any less of an enemy to her. It may even mean she'll come after you now that you'll be easier to manipulate. You might get the peace you want long enough for the old human woman to die, but she will come looking for you sooner or later, and what will you do should she come while the human is still alive? She'll have no issue using her to get to you.

"Kill the pet, and Lelit will have less information. She may even not know you're essentially operating with the mind of a human, and therefore act with more caution. Leave the pet alive, and Lelit will come for you soon in the hopes of getting to you before you regain your strength." Shadows swirl around Leithe's feet, and I realize he probably doesn't need to go through me to get Hunter.

"It's not his fault. You're not going to kill him because of things he was forced to do!" I shout.

"He's in this position because he willingly swore an oath of service in exchange for the status that comes from being a court knight. He knew what he was doing. I'm going to handle it. Please move," he says.

"I wish you would do him no harm," I say. "That's my wish. That's what I want." Leithe freezes and then scowls, but his shadows calm.

"Fine. You take care of it, then. If you care about the old woman, you'll kill him."

"You're free to do whatever you want," I say to Hunter. Without a word, he turns and walks away, his hound limping after him. I hate that I hoped he would stay.

"You did him no favor," Leithe says after Hunter's gone. "He'll be punished for his failure." And he failed because he was too kind to just kill me when he should have.

Then there's Zach. He's been standing quietly the entire time, watching me. Around the arrows sticking out of him, his skin has started to turn to wood.

"What will you do now?" I ask.

"My purpose is fulfilled," he says. As I watch, the thing that once had Zach's face turns into a wooden doll, with what looks like a smear of dried blood across its torso.

"That was excellent craftsmanship," Leithe muses. I glare at him.

There's one more thing to deal with. The kelpie lies on the ground in a pool of brackish blood, his hide peppered with arrows. I kneel down next to him and carefully pull out the arrow in his jaw.

"As promised," I say. He struggles to his feet.

"I must return to the water to recover, if I have your leave ... Your Majesty," he says.

"I'm going to keep an eye on you," I tell the kelpie. "Don't kill any innocent people." He nods reluctantly and limps away.

Near where the kelpie fell, my things are strewn over the ground. My clothes are bloodstained and my phone is surprisingly intact. My reflection in the phone screen looks the same as it always has, save for the long hair.

"What are you going to do now?" I ask.

"Stay with you until your memories come back," Leithe says.

"Oh, no. Nope. I don't *want* to be a different person. Right now, I just want to go home." Oh, God. I have so much explaining and apologizing to Grandma to do. I start walking toward home.

"I told you. It isn't that simple. The Dreaming Court will come," he says, following me. "Do you know how to weave glamour? How to fight? If Lelit has been acting as regent in your absence, at best she will return you to the throne as a puppet-queen. At worst, she'll find some new prison for us."

"Why can't she just leave us alone? Can't she just take the court? I doubt I'd be any better than her. She at least knows what she's doing, right?"

"It doesn't work like that. Rulership is tied to your Name—Mab's Name. Even in exile, you will be the queen. No monarch can truly leave their post," Leithe says. I scoff and kick at the ground.

"Lelit and I never liked each other, but I thought she loved you," Leithe muses, voicing a thought he seems to have been chewing on.

"Mab, not me," I correct.

"She couldn't just attack her queen and get away with it, not unless Mab betrayed the court in some way. Marrying outside the court isn't so rare. It seems strange for Lelit to make such a deal out of it," he continues, looking at me as if I might know something he doesn't. I do. Mab seeking her own death was a betrayal in Lelit's eyes, and she thought Leithe was a means to that end.

"I've only met a dream-version of her, so who knows?" I shrug. How could I tell him that about the woman he seems to love so much, tell him that she may have simply been using him?

"But since I'm *not Mab*, I'm not going to marry you. You don't need to care what happens to me," I say, hoping to veer the conversation in a different direction.

"Whether you remember or not, we are betrothed. We agreed to be married. I don't know what that means for humans, but for us it means that we're bound to one another. We pledged to be allies. I'm not going to abandon you just because you've forgotten that."

"Well, I'm going home. I guess you can come with me. But don't be weird to my grandma." I say.

"Why go back to that house? There are endless places we could go. This pseudo-human life you've lived will soon be a distant memory," he says. "Why choose to stay and act human? You can't turn your back on what you are."

"I'm not turning my back on what I am," I say. "I'm a faerie, and a granddaughter." Leithe gives up arguing for now. We walk in silence for a while, but I realize I don't know exactly where we're going. Leithe is the one who finds a door out of Faerie. We come out near the creek, only a short walk from the bridge. It seems to be evening.

Soon after we reach the road, we come to the bridge where Zach's truck is still parked. I stop and stare at it, clutching the bridge railing so hard the worn wooden corners dig into my flesh.

"What's that?" Leithe asks.

"It belonged to Zach—my friend. He died. Though I guess it never actually belonged to *him*," I say.

"I don't know how humans can handle being around so much iron. It's vile," he says. "How can you even look at it?" I want to snap at him for being disrespectful, but I start to feel the prickling on my face and exposed arms. It's slight but noticeable. Staring at the truck makes my eyes sting.

Experimentally, I approach the truck and stick out my hand. The prickling intensifies, as if my arm has fallen asleep. I touch the truck with my fingertips, and I scream. I imagine it's as if I touched a stove top. My fingers hiss and smoke as I pull them back and cradle them against my chest.

"I don't know what you thought would happen," Leithe says.

"I don't know either," I say. My fingertips are charred black and oozing wisps of smoke. The pain is incredible and makes my breath come in short gasps.

"You'll heal faster if you tell yourself to," Leithe says.

"Neat," I say, and let my burned hand fall to my side.

Further down the road, we find Grandma's crashed truck with a police car parked behind it. An officer is sitting in the car while another one sets out road flares.

"I guess I need to handle this somehow," I grumble.

"Uh, hi," I say, waving awkwardly to the cops. They ignore me.

"Excuse me? Don't you need a statement or something?" I ask, approaching the police car until my eyes sting. They don't even look up at me. Leithe sighs dramatically behind me.

"They can't perceive you. Only those with Sight can see you if you don't allow yourself to be visible to mortal creatures."

"How do I do that?" I ask, looking over my arms to see if they're translucent.

"I don't know how to explain it," he scoffs. "It's like glamouring your clothes, or walking, or anything else. You just *do* it." He sighs and crosses his arms. "I suppose, imagine you're taking a paintbrush and painting yourself a second skin." I try to do as he suggests, but he interrupts me.

"I suppose you don't remember any of the old laws," Leithe says.

"No," I say, scowling at my hands.

"We're forbidden from revealing the Fae to innocent humans, but the words leave room for slip-ups and mischief here and there. If you wish to reveal yourself, make sure you look like something they wouldn't think twice upon seeing. Be sure any glamours you cast on them don't leave them wondering about things they shouldn't," he says.

I envision a paintbrush sliding over my skin, covering me in a layer of paint. I imagine I'm painting myself into a still-life scene.

"Oh, Jesus," the cop in the car says, looking up at me. "I didn't even see you walk up, ma'am."

"It's fine. Um, I hit this tree. There was a ... dog in the road. I was worried about it so I ran off, but now I'm back," I say.

"Do you know if the dog's injured?" the cop asks.

"It seemed fine, but I don't know where it is now."

"Alright. I'll get an ambulance down here," he says.

"No," I say quickly. "I'm not hurt. I don't need one." And being inside a metal box with needles sticking out of me wouldn't help if I was hurt.

"You might have a concussion, miss. You need to get seen," he says, picking up his radio.

"I don't need an ambulance," I say. I try to will the words to be magic; my stomach flips and the words come out rushed and high-pitched, almost a squeak. The officer looks at me critically.

"You seem very nervous," he says. I look pleadingly at Leithe, who has approached to curiously eye the police car.

"You have no confidence when you speak," he says. "You're weaving your will into reality. You aren't speaking a lie. Your words will be true, even if it's only for a short time. You must know that or it won't work."

"I don't need an ambulance!" I say again. The officer pinches the bridge of his nose.

"Then take it up with them when they get here. I have to make the call," he says. I look at Leithe pointedly, and then at the officer. Leithe sighs.

"She doesn't need an ambulance," he says, leaning down to speak close to the officer's ear. The officer doesn't react at all, but simply continues speaking into his radio.

"So ... can I go now?" I ask.

"What? No," he snaps. I glare at Leithe.

Leithe looks thoughtful, and then speaks again. "*The dog is back*," he says. At that, the officer looks up and into the trees.

"Stay there," he says to me. "I ought to catch that dog so we can see who owns it." He trudges off into the woods, whistling and patting his thighs.

"Abandon the glamour you're wearing and leave," Leithe says to me. I try to reverse the glamouring process in my mind, but it's as if the paint is stuck and won't come off. Instead, I just tiptoe until I think I'm far enough away and then run. They'll call Grandma about the truck soon enough anyway.

"I thought you were supposed to be all powerful," I say to Leithe as we turn into Grandma's driveway. "Why did it take you two tries to get that guy?"

Leithe scowls. "I've been asleep for a long time. I just need to regain my strength," he says. He does seem strained. "And it was easier to distract that man than convince him to do the opposite of what he wanted. It's often like that."

"What about the glamour? I can't get it off."

"That's because you're bad at it. Most young ones figure it out on their own with trial and error. You've done it before; try to remember how it feels."

"*I* have never done this before," I remind him. He stays silent, though by the set of his mouth I know he wants to argue.

When we walk through the front door, Grandma is sitting in her chair. She gasps when she sees me.

"Jesus Christ. They found my car on the road. They've been looking for you. What happened?" She stands up and runs over to me, gripping my shoulders as if I might just disappear.

"A lot," I say. "You shouldn't be walking around after what happened."

"It's very strange. I took the seed you gave me. I'm still sore from the fall, but it's much easier to get around. They had no more reason to keep me in the hospital. I tried calling for you to pick me up, but when you wouldn't answer I got worried and had them call me a car," she says.

"I'm sorry. I was trying to fix things. I think I have, at least somewhat," I say.

She touches a lock of my hair. "Is this a wig?"

"No," I say. She looks up at my face.

"You look so different somehow. What happened to you?"

"I ... I don't think I can tell you," I say. I remember what Leithe told me about the laws. I remember what happened when I tried to ignore my deal with him. Grandma gently releases me. She flinches at my words as if they cut her.

"I know there's something ... extraordinary going on. I realize that now. I'm sorry I couldn't listen before, but I'm ready now. I'll wait until you're ready to share it."

"She's close to figuring it out on her own. She won't be innocent, then," Leithe says, turning to face me from where he was examining the kitchen appliances. "Of course, that means you can share everything with her, but then the old law won't protect her. You could lead her to the truth without saying the words yourself, or you could leave her innocent and—mostly—safe. What will you do?" He seats himself on the arm of the sofa and rests his chin on his hands, looking at me expectantly. I resist the urge to snap at him.

"I will tell you," I say to Grandma. "I can't now. But I will."

She sighs. "Okay," she says. "I'll take that."

"Also," I say, "I have someone who might need to stay with us for a while."

She raises her eyebrows. "Who?" she asks. I look pointedly at Leithe. He catches my meaning and his form shimmers for a moment, and Grandma jumps in surprise.

"Excuse me. I didn't even see you come in," she says. The initial confusion on her face transforms into suspicion, but she doesn't say anything more.

"You have a darling home," Leithe says.

Grandma eyes him and turns back to me. "Should I even expect you to tell me who this is?"

"I will—"

"—eventually. I know" She cuts me off and sighs. "Help me fix up the guest room, then."

After making the guest room habitable, I excuse myself to my own bedroom. After several tries, I wipe away the clothes Leithe glamoured for me and curl up on the bed, wrapping myself in a blanket. And then I cry—for Zach, for Grandma's real grandchild, for the lie that was my human life, and for the uncertain future. Everything I pushed down so I could keep moving bursts forth at once. I cry until my head hurts and my eyes burn, until my lungs ache from sobbing.

The next evening the police call to ask about Zach. They ask me if I saw him yesterday, and I say no, though I don't tell them it's because he's been dead for years. They ask if I knew why his truck was parked by the bridge. I say perhaps he went hunting. They say to let them know if I can think of anything that might help, or if he contacts me. I say I'll certainly tell them if he does.

I don't tell Grandma about what happened to Zach, not yet. I don't want her to have to keep more of my secrets than she already is. I assume I'm a suspect, since I so recently returned to the area and have a history of erratic behavior, but they have no reason to look too closely. It will probably be assumed he went out to hunt or fish and suffered an accident. People get lost in the woods all the time.

It's Zach's family that pains me the most. Grandma and I make it a habit to drop by and bring meals while they wait by the phone. Even if I knew where Hunter buried Zach's body, it's still the years' old remains of a child; it would only raise more questions. I'm not skilled enough at glamour to make a body for the police to find in order to offer his family some sort of closure, so I nod sympathetically and join the organized searches when I'm asked. Sometimes I dream of him, but no matter how hard I hold onto him he dissipates like fog when I wake up.

It's during the second volunteer search that I see Tansy the cat watching me from beneath a natural arch formed by two trees. Her eyes glitter as she turns away and walks through the door.

I follow her into Faerie, and the crunch of boots from the search party falls away into bird and insect calls in which I can nearly make out words. Even those noises fade away as Tansy leads me into a small clearing where the witch is waiting. She looks like an old woman, with snow-white hair and skin as lined as aged bark. She's sitting on a boulder and doesn't rise to greet me.

"Is this what you wanted?" I ask, gesturing vaguely to myself.

She smiles. "I'm not disappointed."

"What do you gain from all of this?"

"Nothing, yet."

"Where's the baby Thistledown took?" I ask.

"The child was weak. Why would you assume he survived until now?" she asks.

"Tell me he's dead, then," I say.

"I don't know if he's dead. He still lived when Thistledown gave him to me, and I traded him away," she says. Her casual tone makes my blood boil.

"Who did you trade him to?" I ask, trying to sound measured.

"What will you trade for that information?" she asks. I resist the urge to scream and instead ponder what to offer, but she speaks before I can come up with anything. "I won't trade for it now. Think over what it's worth to you."

I can't hold it in anymore. "*Tell me where he is,*" I say. Power surges through my core, past my throat, and out with my words. I put my will into my words the way Leithe described. And from that one sentence, I feel as drained as if I sprinted for a mile. I feel empty.

"No," someone says from my left. I turn and see the witch as she appeared to me the last time I saw her—as a middle-aged woman. The old woman I was speaking to is still sitting on a boulder in front of me.

"Not even Mab in her prime would be able to command me," someone says from my right—the witch as a young teen.

"There's three of you?" I ask. She doesn't answer. Instead, the dirt beneath me explodes with coiling roots that bind my arms and legs and pull me to a kneeling position.

"We are all many parts that come together to make one being—you, me, a forest, a planet," the old woman says. The roots pull as if they're trying to rip my arms off and I cry out in pain.

"You could transform into a swarm of butterflies or a cloud of smoke," the young girl says.

"Or conjure a beast to break the vines," the grown woman says. From the roots a tree begins to grow, threatening to envelop me.

"I wove the binding that held Mab and her betrothed," she says. The tree grows over me, leaving only my eyes free. Panic keeps me from concentrating on anything that might save me.

"I tended to the prison. I coaxed free a part of the whole," the young girl says. As she speaks, a branch of the tree imprisoning me arches down and a single red fruit drops into her cupped hands. It glows warmly.

"And I hid the fragment where it could grow until it was ready to return. And it did, never straying too far from my calculations." In an instant, the tree vanishes and I'm free. I fall to my hands and knees and take several gasping breaths.

"You are Gentry—the highest of fae, but even so you lack the experience to challenge your peers. You would do well to learn before your court comes to find you," the witch says.

"*Why?*" I ask after catching my breath. "Why create the prison only to arrange for it to be broken anyway?" The old woman rises from her seat and moves to stand over me before kneeling down and grabbing my burned hand. I hiss in pain, but then watch as new, healthy flesh replaces the charred remains of my fingertips until my hand is completely healed.

"True death is a difficult thing for the high fae. The creature who was Mab could only hope to die through a great change. I granted her wish, but I do not grant wishes for free. You are Mab, and you are the inheritor of her debts as well as her Name. One day, when it suits me, I will return for my payment," the witch says. With that, she releases my hand and departs, leaving me alone under the trees.

Read on for a sneak peek at the second book of the Dreams
of Faerie series:

THE QUEEN OF DREAMS AND DUST

Chapter One

"I FINALLY FOUND YOU," Zach says. He looks the same as when he died—the real him, not the witch's wooden doll—a teenager who'd only just started growing into his frame, face tan and hair bleached almost blond from the sun. His throat is cut open, exposing layers of skin, fat, and muscle, though the blood spilling over his shirt is long dry. He studies me amiably, his smile crooked. He has a zit on his chin.

"Now I'm talking to myself," I say. "Of course I'd start talking to myself." Zach and I stand at the beginning of a hallway, the end of which vanishes into the distance. Doors line both sides, crammed together with hardly any wall in between. All kinds of doors. The door to Grandma's house. The door to the shed. The door to Zach's room.

"You're talking to me." Zach sounds indignant.

"And you're not real, because Zach died seven years ago. I just dreamed you up, like everything else here."

Zach. The hallway. The doors. All of it a decorative finish atop the workshop of my mind trying to reclaim the memories of my human childhood while I sleep. It's how all my dreams have been since I broke the prison that once held Leithe. And part of myself, I guess. Since then, I always know when I'm dreaming, which means I'm never really asleep, never really resting.

"If you say so." He steps past me and pushes open Grandma's front door; beyond is a scene from forever ago. The memory settles back into my brain: Zach and I sit on the floor and categorize our Halloween candy while Grandma and Zach's parents chat, beers in hand. Zach was a skeleton.

Zach wanders off and opens another door. And another. Fragments of memories play out before my eyes: my tenth birthday party where the only kids who came were Zach and a girl named Samantha who told everyone at school she'd been a horse in a past life. We were friends because I was the only one who genuinely believed her.

Beyond the next door, Zach's father teaches us to drive his pickup truck when we were thirteen. Brent Foster found it hilarious that I picked up shifting gears faster than Zach even though I was a girl, and at the time I took it as a compliment.

Each mundane memory of my childhood with Zach is another nail driven into my skin.

"If you made me, I could look like anything you wanted. I could be from any of these moments," Zach says. "So why this?" He gestures to his neck.

That answer is easy. "It's the last time I saw you. The real you."

"That's not a reason." He opens another door. The memory beyond isn't new. It finds its way to me every night. The other side is illuminated only by what moonlight sneaks past the forest canopy. We watch ourselves limp over moss and roots.

"I don't want to see this again," I say.

"Then close the door," he says.

I don't close the door. I watch myself lead Zach to Thistledown. To his death. I watch myself scream, cry, beg. I watch Thistledown slit his throat and leave. And I watch Zach die.

"I'm sorry." The words come out as barely more than a whisper.

"About what?" Zach asks.

"I killed you," I say. "I wanted to save Hunter, or maybe I just wanted to win. Either way, you paid for it."

The hallway dims and shudders. Zach's eyes glint in the gloom. "You wanted to save *Hunter*."

"But I didn't save anyone," I say. If I'd been better. If I'd listened to Hunter. If I'd made it through the prison sooner. If I'd been able to stop Thistledown. If I'd been able to do anything but sit and scream. There are countless ifs.

Pieces of the world flake off, leaving behind gaps where early morning light seeps through. I'm waking up. "No," I say. "I don't want you to go. I want you to stay."

Very gently, he takes my hands in his. "Then you should have chosen me."

The drone of the window AC unit drowns out the remains of the dream—a static, unchanging noise that reminds me that I'm awake, along with my sweat-soaked sheets. My bedroom is cast in gray, predawn light.

Zach is gone. Zach is dead. Has been for years, though he's only been officially missing for a month.

If I roll over and close my eyes, I'll once again be kneeling on that patch of blood-soaked dirt.

So I get up. Force myself to cross the hall to the bathroom, where a face that's supposed to be mine stares back from the mirror. It's framed by hair that falls nearly to my hips. Hair I didn't have a month ago. It's missing the tiny crescent scar that once sat above my eyebrow from when I tripped face-first into the kitchen counter when I was nine.

This body isn't the one I grew up in. It's the one that was trapped within the prison tree. Mab's body. The body I wore for over twenty years vanished where it fell from the kelpie's back when Hunter shot me. A tool meant for me to use and discard, just like the thing the witch made of blood and twigs and magic and left in Zach's place. A *fetch*, Leithe had called it.

It was a well-constructed fake. But the freckles that used to dot my knuckles are gone, as are all other marks, blemishes, and old scars accumulated through the course of a life. This new skin is flawless, marked only by the faintest tracery of the veins beneath.

I want to peel it off.

In a burst of savage energy, I yank open the medicine cabinet, take the scissors, and saw off a fistful of hair before throwing the scissors into the sink and hissing in pain. My fingers are red and raw where they made contact with the metal. The stench of burning hair fills the small room. Where the scissors touched, the strands are blackened and curling at the tips.

Half my face is framed by hair that falls in uneven chunks nearly to my shoulders, while the hair on the other side vanishes past the lower edge of the mirror.

I want it gone. Using a hand towel, I take the scissors again, wrap the rest of my hair around my fist at the back of my head, and hack it off.

It looks terrible. The left side is shorter than the right and the back is far shorter than the front. But at least it's something I did myself.

I throw my hair in the trash and rinse my head under the sink to get rid of the burning smell before I go downstairs.

In the living room, Cheeps is perched on the windowsill, staring intensely outside. He doesn't react when I look out over his head. A lone squirrel sits on a low-hanging branch and screams indignantly at something I can't see, tail lashing. Cheeps hates squirrels. That's all it is.

There's nothing else outside. The movement on the ground in the corner of my eye is just the shadow of a branch swaying in the breeze. No faeries. No monsters. No matter what I think I see in the trees at night. No matter how often I consider sneaking Grandma's rifle up to my bedroom.

I take a breath. Force myself to relax. There's nothing outside.

"What are you looking at?" Grandma asks from her armchair.

I jump at her voice. "Squirrels." She gives me a skeptical look, but doesn't push.

"You're up early," she says, coffee mug clutched in her hands. "There's coffee."

"So are you." I fill a mug from the carafe. The bitter coffee lacks the acrid tang of metal that's present in everything Grandma cooks, every dish she uses being cast iron or stainless steel. The smell permeates the house. It makes my nose burn and skin prickle.

Even with the stench of iron hanging in the air killing my appetite, my stomach growls. It hasn't stopped growling since I got this new body. But nothing I eat dulls the pain.

"Bad dreams," she says.

"What kind of dreams?" I ask before I can stop myself. If Grandma remembers that night in the hospital when I tried to tell her the truth, she's never said so. It's simultaneously a relief and a disappointment.

She purses her lips. "Do you want me to even out your hair?"

"No," I say quickly. Too quickly.

"Hm," she says. Her go-to phrase to indicate she's suspicious but choosing not to ask. She hasn't confronted me for answers, not about how my hair grew three feet or why I only use plastic utensils now. I've run through scenarios in my head of telling her the truth. She usually calls me a monster. A murderer. Accuses me of taking the place of her real grandchild. I imagine the scraps of goodwill we'd just managed to cobble together going up in smoke.

Telling her would also mean whatever protection fae laws provide to humans would no longer apply to her. So I tell myself hiding the truth is for her sake and not my own cowardice.

"They're pausing the search for Zach," Grandma says. The sensation of the town of Shrike Run for the past month. There hasn't been anything this interesting here in years. They'd interviewed all the neighbors at this point. A journalist came by to interview me after a picture the Fosters must have supplied ended up in a human-interest profile on Zach for the local paper. Grandma headed them off, wouldn't let them speak to me.

"Oh." She stares at me. That wasn't the right response. I have to sound interested. Invested, like I think there's a chance they'll find something. "Why?"

"Molly called me late last night." Grandma and Zach's mom have been talking every day since his disappearance. "Do you remember Grant Stanley?"

I think. "He was our elementary school P.E. teacher."

"He got separated from the search party yesterday afternoon. They found his body in the creek a few hours later." The creek.

"What killed him?" A dull roar begins at the base of my skull. I already know what Grandma is going to say.

"An animal. He'd been …" Grandma's mouth scrunches up in disgust. "He'd been partially eaten." By the creek. "Molly knows the medical examiner's wife, and she says he's confused as hell because the bite marks look more like an *alligator* than anything we've got around here. They're wondering if it …" She hesitates. "If it might be the same thing that …"

I press my face into my hands. "Okay, I get it!"

"I'm sorry," Grandma says, to my surprise. "That was morbid. I shouldn't have gone into detail."

"It's not you. I'm sorry." It's me. I might as well have killed that man. I pulled the arrow out of the kelpie's jaw and left him free.

"Molly's coming over for coffee in a bit," Grandma says, frowning. "Brent's been fishing most mornings, looking for an excuse to be out of the house, probably, and I don't think she likes being alone right now. Don't tell her I told you, but she's been having awful nightmares. Not sleeping at all."

"Got it." I understand the warning in her words: *pretend to be normal in front of Zach's mom. She's been through enough.*

"How's your job search going?" she asks.

"Nothing yet." Nothing I can do that won't require regular contact with metal. Iron worked by human hands, Leithe explained, including iron alloys, burns fae. And iron is everywhere. It was already hard enough to get a job with no college degree, and now I need to find one that won't burn me alive. *Alleged Faerie Queen* isn't a fit on most resumes.

I take a breath before I launch into the next subject. "I did find some houses online, though. Have you ever thought about Vermont? Washington State?"

She frowns. "We talked about this."

"Seattle is pretty. Or what about Oregon? There's trees there. You could find a place that's just like here." And they're on the other side of the country.

"I'm not moving, Tamsin," Grandma says. "I've been here for forty years and I plan to die here." I must flinch, because her expression softens. "Not that I plan on dying anytime soon."

"What about just into the city? You know, you might want to move closer to civilization soon, so you won't need to drive as much." Do faeries live in cities? How much iron does a place need to be laced with to keep them away?

"Child, I am not even seventy," Grandma snaps. "What is so wrong with this house?"

When a house is haunted, the smart thing to do is move. When your house is in the middle of a faerie-infested forest, the same concept should apply, not that I can say that. "It's just ... there's a lot of memories here. And with Zach

..." I let the words hang. Grandma sighs, and I feel like a monster.

"I understand, but we can't just up and leave while the Fosters are going through this. It's not right." She contemplates her coffee. "I'm not kicking you out, but you know you don't have to stay here, don't you? I'm doing so much better it's throwing the doctor for a loop. You can go back to Boston, if you want."

I can't go back to Boston. My former roommates hate me for breaking my lease and my meager savings were wiped out on the penalties for doing so. But I could still leave. I could sleep on a couch if I was lucky. A park bench if I wasn't—as long as it's not made of metal. Either one might be better than staying. Would Faerie chase me and leave Grandma alone, or would leaving be getting her killed?

"Do you want me to leave?" My voice is small. Vulnerable. I hate it.

"No," she says quickly. "I just mean that you should be traveling, dating, partying, doing drugs responsibly, things kids should be doing. You should be living your life, Tamsin, not trying to babysit me." Something on my face must concern her, because she sighs. "I will *think* about thinking about moving. But it's not happening anytime soon." Then it might not be soon enough. She sighs again and looks up from her coffee, making purposeful eye contact with me. "I know ... things have been hard for you." By the window, Cheeps starts growling deep in his throat like a cat. I whip my head around to look. "*Tamsin,*" Grandma says indignantly. "I am trying to say something important."

"Sorry." I focus on her.

She sighs a third time. "I lost Skye twice." This gets my attention. Grandma hates talking about her daughter. My 'mother.' Skye's son, her real child—Grandma's real grandchild—was taken on the orders of the witch who built Mab's prison. I've seen no sign of the witch after my useless attempt last month to get her to tell me what happened to the baby.

Grandma keeps talking; I force myself to concentrate on what she's saying. "Skye left when she turned eighteen because she didn't get along with her father—and me, I shouldn't downplay my role. She came back after she got pregnant, but you know she wasn't ... she wasn't well." Grandma stares at her coffee, a deep line between her brows. "She was convinced ... she kept going on about ..." She trails off, looking for the words. I see the suspicion working its way through her, the threat that she might start putting things together.

"It's okay," I say quickly. "We don't have to talk about it."

"It's not ..." Grandma sighs and gives up. "I don't know if I will ever see her again. I just don't want that to happen to you."

It won't, I want to say. But I can't promise that. I don't know what's going to happen. If they come for me, from Grandma's point of view, I'd simply disappear.

Acknowledgments

Thank you to the friends and family who donated their time to reading this story in the early stages.

Thank you, Dad, for telling me how proud you were that I never chose a fallback career.

Thank you, Linda and Jonas, for fixing my commas and the occasional homophone.

Thank you, Bec, for telling me what was bad.

Thank you, Ryan, for keeping me fed while I have the writing bug, and for the helping me come up with a long and historically accurate backstory for the gun that gets used one time.

About the Author

Grace Carlisle lives in Maryland. She prefers writing about fictional people rather than herself. Sometimes she posts on social media.

Subscribe to her Substack or visit gracecarlisleauthor. com to stay on top of book news and see the occasional animal picture.